Demure

MODERN LEGENDS OF SIDHE
BOOK ONE

HOPE E. DAVIS

The Fae of Sidhe speak their own version of Irish Gaelic. At times, it may match up with modern Gaelic, sometimes spoken in Ireland, but it's important to note that it is also its own fabricated dialect and any mistakes made in the book in Gaelic are intentional.

Additionally, while the book starts in the city of Dublin, which is a real place, the author has taken many liberties to make Dublin fit her needs, specifically when it comes to the library at Trinity College and the homes of the main characters. This book does not claim to be geographically accurate and should not be taken as a travel guide or tour advice for visiting Dublin or Trinity College.

DEDICATION:

To every woman who has thought her life would be devoid of magic after turning 25.

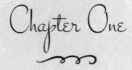

Chapter One

Sierra Lopez rarely went on Tinder dates, but whenever she did, they always went horribly wrong.

That is how she met Aodhan and, like every Tinder date, it ended with Sierra wishing she hadn't gone in the first place.

Well, to be fair, she wished she hadn't gone from the moment Aodhan waltzed up to the coffee shop 30 minutes late, after Sierra had already finished her coffee and was just preparing to call it quits.

"You're late," she said as he stopped by her table, resting his large hands on the smooth surface and shifting his weight from one foot to the other. Sierra didn't even bother looking up from her laptop screen where she was currently making notes for her thesis.

"Yes I am." His deep voice replied in an even tone that conveyed no notes of regret.

Sierra waited for an "I'm sorry" or a "My apologies"—but it never came. Instead, Aodhan silently folded his tall frame into the chair in front of her, looking at her expectantly as he crossed his arms over his broad chest.

The good news was that Aodhan looked just like his picture.

With sandy brown, curly hair that fell to his shoulders and pale, almost translucent skin that gave him away as an Irish native, he looked just as his profile had portrayed. Even down to the black woolen beanie he wore, which covered the top of his hair and most of his ears. Sierra didn't usually go for men who followed the 'skater' style, but while he wore beanies in all his photos, he was dressed in fitted jeans and a long sleeve polo shirt, giving Sierra mixed signals on his true aesthetic.

She had only agreed to go on a date with him because of the way his style in his Tinder photos had intrigued her. They had spoken briefly over the past few days on the app, but he hadn't seemed to be much of a conversationalist. He kept his answers short and to the point, which Sierra also liked, to an extent. She had always been drawn to direct men who didn't play games with women's feelings by trying to impress them by showering them with empty compliments.

"Sierra, obviously." She stated her name, not bothering with pleasantries since he hadn't either. She tugged down the sleeves of her sweater as she swept her messenger bag from the floor.

"Aodhan." He replied, just as deadpan.

Well, this is going great, Sierra thought to herself. She tried to get the conversation going. "Aodhan, is that a family name?"

He shrugged, keeping his arms crossed, his eyes pinned on her messenger bag where she was fiddling with the zipper on one of the pockets.

What a date this was turning out to be.

"So, are you from around here?" She tried again. This was his last chance to try and salvage their date before she called it quits.

"No. Are you?" He raised one sandy brown eyebrow.

The corner of Sierra's mouth quirked up in annoyance. "What, my accent didn't give me away?"

As an expat in Ireland, all the natives knew immediately that she was American. With her dark brown, almost black hair and light skin, Sierra could technically be Irish, but the moment she opened her mouth, they knew. Though, now that she thought about it, Aodhan didn't have the typical Irish accent either. Before she could ask about it, he answered her rhetorical question.

"I didn't know you had an accent."

Sierra rolled her eyes and checked the time on her phone. "Well, this has been great, but I didn't have a lot of time to begin with. You were late, sooo..." She stood, sweeping her notebook and laptop into her book bag. "See you around."

Sierra remembered from Aodhan's profile that he was also a student at Trinity College, just as she was, but she really hoped she wouldn't actually see him around. She was a master's student, studying Aging and Fragility. It was a smaller program marketed to those who had already completed their pre-med studies but didn't want to become full-fledged doctors and preferred to go into medical research. Sierra had chosen pre-med for her under-grad, hoping to one day help support her family, who had always struggled financially. Her parents weren't poor, by any means, but as blue-collar workers with five children, they had always had to use 'creative methods' to make ends meet.

Sierra exited the coffee shop without looking back and began her trudge to the dull and dreary room she called an apartment, pulling her coat closed against the fall wind. She had moved to Dublin on a whim, needing a fresh start, free from her argumenta-tive parents and their radical American lifestyle.

When she had first brought up going to college far away, her parents had assumed she meant in New York or maybe LA (pretty far from her hometown of Dallas, Texas), but they had been beyond shocked when she announced she had been accepted into Trinity College in Dublin. They were more sad than anything because they knew they couldn't afford to visit her during her 1-year graduate program abroad.

Truthfully, that was one of the reasons Sierra had enrolled in the Trinity College program; not seeing her parents for a whole year was a blessing in her eyes and just the break she needed. Although Sierra loved her parents and her siblings, she also felt a little lost. One of the reasons she came to Dublin was to find out who she was, and what she wanted from life, without her parents breathing down her neck and trying to influence her decisions.

Even though she had completed her undergrad in Pre-Med, Sierra wasn't sure what she wanted in life. At home, she had felt forced to continue on the path to becoming a doctor, but somewhere along the way she had lost the passion and drive she had once felt. Now, she felt like she wanted to do anything other than what she had just devoted the past four years of her life studying.

Sierra stopped her brisk walk at the intersection, waiting for the walk signal, only to feel a hand at her elbow. She spun around to tell off the stranger, to find Aodhan standing there.

Trying to suppress her annoyance, Sierra raised her brown eyes to meet his green ones. He was taller than her by at least a foot. At 5'5", Sierra wasn't short for a woman, but she certainly wasn't tall either.

"You're leaving?" Aodhan asked, his eyebrow raised, an unreadable look occupying his face.

Sierra looked around at the sidewalk and the other people making their way across the crosswalk, which had just started flashing the walk signal. "Seems like it, doesn't it." She said, matter of factly. She was just so sick of the terrible Tinder dates that she constantly found herself escaping. At least with Aodhan, she had brought her computer and had accomplished some homework while he was late.

"But..." He started, trailing off as he searched for the words he wanted to say.

"But what?" Sierra cocked her head to the side as the walk signal started blinking red. Great, now she would have to wait for the next cycle.

"Don't you want to meet me?"

Sierra scrunched her eyebrows. "Are you seriously asking me if I want to get to know a man who didn't value my time enough to show up on time for our coffee date? I'll pass, but thanks." Sierra turned back to the crosswalk, pissed that it was red, and she couldn't dramatically exit as she would have much preferred to do.

"Oh."

Sierra spun to face him. "That's it? 'Oh?' You were thirty minutes late for a date we set three days ago, and you didn't even have the audacity to text me and let me know? Or say sorry when you did arrive?" Aodhan had a shocked look on his face, and Sierra had to admit he was attractive. He likely never had to apologize to a woman because they probably fell at his feet at the sight of his long curly hair, pronounced jawline, muscular chest, and crooked smile. That thought just fueled her anger. "You know what? Other women might fall for your looks, but I'm looking for a man who actually values me and my time. Thanks for showing me right away and not wasting my time. Goodbye."

Luckily, the universe heard her silent prayer, and the light turned green. Without a glance behind her, she crossed the intersection and walked briskly down the street.

Sierra didn't live far from the coffee shop where they had agreed to meet, but she walked quickly, so he couldn't follow. She even debated stopping into a grocery store just to ensure he didn't trail her home. But after five minutes of walking, she glanced over her shoulder to see the sidewalk was empty. He hadn't tried to follow her.

She smiled smugly to herself and rounded the corner to the street where her building was located. Checking once more over her shoulder, she reached in her purse for the key and let herself into her building.

Like most buildings in Dublin, the building Sierra lived in had once been something else, and only turned into apartments in the last few decades as the housing crisis had increased. Because of the aftermarket division, almost all the apartments in the building were set up strangely, with some spanning multiple floors and some being just a room off to the side. The two studios on the top floor even had to share one bathroom due to the location restrictions on where plumbing could be installed.

Sierra was just glad she had snagged a studio with a private bath, even though it was smaller than her family's living room in Dallas.

As an international student without much money, Sierra hadn't had much choice but to rent a small studio situated in between the larger apartments. It was still expensive, and Sierra worked at the university library on weekends and some week-nights to help cover the costs. She had financed the cost of her tuition (as most American students did) and planned to deal with it later after she graduated and hopefully had a job.

Sierra made her way up the two flights of stairs to her apart-ment, unlocking the door and tossing her bag on the side table just inside her door. She flipped on the lights before sinking into her second-hand couch.

Her apartment wasn't much, just a queen-sized bed with a sitting area arranged at the end. There was a couch that faced a TV hanging on the wall. To the right of the entrance was the kitchenette, which had a hot plate, microwave, fridge, and sink. A small table with two chairs served as both her dining room and desk. The door to her bathroom was just past the kitchen.

It wasn't much, but it was home—well, at least for the next eight months. The Aging and Fragility program was a one-year master's, and they were already three months into the first semester. She was supposed to return to America after her studies, but Sierra was already looking at other post-graduate programs that she could stay and complete. Even though it was eight months away, she knew she wouldn't be ready to go back to the life she had come to detest just yet.

Sierra pulled her phone out of her pocket and began scrolling Instagram. She liked seeing what her 'friends' were doing on the other side of the world. She hated to admit it, but she didn't think they were real friends to begin with. She had come to Dublin hoping to find people she connected with better than those in her hometown, but even though she had been here for a few months, she hadn't really met anyone she clicked with yet. She had a few acquaintances she had come across in her program, but they weren't at the point of 'hanging out' on weekends.

Although it was challenging to accept, Sierra knew she was lonely, which is why she kept going back to Tinder and going on dates that made her want to gag. Sure, some of the men were attractive, but most of them had no respect for women. Or they partied too much, or they simply weren't her type.

Sierra sighed as she opened Tinder and unmatched Aodhan. Another wasted Saturday evening.

Chapter Two

Sierra pushed the cart through the racks at the campus library, weaving her way around a group tour. The library of the famous Harry Potter books was based on the Trinity College Old Library, and tourists frequently came to the other parts of the library, namely the Berkley Library building, where Sierra worked, by mistake. Plus, campus tours for prospective students had this part of the library complex on their route as well. Sierra typically didn't mind, but on days like today, the tourists congregating in massive, inconvenient groups in the middle of the path made her job reshelving books almost impossible.

Keeping her face neutral, she passed around the group and began shelving the books on the cart in their correct location. Once she finished the ones on this particular shelf, she grabbed her cart and wove her way back through the tour to the other side, fighting not to voice her frustration as she slammed the books into the shelf.

"Whoa there, you know the books aren't the ones sponsoring the tour, right?"

Sierra spun around to find her coworker, Tyler, leaning

against the shelf behind her. Tyler was tall and lean, with a mop of red hair pointing every which way on his head.

"Go away," Sierra muttered as she continued shoving books on the shelf as hard as possible.

"Not until you stop taking your anger out on the poor books. They didn't do anything wrong, you know."

Sierra could feel her resolve melting and a smile cracking through her anger. "How do you always do that?"

Tyler smiled. "It's my secret talent. Plus, as a book lover, I have to advocate on their behalf."

Sierra shook her head as she chuckled. It was well-known around the library that she wasn't a reader. Apparently, all the other staff had gotten jobs here because of their love of books. Sierra didn't know why they had hired her exactly, considering she had been honest in her interview when she said that she read maybe one book a year—and usually only if it was assigned for a grade.

Tyler began grabbing books off the cart and shelving them on the shelf behind her. "I still don't know why Mona hired you."

Mona was the staff manager at the library, and Tyler brought up Sierra's strange hiring at least once a day, even though she had been hired over two months ago. Sierra knew better than to answer Tyler's rhetorical question at this point.

"So, what are your plans for Halloween?" Tyler asked, after a moment of silence.

Sierra pulled her phone out of her pocket and looked at the date. "It's September 30th."

"Exactly. Time to start planning."

Sierra looked up at the ceiling and shook her head. How she ended up with the same hours as her exact personality opposite, she was unsure. She supposed some deity was having a laugh at her pain. "You know I was raised religious. We never celebrated Halloween."

Tyler feigned shock. "What? No Halloween? How did you ever survive?"

"Like most of the world survives without Halloween, I assume," Sierra retorted. Technically, her family had celebrated around this time of the year. But they celebrated Día de Los Muertos, which she didn't feel like explaining, so she didn't mention it.

"How was your Tinder date last night, by the way?"

"Ugh," Sierra groaned, grimacing. "I don't want to talk about it."

Tyler reached to grab a few more books from the cart. "My offer still stands, you know."

Sierra shook her head. "I'm not going on a date with you, Tyler. I already told you, I don't date coworkers."

"If it meant I could have you, I would quit."

Sierra laughed, "And never see your first love again? I highly doubt it."

Tyler looked at the book in his hands. "You're right, I don't know if I could stay away."

Sierra sighed, grabbing the last book on the cart. "I appreciate the flattery, Tyler, but I'm afraid you're not really my type." She shelved the book and began walking back with the empty cart to trade it for a full one, Tyler hot on her heels.

"Not your type? Can you tell me what your type is exactly?"

Sierra spun around, narrowly missing Tyler with the cart. "Tyler, don't ever offer to change yourself for a woman, okay? It won't work out."

Tyler nodded, "Okay, I won't...But if I did, what would I have to do for you to love me?"

Sierra began pushing the full cart toward a different shelf alcove. "I'm not playing the 'what if' game, Tyler. I'm sorry." Although what she said sounded serious, Sierra knew that Tyler asking her on a date was more a joke than anything. He wasn't truly interested in anyone; he just liked the chase and was known around the library as a bit of a playboy.

"I understand," Tyler replied, the smile falling from his lips. He wasn't sulking, but clearly sensed the conversation was over as he grabbed another cart and headed in the opposite direction. Sierra watched him go, knowing that even though he said he understood, he really didn't, and he would ask her out again next weekend and the one after that. It was just who he was.

Sierra turned back to her cart and began pushing, almost hitting a man who had wandered away from his tour. She quickly raised a hand over her shoulder in apology before entering the alcove and returning to her task.

She had been so distracted by what she had said to Tyler that she didn't recognize the man she almost hit until he cleared his throat. She spun around to meet his emerald-green eyes.

"Aodhan." She looked to her left and her right to see no library employees or tour in sight. "What are you doing here?"

He motioned to the shelf behind her. "Looking for a book. Then I saw you."

Sierra kept her face neutral as she crossed her arms over her chest. "What book?"

"Uh...um..." He quickly glanced around, reaffirming Sierra's suspicion that he hadn't come here for a book at all. "Do you have any in Gaelic?"

Sierra raised an eyebrow. "Of course, this is the University library." She snapped before his words sunk in, causing her to pause. "I didn't know you read Gaelic." She motioned to an alcove across the way. "All of our Gaelic books are on that side. I don't read or understand Gaelic, but you can head to the Information Desk to look up a specific title."

Aodhan nodded in understanding but didn't move. Sierra waited, but he didn't say anything, he just stared at her.

"So...is there anything else I can help you with?" Sierra was really trying to be nice, but this man was just so strange. She already wished she could go back in time and never match with him in the first place.

"No. That's it, I suppose." And with that, he turned on his heel and headed for the front of the library.

Sierra turned back to her shelving, but she couldn't get

Aodhan out of her mind. He clearly didn't come to the library for a book, and he didn't have any study materials with him. Plus, he hadn't looked shocked to see Sierra when she had clearly been surprised to see him.

Something about Aodhan set off warning bells in her head, and Sierra made a mental note to check that she had her pepper spray in her bag when she left work. The last thing she needed was some crazy nut of a Tinder date turning into her worst nightmare.

Chapter Three

Sierra doodled a small bird in the margin of her binder as the professor droned on about genetics and its tie to the aging process. It wasn't anything groundbreaking, and any student who had done their reading the night before would recognize the subject matter. But as Sierra lifted her eyes and glanced around the room, she noticed most students furiously jotting down notes. Apparently, she had been the only one home on a Sunday night with nothing better to do than read the textbook.

She continued her doodling, staring at the dark iPhone perched on the corner of her desk. Back in the United States, she had always had 'friends' to text when class had gotten boring. Since she had moved abroad, most of them had shown that she wasn't an important fixture in their lives. Her texts often went unanswered, and while she still followed them on Facebook, they rarely messaged her.

It was okay, though; Sierra would rather it this way. She had always felt that her friends weren't really there for her, and now she no longer had to wonder about the truth as she knew they had never been her friends in the first place. It had made room for her to make new friends in her life, but she had been failing at that, unfortunately.

She must've zoned out, as suddenly everyone was packing their belongings, including the teacher. Class was over.

Sierra quickly put away her notebook and colored pencils, making her way down the stairs of the lecture room and into the hall.

Most of her classes were located in the medicine building, and she passed many of the lab rooms on her way out the door. She couldn't help but glance out of the corner of her eye as she watched various students attending dissections, evaluating plants, and heading into the room she knew likely held the human cadavers. Medical school wasn't for the weak.

As she made her way outside, she brushed shoulders with someone and looked up to apologize, only to see Tyler grinning down at her.

"Hey, coworker!" he said enthusiastically, a smile breaking out across his pale face, his teeth practically blinding her with their intense whiteness.

"Hey, Tyler," Sierra responded less than enthusiastically, trying to think of a way out of talking with him for an extended period of time. The small doses she had of Tyler at work were more than enough for her.

Tyler noticed her energy didn't match his own and quickly adjusted his tactic. "Listen, I know I've made things awkward between us by always asking you on dates, but listen, I really do want to be your friend because work is going to suck if we hate each other."

He had a point. "Alright, Tyler, we can be friends," she conceded.

His answering fist pump in the air made Sierra grimace. Hopefully, he wouldn't be trying to leave the 'friend zone' anytime soon. But as much as she hated to admit it, she really did need to try to start making friends rather than simply complaining about her lack of them.

"As our first order of friendship, we should get dinner tomorrow. I know an excellent pub!"

Sierra held up a hand. "This sounds a little too much like a date."

"No, I promise it won't be, I'll invite my roommates, so there will be four of us. How does that sound?"

Honestly, she wasn't too keen on the idea, even with the roommates. But she knew that she needed to make friends here, and that wasn't going to happen if she kept spending every night at home reading textbooks. Sierra bit her lip and pulled the sleeve of her dark blue sweater over her wrist. "Alright, I'm in."

"Excellent. See you at Mulligan's 18? My last lecture ends at 17." Tyler asked, using the 24-hour clock that most Europeans tend to use.

"Mine, too. See you then!" Sierra turned and headed to her apartment before realizing something and turning back to see Tyler's receding form.

"Wait!" she called, and he turned to face her. "Let me get your number in case plans change."

"Sure thing!" He patiently waited for her to pull out her phone before rattling off his number. She quickly typed it into WhatsApp, sending him a message with her name.

"Thanks, see you tomorrow!" They waved again, heading their separate ways.

As soon as she was off campus, Sierra pulled her hood over her head to protect her ears from the biting wind. Even though it was only the end of September, it was already getting quite cold. Something Sierra wasn't used to in Texas.

She walked home quickly, shedding her jacket as soon as she was in her apartment. Dumping her messenger bag on the couch, she turned to her single cupboard and sifted through it, trying to think of what to make for dinner. She didn't have a whole lot, but that wasn't unusual.

As a full-time student who worked weekends and some weeknights, she found it hard to find the motivation to head to the store in the evenings, as well as cook and complete her homework. She tried hard, but she often ended up grabbing something from a stand on the way home or eating a prepackaged meal from the shop that she could easily pop into her microwave.

She hadn't been to the grocery store since Friday, so her options for tonight were pasta or oatmeal. She didn't have anything else. A quick glance in the fridge revealed some butter, an onion, and half a carton of mushrooms. Just what she needed to make the pasta in her cupboard slightly more nutritious.

Sierra flipped on the TV and began cutting the ingredients for her dinner. She was just about to turn on the stove when her phone began buzzing from her messenger bag. With a sigh, she quickly rinsed her hands and dried them, before pausing the TV and digging in her bag for her phone.

She reached it just as it went to voicemail but saw that it was her mom. With an eye roll, she pressed redial, placed the phone on speaker, and turned on the stove.

Her mom answered after the first ring. "Sierra! *Cariña!* Why didn't you answer on the first ring?"

Sierra winced at the Spanish term of endearment. Her parents had moved to America after they got married, and although they had learned English in school in Mexico, they often mixed in Spanish words when they spoke. Sierra and her siblings also spoke Spanish, as it was necessary for conversing with extended family, but her parents had always insisted on speaking English, or at least mostly English, at home. "I was cooking, *Mamá*."

"Cooking? What are you making? *Arroz con pollo*? Or maybe some *lomo saltado*?"

Sierra let out a sigh. "*Mamá*, I'm vegetarian now. I don't eat meat anymore, remember?" No matter how many times she explained it to her parents, they never seemed to understand her new diet. And Sierra had been vegetarian for over four years.

"Ah, *sí*, I remember now. No meat. *Sin carne*."

"Yes, *Mamá*," Sierra responded, although she knew they

would have this exact same conversation in a few weeks. "How is everyone there? Is Cecilia still enjoying her classes?"

Cecilia was Sierra's younger sister who had just started college in September at the University of Texas.

"Ah yes, yes, she likes her classes a lot! She just told me that she is preparing for an *examen final*."

Sierra dumped the pasta in the water before inquiring about her younger brother. "And Diego?"

Her mother made a *tsk*ing sound through the phone. "He is in trouble again. I do not understand. Antonio was never like this when he was in school."

Antonio was Sierra's older brother by two years, and unlike her younger brother Diego, he had always been a model student. He had recently finished his law degree and was working at a private practice in the Dallas area. "Diego and Antonio are very different people, *mamá*. It's not fair to compare them." She reminded her mom.

"I know, *Cariña*, I just wish he would stop getting detention. His teachers think he will need to go to summer school to graduate next year."

Sierra bit her lip. While she was glad her parents couldn't visit her, she knew they had their hands full with Diego. For whatever reason, Diego had never seen eye to eye with her parents, an issue which had only increased as he entered his teen years. Now, at 16, he was practically unmanageable, and all her siblings had moved out, leaving her parents alone to deal with his shenanigans. "Maybe Maria can talk to him?"

Maria was Sierra's older sister and the oldest child in their family. She had finished medical school and was a doctor in Fort Worth, the city right next to Dallas.

"I don't want to bother her. You know she is busy at the hospital."

Sierra stirred the pot, trying to think if there was anything else she could suggest to her parents. "Maybe the pastor at church could talk to him?" Just because Sierra was no longer religious didn't mean that the pastor couldn't help Diego.

"Church is one of our major arguments. I don't think he will go."

Sierra could hear the sadness in her mother's voice. While she was sad she wasn't there to help, Sierra also knew that this was one of the main reasons she lived abroad, to remove herself from the middle of these situations. "I don't know what else to suggest, *Mamá*. Maybe you should just let him get in trouble? He might not be so proud when he doesn't graduate with his friends next year."

Her mom was silent on the other end of the line.

"But other than Diego, is everything okay there?" Sierra pressed.

"Ah, *sí, sí. No te preocupes.* Everything is fine here, *Cariña*, Diego will come around."

"Okay, *Mamá*, was there anything else you wanted to talk about?" Sierra stirred the pasta again and looked at the clock. She would need to take it out soon, and she hoped to hang up the phone before then.

"What! I can't call my middle daughter just for a talk?"

"Of course, *Mamá*, you can call anytime." Sierra hoped her mom wouldn't get worked up. She was always very dramatic, especially when it came to thinking her children didn't want to speak to her. "I'm just a bit busy, *Mamá*. I'd like to hang up and finish cooking if you don't want to discuss anything else?"

"I see how it is! You move abroad, and you are suddenly too busy for your *mamá*. We will see how you feel when I am dead!" she snapped before the line went dead.

Sierra sighed, set her phone down, and drained the pasta. Her mom would get over it, she always did. But it still annoyed Sierra that she tried to play with her emotions like this. Holding her future death (which was at least 30 years away) over her head as if it would make Sierra sit down and spill her heart out to her mom.

The truth was that Sierra and her mom hadn't been close for

years. Besides the vegetarianism, Sierra had also left the church, something which devastated her mom. She was convinced that just because she didn't sit in a pew every Sunday, Sierra was now worshiping the devil.

Sierra hadn't fit in with her family for a long time. Her older siblings were so successful, and Cecilia was on her way to join them, studying to be a psychologist. Sierra had been pressed to choose a prestigious study, as her siblings did, but in the end, it just wasn't for her. In fact, most days, she felt she understood Diego better than anyone else in her family. It was difficult to live up to perfect older siblings, and at some point, she just wanted to do her own thing, even if it wasn't considered a "successful" path —and upset her mother to no end.

Sierra scooped the mushrooms, butter, and onion into the pot with the pasta, stirring it all together. It was nothing gourmet, but it would do.

Thankful for the silence of her small apartment, Sierra dumped the pasta in a bowl and sat down at her table to eat. She kept her phone nearby as she ate, just in case her mother called her back. But she didn't.

Her phone remained silent for the rest of the night.

Chapter Four

The next night, Sierra found herself in Mulligan's pub surrounded by fans screaming at the TV where soccer, called football in Ireland, was playing.

"Oh, COME ON!" Tyler practically screamed in her ear. She tried to lean away only to find his roommate, Jack, screaming something by her other ear as well. Her eardrums weren't going to survive this.

Tyler's second roommate, Jameson, laughed from the other side of the table. "You actually came when Tyler invited you to a pub? You had to know this was going to happen."

Sierra frowned. "I thought we were coming to spend time together as friends." She emphasized the word 'thought'. "If I had known it was just to watch football, I would have stayed home."

Tyler looked over at her as if suddenly remembering she was there. "Sorry, I just get a little too excited about sports sometimes."

"I see." Sierra took a sip of her cider. This just reaffirmed that he wasn't her type. Sierra wasn't interested in sports at all.

"Oh, come on, Sierra, loosen up a little. Football is fun!" Tyler put his arm around Sierra's shoulders as she grimaced.

"For you, maybe." She huffed under her breath, draining the rest of her drink and ducking out from underneath Tyler's arm. "I'm going to get some fries. Anyone else need anything?"

The guys had their eyes glued to the screen, not even acknowledging that she spoke. Sierra rolled her eyes and headed to the bar.

The bartender was also watching the game as she dried a glass in her hands. As the team on the screen missed a goal and the crowd in the pub cheered, she turned and looked at Sierra. "What can I get ya?" she asked in the Irish accent that Sierra wished she had. The lyrical lilt made everything sound so much more attractive.

Sierra ordered another cider and a basket of fries, handing over her card. The bartender printed the receipt, sliding it back to her. She quickly signed, picking up her cider and turning from the bar, only to run into a wide chest. She would've fallen over if the owner of the chest hadn't grabbed her arms to steady her. Sierra checked to see that her cider was still mostly full before raising her head to find Aodhan's piercing green eyes staring back at her.

Anger immediately coursed through her, igniting beneath her skin. The library at the campus they both attended was one thing, but ending up in the same pub in a city that was nothing but pubs? He was clearly following her.

"You need to stop following me."

Aodhan didn't say anything. He took a step back.

"I'm serious." She tried again. "I'm going to contact the campus police if I keep seeing you."

Aodhan's eyes raked over her, not an ounce of fear on his face, making Sierra feel naked even though she was wearing a turtleneck sweater and jeans. His eyes drifted over to the table where Tyler and his roommates were sitting, anger flickering in their depths. "I just want to know why you will go out with him, but not me."

Sierra cocked her head at the odd words. "Excuse me?"

"You heard me. I'm ten times better than that guy."

Sierra felt her ears getting hot. "You must have some nerve.

That guy is only my friend, and, unlike you, he showed up on time when we made plans. As far as I can see, the fact that he values me should be answer enough as to why I'm here with him." Sierra made to move past Aodhan, but he put a hand on her shoulder, effectively stopping her.

"Listen, I'm sorry I was late on the date. But you're not giving me a chance."

Sierra glanced at the table, wishing that Tyler was paying attention so he could come rescue her. She attempted to duck out of Aodhan's strong grip but it was like iron. Pissed that she couldn't avoid the situation, she retaliated. "Maybe if you had said sorry when you arrived, I would have given you a chance. But with your behavior, following—no, stalking—me, I see no reason in hell to spend any more time with you."

Aodhan raised his eyebrows. "I am quickly noticing that maybe we are not a match after all."

Sierra narrowed her eyes. Who talked like that? Aodhan was clearly off, and she regretted that she had ever granted him a date. But it looked like he was backing off at least, so she added her retort. "Yeah, I guess we aren't. So, bye."

Yanking herself out of his grip caused her cider to splash over the edge of the glass, but at this point, she didn't care.

"You'll regret this!" Aodhan called after her as she stomped back over to the guys, who hadn't even noticed she was gone.

Sliding into the rickety wooden chair at the high-top table they had chosen to occupy, Sierra sipped at her cider, refusing to look around and confirm that Aodhan had left. Instead, she watched the soccer players run across the screen, not really watching the game, or caring which of the teams won.

Something about Aodhan brushed her the wrong way, but the words he was saying weren't technically threatening. Internally, she was going back and forth about whether or not she should speak to someone on campus about her concerns regarding him.

When the server arrived with her fries, she took the opportunity to look around and see if Aodhan was in the bar. When she noticed he had indeed left, she decided she likely didn't have to worry about him. If he showed up somewhere again, then she would tell someone. He was probably harmless, just weird.

At least, she hoped that was the case.

Chapter Five

"That last goal was crazy, huh? Just whoosh—"

Sierra tuned Tyler out as they went about reshelving books the next day. Ever since their shift had started, Tyler had done nothing but talk about the soccer game from the night before. While Sierra was glad to see Tyler happy and excited, she hoped this hadn't given him the wrong idea that she was interested in the sport.

The soccer game breakdown became background noise as Sierra looked at the titles in her hand and found their spots on the library shelves. Like most libraries, this one was organized by the Universal Classification System, which was similar to the Dewey Decimal system the United States used. While she had to learn the UCS system when she initially got this job, she hadn't been familiar with Dewey Decimal in the first place, so it hadn't bothered her much, and she had picked it up quickly. Although she wasn't a reader, Sierra did like studying and organization, two things that the UCS system made easier for students.

Sierra liked the look of some of the book covers as she slid them away, especially some of those in the fantasy section. She wished she liked reading books, but she couldn't get over the fact that it was just so boring to her. She would much rather take a walk or learn a new skill, leaving the storytelling to movies she could consume in a few hours.

Tyler must've noticed she wasn't paying attention, as he suddenly changed the subject. "Oh, is that *Silver Kiss*? I loved that book as a teen."

"Uh," Sierra looked down at the book in her hand, which featured a man biting down on the neck of the woman underneath the title, *Silver Kiss*. "I suppose it is." Sierra squinted to look closer at the image.

"You should check it out, I bet you would like it."

Sierra shook her head. "I don't think vampire books are my thing." She quickly shelved the book in its spot, hoping Tyler would drop the conversation.

"Oh, come on, you're telling me you haven't read *Twilight*?" Tyler was staring at her, open-mouthed.

Sierra shook her head. "No. But I saw the movie. If the book is anything like the movie, no thanks. I'm a huge movie fan and that was just...No." She vaguely remembered a movie with an anorexic-looking man who had fallen in love with a teen girl who was terrified of turning 19. If only her character had been faced with the same situation Sierra was now, she was about to turn 26 and she hadn't done anything but study and had no idea what kind of job she even wanted to work when she was done. Maybe she would just study forever, at least then she wouldn't have to worry about paying her mountain of student loans.

Tyler shook his head. "Ugh, everyone knows the book is better than the movie. From now on, no more watching movies based on books until you read the book first, okay?"

"Like I would ever agree to that," she laughed.

Tyler groaned and put his palm over his face. "And to think I thought we could be friends."

Sierra noticed the smile on Tyler's face, indicating he was joking. "Yeah, well, sorry, I'm such an impossible friend."

Tyler joined her in laughing. "Actually, maybe you not being into books is better. That way, you can't spoil anything for me. If you were into books like me, you would probably spoil all the endings since you read faster than me."

"See? Books are bad." Sierra jokingly nudged Tyler, her sleeve riding up. With a grimace, Sierra quickly pulled back down her sleeve until it covered her wrist, hoping Tyler hadn't seen anything.

Lucky for her, Tyler was fairly oblivious to, well, everything, and he simply continued shelving the books from the cart. The two continued to joke about books and movies until the cart was empty. One glance at the clock told Sierra it was time for her break, so she told Tyler she was heading for lunch before grabbing her bag and heading outside.

The library was located near a small campus café that offered coffee, sandwiches, and pastries. While vegetarian food was becoming more common in Dublin, there were only two sandwiches they regularly offered that came vegetarian, and, of course, today they were out of them. Not wanting to ask if they could make one special, Sierra grabbed a croissant and banana and headed outside to eat.

There were a few benches in the common area, but they were taken, so Sierra sat on the cement with her back against the café building, people-watching as she consumed her sad lunch. She was always curious about people, and she enjoyed watching their body language and trying to guess what was going on in their lives or conversations.

One couple sitting on the grass was clearly arguing during what should have been a romantic afternoon picnic. Another young woman was on the phone, pacing back and forth, clearly dealing with something serious. Feeling for the woman, Sierra hoped it was something she would be able to solve.

After her food was gone, Sierra pulled her homework out of her messenger bag and began working on a lab write-up, which was due the next day. Focused on her work, Sierra didn't notice what was going on around her, oblivious until, at some point, she felt the hairs on the back of her neck prickle. She looked up, confused at the sensation.

Across the campus, seated on a bench, was Aodhan. He was leaning back on his muscled arms as he lay on top of the bench, looking incredibly relaxed and attractive in a way that made her chest tingle. Sierra felt a shiver go through her but quickly brushed it off. Aodhan wasn't looking at her; in fact, he appeared to be observing other people just as she had been before the hairs on the back of her neck had alerted her that something was going on.

Although she was itching to report Aodhan to campus security, Sierra knew that the fact that she had seen him in the common area at a school they both attended was no reason to make a report. He was likely just here by chance, and it looked like he hadn't even noticed her.

Sierra took a moment to take in his profile, which she had to admit was much more attractive than some of the other men she had met over the past few months via Tinder. If only Aodhan hadn't turned out to be an asshole in the end.

Her neck prickled again, causing her focus to leave Aodhan and look around. Why did she feel that something wasn't right, but no one was even looking at her?

A final look around revealed that no one in the common area was even glancing in her direction, but Sierra couldn't brush off the odd feeling that something was wrong. Regardless, a glance at her phone told her that break time was almost up anyway, so she packed up her book and notebook and headed back into the library to resume work.

She was so focused on where she was going, she was oblivious to the green eyes that followed her every step until the library doors closed behind her.

Chapter Six

The rest of the week passed in a blur, and before Sierra knew it, Saturday arrived, along with her full day shift at the library, which started at eight in the morning. It was a struggle to leave her warm and cozy bed to tug on a green turtleneck sweater and jeans, but she knew there would be no mercy from Tyler if she called in sick simply for not wanting to get out of bed.

Sierra brushed her dark hair, which was naturally a bit curly and often unruly, into a low ponytail, before deciding it looked stupid and braiding it instead. Sierra inspected her face in the mirror next. While she normally didn't wear much makeup, she definitely looked tired today, so she applied a small amount of under-eye concealer and some mascara in hopes it would help. It didn't.

As much as it pained her to shrug on her messenger bag and head outside for the cold walk to the library, she reminded herself of her desire to be here; abroad, miles away from her family and the job she had to work at to make it possible.

"At least it's not waiting tables," she said under her breath, as she arrived at the campus and entered the library. Sierra had waited tables all through her undergrad, and she still had nightmares about the fast-casual restaurant she had worked at in Dallas. A shudder went through her at the thought alone, as she crossed through the library and headed toward the employee area.

She tucked her stuff in the employee room and grabbed a cart to go pick up returned books until she noticed something odd. Aodhan was standing in the staff room and looking like he was lost. He was wearing his typical black woolen beanie, fitted jeans, and a green polo shirt, which made his eyes look extra green as they bore into hers. With his arms crossed, she could see his biceps bulging from beneath the short sleeves. She felt her heart drop to her stomach and let go of her cart to confront him.

"What are you doing here?" she snapped as she marched up to him, stopping when her feet were just a few inches from his. "Library visitors can't be back here."

Aodhan glared down at her stoically, his facial features unchanging. "I work here now."

"You—What?" Sierra sputtered as his words sank in, and something in her chest tightened.

Aodhan shrugged. "I was hired yesterday. So, pardon me." He pushed past her and headed for the cart she had just abandoned. Sierra looked around to see if the manager, Mona, was around, but, of course, she wasn't.

Seething, Sierra marched up to Aodhan once again. "If you were hired yesterday, you're going to need training. You can't just start putting books on shelves."

"I know that," he snapped, his green eyes focused on her. "Mona said you would train me. Lead the way." He motioned to the cart.

Sierra narrowed her eyes. She was inclined to believe he was just messing with her. In fact, she was so sure there was no way Aodhan could have been hired to work at the library that she started laughing. "Ha, ha, you got me, Tyler!" She called out, looking around the staff area for him. "Very funny!" Another employee, Sheila, looked up from her cubby in the staff room, glancing around confused.

Aodhan simply crossed his arms over his chest. Apparently this was his signature pose, and Sierra did agree that it suited his brooding personality. "I don't know what you think is funny."

"There is no possible way you got a job here just to follow me around!" Sierra nearly screeched. She couldn't believe the nerve of this guy.

Aodhan arched one of his eyebrows, his jaw clenched. "I didn't. My job here is purely a coincidence."

"Like I believe that," Sierra snapped. It felt like something was crawling beneath her skin, and she felt the sudden urge to scratch her arm.

The room quieted as Shelia passed their little stare down and made her way out into the library. Sierra bit her lip, waiting and praying to a God she no longer believed in that this was some sort of joke.

Aodhan just looked around expectantly, his lips pressed in a firm line. "Well, if this is what you do all day, then this is the easiest job I've ever had." He brushed imaginary dust off his shoulder in a move that was reminiscent of the boys who used to bully Sierra in high school.

Shocked at the sudden flashback, Sierra continued to stare at him for another moment before realizing that it probably wasn't a joke, and since that was the case, she really did have to help train him.

"Ugh, fine," she grumbled, grabbing the cart, and choking down the words she wished she could say to him. "Follow me." She pushed the cart out to the main library and began gathering books that were left on tables or near the checkout at the front. "First thing you should do when you get here is collect any books lying around. Most of them are for library use only, but people don't know how to put them away in the right spot, so we do it."

Aodhan nodded, his jaw still clenched, and began collecting the books and stacking them on the cart.

"Exam weeks are worse, but usually, there aren't too many left out. If there aren't any, or just a few, you can go grab a cart from the returns section and start reshelving those."

"And how do we know where they go?"

Sierra nearly dropped the books she was collecting. "Are you serious?"

His expressionless face gave her the answer.

"I can't believe they hired you, and you don't even know about library shelving systems." Sierra turned her attention back to the books she was stacking. The irony of the fact that she also hadn't known the shelving system was not lost on Sierra, but she didn't voice that small fact, resolving to hold on to her anger at Aodhan instead.

"Where I'm from, libraries are organized based on preference."

"Preference?" Sierra picked up her stack and placed it on the cart. "Who organizes a library based on preference, and how do you know whose preference to follow?"

Aodhan shrugged. "All libraries are privately owned. The owner picks, but if it changes hands, I guess the new owner can change where books are shelved if he wants."

Sierra's brows furrowed as she tried to think of his Tinder profile and whether it said where he was from. When she couldn't find the answer, she asked, "Where are you from again?"

Aodhan placed his books on the cart and, seeing the table empty, went to get ready to push it. "Somewhere up north, you don't know it."

Sierra was trying to be nice, she really was, but this man infuriated her. She took a deep breath before she answered to control her volume. "Up north, where? This is Ireland, Aodhan, there isn't much else north besides more Ireland."

Aodhan began pushing the cart with one of his arms, waving her off with the other. "Never mind. Like I said, you wouldn't know it."

Sierra rolled her eyes at his insinuation, as she followed him to another desk area and began collecting more books. Aodhan must really think she was an idiot. Maybe, in the past, Sierra would have kept this opinion to herself, but her mouth had a mind of its own as it opened. "You must think I'm dumb."

As if it couldn't get any worse, Aodhan shrugged, as if he agreed.

Sierra was about to explode. She took a few more calming breaths, reminding herself that she needed this job if she wanted to continue to live in Dublin. Without any explanation, she snatched the cheat sheet for the Universal Classification System from where it hung on the side of a shelf and slammed it on the desk in front of Aodhan.

"Here's how you organize the books. Figure it out." Then she spun on her heel and went to collect another cart from the employee area before she could say something she would really regret.

She told herself not to look back, but her neck didn't listen to her mental commands, spinning around to see Aodhan squinting at the chart in his hand as if her outburst didn't have any effect. Either way, it only made her feel worse.

Forcing herself to turn away, she grabbed another cart and began working in a different area of the library.

⁓

Sierra managed to avoid Aodhan the rest of the morning. But of course, when she walked into the employee area for lunch, Aodhan was sitting there, staring at the table, a weird expression occupying his face as he frowned at the sandwich in front of him.

Not wanting to deal with his rude comments again, Sierra snatched her wallet and headed for the cafe. She usually ate in the employee room alone during her full-day shifts when it rained, but she was going to get her sandwich and eat outside today, even if her hands froze.

By the time she purchased her lunch and exited the building, it was pouring even harder than when she had entered the café.

Even if she had an umbrella, the wind was blowing the rain every which way, ensuring there was no way she could possibly stay dry. Dismayed, but still not willing to sit in the same room as Aodhan, she leaned against the wall and unwrapped her caprese sandwich in the same place she had eaten earlier that week, trying to shield herself from the rain as much as possible and failing miserably.

The sound of the rain calmed her a bit as she savored each bite of her lunch. Aodhan was a jerk; it was simple. She dealt with jerks all the time in Texas. She could handle him. She would just limit their conversations to work only and avoid him the rest of the time. She could do this.

Finishing her lunch and throwing away the wrapper, Sierra made her way back inside, stopping by the women's room to pat a paper towel on her sopping hair and arms before grabbing one of the carts filled with returns and heading for the stacks.

Sierra loved the peace that came with reshelving books. It was like her own little form of active meditation. It was also a mental challenge to find the right spot for all the books in the cart.

Everything was going smoothly until she pulled out a book that she couldn't read the title of. Not only that but the label on the side, which would usually tell her where to shelve it, was rubbed off, so she couldn't see the number.

While she spoke little to no Gaelic, she was usually able to figure out enough to put the book away. But this book didn't even look like it was written in Gaelic.

Tucking the book under her arm, she went to look for one of the other employees as she normally did when she couldn't find where to shelve a particular book.

Mona, her manager, was behind the main counter, typing something on the computer as she peered down through the glasses perched atop her narrow nose, when Sierra approached.

"Hey, Mona, can you help me with this book?" She set the title on the desk.

Mona had been working at the library for decades, and it showed. While she was still fit and relatively healthy for a woman in her 60s, she definitely looked like a librarian, and it seemed like her blonde hair was constantly coated in a light layer of dust from digging out old, relatively unknown books for research students.

Mona turned to Sierra, pushing her glasses back toward her eyes, only for them to sink down to the tip of her nose a second later. "Let's see here...ah, yes."

Sierra waited patiently, expecting a translation, but instead, Mona turned her head to the side. "Where did Aodhan go?"

"Aodhan? I'm not sure. Reshelving somewhere. Why?" Sierra didn't understand why Mona would be bringing this up now.

"Because he can read old Gaelic. That's why I hired him."

Sierra felt her jaw drop. "He reads old Gaelic?"

"Yeah, I hired him to help organize some of the older texts that even I can't read. We don't have many in Old Gaelic, but they've just been collecting dust for the past few years. It's rare we find someone who reads it and has the time to devote to working in the library."

Sierra huffed, trying and failing to keep the distaste off her face.

Mona didn't seem to notice. "I'm giving him your Thursday shift by the way."

She felt her heart drop. "But why?" Her mind immediately began running over all the problems that would cause her financially. "I really need the hours."

"All student contracts are for 25 hours a week. We've had extra shifts, so I didn't mind that you were working more, but I had to offer Aodhan the same contract. You'll still get your 25 hours, just not more unless another employee requests vacation."

Sierra knew better than to argue, as she reached out and took the book back from Mona's outstretched hand, feeling as if she were in a daze. Without another word, she started walking toward the other side of the library, peeking down each aisle, looking for Aodhan. She hadn't liked him before, and now she downright hated him. Following her was one thing, but getting a job at her work, which cut into her income, was another thing.

It didn't take long for her to find his large frame staring at a bookshelf with a book in one hand and rubbing his angled chin with the other. It was clear he was having some trouble.

Aodhan must've heard her approach, as he turned toward her even before she was standing next to him. She held out the book, ensuring she was a full arm's length away, keeping her eyes on the book so she didn't have to look at his face. "Can you let me know what subject this book is?"

Aodhan didn't even blink. "It's a religious book," he replied, turning back to the book in his hands.

Sierra didn't know what to think. First, she found out he knew how to read a language that had been dead for over 1400 years, and he didn't even take time to study the title. It was like he just inherently knew it.

Not willing to talk to him more than necessary, Sierra turned to head back to her cart.

"Wait, can you tell me where this book goes?" He held out the book in his hands, his face as impossible to read as always.

Sierra plucked it from his outstretched hand, careful to avoid her skin touching his, noticing the cover label had worn off, just like the religious book she had brought to him. She flipped the book open to the first page.

"It's an astrology book. I'll take it to get relabeled, and I'll reshelve it."

Sierra figured that was the end of their conversation. But before she exited the aisle, she heard Aodhan say, "What's astrology?"

Sierra spun back around, checking to ensure her mouth was hanging open. "You seriously can't tell me that you can read old Gaelic but haven't ever heard of astrology?"

In typical Aodhan fashion, he shrugged, turning back to the shelves, his face completely passive. Sierra didn't bother to explain, choosing instead to go back to the front desk to have Mona relabel both books. Aodhan could figure out what astrology was on his own.

Chapter Seven

Sierra managed to avoid Aodhan the rest of Saturday, however, when she clocked in for her Sunday shift, she wasn't so lucky. Aodhan was leaning against the wall right by the carts, clearly waiting for her when she arrived.

Ignoring him, Sierra went to grab a cart, only for Aodhan to wrap his fingers around her arm.

"Why are you so mean to me?" he demanded, his green eyes appearing darker than normal. His lips were pressed into a frown, which normally wouldn't bother Sierra, but she had never seen him express anything but passivity, so this was something new.

Sierra looked down at where his hand encircled her forearm. His grip was warm and firm, and she could get away if she wanted with his arm in this position, but she was itching for a fight after having not slept well the night before, for the second night in a row, and decided to answer him instead.

"Why am I mean to you? You have been nothing but rude to me since we met! You act as if I'm nothing, and you basically called me stupid yesterday. You can't seriously be suggesting that you don't know why I don't like you."

Aodhan didn't say anything for a moment, his green eyes

assessing hers. He appeared to be having an internal debate. Finally, he said, "That doesn't mean you have to be rude to me. I deserve respect."

Sierra couldn't help herself, she burst out laughing. "Oh my god, what century are you from, Aodhan? This isn't 1750 anymore, women have rights. You don't get the respect of a woman just because you were born a man."

This seemed to confuse him, and he tilted his head to the side. "I still think you should respect me."

Sierra shrugged. "Well, that's just too damn bad. I'd love to not be a poor university student with no direction in life, but here we are. You don't always get what you want, okay?" She looked down at where his hand was still on her arm. "If you would let go of my arm now, that would be great."

His eyes narrowed, but he dropped her arm and Sierra quickly pulled her sleeve over her wrist. "You don't like me? Well, I can assure you, the feeling is mutual," he snapped.

"Good. If you don't like me, then stay away from me," Sierra retaliated, entirely unsurprised to find out they shared a mutual distaste for one another.

Aodhan opened his mouth to say something else, but Tyler chose that moment to arrive and dump his happy attitude on everyone in the vicinity.

"Hey, Sierra! Happy Sunday!" His grin was infectious, and Sierra couldn't help but return it as she maneuvered the cart out from the wall, around Aodhan, and began to walk toward the other side of the library. Tyler fell into step beside her.

"Tyler! How was your Saturday?"

Tyler smiled. "Excellent. Went to a football game. You should've come."

Sierra shook her head. "I told you that football wasn't my thing. Plus, who else would shelve the books in your absence?"

Tyler laughed, opening and holding the door as she passed through with the cart. As Sierra turned around to face Tyler, she saw Aodhan over his shoulder, still standing where they left him. But unlike before, when his eyes had been curious, they were now filled with rage. And he was looking right at her.

The morning portion of work went without incident, but as Sierra went to eat her lunch, Aodhan was once again taking up residence in the staff room at the table they all had to share. She grabbed the sandwich she had remembered to bring from home for once, and her jacket, before heading outside to lean against the wall and eat. At least it wasn't raining cats and dogs today.

In between bites of her sandwich, she scrolled through her Facebook feed, silencing a call from her mother when it rang. She didn't want to deal with her mother's dramatics, not today. She had enough other things on her mind.

But when her mother's name flashed on the screen a second time, she groaned before reluctantly pressing the talk button.

"What is it now, *mamá*?"

"That is how you answer the phone when speaking with *tu madre*?"

Sierra rolled her eyes, knowing she had just made a huge mistake. Before she could even answer, her mother was off on a tirade in Spanish, attacking everything from Sierra's decision to move abroad to her choice to leave religion. Sierra was pretty sure she even called her a vegetarian heathen at some point, but she couldn't be sure as she had to hold the phone a few inches from her face, so her mother's screeching didn't break her eardrum. At some point, the line went completely dead, and Sierra knew her mother had likely hung up the phone in exasperation.

As she finished the last bites of her sandwich, she walked over to the trash, only to see Aodhan standing along the other side of the building, staring at her intently. Sierra grimaced, realizing he likely overheard her one-sided phone conversation. Sierra tried to think of something smart to say, but nothing came to mind, so she decided it was better to say nothing as she tossed her wrapper in the can.

Aodhan opened his mouth as if he was about to say something, but before he had the chance, a blonde student approached him. "Well, I haven't seen you leaning around here before," she said as she leaned on the wall between them, blocking Sierra's view of Aodhan.

For some reason, anger flickered within her stomach, but just as that thought reached her, she brushed it off, reminding herself she didn't care about other women looking at Aodhan, and headed inside. What Aodhan did or who he liked was none of her concern. She tucked her coat away in the staff area and headed back to the mundane task of reshelving books.

Just as she rounded the corner, Aodhan was standing there, no longer wearing his coat. How had he passed her? Had she been moving that slowly?

Confused, but resolving not to let this man infuriate her anymore, Sierra began shelving books, only for Aodhan to walk over and begin shelving right next to her without a word.

By this point, Sierra was tired of the drama between them and decided to leave it be, continuing her shelving without looking over at him. The air between them buzzed with electricity, and Sierra's shoulders tensed, worried about what might happen if either of them said anything. Sierra glanced at Aodhan once or twice, but if he felt the tension between them, he didn't say anything. He looked like he respected her resolve and remained quiet as they continued to shelve, side by side, until the cart was empty.

Sierra headed to get another cart, watching as Aodhan walked up to Tyler and began helping him shelve his cart. Apparently, he was just being helpful to everyone. Sierra couldn't explain it, but she felt a little sad at the thought that he hadn't been trying to be nice to her specifically. She quickly brushed it off. There was no reason Aodhan had been helping her other than because it was his job. Just as it was his job to help Tyler as well.

Sure, Aodhan was attractive, but he was a jerk, and Sierra wanted nothing to do with him. But even as those thoughts passed through her mind, her resolve was melting. She didn't like Aodhan...right?

Chapter Eight

I t was Monday night, and Sierra was inspecting herself in the mirror as she prepared for her date. Despite what she had told herself before, she had started speaking to a new guy on Tinder last night when she got home from work, and he had asked her out on a dinner date tonight. Even though she knew she would likely regret it, Sierra had said yes.

Plus, he was buying, and she was really ready to eat something that wasn't a sandwhich that she didn't have to cook herself. They were meeting at a pizza café. Sierra loved pizza.

Adjusting the collar on her skin-tight black turtleneck shirt, she made sure it was even as she hung a pair of small silver hoops from her ears. Her dark hair fell in waves past her shoulders and over her average-sized breasts. Thanks to the student diet of sandwiches and skipped meals, Sierra's stomach was flat, but due to her Hispanic heritage, she had hips that meant she had to wear form-fitting clothes or risk looking like she was trying to hide a pregnancy. The black sweater she had chosen fit the bill perfectly, clinging to her curves to show them off.

Paired with dark blue skinny jeans and knee-high black leather boots, Sierra knew she looked good. Her date, whose name was Paul, had seemed like good company during their text conversation last night, and she hoped that he proved to be the same charismatic guy in person, but she wasn't holding her breath.

Grabbing her small clutch purse, which usually lived inside her messenger bag, Sierra slipped on her gray peacoat and headed out to the restaurant, which was only about 15 minutes by foot from her home. That was the best part about living in the center of Dublin; everything was close, and there was no need to even consider driving a car.

She arrived at the restaurant on time and found Paul right away, as he had taken it upon himself to arrive early, it appeared. He didn't look exactly like his picture, but close enough that Sierra wasn't going to be mad about it. He had blonde hair and blue eyes. While he wasn't as fit as other men—*Aodhan,* her mind reminded her even as she pushed the thought aside—he was lean and attractive. He had commandeered a table for two in the corner, and Sierra slid into the empty seat across from him.

"You must be Paul," she said with a smile on her face.

Paul's eyes roamed over her as he returned her smile. "I am, and you, Miss Sierra, look just like your photo. I am impressed."

While it wasn't the best greeting and bordered on those flimsy compliments Sierra hated, she liked that he had been on time, unlike some other people she had been on a date with recently. *Aodhan.* "Thanks, I guess."

Paul placed a hand on hers. "So sorry if I offended you. I'm very direct. It can scare girls away sometimes, so I apologize in advance."

Sierra looked down at his hand resting on hers and decided she didn't hate the warmth that radiated from his skin onto hers. "No worries. I am also direct."

"Awesome." He picked up the menu. "All we have to do now is pick a pizza. What do you like? You're American, right?"

Sierra picked up her own menu, her eyes falling on the 'American' pizza on the menu, which was loaded with every kind of meat imaginable. It was typical for them to assume all Americans love meat. "I am, but I am actually vegetarian, so if we could pick something with less meat or do half and half, that would be great."

Paul's eyes met Sierra's. "No worries, I'm not a big meat eater anyway. Why don't we get the Veggie Delight?" His slight Irish accent made her smile, it was endearing.

"Sounds amazing."

"It's done." He waved to a waitress who quickly came over to take their order. Paul ordered a large veggie delight pie and a plate to split it. Sierra ordered a water to drink, and Paul ordered a beer. After the waitress left, he turned back to her. "I'm glad you like pizza."

Sierra shrugged. "I'm pretty sure if you don't like pizza, they kick you out of America. It's a prerequisite to living there."

Paul laughed. "Is there any culture where not liking pizza is acceptable?"

She thought for a moment. "Probably not, now that I think of it."

The conversation lulled for a moment, but Paul was quick to pick it back up before awkwardness could overtake the air between them. "So, I know you're a student. What are you studying?"

Sierra leaned her chin on her hand. "Age and fragility. You finished your studies a couple of years ago, right?"

He nodded, clearly impressed that she had read his profile. "Yes, I'm 28 now. Finished my bachelor's a couple of years ago. I'm working full-time right now as a graphic designer. But enough about me; tell me about your studies."

Sierra opened her mouth to answer him when a firm hand landed on the table between them with a thump. Both she and Paul looked up in shock, only for Sierra to, unfortunately, recognize the man in the black beanie putting his large hand on their cozy table.

"Aodhan," she said solemnly. What was he doing here? Had she somehow summoned him when she had thought his name just a few moments before?

"Can I talk to you outside?" He motioned to the door of the pizza place.

Sierra looked at Paul, who she could see was quickly beginning to rethink her date with her. Great, he likely thought Aodhan was an ex, or some other type of baggage he didn't want to deal with, and she was just starting to like him. Either way, Aodhan had ruined their cadence, and likely the date. She sighed. "Yes, one moment." Aodhan stalked toward the door as she looked at Paul, hoping he would understand. "He's my coworker. Let me find out what he wants."

Paul nodded, but his eyes were no longer lit up like they had been before Aodhan slammed his hand on their table.

Sierra slipped on her jacket and walked toward the door. Aodhan held it open for her as they stepped out into the night. Sierra turned and watched the door close before she spun toward Aodhan and let him have every ounce of fury that had been building under her skin this past week.

"What the fuck do you think you are doing?!"

Aodhan seethed. "What am I doing? What are you doing out with a man like that?" He motioned to the door. His face held emotion for once, lips poised in a snarl of sorts while his eyebrows scrunched in anger. Sierra had to admit, he actually looked kind of attractive.

Brushing off that thought, Sierra was quick to continue her rampage. "What am I doing? We—" she motioned between them with her finger, "Are nothing, absolutely nothing. I am my own person, and I can date whoever I want!" He opened his mouth to answer, but before he could say anything, she cut in again. "You know what? I don't owe you anything. Not even this argument. We spoke like six sentences to each other and had one failed date. You have no right to be—"

Before she could say anything else, Aodhan was pushing her up against the wall with his muscular frame, his full lips pressing onto hers.

For a second, Sierra was so shocked that all she could do was stand there, his mouth moving forcefully against hers. But it was just a second, and then she was back to her fury, gathering her strength and pushing him off her.

He took a step back, breathing heavily, and she regained her footing now that he was no longer pressed against her. She looked down and quickly adjusted her jacket before looking up to bring her eyes to his. She knew the shock was evident in her eyes, but it became even more pronounced when she noticed his eyes were still trained on her lips, and whatever anger had been occupying his face was now replaced with another emotion that Sierra couldn't quite read.

She thought of what to say, expletives coming to the forefront of her mind, but as the silence between them grew, she began to feel awkward, making it even more difficult to know how to navigate this situation. Why the fuck was Aodhan kissing her? And why did she sort of...like it?

Then she did the only thing she could think to do, and that was spin on her heel and reenter the restaurant, sliding down into her seat in front of Paul, trying to keep her breathing calm so she wouldn't alarm him.

Aodhan, thankfully, didn't follow.

Chapter Nine

L ater that night, Sierra lay in her bed in the dark, staring up at the ceiling, the day's events spinning around in her head.

As much as she hated to admit it, whatever she had seen in Paul had been gone when she had returned from outside speaking to Aodhan. Whether it was on his end or hers, she didn't feel as excited by the rest of the date as she had in those first few minutes. They had enjoyed their pizza, and the conversation had flowed, but it had been nothing special.

It was the first Tinder date she didn't regret, however, as she did have a good time. But at the end of the night, as they had bid each other farewell, Paul hadn't tried to kiss her, nor had he said anything about another date, he had just said he had enjoyed it before walking off into the night without looking back.

What transpired outside the restaurant during said date rose to the forefront of her mind, and she brought her hand to her lips as she remembered Aodhan's forceful kiss. Although it hadn't been welcome or expected, it hadn't been bad. Actually, it had been one of the better kisses she had shared in the last few years.

Sierra rolled over, trying to find a comfortable position so she could get some sleep. But her thoughts were running wild, wondering why Aodhan had kissed her like that.

Sure, she had dated in the United States, but her studies had always come first, leading her to more frequently date fellow students who were inexperienced in the more physical aspects of a relationship. She had honestly had more bad kisses than good ones.

Did Aodhan like her? She didn't think so. At least the way he acted didn't make her think he did...but then again, he was strange. Maybe this was his way of showing affection, like some kind of prepubescent boy?

Sierra groaned and sat up in bed. She wasn't going to get any sleep with her thoughts swirling like this. Wanting a little mindless relief, she made her way to the couch and flipped on the TV, looking through her Netflix account for something to watch. She had class tomorrow, so she didn't want to binge all night, but she definitely couldn't sleep with the way her thoughts were whirling around in her brain.

The conversation with Tyler came to her mind, and she skipped over a few movies that she knew were books. Although she didn't owe Tyler anything, she wondered if he had a point about books being better than the movie. Maybe she would have to read one eventually and see for herself.

Just as she selected a random comedy movie that looked decent that she wouldn't mind missing the end of, her phone lit up with a call.

It was her older sister, Maria.

"Maria," she said sternly as she answered the phone. Her sister rarely called her for social purposes.

"Hello, Sierra, that's all I get? My name? Not even a greeting?" Her sister's voice replied sarcastically.

Sierra sighed. "You and I both know you don't make phone calls for social reasons unless you lost your job at the hospital recently and were calling to tell me that."

"No, you're right. But you don't have to be so blunt. I'm

sorry I don't call more." Maria's voice sounded sincere, but Sierra kept her guard up. It wasn't the first time she had apologized for not being part of Sierra's life, and she was sure it wouldn't be the last.

"So...what is it this time?"

"Mom says you won't talk to her."

Sierra groaned. "You've got to be kidding me."

"She said you won't take her calls." Sierra heard background noise which sounded suspiciously like papers sliding on top of one another.

"Are you calling me from work?"

Maria huffed. "Okay, yes, I am calling you on my coffee break; now, will you tell me what's up with you and Mom?"

"Okay, so I skipped one call from her because I was at work on my all too short lunch break after she basically hung up on me for not disciplining Diego for her. You happy now?"

"Geez, you don't have to be so dramatic."

"Neither does Mom! I swear, I'm halfway around the world, and it still isn't far enough away to avoid this pettiness. Tell Mom if she wants to talk to me, she can text me and arrange a good time to call."

Maria sighed. "Come on, Sierra, don't do this to *Mama*."

"Do what? Have boundaries? I am twenty-five years old. I don't need my mother breathing down my neck when I don't even live in the same country. Now, Maria, respectfully, back off."

"Alright, calm down, Sierra. I'll tell Mom." The line went quiet. Sierra was waiting for her sister to ask how life was going and to ask how she was doing, but she just heard papers shuffling in the background.

"I'm sorry, Maria," Sierra said at last. "I don't mean to raise my voice at you. I know you didn't put yourself up to this. How's work?"

The papers shuffled in the background, and she heard a beeping sound. "Fine, speaking of work, that's my pager. Gotta go," Maria said in a hurry before the line went dead.

Sierra removed the phone from her ear, looking at the background behind her apps, which was some stock photo of the mountains that had come with the phone. She was so tired of the petty drama her family engaged in. She wished she could brush this off as a one-time thing, but it had already been happening for years, and apparently, even living in Dublin wouldn't stop it.

With a sigh, Sierra pressed play on the TV, and the opening credits for the movie she had chosen began. She looked down at her phone, wishing she had someone she could talk to. She briefly thought of calling Diego but quickly pushed the thought aside. It would only make the current situation worse.

She also thought about texting Tyler since he had said he was serious about being friends, but a quick glance at the time told her he was likely asleep since it was already past midnight, and she certainly didn't want him thinking it was a booty call. Not seeing any other viable options, Sierra grabbed her fuzzy blanket off the back of the couch and tucked it around her. It was just her and Netflix tonight.

Chapter Ten

Sierra could feel her energy lagging the next day at work as she added new labels to the books the library had ordered. It was normally pretty easy for her to stay awake when she was walking around reshelving books, but sitting at a desk was causing her eyes to droop. She had never been cut out for office work.

After the third time of almost drifting off, she grumbled, pushing her chair back to stand. If her body wouldn't stay awake while sitting, standing and labeling it was.

It had taken hours for Sierra's thoughts to calm the night before, and she hadn't headed to bed until after three in the morning, which only gave her about four hours of sleep before she had to get up for her eight o'clock lecture. Sleeping issues weren't new to Sierra, but she had hoped they would go away as she kept busy with her job and school. Unfortunately, it looked like that wouldn't be the case.

Sierra heard the door open, only to feel her eyes narrow of their own accord when Aodhan walked in. She had looked at the schedule when she clocked in, and he hadn't been on it, which meant he was covering for someone—or was just here to annoy her. Sierra had known she would need to see him sometime, she had just been hoping to at least have a day of peace beforehand.

Aodhan had his head down as he crossed the room, and his eyes rose to meet hers as he stopped in front of the cubbies where they could store their personal items during their shift. Sierra waited for him to say something, maybe an apology for the night before, but he said nothing.

Well, silent treatment it is then, Sierra thought, turning to pull the next book out of the box. Two could play at that game.

Instead of heading out of the employee area to reshelve books, Aodhan slid into the seat across from where Sierra was standing and working. She ignored him at first, but after a few moments, she looked up to see his eyes assessing her.

"Aren't you supposed to be reshelving books?" she asked, looking back down at the book in front of her.

"Yes, but I have a few minutes before my shift."

Sierra looked up at him, scowling. It was his right to be here. He was an employee. At least now she knew he was covering for Sheila. Most days, the library had 2-3 employees on reshelving and just generally being available for customer questions as needed. There was also at least one at the checkout, though most shifts had two during the school year because it was so busy. Then, there was additionally someone who was assigned to work in microfilm, helping students set up the machine and retrieving records as needed. The last employee they had on each shift, besides the manager, was a 'float' who could either help with reshelving, the checkout, or book labeling, depending on where it was busy at the time. This was the position Sierra was working in today. All of the employees could work any of the positions except for microfilm, as this required special training on the machines. While Sierra mostly reshelved by preference, she was also assigned float and checkout from time to time.

The silence stretched between them. Feeling the awkwardness grow, Sierra said, "So you're covering for Sheila, I take it?"

Aodhan nodded, his mouth remaining pressed in a thin line.

Sierra couldn't explain it, but she had a weird feeling in the pit of her stomach when she thought of Aodhan talking to Sheila. She brushed it off. "That's nice."

He nodded. "You don't look like you slept well."

It was Sierra's turn to answer nonverbally with a shrug. She really didn't want to discuss her sleep problems with Aodhan.

To her surprise, the next thing that came out of his mouth was, "Do you want to talk about it?"

For some reason, that was the absolute last thing she expected him to say, and she almost choked on her saliva, swallowing the retort she had prepared for what she had thought would be an insult coming her way. She lifted her eyes to meet Aodhan's, a little at a loss for what to say, but knowing she didn't want to discuss anything with him.

"No thanks," she finally managed to squeak out.

Aodhan didn't say anything else as he rose from his spot at the table and headed out the door, pausing only for a moment to throw a concerned glance her way. Something in the air buzzed between them, but Sierra couldn't put her finger on it.

Sierra shook her head at the odd encounter, turning back to the book in her hands. Whatever was going on between her and Aodhan, it was only blossoming to become more uncomfortable, and it needed to stop now.

Aodhan was her enemy. Her archnemesis. Even he himself had said that he didn't like her. The last thing he should be doing is feeling concerned for her.

It took about two hours for Sierra to finish all the labeling of the new books. Once she was done, she grabbed a cart and began loading the books by the section they would need to be shelved in. The employee area was quiet, and she was able to work efficiently. A song she had added to her Spotify playlist circled in her mind, keeping her occupied and awake more easily than those few hours prior.

As soon as the books were labeled and loaded, she made her way into the main part of the library, which was mostly empty, usual for this time of night.

She made her way over to the first section she needed to shelve books in, glancing at the clock on the wall. It was 20:00, giving her two hours to shelve the books before her shift ended at closing time. If she stayed focused, she knew she could definitely finish during that time.

After completing the first section of shelving, she maneuvered her cart to the next, only for a commotion at the front entryway to catch her attention. There was a group of students trying to enter the library, and they sounded intoxicated.

"C'mon man, I dare ya'."

The taunt reached Sierra's ears as she turned and made her way down another section. It didn't happen often, but sometimes, students would come through campus buildings on their way back from partying. They were loud and annoying, but usually harmless.

Sierra zoned in on the task at hand, pushing their drunken taunts to the back of her mind, hoping they would get bored with whatever they were doing and make their way back to their dorms.

She was so focused on ignoring the drunkards that she didn't realize one was behind her until he was pushing her up against the bookcase, his fetid breath blowing in her ear. Sierra tried to shove him off, but he was amazingly strong despite his intoxication.

"Get off of me!" she shouted. Looking around as much as she could with the side of her face pressed up against the books, only to notice that there were no other students in her line of sight. Great, she was on her own.

"I caught one!" The drunkard yelled, breathing his disgusting breath on her face a second time. Sierra gagged, trying to keep the contents of her stomach calm. She pushed against him again, and this time, she was able to get him to stop actively leaning against her, but she fell to the side as one of his hands still encircled her arms. She tried to pry off his fingers.

"Hurry! She's feisty!"

Sierra looked around, but none of his drunk friends were nearby. She almost felt bad for him for a second, as it was obvious this was some form of prank gone wrong, but then she remembered he was still holding on to her forcefully, and her anger renewed with a vengeance.

"Let. Go. Of. Me." she yelled, hoping that one of the other employees would hear, and come to her aid.

The drunk man started trying to drag her to the exit, but Sierra dug in her heels and began yelling for help. It felt like an eternity, though in reality it must've been only seconds later, when a shape came around the corner of the shelf. It was Aodhan. Sierra would've much preferred to see someone else's broad shoulders, but at this point, she would take anything she could get to stop breathing in the drunkard's booze breath.

"Let go of her this instant," he said, his voice sounding strange to Sierra, even though she had heard it multiple times over the past week. The drunkard dropped her arm instantly, and Sierra fell, catching herself on her palms at the last minute. Rolling into a sitting position, she reached to rub the part of her arm where his hands had been, sure she would have a bruise later.

"Leave," Aodhan said, in the same tone as before.

Without a single word, or argument, the drunk man stumbled past Aodhan and back toward the entrance.

Sierra pushed herself off the ground, so she was once again standing. "Geez, I gotta learn how to do that." As soon as the drunkard was out of sight, Sierra brought her eyes to meet Aodhan's, only to find them looking at her with irises that were ablaze.

"Did he hurt you?" Aodhan questioned, his teeth clenched together.

Sierra shook her head, rubbing her arm again. "No, I'm fine, he was just drunk."

"Let me see your arm." Aodhan reached for the sleeve of her shirt, but Sierra stepped back out of his reach.

"I said, I'm fine."

Aodhan stepped toward her. "And I asked to see your arm. Now show me."

Sierra went to step back again, but Aodhan was too fast. At what looked like inhuman speed, he grabbed her hand in one of his, and his other hand went to her sleeve. Sierra tried to protest, "No, don't—" but before she could finish, he pushed her sleeve up to reveal her forearm. He went still, staring at her skin.

Sierra knew why. Her skin wasn't pretty to look at. She suffered from a skin disease known as psoriasis, which left angry red lesions marring her light skin all over her body. While she had once had the condition under control, the stress of moving across the world had brought it back in full force. She knew what was coming next. Whenever anyone saw her skin, they were always disgusted, and they always assumed it was contagious. Sierra opened her mouth to reassure him that he wouldn't get it, but before she could, he growled, "Who did this to you?"

Taking a deep breath, Sierra stepped back, successfully removing her hand from his while pushing her sleeve down with her other hand. "No one. Well, I guess if there is a God out there, he did. It's a skin disease I've had since I was a child."

"Oh," Aodhan replied, his eyes meeting hers once again, the fire in them finally seeming to fade. "Does it hurt?"

Sierra shrugged. "Sometimes. Mostly, it just itches. I'm used to it. It's not contagious, by the way."

"I assumed not," he replied. "If it was, I assume you wouldn't be here." He looked back at her arm, which was now covered with the sleeve again. "Is that why you always wear long sleeves?"

Sierra nodded. "It's, uh, all over, and I don't really like talking about it."

He tilted his head to the side, his eyes roving all over her body in a way that made her feel self-conscious. "I might know someone who can help you."

Sierra shook her head. "I've been seeing doctors for this condition my whole life. There isn't a lot they can do. I've got some creams which work, but as soon as I run out, they come back—"

He interrupted her. "Not a doctor, a healer."

Sierra scrunched her nose. "A healer? Like with crystals and spells and stuff?" The idea sounded so outrageous that Sierra started laughing. "Only in Ireland would someone suggest I see a healer."

"No, not in Ireland, but where I'm from in—" Before he could mention where he was from, Mona came tearing around the corner of the shelves.

"Are you two okay? I saw what happened on the security cameras from my office. Those drunks, I swear, I don't know who they are, but I called campus security, and they're on their way over." The words came out in a rush as Mona's eyes bounced back and forth between the two of them. Sierra held up her hand.

"I'm fine. Aodhan helped me. No harm."

Mona raised an eyebrow. "Are you sure? I can have you go to the clinic to get looked over."

Sierra shook her head. "No thanks. I'd actually just like to go home at this point, but I'm a little nervous to walk back alone in case those guys are still around. Do you think security would walk me home?"

Mona bit her lip. "I'm not sure, but I can ask."

"No need, I'll walk Sierra home. It's almost closing time anyway." Aodhan interrupted, his emerald eyes roving over Sierra in a way that made her mentally shiver.

Mona nodded, looking at the full cart of books Sierra hadn't finished shelving. "Just put the cart behind the desk, and I'll have the morning shift finish it tomorrow. Niamh and I will lock up."

Sierra nodded, reaching to grab the cart, but before she could, Aodhan was there, pushing it back toward the desk while Sierra trailed behind. She didn't know if she was in shock or just off her rocker to allow Aodhan to walk her home, but she didn't argue as Aodhan collected his jacket while she collected hers. She knew that she should probably argue against him walking her home, but she just felt so drained that she didn't want to deal with trying to find someone else to take her.

The two of them walked out of the building side by side and began making their way to Sierra's house. Neither of them said anything. Sierra didn't know what to say now that Aodhan knew one of her darkest secrets, and she had a feeling he didn't know what to say either.

She was so concerned with thinking of what to talk about, it wasn't until they were nearly at her door that she realized she hadn't been paying attention to where they were walking, but he had somehow led her directly to her street. She stopped in her tracks.

"How do you know where I live?"

Aodhan turned to face her, his face neutral.

"Did you follow me after our date?" she accused, her tone dripping with acid.

Aodhan shrugged. "No. Well, not really." He motioned to a building just a few buildings back along the street they had just walked on. "I'm staying there."

"Oh."

"After our date, I watched you walk ahead of me around this corner. I don't know the way from here."

Sierra felt herself blush. She felt bad that she had accused him so quickly. "I live just there." She motioned to her building, which was halfway up the block.

He nodded, and they continued on their way until they were at her door. As Sierra dug out her keys, the awkwardness stretched between them. She really wasn't sure what to say or how to fix the weird tension that was clearly between them. She knew she would regret leaving this tension to fester for another day, but she didn't see another solution. She just couldn't deal with this—or the fact that they had kissed the night before—right now.

Instead, she unlocked the door, and as soon as it was open, she turned over her shoulder, called "Good night" to Aodhan, and slipped inside. She closed the door quickly behind her, not even waiting to see if he called goodnight in return.

She made her way up the stairs, ducking into her apartment and locking the door behind her. Heading directly for the bathroom, Sierra flipped on the shower, turning the water up as warm as she could stand before stripping and stepping in. She usually preferred showers and didn't mind the fact that her apartment didn't have a bathtub, but she would give anything at that moment to be able to soak in warm water.

Sierra just stood under the stream of water for several minutes, not even moving to wash her hair or body, replaying the events of the evening behind her closed lids.

She was supposed to hate Aodhan. He had been late, following her, and just generally a pain in the ass, but something had changed between them tonight. Sierra couldn't put her finger on it, and she didn't know what it would mean for them going forward, but she really hoped she wasn't making a huge mistake.

Chapter Eleven

The next morning, Sierra felt weird as she went about her morning routine. The events of the night before continuously raced through her mind, crowding the front of her consciousness so tightly that she could barely discern where one thought ended and the next began. It wasn't that she was still afraid of what happened—as she had been the night before—but she was having a difficult time coming to terms with the fact that she had both let Aodhan walk her home and that she had told him about her psoriasis.

Sierra normally didn't like to tell anyone, and not even her friends in high school had known. Her family knew, of course, but she had always kept others at arm's length, not wanting them to see her lesions for fear she would have to explain them, or face their ridicule, or worse.

She winced internally as she remembered the last guy she had dated for several months in Texas. He had seen her skin when things had begun to get physical between them and had assumed it was a communicable disease. Sierra had tried to explain that it wasn't contagious and that he had nothing to worry about, but the relationship fell apart shortly after because he never seemed to believe her, always accusing her when he would get anything, even just a cold, as if there was some sort of connection to his sniffles and the red marks on her skin.

Sierra had really liked him, but in the end, she couldn't deal with his toxic behavior, and she had ended it before it had really taken off. Sadly, this wasn't the only story she had like this.

The residents of Texas were, unfortunately, some of the most vain in America when it came to appearances, making it really hard to fit in as a second-generation Mexican-American, and even more difficult when she didn't meet the appearance standards others expected her to meet.

Sierra looked in the mirror as she pulled on her red sweater, ensuring it covered as much of her skin as possible. One of the reasons she had been so glad to move to Dublin was because of the fact that it was quite chilly almost year-round. Sure, there was a summer, but she wouldn't be expected to wear the same skimpy shorts and tank tops that most female residents of Texas wore with pride from May until September.

With one last glance at her reflection in the all-too-honest mirror, Sierra grabbed her bag and headed down the stairs. She had a class at ten, followed by an afternoon shift at the library.

As she exited her apartment building into the blinding but chilly sun, she noticed a masculine figure leaning against the wall. She nearly panicked for a moment until the man looked up, and she recognized Aodhan's green eyes.

"Aodhan," Sierra gasped, looking around the street as if she was expecting someone else. "What are you doing here?"

He shrugged. "Thought you might want to walk to class together." Aodhan was wearing a fitted long-sleeve blue t-shirt and tight black jeans. While he was wearing his signature black beanie, Sierra was surprised to see he didn't have any sort of coat with him despite the fact that it was a chilly fall Dublin morning.

Sierra raised an eyebrow, pausing to cross her arms over her chest. "How did you know I had class this morning?"

"I didn't," he replied, his nonchalant shrug irking Sierra. "I just came early and figured you would come down at some point."

Sierra rolled her eyes as she began walking towards the University, and Aodhan fell into step easily beside her despite her brisk pace. "So, you were just going to wait there on the street until I came down? And what if I didn't have class today?"

"Then I would've left at some point, I suppose." Aodhan's tone didn't give Sierra any insight into his thoughts. She truly couldn't tell if he was being serious or making a joke. "I just thought you would feel better having someone walk with you."

"Hm." Sierra was quiet for a minute, the only sound of their footfalls on the cement leading her to conclude he hadn't been joking. He really would've waited outside her building for hours, maybe he already had. "And what about your own studies? Don't you have classes or lectures today?"

"Not really."

Sierra groaned internally at his continued non-answers. They walked on for a few moments while Sierra ran his words under the microscope in her mind. Realizing he had never given her a straight answer, well, ever, she planted her feet where she stood. It took Aodhan a moment to notice she wasn't beside him before he turned around to see what was going on. The moment his eyes met hers, Sierra's blood boiled, which had been building since she met Aodhan the week before, and she exploded.

"That's it, THAT'S IT!" She took a deep breath. "I am so tired of your non-committal answers and never telling me anything about yourself. This isn't how friendships or relationships of any sort work, Aodhan, and frankly, I don't even know which of those you want. I know we had a little moment last night, but you don't owe me anything, okay? You can just walk away, and we can go back to our regular routine of hating each other."

She paused for a moment, but before he could answer, she continued her verbal rampage. "I have a ton of fake friends at home, Aodhan. I don't need any more. I am also perfectly happy on my own, and don't need a relationship to complete me. So, if you want to be my friend, or more, or whatever your end game is, you've got to start talking to me. Otherwise, I don't want to see you waiting at my doorstep, or coming to my rescue at work, or within a few meters of me at a bar. Is that clear?"

The silence stretched between them as Aodhan's eyes searched her face, confusion clouding his features. "I understand," he said after a few moments.

Sierra was so busy preparing for him to argue with her, it took a second for the fact that he agreed to sink in. When it did, she wasn't sure exactly what to say. "Soo…" she started.

"What do you want to know?" he asked, his face impassive.

"Just tell me about yourself. You know, be a regular, friendly human."

Apparently, her words didn't register because he said nothing. Sierra internally groaned, wishing they were already at school so she could avoid finishing this conversation, which apparently wasn't going to change anything that was going on between them. "You could start by telling me where you are from," she tried again.

"I'm from the north," Aodhan answered as they began walking again, him shortening his large strides to match hers. "My father works in politics, and I have a younger sister."

Well, that explained the protective instincts. "And your mother?" Sierra asked, afraid that if she were to pose the wrong question, he would clam back up again.

"She doesn't do anything."

"Hm." Sierra knew that having one parent as a stay-at-home parent was not financially feasible in Dublin. "So, you must be from a smaller town, then?"

"You could say that. My parents own a lot of land, so there isn't much else around anyway."

"And what's the closest city to your parent's place?" Trinity College came into view, and Sierra was almost sad that her first real conversation with Aodhan was about to end so soon; now that he was finally talking to her.

"You wouldn't know it. But the closest city you know would probably be Culkeeny."

Sierra wracked her brain, but her Ireland geography wasn't very good, so she just nodded, letting him think that she knew the town. "And what are you studying here?"

"Uh, history."

Sierra raised an eyebrow. This was the first answer he stumbled on, which made her think he wasn't being fully honest. "What kind of history?"

"Of the Gaelic language, it's why I speak it."

Sierra still had a feeling he wasn't telling the entire truth, but she brushed it off. She'd already confronted him once today, and the anger rushing through her blood had just finally settled. The last thing she wanted to do was get herself riled up again right before class. "And how long is your study?"

"Just a few more months. It was one year total, but I started in January. I'm almost finished."

"Well, that's exciting." Sierra came to a stop outside of the building where her lecture was. "This is me. I'll see you later?" It was more of a rhetorical question, but Aodhan didn't seem to notice.

"Yes." His reply was succinct, making it clear he would be seeing Sierra later.

As Sierra turned to enter the room, she swore she saw the corner of his mouth twitch into the hint of a smile, but as quickly as it appeared, it was gone, and he was once again the stoic Aodhan.

Sierra exited the classroom after her lecture on theories to delay aging had finished, only to nearly collide with Aodhan's muscular chest.

"Okay, this is getting a little weird. You must seriously be following me," she snapped as he began walking next to her again.

"No, I just happened to decide to study in the hall and figured I would walk with you to the library since I was just studying anyway."

Sierra bit her lip. It didn't sound like a lie, but it didn't sound honest either, and she was reminded of how he hesitated when she asked what he was studying earlier. For the second time today, she brushed off his comment. "Since you decided we are walking together apparently, I guess you can answer some other questions I have about you."

Aodhan looked at her apprehensively out of the corner of his eye. "Sure."

Sierra smirked, proud that she had won this round. "What's your sister's name?"

"Aislin," he answered, without missing a beat.

"That's a pretty name."

Aodhan nodded.

"I just realized I don't know your last name either." Tinder was well known for the fact that it only showed the individual's first name, age, and usually a less than stellar picture.

"It's a hard one in your language. It's De Thuaidh." His lips both curled and pressed together as he pronounced his last name in a way that Sierra knew she would never be able to recreate.

But her mind caught on something else he had said. "In my language?" Sierra asked, as they turned a corner and headed toward the library, both of them twisting and stepping aside as other students passed by them.

"Yes, in English. It's much easier for Gaelic speakers to pronounce."

That reminded Sierra of something else she found weird about Aodhan. "How did you learn old Gaelic anyway?"

"My family all speaks it. It's much more common where I am from."

"They speak old Gaelic in Culkeeny?"

Aodhan shook his head, stopping to open the door to the library for her, placing his large hand against the top of the glass so she could walk underneath. "Not in Culkeeny, but in my village, yes."

"How did you learn to speak English so well, then?"

"Everyone in my village has to learn it in school in addition to Gaelic."

Sierra and Aodhan made their way back to the employee area, Sierra lifted a hand to Mona, who was at the checkout desk, in greeting as they passed.

"I believe it's my turn to ask some questions," Aodhan said as they entered the employee break room.

Sierra winced as she removed her jacket. He was right, she couldn't demand he talk about himself and not do the same in return, even though she hated it. "I guess."

She looked over to find Aodhan's eyes on her. "That makes you nervous. Why?"

Sierra looked around the room, glad to see it was empty of other employees. "I just don't like talking about myself, or my family, or...my condition."

"Okay, we don't have to talk about those things then." He hung Sierra's jacket on a hook for her. "Where are you from?"

"Dallas, it's a city in Texas in the United States."

He nodded. "I've heard of it." Sierra looked at her jacket on the hook, before putting her messenger bag in a cubby and heading for a cart in the hall. Aodhan followed. "Why did you come to Ireland?"

Sierra pretended to be busy grabbing a cart. She knew it was a normal question and that he couldn't know how uncomfortable it made her feel, but before she could answer, he surprised her with the next words out of his mouth. "That makes you uncomfortable, why?"

"You're very intuitive, I see." Sierra began pushing the cart to the section where she would be shelving the books.

"When I want to be," Aodhan corrected. The two began working in silence, but Aodhan wasn't going to let his unanswered question go. "So, I'll ask again: why did you come here?"

Sierra sighed. "To get away from my family."

Aodhan put down the book he was shelving. "Why? Do they hurt you?"

Sierra shook her head, touched by his concern for her well-being. "Not physically, but my mother is very controlling and not very understanding."

Aodhan didn't say anything, so Sierra continued, switching the subject. "What about your parents? Do you guys get along?"

"For the most part," he replied. "I've been an adult for a long time, so..."

Sierra nearly dropped the book she was holding. "I thought your Tinder profile said you were 25?"

A weird look ghosted over Aodhan's features, but before Sierra could properly analyze it, it was gone. "Yes, I am 25. I guess I've just felt like an adult for a long time."

Sierra was about to respond, but she was forced to swallow her question, nearly choking as Mona walked up. "Hey Sierra, would you mind covering the checkout? Sheila is ill."

"Of course! I'll head over there now." Sierra set the book she was holding back on the cart and turned to follow Mona. "See you later," she said awkwardly to Aodhan, mentally slapping herself for how idiotic she probably sounded.

Mona led her over to the main register and helped her get logged in to the checkout screen. Sierra had manned the checkout desk before, but it had been a while. She much preferred shelving, and the students who normally ran the checkout apparently preferred it, so everyone was happy. Except like today, when someone got sick.

The only nice thing about managing the checkout is that you were allowed to work on homework or read if it wasn't busy. Sierra thought about going to grab her textbook to study but decided she deserved a little time between customers just to think.

As the afternoon hours stretched into the evening, Sierra found herself thinking about all the things Aodhan had said over the course of the day, as well as what he had said during their previous encounters. At one point, she took out her phone to see where exactly Culkeeny was, wrinkling her brow as she realized it was on the very northern tip of Ireland. She zoomed in on the map, hoping to see small villages nearby that could show where Aodhan was from.

Not seeing any small villages on her map at all, Sierra decided to try a different tactic and googled if there were any villages still speaking old Gaelic in Ireland, and unsurprisingly, there were not.

Sierra looked up from her phone to glance around the library, which was quickly darkening as the light of the setting sun faded, hoping to see Aodhan around. But, in true Aodhan fashion, he wasn't in her line of sight from where she sat at the register.

Turning back to her phone, Sierra tried a different tactic, typing Aodhan's last name, or what she thought was his last name, in the search bar of Google. He had said his father was in politics, so she figured something had to come up.

Nothing did.

There were a few actors with a similar first name, Aodhan, but she didn't see anything about the last name. She tried just the last name next, and to her surprise, it came up with some results.

It wasn't a family or even a person; rather, it was a translation. De Thuaidh was old Irish for "northwards."

Sierra groaned. Aodhan was totally playing her.

Before she could dive into another internet rabbit hole, a few students came up to check out some books, and Sierra had to tuck her phone into her pocket. They each had several books, one of which was reference only, which Sierra had to explain to the student that she couldn't check out. This led to an argument, and before she knew it, she was calling over Mona to settle the dispute.

Mona settled it quickly, somehow explaining it better than Sierra had. After the students exited, she turned toward Sierra. "Why don't you take your break? Since I'm already here."

Sierra nodded, sliding off the stool and heading to the break-room to grab her jacket. Along the way, she looked down each aisle to see if she spotted Aodhan anywhere, but he wasn't there. She would find him later.

She entered the breakroom, grabbed her jacket and wallet, since once again she had not packed food for herself, and headed for the kiosk.

As she passed through the library, she looked for Aodhan once more, but he and his distinctive black beanie were nowhere in sight.

Sierra stood in line to purchase her sandwich, wondering whether she should confront Aodhan again. Clearly, something fishy was going on because there was no village that spoke old Gaelic, and she sincerely doubted that a village existed that wasn't on the map; this was 2024, after all.

That got Sierra thinking about the other weird thing Aodhan had said. He said he had been an adult for 'a while' but last Sierra checked, she was 25 and still didn't feel like a real adult most days. Which meant he was probably older than 25 and had lied on his Tinder profile.

Sierra ate her sandwich in a daze, her mind spinning in circles. She didn't know why, but she kept thinking of the line in the *Twilight* movie where Bella had asked Edward how long he had been 17, and he had said 'a while.'

Sierra knew it was crazy, but she couldn't brush off the feeling that she was on the right track to solving the mystery that was Aodhan as she tossed her sandwich wrapper in the trash and headed back into the library. Tossing her jacket on a different hook than it had been on before, she headed for the fiction section, going straight to the M shelf where she knew Stephanie Meyer's famous book would be. She had just slid one of the three library copies of *Twilight* out of its spot when a large hand stopped her.

"What are you doing?"

It was Aodhan.

Sierra slid the book back into its spot, seeing as his hand was blocking her from getting it out anyway. "Oh, nothing. I was just thinking about doing a little reading."

"You hate reading." It wasn't a question.

Sierra bit her lip, unsure of what to say, when she realized she had never told Aodhan that she didn't like reading, just Tyler. "How did you know that?" she questioned.

"Tyler told me." He crossed his arms over his muscular chest, leaning his muscular shoulder against the bookshelf. "So why are you interested in that book?"

"No reason." Sierra bit her lip nervously and glanced at her phone, noticing her break was almost over. "I've just seen the movie and thought I might like the book, but now that I think about it, I'll never be able to get through a book that big, so I should just head back to the checkout. Later."

Before he could say anything else, she rushed back to the register, taking over from Mona. Once she was situated, she looked back at where Aodhan had been, but he was, once again, somewhere out of sight.

There was definitely something weird going on. The only reason Aodhan wouldn't want her to check out *Twilight* would be if he had something to hide. And she was pretty sure, at this point, that he was hiding something. Whether or not that meant he was a vampire, she was unsure, but she was going to find out.

Chapter Twelve

Thoughts of what Aodhan could possibly be hiding consumed her mind for the rest of her shift. Sierra barely noticed what was going on around her as she went through the motions of scanning books for checkout and answering student questions about where to find certain books within the library.

Before she knew it, the clock on the computer changed to 22:00, and she was off for the night.

Sierra wasn't shocked when she went to grab her coat that Aodhan was waiting for her. She donned her jacket in silence while Aodhan's eyes appraised her. Once she was finished and had grabbed her messenger bag, they both exited the library with the rest of the employees as Mona locked the door behind everyone.

Sierra bid the other employees goodnight, then began her walk home with Aodhan at her side, even though she hadn't asked or even hinted that she wanted company. Once they were off campus, and they were mostly alone on the sidewalk besides the occasional person passing in the other direction, he turned to her.

"You have questions." It wasn't a question and his eyes sparkled in a way that was beginning to make Sierra think he could read minds.

"I do," she replied, "But will you answer them?" She kept her voice calm even though her heart was jumping within her chest, nervous about what she would find out and wondering, if Aodhan was actually a vampire, what she would do. She wasn't much of a runner, and she knew from the *Twilight* movie that if he was a vampire, she wouldn't be able to outrun him anyway.

Aodhan paused before answering, giving Sierra even more time to plot worst-case scenarios in her overactive mind. "Probably not."

The sound of their footsteps echoed on the empty street as they passed several darkened storefronts and restaurants. Sierra tried a different tactic, "Will you just answer one question for me?"

"Possibly."

"Are you a vampire?"

Aodhan's mouth ticked, but he didn't laugh. "No, Sierra, vampires aren't real."

Sierra didn't believe it. She was pretty sure he was just trying to cover something up. "You're just saying that because I'm on to you and your secret."

"No, I'm not. If vampires were real, I would know about it. Trust me."

That was the problem, Sierra didn't trust him. They walked side by side in silence, with Sierra stealing frequent glances at his imposing form. He had pale skin, that part checked out, but then again, it was Ireland, so no surprise there. Tons of people who lived here had that skin tone. He had said he was an adult for a while when he was physically 25, so he was a type of immortal. The only thing Sierra kept getting stuck on was the black beanie that he never removed. Plus, she had seen him during the daylight before, and he hadn't sparkled or turned to ash which did make it seem like he was being honest about not being a vampire.

Sierra's thinking must've been going on longer than she thought because the next thing she knew, they were standing on her doorstep, the dark green door at her back.

"So, you're really not going to tell me then?"

"No," he replied. He didn't look angry, but his mouth was pressed into a tighter line than normal.

Sierra tapped her finger on her chin as she appraised him. Earlier, she suspected he had been reading her emotions. There had to be something she was missing here. Her eyes again settled on the beanie that was always on Aodhan's head...covering his ears.

Sierra's eyes widened. She was on the verge of a breakthrough. But before she could shout her assumption to all who lived on this side of Dublin, Aodhan put a finger to her mouth. "Not here."

Sierra looked around at the empty street. She wasn't too keen on having this strange...man, or whatever he was, in her apartment, but she knew exposing his secret to everyone on the block would only make him attack her...if he was somehow dangerous. But at least he said he wasn't a vampire, so that meant she didn't have to worry about the dangers of inviting him over the threshold.

So, she nodded, digging her keys out of her bag, and opening the door. She ushered him up the two flights of stairs and into her small apartment, closing the door behind her. She remained standing in front of the door, so he couldn't change his mind and escape without answering her questions.

"So, you're an elf," she guessed.

Aodhan's responding wince made her feel like she'd gotten it right, but he shook his head. "No, I'm not, and let's leave it at that."

"No way." Sierra crossed her arms over her chest. "I refuse to have you keep lying to me, and I know you're not human, so you better just tell me before I lose my cool."

"Maybe we shouldn't be friends after all," he tried.

"It's too late for that, Aodhan. You can't just walk away now."

Aodhan shook his head, either in denial or annoyance. Sierra couldn't tell, but her attention was inadvertently drawn to his black beanie, which pressed his curly brown hair to his head, other than the few curls that peeked out from the bottom.

In what she thought was a fast movement, Sierra uncrossed her arms, lunging for Aodhan and reaching up to remove the beanie from his arrogant head. But somehow, he was faster, and Sierra found herself falling to the floor, grasping at nothing but air.

She caught herself and looked around, trying to see where Aodhan had ducked off to, only to see he wasn't there at all. He had vanished entirely.

Sierra quickly stood, glancing around to ensure he wasn't playing a joke on her, but her apartment was too small to really offer anywhere to hide. After a moment, she said, "You can just disappear, too?"

Nothing but silence reached her ears. She reached into her pocket to pull out her phone, only to find it wasn't there. She turned back to her messenger bag, only to nearly jump out of her skin at the sight of Aodhan's large frame leaning against her door.

"What. The. Fuck." she gasped, feeling as if the wind had been knocked out of her. "Tell me what you are," she demanded, her voice dripping with vinegar.

He tapped his chin with his finger. "Hm. No." Then he disappeared again.

"Get back here!" she yelled, knowing that she probably looked and sounded like a crazy person right now. "Aodhan!"

Sierra nearly growled at her frustration with the man, or whatever he was, but before she could lose her composure entirely, she took a deep breath and stepped toward her messenger bag. Aodhan was infuriating, but she was smart, and she knew she could figure this out without him.

Chapter Thirteen

Without another word, she grabbed her phone and sank into her couch, opening up the web browser to begin her search. She knew Aodhan was wearing his beanie for one reason or another, so she would start with that.

She typed in 'creatures with strange ears,' and the results came through almost instantly. There were six possible answers: elves, fairies, pixies, hobbits, vampires, or orcs.

Sierra quickly memorized the list and cleared the search bar. Aodhan had said he wasn't an elf, and for some reason, she was inclined to believe him. So, she searched 'fairies' first, scanning through the first few web pages in the results. Fairies had a human appearance except for their ears, so that was a definite contender. Pixies were similar to fairies; except they were often depicted as smaller than humans. While she wanted to eliminate them, she kept them in mind because their mischievous nature did sound a bit like Aodhan, especially based on the very recent developments within her apartment. She quickly eliminated hobbits, vampires, and orcs, mostly because Aodhan didn't have what seemed to be the basic characteristics.

Sierra looked up from her phone and looked around the

room. Although she couldn't see him, she had a feeling he was still hanging around, "So, fairy or pixie, which is it?"

In an instant, Aodhan materialized on the couch next to her. Sierra might have been startled under any other circumstances, but after the events of the past hour, nothing he could do would surprise her right now.

Aodhan sighed and leaned back. "No one calls us fairies anymore. We are just known as the Fae."

Now, Sierra had been expecting some big confession to come out, but hearing the words come out of his mouth wasn't the same as theorizing in her head, and she suddenly found herself not knowing what to say.

"Fae..." The word came out of her more as a gasp, but Aodhan could hear her.

"Yes."

Her heart was pounding in her chest. "So, you're really...?" Her thoughts were one big jumble, and she touched her hand to her forehead, pinching her eyes shut as she tried to come to terms with the realization that Aodhan wasn't human.

"Yes," Aodhan repeated, removing his beanie with his left hand. As soon as it was off his head, Sierra could see his pointed ears poking through his long brown hair.

Sierra reached up as if to touch them, but before her hand reached his ears, she realized how rude it was to touch someone without their permission and yanked her hand back.

"It's okay." He lifted his chin in the direction of her hand. "I don't mind if you touch my ears."

Sierra nodded but kept her hand in place, trying to think of what to ask next. "So...Fae..."

Aodhan let out a short chuckle. "Yes, we've covered that."

Sierra tried to swallow, her throat feeling dry. "I...uhh...want to ask some things, but my throat is dry. Do you want water?" She stood up and walked to the kitchen. "Wait, can you even drink water?"

For the second time in the last few minutes Aodhan laughed;

a new record in Sierra's eyes. "Yes, I can drink water. You humans always say the darndest things."

Sierra grabbed two glasses out of the cupboard, filling them with water from the tap before walking back to the couch and handing one to Aodhan.

She folded her legs beneath her, situating herself so she was facing him. "So, do you eat food too?"

"Of course. Food in our land is a bit different, but we can eat human food all the same."

"And can humans eat your food?" Sierra asked, thinking of one of the articles she had skimmed, which said humans who ate fairy food would be trapped in fairyland.

"Yes. I'm not sure where the rumor came from that humans couldn't. Our food is different, but it won't enchant or trap you."

"Ah, okay." Sierra sipped her water, her heart racing, as Aodhan took a sip of his. "And can you do magic?"

He nodded. "Sort of. You already saw that I can shift myself to other places, and I can also make it so you cannot see me. I think it is a defense mechanism, as most Fae can do it. I'm better at shifting location than most of my kind, though. Many of us can also use compulsion, which you saw last night in the library. And there are those of us who have special and more unique powers."

Sierra thought back to the drunk student who had been so intent on dragging her out of the library and how he had suddenly done everything Aodhan had said. She tried to think if there was any situation when Aodhan might have used compulsion on her, but she couldn't remember doing anything she hadn't wanted just because he had said to. Still aghast and unsure what to even ask, she decided to see what information he would offer of his own accord. "Anything else I should know?"

Aodhan let out a breath. "Many believe that the Fae were an early race of humans. And most of my kind believe the same. But over the past few centuries, many have come to the human world and married humans, and some have even brought their partners back to The Hills. As a result, many of us don't have very strong magic anymore. That's what makes my abilities unique."

Sierra raised her eyebrows, "The hills?"

"My people, besides being called Fae, are often referred to as the *Sidhe*, which is Gaelic for 'people of the hills.' What they don't know is that the word actually comes from the name of my world, which has been called Sidhe for hundreds of years. When I refer to my home in your language, I just call it 'The Hills' to make things easier."

Sierra nodded. "And back to the powers thing? How do those work?" Sierra knew she should be feeling some form of shock right now at all of these revelations, but honestly, she had spent most of the day mentally preparing for him to be a vampire or some other sort of blood-sucking beast, so this Fae discovery didn't seem so bad.

"I can sense emotions. But I've heard that many generations before me, my gift, or 'powers' as you call it, was to be able to influence and change emotions as well."

Sierra tilted her head to the side, somewhat in disbelief that they were having this conversation. "I'm a little confused. So, for people who had your gift in the past, it was different?"

He took a sip of his water. "Yes. Our magic tends to manifest in very specific ways, and it is often passed through familial lines. For example, if your mother is good at healing, you likely will be too."

"Ah, I see. So your parents are both good at feeling emotions?"

Aodhan shook his head. "Just my mother, and she, like me, can only feel them but not change them. Her mother, my grandmother, reportedly could change the feelings of an entire army and convince entire kingdoms to surrender during her lifetime."

"Interesting." Sierra drained her glass and set it on the side table. "And your father has no gift or magic?"

Aodhan continued, "My father's family is from a line that could once control the weather. But, like most lines, intermarrying has weakened the magic. Now, my father can just sense the weather."

"But you can't?" Sierra asked.

He shook his head. "No. Fae can sometimes receive both of their parents' magic, especially if the bloodlines are strong. But my father's line is so weak that both my sister and I only received magic from our mother."

"That's sad."

Aodhan brought his eyes to meet hers, and she could see something, maybe pain, reflected in their depths. "It is."

Sierra thought back to the other things she had read. "Can the Fae tell lies?"

"No. But it's interesting that as the bloodlines of magic have grown weaker, our ability to avoid the truth or to deflect questions has increased. But we cannot outright lie. It's one of the main things that sets us apart from humans."

"And what about the dangers of making deals with the Fae?"

"Somewhat true. Because we live so long, and we cannot lie, the word of a Fae means a lot and is considered binding law in Sidhe." Sierra looked confused, so Aodhan continued, "No, we can't trick you into crazy things like in the stories, but never make a bargain with a Fae you don't intend to keep because we will force you to follow through. And while some Fae have become more modern over the years, there are many who will kill a human for backing out of a bargain."

Sierra was digesting everything he said, and her mind caught on his mention of their lifespans. "So, how long do you live?"

"A long time." Sierra raised an eyebrow, as Aodhan went on. "We age about five times as slow as humans meaning an average lifespan is 400-500 years. But we also aren't afflicted by as many diseases or illnesses as you are, so it is possible to meet Fae that are 800 or 900 years old, though they are often feeling their age at that point."

"So, I'll ask you again. How old are you?"

The corner of his mouth twitched in a way she now knew

meant he was fighting a smile. "I didn't lie to you. Fae don't track our ages the way you do. We are only either immature, which is any Fae who hasn't been alive for what is about their fiftieth human year yet. Once you pass your fiftieth year, you are a mature Fae or an adult. You remain an adult unless you pass something around your five-hundredth year then you become an older Fae or an elder. But we don't really track years. It's more how you look and feel. An immature Fae looks like a human kid or teen until sometime around their fiftieth year. Then they look the same till around their five-hundredth year when they begin to show age, such as gray hair." He ran his right hand through his hair. "You humans are always so obsessed with age, so when we visit your realm, as I have, we usually choose a human age to align ourselves with based on our expected lifespan. So, I align myself with 25 because I feel I am about a quarter of the way through my expected life of 500 years."

Sierra quickly did the math. "So, you're close to 125 years old?"

"Again with the counting, but if I was keeping track, I'm sure it would be somewhere around there, yes."

"Interesting," Sierra replied, thinking of how nice it would be if humans weren't so obsessed with age and instead focused on how old they felt. She then ran over what she had read online one final time but found he had answered most of her questions. In fact, she only had one left. "Why did you come here?"

Aodhan looked toward her dark TV briefly before meeting her eyes once more. "I came to study. I wasn't lying when I said I was studying history."

Sierra narrowed her eyes. Something about the way he said it didn't sound right, and she suspected he was deflecting, as he had mentioned earlier. "Are you studying at the university?"

A full smile spread across Aodhan's face. "You really are smart for a human." He leaned toward her. "I came here on a personal study to try and figure out why Fae magic is weakening and see if there is anything that can be done to preserve our race. While intermarrying is part of our magic weakening, the pace of the weakening has begun to accelerate, and I suspect it is something more than just genetics thinning the magic in our blood."

Sierra couldn't hide the look of surprise on her face. "And you can find that out in Dublin?"

"Yes, you have some of our ancient texts here. But you act like they are the holy grail or something, so I often have to wait for the one I want to see to be on display—or sneak around after hours."

Sierra laughed, thinking of all the times she had been looking for Aodhan in the library and had been unable to find him anywhere. "I knew you were up to something suspicious at the library."

To her surprise, Aodhan smiled back, marking perhaps the first real smile she had seen on his face. Something in her wished she could take a picture to save the moment, but she quickly brushed off the intrusive thought.

"Of course, the humans who work in the library are often very bright, and that has caused me to be here longer than expected," Aodhan elaborated.

Sierra thought back to when she had first seen Aodhan on Tinder. "How long is that?"

"Almost a year now."

"Oh wow, and you just now decided to get a job at the library?" she joked.

The smile fell from his face. "I wanted to try things the right way first. But then when I realized how difficult it was to get around the librarians, I knew I would have to figure out another route." He leaned toward her. "It's partially because of you, you know. I never thought of getting a job at all until I met you, and you mentioned you worked at the library."

Sierra rolled her eyes. "If you get caught sneaking around at some point, please don't spread around the fact that I inspired your crime spree, that will truly ruin my reputation." She was joking; it wasn't like she had a reputation in Dublin to ruin in the first place, and her reputation in America was already non-existent.

"Don't worry," Aodhan said, brushing his hand lightly across her cheek. "Your secret is safe with me."

The words hung in the air between them, and Sierra knew he meant that in more ways than one. Suddenly, she remembered she had one more question she had been wanting to ask him. "So, why Tinder, and why did you kiss me outside of the pizza place?"

Aodhan broke eye contact to look away, hanging his head slightly. "I joined Tinder because...well...I was lonely, and I wanted to look for someone..." He trailed off, grimacing at something he left unsaid. "With the kiss, I...I don't really know how to say this, but I like you, Sierra. Not just like, I feel drawn to you for reasons I can't explain. I know I didn't go about courting you the right way, and I feel bad about it. But I would like it if you would give me another chance."

Sierra tapped her chin with her finger, a mischievous look on her face. The past twenty-four hours had made her realize that while she had been angry at Aodhan and annoyed these past few weeks, she hadn't really hated him. And the reality was, she hadn't thought of him as her enemy since the day she had seen him at the pub the week before. She had already decided during this conversation to give him another chance, but he didn't know that.

"Another chance, you say?" She kept her face straight, but internally, she was laughing at the fact that he had actually used the word 'courting' in a sentence. He really was from another realm.

She'd forgotten, however, that Aodhan was able to feel her emotions because a smile spread across his face as he said, "You're feeling pretty proud of yourself, as well as a sense of resolve, so I'm guessing that means you have decided to give me another chance?"

She nodded. "I have. But listen, honesty is really important to me. So, if we are going to give this," she motioned between them with her finger, "Another try, you have to be honest with me."

He set his hand on her forearm. "Sierra, I promise you. I cannot lie, and going forward, I won't attempt to obscure the truth from you in any way, okay?"

She smiled, setting her hand on his. "Thank you." She glanced down at her phone, noticing it was almost midnight. "It's getting pretty late, and I have another seminar tomorrow. But I don't work at the library, so maybe we could have that coffee afterward? Start over with the date you were late for?" She rose from the couch, and he followed, reminding Sierra of their height difference as he towered over her.

"I'd like that." He smiled. "And I promise I will arrive on time, okay?" Sierra laughed as she led him to the door even though she was pretty sure he could just shift himself out of the room if he wanted. Just before he exited, he turned to brush a strand of her hair behind her ear, leaning in to kiss her cheek. "Until tomorrow, Sierra."

Sierra grinned like an idiot, watching as he walked down the hall toward the stairs. She didn't close the door until he was completely out of sight, unable to stop smiling at the memory of his kiss.

Chapter Fourteen

T he next day, Sierra was pleasantly surprised to find Aodhan outside of her building waiting to walk her to class in the morning, as well as waiting outside when her seminar for the day finished. He really had been serious about being on time this time, something that made Sierra chuckle to herself as they made their way through the small Dublin streets to Sierra's favorite coffee place, which had shelves of old books along the wall as well as decorative branches and lights hung from the ceiling. Having a coffee there was truly a relaxing and satisfying experience, though it was also a cute place for first dates—if you could ignore all the other women trying to take pictures of themselves at the best angle possible.

Due to her skin condition, Sierra had never been one for pictures; rather, she avoided them whenever possible unless they were required for her school ID badge or driver's license. Of course, she had a few images on hand from family events, and it was one of these images she had cropped for her Tinder photo.

Because of her severe lack of images and the fact that she didn't really enjoy telling others about her life, Sierra didn't have any social media profiles other than Facebook, which her 'friends' had forced her to make when she was 15 and had logged into maybe five times over the years—until she had found herself lonely in Dublin that is. Even when she did log in she mostly just scrolled through her feed mindlessly, never posting, liking, or commenting on anything. Basically, it was safe to say that Sierra was as off the grid as was possible in the twenty-first century, though Sierra was starting to think that she might have met the only man who was more off the grid than her.

"So, tell me about your family," Aodhan said as they began their walk to the coffee shop.

Sierra grimaced. "I don't know what there is to say, really."

Aodhan looked at her apprehensively, "I heard your phone call that day, you know."

Sierra knew exactly what day he was referring to, when her mother had just screamed at her and hadn't let her get a word in edgewise. Now she knew that with his Fae hearing, he had likely heard every word. At least he probably didn't know Spanish. "My mother and I...we've never really gotten along," she volunteered hesitantly.

"I understand. Does that type of call happen often?"

"When she's angry at me, yes."

"And how often is she angry at you?" he pressed.

"Since I moved to Dublin? Nearly all the time." Sierra groaned before realizing how harsh that sounded. "But I promise my mom means well, she just doesn't know how to deal with me. I'm not the type of daughter they usually teach you how to raise in those parenting handbooks."

"Parenting handbooks?" Aodhan was obviously confused.

Sierra chuckled, "Yes, we humans write books to help other humans raise their children." Now that she was saying it out loud, she realized how ridiculous it all sounded.

"So, you're telling me, that humans have children when they don't even know how to raise them?" Aodhan's eyes were wide. "Just when I thought this world couldn't get any crazier."

"It's not like that where you're from?"

"Not at all." Aodhan shook his head before changing the

subject just as the coffee shop came into view. "So, do you have brothers and sisters?"

"Yes, I have four," she answered, reaching for the door handle. But before she could grab it, Aodhan was pulling it open so she could walk through. Such a gentleman.

As they walked in the door of the coffee shop, the warmth from the interior overpowering the cold of the day, Aodhan motioned to the long queue, which wasn't abnormal for the shop. "You find somewhere to sit, and I'll get some coffee, okay?"

She nodded but didn't move just yet as her eyes surfed the menu, and her hands loosened the top buttons of her jacket. "Aren't you going to ask what kind of coffee I want?"

Aodhan's eyes widened. "There are different kinds?!"

Sierra couldn't help the smile that spread across her face at his lack of knowledge of the human ways. "Only like about a million."

"I had no idea," he said honestly, scratching his chin. "I only thought there was regular coffee and Irish coffee. So, what kind of coffee do you want?"

"A latte, please, with almond milk."

"Okay, latte, almond milk. I can remember that."

Sierra looked around and decided to sit on one of the plush chairs in the corner. There was another plush chair next to it and a small table in between. It was cute, cozy, and perfect for a date. It was rare that she came here without her computer, and she wanted to take advantage of the comfy chairs for once. She watched as Aodhan waited in line for his turn, then approached the barista and ordered their coffee. He had worn a coat today, Sierra noted, which made his signature black beanie stick out much less than it had the day before. Sierra wondered if he ever tired of hiding his ears. Within a few minutes, he was walking toward her with two paper cups in his hand. He handed her one without looking.

"Are you sure this is mine?" she asked, spinning the cup to the label.

"Yes, I got two of the same."

Sierra was a bit surprised, but considering Aodhan didn't even know that different types of coffee existed, she supposed she shouldn't be too shocked. "Well, I hope you like it then."

"I'm sure I will," he replied as he took the plush chair next to hers, setting the coffee on the small table and leaning his arm on the armrest closest to her. "So, picking up our conversation from before, let me get this straight: you have four brothers and sisters?"

"Yes, two brothers and two sisters. I'm impressed already that you remembered that."

He took a sip of his coffee, wincing at the temperature before giving the cup a skeptical look and setting it aside. "Well, it's not every day that you meet someone with such a large family, but also, we just spoke about it a few minutes ago."

Sierra shrugged, blowing lightly on her coffee. "In America, it's quite common to have several children."

"Really?" he asked. "In my culture, most families are lucky to have two children, if that. You hear of three children from time to time, but it's very rare. My...people," he improvised, "have a hard time conceiving and carrying a child to term."

Sierra sipped her coffee as well, noting that it was indeed quite hot. "Yes, here, some women also have trouble, but most people can have quite a few children, and they do."

"Where do you fall in the birth order?" He reached over and set his hand that wasn't holding the coffee on hers.

She had never heard anyone use 'birth order' to ask that question, but Sierra was surprised to find it was more polite than the other ways people have found to ask her about her siblings. "I'm directly in the middle, and I hate it."

He tilted his head to the side, rubbing the back of her hand with his thumb. "Why?"

Sierra looked around the coffee shop, searching in her mind for a way to say it that wouldn't sound mean. "I just feel forgotten sometimes. I feel like I came too late to set my own path in life, but too soon to reap the benefits and resources available to the last child."

"Hm," Aodhan replied, his mouth pulling into a frown. "I guess I wouldn't know about that."

"I think things are different for you as well, at least from what you told me. It sounds like the same issues large families have here wouldn't affect people in your...home."

"That's true. Do you think things will be the same when you have children of your own?"

Sierra grimaced. This was the part of most relationships where she tended to scare men off. "No. I've never wanted children of my own. It's not for me."

To her surprise, Aodhan didn't react shocked as most men would. Instead, he just nodded in apparent understanding. "I understand. I feel the same way."

Wanting to change the subject to something more light-hearted, Sierra asked if he had any hobbies.

"Hobbies?" He tilted his head to the side. "Are those a type of animal?"

Sierra couldn't help but chuckle, "No, hobbies are something you like to do in your free time. For example, my hobbies are watching movies, going for a walk, and exploring new places."

"Oh." Aodhan rubbed his chin for a moment. "I guess I like those things too, except instead of watching movies in the hills, we read."

Sierra rolled her eyes. It was obvious she hadn't done a good job of explaining hobbies, but she would circle back to the topic later.

They settled into a comfortable cadence, talking about their families as well as some of their likes and dislikes. There were so many differences between their upbringings that they never ran out of topics, as Sierra came up with new questions about everything from school in Sidhe, to the types of foods they had there. As it turned out, Aodhan had a private tutor growing up, something which was vastly different from Sierra's own experience in the American public school system.

Sierra found Aodhan was much more talkative than when she first met him, and she wondered if it was because she now knew his secret and he could speak more freely, or if he was really putting in an effort because he liked her. Either way, it was hard to admit to herself that the man she had sworn to avoid just one week ago was now telling stories that pulled at her heartstrings and made her want to get to know him even better.

As afternoon turned to evening, Sierra decided to broach the question of their next meeting. "So, since this went well, maybe we should plan a more official date?"

Aodhan looked confused. "An official date? Was this not an official date?"

"Yes, but in...our culture, when two people are getting to know each other romantically, they set up multiple meetings, or dates, to spend time together. How does it work for your people?" Sierra tried her best to keep her questions vague since they were still in a public place.

Aodhan thought for a minute. "I'm not sure, to be honest. I haven't really courted anyone." Sierra giggled at his use of the word courting. "In my home, arranged marriages are still common, especially with the...bloodline...issue. And if you are lucky enough to choose your own partner, I think it is usually someone you knew before as a friend, so things just sort of... happen. But I'm not sure."

"Ah, okay." Sierra couldn't imagine her parents picking a partner for her, and the thought alone made her grimace. "Well, what do you say we have dinner tomorrow? I can cook, or you can cook?"

He shook his head. "I can't cook at all. But if you don't want to cook, we can go somewhere for dinner."

Sierra was surprised. "You can't cook at all?"

"No. But in The Hills, it's common to live with your parents until marriage or until their death if you don't marry, so my mother does all the arranging of meals, and we have servants that help with tasks that go into meals like cooking and cleaning."

Sierra knew that things were different in his home, but the fact that they had servants meant he had some money. Well, the private tutor had been her first indication, but now she was certain he had a wealthy background. But that thought reminded her of something else: did they use the same money in his land?

"I just realized something. How do you, you know, pay for everything?" She motioned to their empty coffee cups on the table.

"We have our own currency in The Hills. And if we decide to come here for a visit, there is a service that will help you exchange your money. Many of my kind who have moved here maintain bank accounts in The Hills and here, and they will give you some of the money you need in exchange for currency back home."

"That sounds a bit complicated."

"It is," he agreed. "But they don't take my money here, so I don't really have an option. Sometimes locals in The Hills will let you buy gold off them, which can be switched for money here, but that's not always an option."

Sierra understood. "Alright, well, since you can't cook, you'll be subjected to my subpar cooking skills then. I work tomorrow, but we could eat a late dinner after I get off?"

He nodded. "I'm working, too. We can leave the library together."

Sierra smiled. "It's a date."

Chapter Fifteen

Sierra floated through the next day on a sort of cloud nine. She didn't usually get this excited about a date with a guy, but she was really starting to feel some chemistry with Aodhan. Plus, they had already surpassed the awkward part where she had to explain her skin disease, so she felt she could really talk to him, something she couldn't say about the other guys she had dated from time to time while living in Ireland, or even the United States, so far.

She had woken up early that morning to go to the store and buy all the ingredients she would need to make tacos with him later that night. It was still a little weird to her that he wasn't, well, human, but Sierra was sure she would get used to it. She couldn't explain it, but now that he had been honest with her, the attraction between them had seemed to increase. She now felt drawn to him, in the same way he said he had initially been drawn to her, but she had been keeping the reins on her emotions, knowing it was too soon to jump to any conclusions yet.

Walking into work, Sierra ran straight into Tyler, who was hanging up his coat just as she was clocking in.

"Sierra! Hey!" He waved enthusiastically.

She gave him a small wave back, heading directly for a cart of books. She didn't want things to get awkward with Tyler, but the fact she had agreed to a date with Aodhan after telling Tyler she didn't date at work was making her feel a little guilty. Knowing Tyler, the best way not to tell him about the date with Aodhan was to avoid him altogether.

Her avoidance tactics didn't work, however, and within a few seconds, Tyler was walking alongside her as she made her way to the first section for reshelving.

Sierra began shelving as Tyler started talking about whatever it was he had done the night before. Sierra tried to smile and nod at the right parts, but found herself zoning out.

She couldn't stop thinking about everything she had learned over the past few days. Aodhan wasn't human, and he came from a place that humans couldn't access. That thought made her pause for a moment, wondering how things would progress if their relationship worked out. Would she go back with him to The Hills? Or would he stay here with her? And what would her parents think? Sierra quickly pushed the thoughts away; this was just date number two, she shouldn't be thinking like this yet.

She had been so deep in her thoughts, she missed a part of the conversation during which she was supposed to respond, leading Tyler to resort to waving his hand in front of her face.

"Hello, earth to Sierra! Where did you go?"

"Sorry," she muttered, quickly finding the spot for the book in her hands. "I've been busy lately, and it's causing me to lose sleep and zone out a lot."

"Busy, hm? With what?" Tyler looked over at her, his eyebrows raised.

"Just studies and...stuff." Sierra grabbed another book, slipping it into its place.

"Stuff? What kind of stuff?" Tyler wasn't going to give up that easily, apparently.

Sierra said the only thing she knew would shut him up. "It's personal, Tyler. I don't want to talk about it, okay?"

Tyler looked a bit taken aback, and Sierra couldn't blame him, as she didn't usually talk to him that way. "Okay, point taken." Without saying another word, Tyler went and grabbed the second cart, heading to a different section of the library.

Sierra felt a little bad that she was blowing him off, but she just didn't have anything in common with Tyler beyond the job, and she couldn't exactly tell him about her current predicament.

She continued shelving books, trying to focus on the task at hand and not let her thoughts slip to Aodhan, but they continued to end up there anyway, no matter how much she tried to rein them in.

At least it helped the time go by quickly, and before she knew it, her shift was almost over. She began grabbing the books off the tables that needed to be reshelved, fighting to keep her eyes on her books and not on Aodhan, who was a few tables away, folding his tall frame over a table to do the same thing. Tyler was nowhere in sight.

Both Aodhan and Sierra were quiet as they clocked out, grabbed their things, and left the library. It wasn't until they had crossed the street and were officially off campus that Sierra even turned to look at him.

"So, how was your day?" Sierra cringed at how cliché that sounded, but she wasn't sure how else to start a conversation based on where they had left the last one.

Aodhan looked surprised at her basic question, glancing over at her before turning back to look in the direction they were walking. "It was good. Except I didn't get to walk you to the library before your shift."

"I can walk to campus myself, you know." Sierra hedged while fighting a grin. She found it cute that Aodhan wanted to walk her places.

"I know, but I like walking with you." His arm brushed hers, and Sierra thought for a moment that he might use the opportunity to grab her hand, but he didn't.

Sierra could feel herself blushing from his words. "Thanks. I guess I do like it when you walk with me."

The tension sizzled between them, and Sierra wasn't sure how to bridge it, especially while they were limited in what they could say in public, so their walk continued in silence until they rounded the corner and entered her apartment.

As soon as her jacket was off, Sierra headed to the kitchen. "I hope you like tacos because that's what I am making for us."

"Tacos." He repeated, his voice pensive. "I've never heard of them."

Sierra smiled. "I figured, but not to worry, everyone likes tacos." She began collecting the ingredients from her small fridge, watching out the corner of her eye as Aodhan evaluated the décor, or lack of décor, in her apartment. She did have one picture of her family, which was pathetically taped to the wall without a frame, and a small ship in a bottle, which was the only decoration on her coffee table.

"See anything you like?" she flirted over her shoulder as she turned on the stove. It had been a long time since she had seriously flirted with a guy.

"I do."

Sierra nearly jumped out of her skin at the feel of Aodhan's breath on her ear. She put her hand on her chest to slow her heart. "Don't do that." She looked over her shoulder to find Aodhan grinning right by her ear, their lips inches apart. "You're going to give me a heart attack."

Aodhan didn't reply. Instead, he took a step back but stayed standing behind her and watching as she poured a can of black beans into the pan for sautéing. He was close enough that she could feel his body heat, and a moment later, his hand ran up and down her back in a calming manner. "Relax," he whispered huskily in her ear. "I don't bite."

Shivers ran down her spine. She took a deep breath, trying to focus on the hot stove and the beans she was stirring. At least she had picked an easy dinner that she could cook with her eyes closed if necessary.

Aodhan apparently noticed that he was distracting her, and

stepped back to sit in one of the chairs at her tiny table. She couldn't help but notice that his large body made her table look even smaller than it was. He was probably used to some massive banquet hall and gourmet cooking back in The Hills. She wished now that she had chosen to make something nicer, but knew it was too late to change anything. Sierra grabbed the other ingredients from the fridge, quickly cutting the onion and tomato. She set them on the table, along with the cheese, tortillas, hot sauce, and lettuce, as Aodhan observed her every move in silence. Just when the quiet was about to get awkward, the beans began to steam, so she turned off the stove and scraped them into a bowl, setting it on the table as well.

Aodhan looked at all the things sitting on the table in front of him. "You're going to have to show me how to eat this, I'm afraid."

It was Sierra's turn to smile. "I figured as much. Here, I'll make your first one for you."

She quickly grabbed a tortilla, filling it with a little of everything and handed it to him.

He looked at the folded taco in his hand, holding it like it might bite him, before looking back at her. "So, I just eat it with my hands?"

"Yes," Sierra replied, already filling her own taco. Aodhan waited until she took the first bite of hers, observing exactly how she did it, before bending his neck down to take a bite of his own.

"Delicious," he said between large bites, devouring the first taco in moments. Sierra was about to offer to make him a second one, but he seemed to get the idea and quickly made his own. "How did you learn to make these?" he asked before eating the second taco in three bites.

"My family, I guess. We are originally from Mexico, well, my parents. I was born in the US, but my parents were born in Mexico and came over as young adults."

Aodhan's mouth was full of food, and as Sierra finished off

the last morsels of her first taco, he was already making his third, heaping on more than Sierra would have dared.

Aodhan noticed her eyes on the nearly overflowing taco in his hand and quickly explained, "I don't normally like human food, but this is delicious."

Sierra began making her second taco, pausing at his words. "You don't like human food usually? Why?"

Aodhan shrugged, his mouth full of his third taco which looked like he would once again be able to eat in three bites, despite it being overfilled. "We Fae, because of the way our existence is tied to the environment and nature, normally choose not to eat animals. Some of the Fae who move here—to the human world—learn to enjoy meat, and some in The Hills have taken to eating meat regularly, but I never have."

"Hm," Sierra replied. "Well, none of this is meat, as I also don't eat animals."

It was Aodhan's turn to look confused. "I thought all humans liked eating animals?"

"Not anymore. Many in our—" Realizing Aodhan was born over 100 years before, she quickly edited her statement, "—my generation have chosen not to, either for health or environmental reasons."

"Makes sense." Sierra's eyes widened as Aodhan began making his fourth taco. "There are many Fae who believe that the mother earth is mad at the Fae for the increased meat consumption, and that has also contributed to our shorter life span. It is generally not legal to hunt in Sidhe, so Fae who want to eat meat must do so illegally or import it from the human world, which is expensive and challenging."

"It doesn't sound like eating meat in Sidhe is a good idea." Sierra had studied vegetarianism and its longevity benefits as part of her master's program, but she had become vegetarian even before moving to Dublin because of the health concerns associated with eating meat.

Sierra finished her second taco, sitting back as Aodhan again devoured his fourth in just a few bites. She had only bought eight tortillas, and now she was wondering if she should have bought a second package. Aodhan reached to make his fifth taco, suddenly realizing Sierra had stopped eating.

"You're done?"

Sierra looked at the dwindling stack of tortillas. "I think I'll eat one more. But I want to make sure you have enough. I only bought eight tortillas."

Aodhan looked at the tortilla half-filled in his hand. "Do you want this one? So we each have four?"

Sierra held up her hand. "No, you eat that one; I just didn't know if you would want one more."

"No, you eat the last one. I don't need anymore."

They finished the last of the tacos quickly, and Sierra began to clean. As she picked up all the dishes and moved to carry them to the sink, they suddenly disappeared from her hands.

"What the..." She looked at the table, aghast to find it was also empty. She spun to the sink to find Aodhan leaning against it, a smug smirk occupying his face. "What did you do?"

"I shifted the dishes."

Sierra felt her mouth drop open. "To where?"

"Where I'm staying. The servants there can do them, and then they'll shift them back when they are done."

Sierra was aghast. "Aodhan. You can't just be having other people do my dishes for me. I—"

Before she could say anything else, his lips were on hers, and he was pressing her up against the wall.

Unlike before, when his kiss had been entirely unwelcome outside of the pizza restaurant, Sierra felt her body come alive as their lips touched. Her arms came up to settle on his shoulders of their own accord as his hand came to rest on her waist, and their lips moved in a comforting rhythm. Aodhan braced his other hand against the wall behind her, keeping his weight off Sierra as he pressed his body to hers.

After a few seconds, Aodhan broke the kiss, resting his forehead against hers. They were both breathing heavily. Before Sierra could say anything, his lips were on hers once again.

She wasn't sure how long they kissed, but at some point, he pulled her to the couch, settling her in his lap. Sierra slipped her hands beneath his shirt, resting them against his firm abdomen. She could feel him toying with the edge of her sweater, and somehow, she knew he was waiting for her permission to remove it. Sierra was torn; on the one hand, she was really enjoying this make-out session, as was her body, which was on fire at the idea of a sexual encounter after so long of having gone without, but on the other hand, she wasn't sure if she was ready to show him everything. While her condition affected most of her body, it was at its worst on her back and stomach, and she was severely self-conscious about it. After all, this was basically only their second date.

Just as she was forcing herself to come to a decision, a clatter reached her ears, and Sierra broke the kiss to see what had happened.

Her eyes connected with a stack of dishes on the counter, all clean and dry.

"Dishes are done," Aodhan whispered against her neck as he began to apply a soft line of kisses down her neck to the edge of her sweater.

"I—er..." Sierra didn't get to finish that question as her phone began buzzing on the counter. With a sigh, she detached herself from Aodhan's embrace and went to see who it was. Considering she had no real friends in Dublin, it was either her family or someone from work.

Sierra groaned as she saw 'Mama' on the screen.

Aodhan's arms wrapped around her waist from behind as he rested his chin on her shoulder, lightly nuzzling the crook of her neck. "Do you need to answer that?" he whispered in her ear in a way that shot a shiver down Sierra's spine.

Sierra knew that she should answer the call, but she also really wanted to see where this was going.

Sensing her indecision, Aodhan took a step back. "I should go anyway. I don't know that I can keep acting like a gentleman if I stay here much longer." Sierra's insides warmed at his words. "But I'll see you tomorrow?"

Sierra bit her lip. "Sure. I'm off work tomorrow."

"Me too." He smiled as he played with a loose curl which had fallen from behind Sierra's ear to hang in her face. "Shall I come over?"

Sierra's phone stopped buzzing but started again soon after. Her mom wasn't going to let this go. "Why don't we go to your place? I'd like to see it," she suggested.

Aodhan nodded. "We can do that. I'll come to collect you at 10?"

"Sounds good."

Aodhan leaned in, placing a single, chaste kiss on Sierra's lips. "Tomorrow."

Before she could say anything else, he disappeared, leaving Sierra looking at her phone, which was still buzzing. Running her hand through her hair and letting out a breath to calm her heart, Sierra pressed the green button and put the phone to her ear. "*Hola, mama.*"

Chapter Sixteen

Sierra groaned as her alarm projected its shrill tone throughout the small apartment, and pulled the pillow over her head. She wanted nothing more than to sleep just a little longer, but she had set her alarm for nine, only giving her an hour to get ready before Aodhan would arrive to 'collect her', as he had worded it.

Sierra's call with her mom had gone late into the night, but nothing had been resolved. Mrs. Lopez desperately wanted Sierra to fix her problems with her youngest son. But Sierra was done being the peacekeeper between them. It was time for her mom to figure it out on her own. Not to mention that Sierra was halfway around the world, and she didn't see what she could possibly do to rectify the situation. Sure, she could call Diego, but she also saw his side of things, and she wanted her mother to grow up and learn how to rekindle her relationship with her youngest son on her own.

She wished that she had left the conversation in a better place, but it had ended with her mom hanging up on her again. She figured now that it was only a matter of time until one of her other siblings called on her mom's behalf. They were probably drawing straws now, but Sierra figured it would be Antonio or Cecilia since Maria had called the last time.

Sierra begrudgingly climbed out of bed, groaning as she flicked on the light, and headed into her tiny bathroom to shower. As she stripped off the shorts and t-shirt she slept in, Sierra tried to avoid looking in the mirror. She loved how her face looked, but her skin always made her cringe, and after the events of the night before, she was feeling even more self-conscious than normal.

She showered as quickly as possible, trying to leave enough time to dry her hair. It had been getting colder in Dublin as winter drew closer, and she didn't want her hair to freeze on the way over to Aodhan's.

Slipping on one of her few matching bra and panty sets, Sierra chanced a glance in the mirror, only to grimace. Brushing off her embarrassment at the sight of her skin, she slipped on an under-shirt, sweater, and jeans over the cute matching set. Sierra wished she had a different body; one she wouldn't be embarrassed to see when she looked in the mirror.

As she brushed out her hair and slipped in her silver hoop earrings, Sierra wondered what Aodhan's place would look like. All she knew was that it was close to here and that he apparently had servants who had done her dishes last night. She knew he was wealthy in his world, but she wasn't sure how that translated to this one.

She had just finished braiding her hair in the mirror when Aodhan's face peeked around the bathroom doorframe. Even though she was now aware of his talents, it still made her heart skip a beat with how quickly he appeared and disappeared.

"Good morning." He smiled as his eyes roamed over her outfit. "You look absolutely breathtaking."

Sierra blushed at the compliment. While she always received them in the US, it was different when the compliment came from someone you were romantically interested in.

"Are you ready?" Aodhan asked. Sierra nodded and left the

bathroom, coming to stand in front of the door to her apartment with Aodhan just a step behind her.

"Are we walking or..."

"Yes, we will walk. While I can shift myself and things, most Fae can't shift people. Only very powerful ones, and even then, not far and only within the Fae realm."

Sierra slid her feet into her boots. "Interesting."

"Very. And since magic has been disappearing, I haven't heard of anyone who can shift people or other Fae in a long time."

Sierra slid her arms into her jacket and her purse over her shoulder. Aodhan took the lead and held the door open for them. Sierra locked it, and they headed down the stairs.

"So, tell me more about your place," Sierra asked once they were on the sidewalk, wanting to be prepared for what she was about to see.

"Well, it is very hard for my people to find homes here since we don't have personal public service numbers like other Irish residents do. We also frequently don't have bank accounts or credit histories, and very few landlords are willing to rent to us without these human things."

"Oh." Sierra hadn't thought of that, as she, even on a student visa had been issued a public service number so she could get healthcare while she was here. She hadn't even considered how hard it would be to live here without one.

"As a result, we almost always have to stay with other Fae that have relocated here with a human partner, or in a place owned by a Fae family for hundreds of years, before public service numbers were invented."

They turned the corner. "Makes sense. So, who do you live with?" Sierra looked up at Aodhan, but his eyes remained straight ahead.

"An old friend of my family, Braan. He came here about a decade ago to be with his human wife, Kaye."

Sierra was quiet for a moment. "But won't she, you know, die long before him?"

Aodhan glanced at her out of the corner of his eye before looking forward again. "There are many complications when a human and Fae fall in love. The main one is the aging; the second is that the human world can be tough for a Fae to reside in permanently, and many humans don't ever feel fully comfortable in the Fae realm, even if they live their whole lives there. But," he took a breath, "when you agree to date someone, there is no guarantee they will live the same amount of time as you will anyway. You could fall in love with a human your exact age, and they could die tomorrow. Time is never promised, and it's not worth not enjoying the person you love because there is a risk that they might die before you."

Sierra had never thought of it that way, but Aodhan was right.

Aodhan cleared his throat. "As for Kaye and Braan, Braan was over 60% through his lifespan when he met her. While she will still likely precede him in death, it may only be by a few decades."

Sierra was so wrapped up in her thoughts that she hadn't noticed that they had come to a stop in front of a large house, something which was uncommon in the Dublin city center. It was built of brown bricks and looked to be at least a few hundred years old. Vines climbed up the side of the house, and empty flower boxes lined the windowsills of the white framed windows. The curtains in all the windows were closed, ensuring that no one on the street would be able to see what was going on inside.

"Are you ready to go in?" Aodhan turned to face her.

Sierra looked from the house to Aodhan. "Almost. I wanted to ask one thing more." Aodhan's eyes bore into hers, and Sierra took that as permission to do so. "Is there any way for a human to become Fae? Or vice versa?"

Aodhan froze. Sierra could tell he knew the answer, but instead of opening his mouth, his eyes searched her face, clearly scavenging for a way to avoid answering the question.

"You promised not to lie to me." Sierra reminded him.

Aodhan let out a breath, "I've heard rumors...that humans can become Fae, but it is very complicated and rare."

"What do you mean?"

"For a human to become Fae, they must petition Mother Nature, also called Gaia, that they are needed for a purpose and that being human would impede that purpose. Mother Nature has the final say, and she may or may not make the change. If it is discovered you asked for selfish reasons, she could also leave you with a curse."

"Do you know anyone who has been changed?"

"No."

"But you just ask?"

"Sierra, I really don't want to discuss this right now."

Sierra bit her lip; Aodhan's angry tone wasn't one she had ever heard him use before, not even when they had been arguing. "Okay, let's go inside then." She replied as she took a tell-tale step back, putting a buffer of space between them.

She expected Aodhan to reach past her to twist the doorknob, but to her surprise, the door floated open on its own as they said the word 'inside'. She raised her eyebrow at Aodhan, but he just laughed. "You'll get used to it."

Aodhan stepped in first, and Sierra followed. They were barely in the door when it drifted shut behind them. Before she could ask about anything else, two forms filled the hallway in front of them. One was a man, who was clearly Fae by the look of his pointed ears. His hair was a similar sandy brown tone to Aodhan's, and he had a similar height and build. Sierra hadn't asked, but now she was wondering if they were somehow related. The hallway was wide with tall ceilings, but the man was imposing enough that it almost felt crowded to Sierra. The house had clearly been built in a previous century, as Sierra noticed the wooden floor creaking as she shifted her weight. Her eyes were also drawn to the opulent chandeliers, of which there were at least three, though the hallways continued around a corner and out of sight, so she couldn't be sure. Directly to her right was a large staircase with a bright blue runner covering the centermost part of the steps. But Sierra found that, despite all of the obvious opulence, her eyes kept returning to the woman who stood next to the man.

She had fiery red hair, which fell in waves around her distinctly human ears. She was taller than Sierra and very beautiful, even in her comfortable-looking oversized sweater and leggings. She looked to be in her early thirties. Sierra figured this must be Kaye.

Both of her suspicions were confirmed when Aodhan stepped forward and introduced them. "Sierra, this is my cousin Braan and his wife Kaye."

Well, that answered her question about the family resemblance.

"And this is Sierra," he told Braan and Kaye.

Sierra stuck out her hand, but to her surprise, Kaye enveloped her in a hug, and when she was done Braan followed suit and did the same.

"Welcome to our home. Aodhan has told us so much about you," Braan said with a warm smile.

Sierra looked at Aodhan, whom she had only really been on good speaking terms with for a day or two. "That's concerning."

Everyone burst out laughing, which made Sierra smile, but she truly wondered what he could've possibly told them since they weren't even officially dating just yet.

"Nothing bad, we promise." Kaye took her hand. "Come and sit. We have prepared tea."

She practically pulled Sierra into an old-fashioned sitting room. She wasn't familiar with interior decorating trends, but if she had to guess, no one had ordered new furniture in at least a century. The room was lined with bookcases on every wall and a fireplace at one end. There was one window, but it was covered by the heavy blue drapes she had observed when they were standing outside. A lamp sat in the corner, providing most of the light in the room. The center was occupied by several Victorian-style chairs and couches around a coffee table which held a tea set and several plates of sweets and cakes. Kaye released Sierra's hand by the couch, which Sierra took as a sign for her to sit. Aodhan sat next to her while Kaye and Braan made themselves comfortable on two of the chairs on the other side of the coffee table. Aodhan slid off his beanie, revealing his ears, which he clearly didn't need to keep hidden here.

"Sooo, Sierra, Aodhan mentioned you work at the library together." Kaye picked up the old-fashioned teapot and began filling the dainty teacups with hot water.

"That is true," Sierra replied.

"And you're studying at the university?" Kaye finished filling the cups and passed around a wooden box filled with tea bags. Sierra chose a clove tea.

"Yes, aging and fragility."

"That's an interesting course of study," Braan replied, as he chose his own tea bag and a second one which he placed in Kaye's cup.

"It is. I am very interested in medical sciences." Sierra picked up her cup, blowing the steam from the top as the tea steeped.

"Have you thought of becoming a doctor?" Kaye asked.

Sierra winced. Although this topic frequently came up, she still didn't like discussing the reasons why she wasn't becoming a doctor. "I studied pre-med already. However, I am much more interested in the science behind medicine rather than treating people for illnesses." Sierra scoped out the treats on the table, careful to avoid eye contact.

"Help yourself," Braan encouraged.

Sierra reached for a brownie, setting it on the plate next to her teacup. "So, you're Aodhan's cousin." It sounded dumb, but Aodhan hadn't exactly prepared her properly for this type of social event, and Sierra felt uncomfortable and desperately wanted to get the attention off her.

"That's correct," Braan answered. "Our fathers were brothers."

Sierra noticed the word choice. "Were?"

"Yes, I'm sure Aodhan has told you, but it is very hard for the

Fae to have more than one child. When Aodhan's father was born, mine was already well into the middle of his life. He passed to the next life some time ago."

"I'm sorry to hear that," she replied sympathetically, wondering what Fae believed the next life to be, but feeling it was an inappropriate time to ask.

"Don't worry about it. It was over a hundred years ago."

Sierra nearly choked on her first sip of tea at Braan's statement. "I forget that time is different for you," she explained, blushing at her faux pass.

Kaye shrugged, fixing her hazel eyes on her husband. "You get used to it. Sometimes, I am very envious, as I feel we humans aren't given the same time to properly heal from mental traumas and the trauma of loss as we would get if we lived longer."

"I understand." Sierra surveyed the table again, hoping they wouldn't judge her for taking more than one treat as she hadn't had anything to eat yet today. "Not to give you false hope, but there are many advances in the study of aging and why humans age. So maybe by the time you have to worry, human science will have solved some of the major causes and effects of aging."

Kaye smiled, showing off her beautifully straight teeth. "I sure hope so." She looked between Sierra and Aodhan, an emotion Sierra couldn't read dancing in her eyes. "So, how did you meet Aodhan here? He wouldn't tell us."

Sierra laughed. "Believe it or not, Tinder."

Kaye and Braan both laughed. "Us too! But it was over ten years ago, before Tinder was as widespread as it is now."

Sierra took a bite of her brownie, smiling as the delicious chocolatey taste filled her mouth. She chewed slowly. "Oh my, this is delicious."

Braan smiled. "That's because we mostly cook with Fae ingredients."

Sierra must've looked confused because he continued. "We work as traders between the Fae and human worlds. Though many Fae have come to work and live here, they still miss products from home. So, we make trips home to keep them stocked."

Sierra's eyes widened, realizing she hadn't yet asked Aodhan how one got from the Fae world to the human world. "How often do you go back?"

"Not too often. Sometimes, when I know someone is coming this way, I have them bring stuff with them."

"And you can't just shift the items?"

It was Aodhan who replied. "As I mentioned before, while all Fae have shifting abilities, they aren't what they used to be. Plus, shifting between our home realm and here doesn't work."

"Why not?" Sierra was still trying to get her mind around this shifting thing.

"We aren't sure," Braan replied. "But we think it's because we can only shift things that share the same plane. Most Fae believe the realms are stacked and, therefore, have different planes. Even bringing stuff back and forth is tedious, as only what can be carried can be brought at one time. Usually, we have a vehicle on one side of the barrier and go back and forth a few times to fill it with everything we plan to bring."

Sierra saw her chance. "The barrier?"

Aodhan cut in a second time, "The barrier, or the door between our worlds, is located up north by Culkeeny, which is why I said I was from there when we first met. It's not a visible barrier, but if you know where to look, you can see the place where the air twists. Well, at least we Fae can see it. I guess I never asked a human." His eyes drifted to Kaye.

She nodded enthusiastically, "I can see it as well." She looked to Sierra, who was taking bites of something she assumed was a scone. "Many humans have stumbled into Sidhe over the years out of curiosity when they see the way the air glimmers differently."

Sierra was having a difficult time picturing this portal and wished it was closer so she could see for herself. Sierra looked at Aodhan, and he must've been reading her emotions because he stood from the couch and announced, "I'm going to take Sierra on a tour of the house now."

"Oh yes, of course, go ahead. We will catch up to you later." Kaye and Braan looked at each other, something unspoken passing between them as Sierra rushed to swallow the large bite of food she had just taken and brushed the crumbs from her lap onto her nearly empty plate.

Before Sierra could say anything else or take a last sip of her tea, both Kaye and Braan stood and left the room. Sierra looked over to see Aodhan had also stood and was holding out his hand to her. "Are you ready?"

Chapter Seventeen

The tour of the house took longer than Sierra anticipated. Even though Sierra had been able to tell that the house was large from her view of the street, she had not realized how far back it went. There were rooms upon rooms; she was sure this house would cost a fortune if it was sold today, but she was reasonably sure that Braan and Aodhan's family had owned it for a long time, or at least knew the person who did, to be able to afford it without all the requirements Aodhan had mentioned previously.

As Aodhan took her from room to room, explaining the function of each room and who had visited, when unease settled in the pit of Sierra's stomach. For some reason, the looks Kaye had given her during their teatime were in the forefront of her mind. Something about them had brushed her the wrong way, but she couldn't say why.

Sierra *hmm*ed and *ooh*ed at the appropriate times as Aodhan explained yet another statue sitting on a table in this hallway, which she now swore went on forever. The hairs on the back of her neck prickled.

Sierra spun around, only to set her eyes on the empty hallway behind her. Once she was satisfied that there truly was no one there, she turned back to find Aodhan studying her curiously.

"Are you okay?" he asked, his eyes alternating between searching her face and the empty hallway, which had drawn her attention away from him.

"Yeah, I thought I felt someone watching me."

"Hm." Aodhan looked over her shoulder. "Could be one of the servants they have on staff."

Sierra laughed. "I still can't believe you guys have servants."

The corner of Aodhan's mouth ticked up. "What can I say? I'm privileged enough to be able to live with some pretty wealthy Fae."

Sierra's eyes widened as she thought of something she had yet to verify. "The servants, are they human?"

He nodded. "Of course."

"Even in...The Hills?"

He nodded a second time. "Obviously. How do you think the bloodlines started mixing in the first place? While I can admit your world is pretty liveable now, I know for a fact it was no walk in the park in the 1400s and 1500s."

"Hm." Sierra responded, not sure how she should feel about that. The way Aodhan had mentioned humans as 'obviously' being servants made her feel like he thought of them as less than the Fae.

Before she could pursue that thought further, Aodhan pushed open the door they had stopped in front of. "And this is my bedroom."

Sierra poked her head in, cataloging the large king-size bed covered in a black bedspread. The bed itself looked to be made of white wood, which matched all the other furniture in the room, most of which was in pristine condition and looked newer than the furniture she had seen in the sitting room. While it was certainly a nice room, she also felt it lacked character. There was nothing in here that told her anything about who Aodhan was, and it looked as if he hadn't really brought much from home when he had come here.

Aodhan walked up behind her, slipping his hand into hers and leading them to the bed. As Sierra sat stiffly next to him, the uneasy feeling she had felt in the hallway only increased.

"Are you sure you're alright?" Aodhan asked, running one of his hands up and down her arm which was covered in goosebumps.

Sierra knew he was just trying to be comforting, but his touch only increased her anxiety. Without thinking, Sierra stood up, not realizing that was her intent until she was standing in front of Aodhan, who was leaning back comfortably in her presence. She opened her mouth to say something, then closed it again.

"I can feel your emotions, you know." His eyes remained trained on hers. "Now tell me what is wrong."

"I...uhh..." Sierra knew she couldn't talk about the odd looks she received from Kaye and Braan here, as she wasn't sure just how good Fae hearing was, but she figured asking about his room was innocent enough. "I guess I just thought your room would tell me more about you. But...there isn't much personality in it at all."

Aodhan took his eyes off her face to look around the room. "You're right. I guess when I came here, I didn't expect to stay long, so I didn't bring much."

"That makes sense," Sierra replied, but she still felt apprehensive for some reason. Even though she was only living in Dublin for a year or two, she had done way more to her space than Aodhan had.

"Come, sit." Aodhan patted the spot on the bed next to him, and Sierra sank down into it. While she had hoped his explanation would calm her nervous stomach, it hadn't.

Aodhan placed his hand on her knee, probably still able to feel the apprehension rolling off her. "Do you want to stay in here?"

Sierra knew what he was alluding to, but there was no way she would be in the mood for a make out session, or more, anytime soon. Not with her stomach like this. "Uhh. Not today." She said, trying to let him down easy.

Aodhan didn't seem upset or disappointed as she thought he might be. Instead, he just nodded, grabbing her hand and leading her to the door. "Do you want me to walk you home?"

"Should I say goodbye to Kaye and Braan first?"

As if they had been waiting to hear their name, the two of them stepped out of a doorway a little further down the hall.

"Leaving so soon?" Braan asked, answering Sierra's questions about how powerful Fae hearing could be.

"Yes, but I would love to come back another time."

"Of course!" Kaye beamed as they approached. When they were close enough, she leaned in to give Sierra a hug, and Braan followed suit. "Feel free to come anytime. Even if Aodhan isn't here. I really miss having girlfriends since I can't really tell anyone about Braan's heritage."

Sierra understood, and what Kaye said reminded her of something else she needed to ask Aodhan.

Aodhan and Braan said goodbye in their native language, which Sierra assumed was ancient Gaelic, and the pair made their way down the stairs. Once they were on the sidewalk and a few steps away from the house, Sierra asked her question.

"Is there a punishment if someone finds out you told me that you are Fae?"

"No," Aodhan replied as they started the walk to her place. "There aren't really any rules. The Fae and humans have always lived in harmony in The Hills, and even if you could find the entrance, you would need a Fae to get beyond the forest. There's no need to worry about proverbial witch hunts."

"You don't think someone would hurt you if they knew?"

Aodhan glanced at her out of the corner of his eye. "While I am still relatively young for one of my kind, I know that sentiment about us comes and goes with the ages. If I was alive during the witch hunts a few hundred years ago, I might be more careful, but right now, feelings about us and other beings from my world are at the best they've ever been." He paused, considering her original question before continuing, "If someone really wanted to hurt me, they could try, but with my shifting ability, I would probably avoid it. Plus, in Ireland, the Irish have always been very...accepting of us. Perhaps if I traveled somewhere else, I would worry. But here, I feel quite safe."

His answer only led to another question in Sierra's mind. "So, are the Fae stronger than humans?"

"Somewhat. I wouldn't say we are as strong as human body-builders, but we are more in tune with our body, more physically fit, and we have many more years to work on building our strength to the best it can be. You humans have so little time to really come to your full potential."

Sierra's feet came to a stop on the sidewalk. They were just around the corner from her apartment, but she couldn't keep her thoughts inside her mind any longer.

"Aodhan, I need you to be 100% honest with me. This—" she motioned between them, "—is it even possible it will work?"

Aodhan looked at her, and Sierra could see that the answer he was about to give was painful for him. "I...I don't know." He let out a breath, his shoulders sagging in her presence for the first time she had ever seen. "I want it to," he added, bringing his hand up to cup the left side of her face.

"Is that why Kaye and Braan were giving me weird looks? Because they know it won't work?" Sierra asked, at last, the burning in her stomach calming the minute the words passed through her lips.

Aodhan lowered his hand from her face to clasp her hand in his. "I can't lie to you. I felt doubt coming from them. But I don't think it had anything to do with you being human. They don't judge like that."

Sierra removed her hand from his, turning away to walk more quickly to her home.

Aodhan had no problem keeping up with her brisk pace, and right before she reached into her pocket to grab out her key, his hand landed on her wrist. "Give us a chance, Sierra. Just because we're going on a few dates doesn't even mean this will be long-term anyway."

Sierra pulled her wrist from his hold, grabbing her key. "You're right." She took a deep breath, unlocked her door, and began her walk up the stairs. Aodhan followed silently.

Once they were both inside her apartment, she closed the door behind them. "I'm getting ahead of myself. It's just meeting them, it felt a bit...permanent to me, and the way they were looking at me made me nervous."

"I understand. I wasn't planning to introduce you to them so early, but there was no way for you to see my place without meeting them. As you saw, there is no way to evade their attention in their home."

Sierra bit her lip. She wanted to add that she was uncomfortable with the way he had referred to the human servants, but she held back. That was a conversation for another day. Plus, he probably didn't mean it the way she thought he did. She was overreacting and on edge because of the discomfort she felt.

"I understand," she told Aodhan before her eyes landed on her messenger bag. "I did have a good time with them today, I just didn't feel comfortable at all."

"I could tell." Aodhan reached up, brushing a loose tendril of Sierra's dark hair from in front of her face. "But I would like the four of us to spend more time together. You'll get used to them; I promise."

Sierra nodded. "Okay, we can try that." She had no idea what time it was, but she felt like she needed some time alone, and she definitely needed to study as she had barely done any studying all week. "If it's okay with you, I'm going to study for the rest of the day, I think."

Aodhan was a bit disappointed, but he nodded in understanding as he pulled her into a tight hug. "Are you working at the library tomorrow?" His voice was muffled by Sierra's hair.

"Yes, are you?" Sierra answered from where she was, tucked into his chest.

"Yes. I will see you there, *mo ghrá*."

"What does that mean?" Sierra asked, tilting her head to the side.

Aodhan's lip turned up at the corner. "You'll have to learn Gaelic, I guess."

Sierra opened her mouth to argue that she wanted to know now, but before she could even breathe a word, he leaned down, capturing her lips in a kiss. Sierra moved her lips against his, feeling some of the tension drain from her body as his arms came up to embrace her. The kiss felt like just what she needed to soothe her worries about their relationship, and as Aodhan held her tightly, his mouth pressed to hers, she considered changing her mind about being alone. But before she could, Aodhan stopped the kiss, hugging her tightly once more before letting go.

"Until tomorrow," she whispered, as he ran his hand down the side of her face.

"Until tomorrow," he repeated before disappearing from her room.

Chapter Eighteen

Sierra pushed her cart along the aisle, reshelving books, as Tyler prattled on about something behind her, as per usual. She had lost track of what he was talking about. The conversation had started about the book he was currently reading, but now he was just going on about some author that Sierra couldn't care less about.

"...And that's why I'm pretty sure she is out of ideas and that she should fess up, you know? Before she releases another book of nothing."

"Yeah," Sierra agreed halfheartedly, as she inspected the book in her hand, turning the worn cover over and running her fingers along the embossed gold lettering.

"What's going on with you these days?" Tyler asked, drawing Sierra's attention away from the book and up to his face, where his lips were pressed in a tight line.

"Nothing," Sierra replied, slipping the book onto the shelf before realizing she had put it on the wrong one, so she had to pull it back out and slide it on the shelf beneath where it had been.

"Bullshit." Sierra opened her mouth to argue, but Tyler held up his hand. "You haven't wanted to talk to me all week. I know I may have been a bit forward in the past, but come on, we're friends."

Sierra knew he was right. But before she could apologize or mention what had been going on in her life, Aodhan came around the corner with a cart of his own, his eyes alight with what Sierra assumed was jealousy. "What is going on here?" he questioned, his eyes bouncing from Tyler to Sierra.

"Nothing, Aodhan." It came out as a sigh, and to emphasize, Sierra turned back to her shelving, ignoring his questioning and intrusive glance.

"We're just talking." Sierra saw Tyler cross his arms over his chest out of the corner of her eye, and without looking at Aodhan, she knew he had probably done the same.

"Hm, well, if Sierra wants to be left alone, you should leave her alone." Aodhan's voice was low, and Sierra could tell he wasn't happy.

"She can tell me that herself," Tyler insisted, not backing down. "She doesn't need you to speak for her."

Sierra spun around to face the guys, confirming indeed that they were both standing with their arms crossed in standoff mode. Aodhan noticed her look and raised one of his eyebrows. "It's fine, you guys, settle down. I'm just trying to work here," Sierra assured them both, hoping it was the end of whatever this situation between them was becoming.

It looked like neither Tyler nor Aodhan bought her excuse. They both continued to stare at each other for another minute until Tyler backed down and made an excuse about how he needed to leave. He didn't meet Sierra's eyes as he grabbed his cart and made his way toward the employee room.

"Great. Just great." Sierra grumbled.

"What?"

Sierra set the book in her hand back on the cart, turning to face Aodhan. "You know, you can't go around scaring all my friends, okay?"

Aodhan lifted one eyebrow. "Are you two really friends?"

Sierra knew he was right. She had no friends here, and Tyler was a sad excuse for one. "Does it really matter?"

"Not really, but if it were up to me, you wouldn't be talking to another male besides me for the rest of your life."

Sierra raised her eyebrow. "Aodhan, this is the 21st Century and I will talk to whomever I please, no matter what their gender is."

"Their funeral then, because I will not stand by and let anyone, male or female, make you feel the way you are feeling right now."

His words made Sierra pause from spilling the retort she was about to make. What was she feeling that was strong enough to draw Aodhan to her side? Sad, yes, maybe even something a little more serious, akin to despair. But these emotions were not about something Tyler had said, but rather because Aodhan had pointed out the fact that she had very few friends and that not even Tyler was truly her friend, despite what he may say.

"Oh," she sighed. "These feelings aren't because of Tyler. It's because I don't really have any friends here in Dublin...or back at home...or at all really."

It was as if a lightbulb suddenly flicked on in Aodhan's head, and the anger on his features diminished immediately. Aodhan then placed his finger under her chin, lifting it to bring her eyes to meet his. Sierra thought he might say something, but instead, he gave her a quick but passionate kiss on the lips before whispering, "Meet me outside at lunch."

Sierra could only nod as Aodhan released her face, grabbed his cart, and maneuvered away from her.

~

Her lunch break arrived quicker than she anticipated, and Sierra rushed into the employee room to grab her purse and jacket before heading outside. She wasn't sure what Aodhan had in store, but she was excited at the prospect of some sort of surprise, despite her earlier annoyance at his actions.

As she rounded the corner just outside of the glass doors to the library, her eyes met Aodhan's as he was leaning against the wall, but then she noticed someone standing next to him. The other person was wearing a hood, but it only took her a second to recognize Kaye's fiery red hair peeking out from the sides.

"I thought we could all have lunch together," Aodhan explained, leading the two of them inside the café area. They quickly found a table for four, and as Sierra and Kaye sat, Aodhan headed to get in line to buy them all lunch.

"I've never sat in the café before," Sierra mused as she surveyed the large number of students and campus employees eating their lunches. Usually, she was in such a rush to get her food and leave, she hadn't really taken a good look at the café.

"Where do you normally eat?" Kaye asked as she looked at the variety of people in the room.

"Outside," Sierra replied. Kaye raised an eyebrow. "I, uh, tend to try to avoid people as much as possible."

"That would explain why you don't have any friends then."

While her voice was critical and a bit blunt, Sierra recognized that Kaye was just trying to help her with the issue that had brought this on in the first place. "Did Aodhan put you up to this because I don't have friends?"

Kaye smiled. "Maybe. But I also think he really wants us to get along."

"It's not weird for you?" Sierra asked.

"Is what weird?"

Sierra glanced around before leaning in. "Being forced to be my friend because of Aodhan?"

Kaye tossed her head back and laughed. "Any friend of Aodhan's is automatically a friend of mine. Plus, Aodhan knows I also struggle to find friends here, so this is as much for me as it is for you, I think."

Sierra tilted her head in confusion. "I thought you were from here?"

"Oh no." Kaye placed her hands on the table. "I'm from up north, closer to The Hills."

"Oh."

"Don't worry about it. It's not like I expected Aodhan to mention it."

"So, you came down here for Braan then?" Sierra noticed that Aodhan was almost at the register.

"Yes and no. Dating someone who is...different...can be hard, even here in Ireland." Sierra's mind backtracked to Aodhan's nonchalant explanation from the day before. "My parents have no idea that I'm with a Fae, and they're a bit traditional, so Braan and I don't feel comfortable telling them."

Sierra hadn't thought about the challenges that came with dating someone different, nor had she thought of the challenges of explaining to your parents that you were dating someone of a different species. As quick as the thought came, she pushed it away because she knew thinking of her own family right now would only stress her out. Instead, she asked Kaye, "So, what do they think you are doing then?"

Kaye sighed. "Well, they think I'm working as a travel psychologist. I travel home from time to time, without Braan, of course."

"And you don't video call or anything?"

Kaye smiled again, but it didn't quite reach her eyes. "Yes, but I call from different rooms of the house, pretending that it's a different hotel."

"Hm." Sierra rested her head on her hand as Aodhan made his way over, sandwiches piled precariously in his hands. "Does it bother you?"

Kaye shook her head. "My parents are much too religious to accept the idea that I love Braan no matter what he is—or isn't. And honestly, I don't get along with them well anyway, so at least this way I can control when I see them."

Something Kaye said resonated with Sierra. Her own relationship with her mother and siblings were so strained she wondered if a situation like Kaye's would be better for her in the future. At least then she would be able to control when she saw her parents, and not feel like she was spiraling out of control when they randomly just showed up in her life, wanting her to solve their problems.

She didn't say anything as Aodhan sat at the table, handing them their sandwiches. Sierra looked at the label, noticing he had chosen her a vegetarian cheese sandwich. She assumed he had chosen the same thing for himself, and maybe Kaye as well.

Sierra unwrapped her sandwich and took a bite. They ate in silence for a few moments until Sierra decided to break it. "Thanks for lunch, Aodhan."

"You are welcome," he answered, his sandwich already devoured, hands occupied with unwrapping a second. "Can't have you going hungry."

Sierra rolled her eyes. She knew he had orchestrated this whole thing just so she could spend time with Kaye, but she enjoyed the sentiment regardless.

The trio spoke of the weather, and something about The Hills, which Sierra didn't quite understand as Kaye and Sierra finished eating. Even though she wasn't able to chime in about all the subjects, Sierra enjoyed sharing her lunchtime with others instead of keeping herself sequestered as she normally did.

As Aodhan gathered the trash to throw away, Kaye waited until he walked away from the table to say something to Sierra under her breath. "I like you, Sierra, and I hope things work out for you and Aodhan." She gave Sierra an awkward hug over the surface of the table. "And I meant what I said, you are welcome at our home anytime."

Sierra could only nod as Kaye pulled away and stood, giving Aodhan a wave before heading out the door.

Once he was back at her side, he placed a hand on her lower back and guided her out of the café. "What are you doing after work?" he asked, as they made their way back to the library, the fall breeze causing Sierra to pull her coat more tightly across her body.

Sierra felt like being a little coy. "Hm, I'm not sure. I might have a date."

Aodhan, who was likely picking up on her emotions, played back. "Oh, really now. With who?"

"Oh." Sierra tucked her hair behind her ear. "You don't know him."

"I don't?" Aodhan appeared to be second-guessing their game for a moment, and Sierra could see his jealousy rising like it had that morning in the library.

"Nope, but I'd like to introduce you to him. Maybe you can come to my place after work." Sierra kept a smile on her face as she invited him over, and to her relief, he smiled back.

"I guess I can set aside time for that."

He gave her another quick kiss on the lips, before opening the door and holding it for her.

"It's a date then," she said as they made their way back to the employee area.

"It's a date," he confirmed, before they parted ways and returned to work. Well, at least Sierra returned to her work. Aodhan pulled his normal disappearing act, and Sierra didn't see a single glimpse of him for the rest of the afternoon.

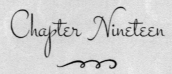

Chapter Nineteen

Sierra collected the dishes from their dinner, setting them in the sink. The minute they were out of her hands, they disappeared.

"Aodhan," Sierra grumbled, turning around to find him trying to look innocent as he seated himself on her couch. "You can't always be shifting my dishes to the servants your friends pay for."

"Why not?" He seemed genuinely confused as to why it wasn't appropriate to have Kaye and Braan's servants cleaning up after them.

"Because Kaye and Braan pay them to clean up after them, not me."

Aodhan lifted one eyebrow. "I disagree." Sierra rolled her eyes, but before she could say anything, Aodhan added, "They also pay the servants to clean up after me, and half of those dishes were rightfully my mess, so it's fine."

Sierra narrowed her eyes at Aodhan, but he just motioned to the couch. "Come, relax a bit. You deserve it."

Sierra took a deep breath, telling herself to let the argument go, and walked over to the couch, settling next to Aodhan. Once she was in place, Aodhan reclined back, pulling her head onto his shoulder with one arm, while he turned on the TV with the other.

"Now, what would you like to watch?"

"Anything is fine," Sierra replied. She was surprised he knew how to work a TV, considering they didn't have them in The Hills.

"I only know a few shows, mostly what Braan and Kaye watch, so—"

Sierra cut him off. "I'm sure it's great. Put it on."

Aodhan selected some Irish comedy that Sierra had seen ads for, but never watched herself. The screen filled with the characters who looked to be in their late teens and early 20s.

Sierra tried to pay attention, but all she could really focus on was the sensation of Aodhan running his large hand up and down her arm. She knew it was just supposed to be comforting, but it was having an entirely different effect, and she was feeling light tingles wherever his hand touched. It had clearly been too long since she'd had sex.

Probably feeling her hesitation, or maybe something else, Aodhan whispered in her ear, "Is it okay to touch your arm like this?"

Sierra nodded. "It's fine."

"Are you sure?"

His breath on her earlobe sent chills up her spine, and Sierra let out a light gasp. Aodhan stilled, and before she could second guess herself, Sierra turned to him, placing her lips on his.

Aodhan immediately began kissing her back, moving his hands to run up and down her sides instead of her arms, his thumbs caressing the underside of her breasts with each pass, setting fire inside Sierra's core.

Her breathing became even heavier as Sierra felt her arousal growing. But along with her arousal came her usual nerves at the fact that sex required taking her clothes off.

Pushing down her anxieties, she reached her hand around

Aodhan's neck to keep his face pressed to hers in case he felt her nerves and decided they should stop.

Taking that as a go-ahead, Aodhan slipped his hands beneath her shirt, caressing her breast through her sports bra. He broke the kiss, breathing hard, and pressed his forehead to hers. "Is this okay?"

Sierra nodded, moving one of her hands down to his waistband, where she could feel his arousal through his jeans.

"If you get uncomfortable, just tell me to stop. We only do what you are comfortable with, okay?"

"Okay." It came out as a breath, and before she could question whether he had heard her, he pulled her shirt over her head before placing his lips back on hers.

The minute the cold air hit the lesions on her back, Sierra's self-doubt reared its ugly head, and her heart pounded in her ears. Instead of focusing on the sensation of Aodhan's lips on hers, and the feel of his hands on her skin, her mind roared her insecurities on a continuous loop, wondering what Aodhan thought of how her skin looked. The effect was instant, and her arousal evaporated.

Aodhan pulled back. "What just happened?"

Sierra hastily grabbed her shirt, holding it in front of her body, even more worried now that he had nothing to distract him and could look at her skin and see how terrible it truly looked. But to her surprise, when she raised her face to meet his eyes, they were focused solely on hers, and he wasn't staring at her body at all.

"Tell me what's wrong, *mo ghrá*," he whispered, pulling her into his chest and resting his head on hers.

"I..." Sierra started, but then stopped. She wanted to explain, but she was sure Aodhan would laugh. "I'm sorry, I'm just not in the mood."

"No," Adohan said, sensing her dishonesty. "Don't lie to me, Sierra; you were in the mood, then I took off your shirt, and then you felt insecure and stopped. So, let's try this again: why did you feel insecure without your shirt?"

Sierra could feel the tears gathering in the corner of her eyes, and she pushed them down. She was stronger than this. "I was just worried that you were going to see my skin and then decide you didn't want me."

She waited for him to yell or tell her she was being dumb. But instead, he took her chin in his hand and turned her face to look up at his. He used his other hand to grab hers. "Listen to me, Sierra, I desire your body because of who you are, not because of the way you look." He took the hand that was holding hers, pressing them both into his lap, where she could feel he was still hard through his jeans. "I'm attracted to your heart and your soul, and no matter what you look like on the outside, you are beautiful to me. Understand?"

Sierra's emotions bubbled to the surface, and although she tried her hardest to press them back down, a tear slipped from the corner of her eye. Somehow knowing she couldn't find the words to speak, Aodhan pulled her back into his arms as more tears spilled from her eyes. "I've got you; everything is okay," he whispered into her hair as she cried.

Sierra didn't know if it was all the stress from the past few months, or the fact that no one had ever been so accepting when their relationship had gotten to this point, but the tears she was crying relieved some of the pressure she felt in her soul, and once she started, she couldn't stop. Aodhan didn't mind though. He simply sat there, holding her body against his, running his hand down her hair and her back, which was still bare.

She let her soul weep, and she must've needed it because, at some point, she drifted off to sleep, having her first restful sleep for as long as she could remember.

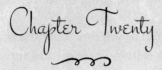

Chapter Twenty

Sierra woke to the sunlight streaming in through the single window in her apartment. For a moment, she just looked at the blue sky (which was rare for Dublin) until the events of the night before came rushing back.

Sitting up straight in bed, Sierra looked down to see she was still wearing her jeans and bra from the day before, and before her mind could follow that concerning thought further, Aodhan set his hand on her shoulder.

"I didn't want to cross any boundaries, so I put you to bed in what you were wearing."

Sierra nodded mutely before turning to find Aodhan tucked into bed next to her, still wearing his shirt from the day before. "I also thought it might scare you to wake up next to me in nothing but my undergarments, so I am still clothed too."

Sierra let out her breath. It was like Aodhan already knew all her anxieties without her having to explain them and had taken steps to make sure she woke up as comfortable as possible. The thought made her warm inside, even though she knew his extreme attentiveness was likely thanks, for the most part, to his gift.

"Are you okay?" he asked. "I thought about leaving, but I thought that might also cause you stress."

Sierra swallowed before answering, her mouth dry from crying the night before. "I'm okay. I'm sorry about...that."

Aodhan shook his head. "You never have to apologize for having emotions. It's part of being human."

The word 'human' caused Sierra's eyebrows to shoot up. "Is it different for Fae?"

Aodhan shrugged. "Yes and no. I think, as Fae, we are more in tune with our emotions and their causes than humans are, but we also have more time to figure them out, so it's not a fair comparison. As to feeling the same emotions, I think humans and Fae feel all the same emotions, yes."

"That makes me feel better, I guess."

"Listen, Sierra," Aodhan waited until her eyes rested on his before he continued, "I don't want you to feel like you have to hide your emotions from me, okay?"

"I won't." The corner of Sierra's mouth ticked up. "You're like no man I've ever met, Aodhan."

"I know."

The air in the room felt a bit heavy, especially after her breakdown the night before, so Sierra decided it was time to lighten the mood a bit. "Who knew this whole time all I needed to do to find an emotionally mature man was to date someone a little older."

"Hey now," Aodhan said teasingly, a smile dancing across his lips. "I don't want to see you dating any other Fae, understand?"

"Why?" Sierra stepped out of bed and headed toward the bathroom, looking at Aodhan over her shoulder. "Jealous?" Even though she was just in her sports bra and jeans still, she found that the insecure voice in her head remained quiet.

Aodhan's eyes darkened. "Yes," he replied honestly. "Plus, the only Fae I know in the area is Braan, and that would cause problems for numerous people."

Once she was out of view, Sierra pushed the door closed, leaving it open a crack so they could talk as she undressed. "I would never do that to Kaye," she replied in earnest.

"I know," came Aodhan's answer from the other side of the

door as Sierra turned on the shower and stepped under the spray, washing away the shame and anxiety of the night before. Today was a new day, and Aodhan was still here.

She washed quickly, wrapping herself in her favorite extra-large towel, which covered most of her torso and legs, before reentering the bedroom. Aodhan was right where she had left him, sitting up in bed with her blue comforter covering his lower half, his bare chest on display, giving Sierra the perfect opportunity to ogle the impressive abs she had felt during their previous make-out sessions. "Do you want to shower?"

"That would be preferable, yes," Aodhan answered, his voice husky in a way that made goosebumps appear on Sierra's skin.

Knowing that now wasn't the time to try a repeat of last night, even though other parts of her body disagreed with that sentiment, Sierra grabbed her second towel from the bathroom cabinet and handed it to him on her way across the room. "Here you go."

Aodhan disappeared into the bathroom, leaving the door open a crack as she had. As soon as she heard the water running, Sierra moved to her dresser, dropping her towel to pull on jeans and a long-sleeved turtleneck sweater. She swapped the towel to her head, hoping her hair would dry a bit before she had to head to her lab.

With a glance at the clock, Sierra confirmed she had another hour until she would be late. For the first time in a while, she was glad she didn't have any early lectures. While later lectures made it harder to arrange shifts at the library, at least she didn't have to worry about the fact that she hadn't set an alarm before falling asleep during her mental meltdown the night before.

Remembering that it was morning and that Aodhan might want breakfast, Sierra moved to her kitchen corner to see what she could scrounge up. One glance at the half-sized fridge in her tiny kitchen confirmed it was indeed nearly empty, and the cabinets were just as bare. With a grimace, Sierra started the hot water pot and grabbed two tea bags and two granola bars from her snack stash. It would have to do.

She turned around, only to come into contact with a wide, chiseled, and slightly damp chest. Sierra dropped the tea bags and the granola bars, lifting her chin to meet Aodhan's green eyes, which were burning with desire.

Aodhan ducked, pressing his lips to hers in a kiss that left her breathless. The kiss continued until the hot water kettle beeped, and Sierra reluctantly tore herself away. Aodhan backed up a step, but Sierra could see he was clearly aroused by their morning inter-action. But before she could come up with something else to say, the hot water kettle beeped a second time, furious that Sierra hadn't pressed the off button yet, and she had to turn away.

When she turned back, she saw Aodhan's back as he stepped back into the bathroom, closing the door to assumably get dressed.

Sierra gathered the tea bags and granola bars from the floor, setting them on the table, before filling two mugs with hot water. By the time she was finished putting the tea bags in, Aodhan was back and fully dressed in the same clothes he had been wearing the night before.

"Are you working today?" he asked as he slid into the chair, pushing his damp curls from where they fell in front of his eyes.

She shook her head. "No, I have a lab and a lecture today. Are you working?"

He shook his head as well. "No, I'm off today."

Sierra thought maybe the sentence would end with an invita-tion to spend time together that night, but the silence stretched through her kitchen.

"So, when will I see you again?" she asked, as she unwrapped her granola bar and took a bite.

"I want to take you on a date. Tomorrow night, maybe?"

Sierra's eyes widened. "Okay," she breathed.

Aodhan placed his hand on hers. "Are you working?"

Sierra was glad one of them still had some sense because all thoughts of her job had left her head at his mention of a date. "Oh yes, I'm closing." She winced.

"No problem," he assured her. "This is Dublin, we can do a late-night date when you get off."

"Sounds perfect," Sierra replied, her mouth full of granola bar.

"Okay, see you then." As soon as she swallowed, Aodhan leaned over and gave her a peck on the lips. "Did you want me to walk you to class?"

Sierra thought about it for a moment. While she enjoyed their walks together, she also enjoyed walking alone, having just some time for herself and her thoughts. Plus, after the previous night, she definitely needed some space. "I'll be okay on my own."

"Alright," Aodhan leaned in to press a second kiss to her lips. "Have a good day at class, okay?" Sierra nodded in response as Aodhan disappeared from view.

It must be nice to practically teleport everywhere, Sierra thought as she stood to get ready to walk to class. She looked down to see he hadn't touched his tea or the granola bar, and Sierra realized he probably had a breakfast buffet waiting for him at home. Oh well, more for her. Sierra grabbed the second granola bar, slipping it into her messenger bag before heading out the door for her lab. She couldn't wait to see what Aodhan had in mind for their date.

Chapter Twenty-One

Sierra floated through her day, unable to stay focused during her lab, thoughts of Aodhan flitting every which way in her brain. As a result, she very nearly burned her partner with the hydrochloric acid they were working with when she spilled their bottle of it mid-experiment. Though she apologized profusely, her lab partner was less than enthusiastic, and Sierra knew she probably wouldn't be willing to work with her again.

Ah well, that was future Sierra's problem.

Sierra's mind drifted just as much, if not more, during the following lecture, making her feel like a high school girl again. Sierra wasn't a virgin by any means, but she hadn't been this consumed by the thought of sleeping with a guy, or almost sleeping with a guy, in years. She wished now that she had some kind of best girlfriend because she would love to text her and get her thoughts on the entire situation. Sierra briefly thought of texting Aodhan to get Kaye's number, but then realized it was too new of a friendship for that kind of conversation just yet.

Sierra must not have been the only one wishing they had spent more time together the night before, because when Sierra exited her classroom after her lecture, she found Aodhan leaning up against the wall outside, his eyes trained on the door she had just exited.

"Aodhan!" she said, her voice conveying her shock as it rose to a higher pitch than usual. "What are you doing here?" Although she was shocked, this didn't stop a smile from spreading across her face.

Aodhan's dark eyes bore into hers as he stepped closer, forcing Sierra back, her spine pressed up against the brick wall, his palms flat on the wall by her sides. "I couldn't stay away." Sierra had never heard a man growl, but the tone was definitely one that she would consider a growl.

Sierra looked around at the rapidly emptying hallway, trying to keep her cool. "I see. Didn't you have plans today?"

"No, I had been planning to spend some time at home today, but I missed you too much." His lips ghosted over her jawline, and Sierra felt her blood begin to sizzle. After how he had cared about her the night before, her body was definitely ready to take this to the next level. Sierra just hoped her mind would allow it to happen.

With another glance at the hallway, Sierra knew she would never be comfortable enough to kiss him back here. "We need to go somewhere else," she whispered as Aodhan trailed kisses up and down her neck.

Aodhan didn't stop his kissing as he replied, "Where would you like to go, *mo grá*?"

"Somewhere...more private," Sierra whispered. She didn't want to say her apartment because suddenly that felt very far away, but she knew she didn't want to stay in the hallway either.

Aodhan's green eyes connected with hers, fire flickering within their depths. "I have an idea."

Aodhan tucked his hand under her arm and started leading her out of the lecture hall. Sierra thought maybe he was taking her to her apartment after all, when he suddenly made a turn and headed toward the library.

"What's this idea?" Sierra gulped. The last thing she wanted to do right now was run into Tyler.

"You'll see," Aodhan replied, not calming her fears any.

Aodhan led her through the front doors of the library, but before anyone could see them, he took a sharp right, leading her down the stairs to the microfilm area. Sierra was about to argue that they shouldn't be down here, when Aodhan stopped in front of a door and pushed it open, pulling Sierra in behind him.

Inside the room, it was pitch black, and Sierra reached out her hand to see if she could feel where they were, but her hand encountered nothing. She heard the click of a button lock engaging behind her and assumed Aodhan was locking the door.

"It's one of the microfilm storage areas," Aodhan explained, pulling her body into his and resuming his trail of kisses. "I found it during one of my hunts for texts."

"Isn't there someone down here to monitor?" Sierra asked hesitantly, as the fire in her lower stomach resumed its burning.

"Not today. I came in looking for some stuff this morning, and Mona said Carl is out sick."

Sierra nodded as his lips made their way along her jaw, and his hands slid around her back to cup her ass, giving it a squeeze. Sierra let her messenger bag slip from her shoulder, coming to rest on the floor with a soft thump.

"And I was thinking, we might keep the light off, so you feel more comfortable," he explained in a rough whisper, as he kissed the corner of her mouth. Sierra's heart warmed at the fact that he was thinking of what would make her feel best. And he was right, she liked the idea that he couldn't see her in the dark, and she wouldn't have to worry that he might stare.

Instead of answering with words, she pressed her lips to his, one of her hands coming to rest on his shoulder, the other sliding down to his waistband.

Aodhan slid his hands under her shirt, resting them on her sides. "Is it okay if I take off your shirt now?"

"Yes," Sierra replied, glad he was asking for permission and not assuming. In one smooth motion, Aodhan tugged both her undershirt and sweater over her head, leaving her in her bra and jeans. As soon as her head was free from the sweater, Aodhan's lips met hers again.

"Can I take off your shirt?" Sierra whispered when they paused.

"Please," Aodhan groaned, as Sierra slid her hands under his shirt. She wasn't nearly as smooth as he had been, but then the cloth between them was gone, and Sierra ran her greedy hands over the muscled plane of Aodhan's chest.

Aodhan's hands rose to do an exploration of their own, running over the cups of her bra where Sierra was sure he could feel her nipples poking into them from below. "Can I take this off too?"

"Mm-hmm," Sierra replied, as one of his hands snaked behind her back and undid the clasp in one fluid motion.

"If you start to feel uncomfortable, tell me, and we can stop." Aodhan's voice was husky as one of his hands cupped her breast, and he ran his thumb over the nipple.

"I think...I think I'm ready for this now, Aodhan, really," she breathed into the darkness. "But I will tell you if that changes."

Aodhan returned his lips to hers, the darkness around them seeming to amplify the intense sexual tension between them. Sierra's hand lowered, rubbing the front of his jeans where she could feel his very large erection beneath his zipper. If it was even possible, Sierra felt herself becoming more aroused.

Aodhan's breath caught as she continued to rub him. "I want you more than I've ever wanted any other woman. I want you to know that," he said with a groan, as she continued her ministrations.

"Are you sure you're not just saying that to get into my pants?" Sierra teased, enjoying the feel of Aodhan's thumb circling her nipple.

"I promise, I'm not," Aodhan replied. "You are the most attractive woman I've ever met."

Somehow, Sierra highly doubted that, but she didn't want to ruin the moment with an argument, so in response she reached for the button on his jeans.

"Wait," he said, moving her hand away. Sierra heard rustling, but before she could figure out whether or not he'd removed his pants, she felt his lips enclose around her nipple. At the same time, his hand connected with the opening of her jeans, rubbing the heel of his hand against her clit through the cloth barrier.

He continued this for a few moments before his fingers lifted to undo the button on Sierra's pants, followed by the zipper, and then slowly, he pushed them down her legs. Sierra put her hands on Aodhan's shoulders for support as she stepped out of her pants. Sierra realized that this must've been part of Aodhan's plan because it put her nipple right next to his mouth, and he quickly sucked it in, teasing the hardened tip gently with his tongue.

Sierra expected Aodhan to stand back up, but instead he sat with his legs out in front of him, pulling Sierra onto his lap so that she was straddling him with her knees on either side of his thighs. She felt her bare skin against his, realizing he had indeed taken his pants off earlier.

He pulled her mouth to his, his erection pressed between their bodies. Sierra reached down and began to rub him up and down gently, causing him to moan.

Aodhan kept one hand on Sierra's hip to keep her in place while the other ventured into her underwear as he ran his finger up and down her slit gently.

"And here I was worried you wouldn't be ready," he whispered in her ear teasingly, as he began to gently apply pressure to her clit. Enjoying the feel of his fingers, Sierra began to move, pressing herself down on his hands to increase the pressure.

It usually took Sierra a while to orgasm, especially the first time she had sex with a guy, so she was surprised a few minutes later when she felt her orgasm beginning to build without needing several minutes of foreplay.

"I'm getting close," she whispered, but Aodhan didn't

answer, he just continued the pressure, bending his head down to suck on her nipple.

Within moments, Sierra was falling over the edge as waves of pleasure pulsed through her body. As soon as her orgasm finished, she collapsed against Aodhan, panting hard.

"Mmm," he breathed in her ear, nibbling on her earlobe. "That was hot."

As soon as she caught her breath, Sierra moved her hand to his boxers, pushing them out of the way so his cock could spring free. Without hesitating, Sierra wrapped her hand around his cock and began pumping him. He was so large that even with both of her hands, she didn't quite cover his entire dick. She was so ready to feel him inside her, but suddenly, her medical schooling came to the front of her mind.

"Do you have a condom?" she asked.

"Yes," Aodhan whispered back, pulling the foil packet from somewhere Sierra couldn't see, but she assumed it must've been in the pocket of his pants. She heard the sound of the wrapper tearing, and then Aodhan paused her hands to roll it on.

As soon as it was in place, Sierra lifted herself, slipping off her underwear before moving to hover just above him. Aodhan still held her with one hand, using his free one to guide himself into her. When he was properly lined up, Sierra lowered herself inch by inch.

Aodhan's breath caught as soon as he was fully sheathed in her, and Sierra found she was already close to a second orgasm, just from the feel of him inside her. He fit perfectly and touched all the right places, something she couldn't say about the men she had been with back in Texas.

Sierra began to move, rolling her hips forward. Aodhan groaned, his hands coming to rest on her hips. "I'm not going to last long if you move like that," he breathed.

Sierra felt a surge of pride shiver through her body, and she repeated the hip roll, causing Aodhan to moan softly again, much to her delight.

Before she could do it a third time, Aodhan took control, using his hands on her hips to guide her motions, pushing her forward so that her clit rubbed against the area below his abs. Combined with the feel of him hitting her g-spot on the inside, it wasn't long before Sierra came again, clenching herself around him.

After she collapsed against him, he waited a few moments to allow her to catch her breath before he began moving again. He moved her back and forth across his lap a few more times, then cursed as he shuddered and came.

The sound of their panting echoed throughout the room as they came down from their post-coital high. Sierra leaned against Aodhan's chest as he used one hand to hold them up and the other to rub up and down her back.

Sierra broke the silence. "So, do they also use condoms in The Hills?"

Aodhan chuckled, clearly not expecting that to be the first thing out of her mouth after their first time sharing their bodies with each other. "No, but we use something similar, so I was able to figure it out with some help from the internet, and an awkward conversation with Braan."

Sierra nodded into his chest, looking around at the darkness that surrounded them. "Now for the hard part. I guess we have to find everything and clean up in the dark."

Aodhan chuckled a second time. "That's no problem. All Fae can see in the dark."

Sierra froze, shock running through her core. "So even though I can't see you...you can see me?" she squeaked.

"Yes."

Sierra felt coils of embarrassment building in her stomach, climbing up to her throat. Aodhan, clearly sensing her emotions as usual, put his hands on either side of her face, bringing her forehead to his.

"Hey now, no need to be embarrassed. I already told you that you are the most beautiful woman to me. Spots included."

Sierra wished the words would bring relief, but they didn't. But at least it was quiet inside her head, and she didn't feel like she was going to burst into tears.

"The darkness was for you. You are the one holding yourself back. That's okay, but I just wanted you not to worry about it for a few minutes. Now breathe."

Sierra didn't realize she wasn't breathing, but the moment he said the words, she gulped down a breath, trying to keep the panic at bay. But as she breathed, she realized he was right. He never said that he couldn't see in the dark, just that he wanted her to feel better, and she did.

"I'm sorry," she whispered finally.

"Shh. Don't do that. Don't ever apologize for being yourself. Your nervousness about your skin is part of you. I wouldn't wish you to be any different."

"Even if it means we could've had sex sooner?"

"No, we had sex at the perfect time for us. I wouldn't have wanted it to happen any other way. Plus, how many people get to have sex in the microfilm storage room at their university?"

Suddenly remembering where they were, Sierra cringed and began to stand. "I forgot we were in the microfilm room."

"I know. Me too, for a moment." She heard the sound of rustling fabric before the soft fabric of her sweater pressed against her arm. Grabbing it, she quickly felt for her bra, which Aodhan also included in the stack, and began slipping on her clothes one by one. Once she was all put together, Aodhan found her hand with his, handing her the messenger bag and tucking her under his arm.

"Now, I know I said I would take you out for a date tomorrow, and I still want to do that, but how does grabbing some takeout tonight sound?"

"Lovely," Sierra replied, as he guided them toward the door.

She heard the pop of the button lock as he turned the doorknob. "Brace yourself."

Sierra didn't have a chance to respond before he pulled her

into the bright light of the library, closing the door to the micro-film room behind them.

Squinting, she looked around the library basement, relieved to see it was unoccupied.

"I'm going to stop by the bathroom, but wait for me outside, okay?" Aodhan whispered in her ear.

Sierra nodded, shivering slightly at the feel of his breath tickling her earlobe. They walked up the stairs, hand in hand, before Aodhan split off to head to the bathroom, while Sierra slipped outside and around the corner as quickly as possible, hoping not to run into any of her coworkers.

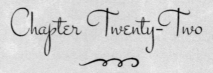

Chapter Twenty-Two

Aodhan joined her outside a few minutes later. Without a word, he slipped his hand into hers, and they began the walk back to her apartment.

They walked in silence for a few minutes, but something between them felt off to Sierra. She wasn't sure if it was because their first time having sex had been in the library microfilm room, or if it was something else. Normally, she would be too shy to say something and brush it off, but Sierra knew that wouldn't help if everything wasn't okay.

"Umm..." She cleared her voice. "Is everything okay?"

Aodhan nodded but kept his face forward. "When I went to the bathroom, Braan texted me and said someone from home tried to contact me today."

Sierra rolled the words over in her mind. "What do you mean tried to contact you? And who?"

Aodhan glanced at her briefly before returning his vision to the path in front of him. "My father. And...it's a bit complicated. Since my world isn't your world, we can't use modern methods of communication. We use a method similar to what humans call scrying. It isn't perfect, but we can speak to each other while we are in different worlds at least."

Sierra had never been more disappointed that she hadn't been more into reading, as she didn't want to ask what scrying was, but she didn't really know either.

Sensing her embarrassment, Aodhan jumped into an explanation. "Scrying is an ancient method used by witches to see the future using water." They turned the corner, drawing close to her apartment. "Now, we can't see the future or anything, but we can use the water as a connection and speak to each other through it."

Sierra felt her eyes widen at the realization that witches also existed, and turned to Aodhan to ask a question, but he held up a finger before she could.

"There's quite a few...caveats. The water must be from the same source, and it grows...stale after a while. So, every few years, more water has to be brought here from The Hills to replace the water we have on hand for communicating."

"And the water is just kept in a jar...or something?"

They came to a stop in front of her apartment door, and Aodhan turned to her. "Not quite. It must be stored in stone. So, it is brought here in a stone jar, and kept in a special stone bowl. Which brings up the other problem. There is no way to let someone know you want to communicate, so you have to just go for it and hope that someone is near the bowl to fetch the person you want to speak with when you call."

"I see." Sierra unlocked the door, and they made their way up the stairs. "And you weren't nearby today."

Aodhan waited until they were inside her room before he replied. "Exactly. But that's the weird thing. Last night, I felt I needed to be home today, which is why I didn't make plans. And then someone calls."

Sierra removed her jacket and set her messenger bag on the table by the door as his words sank in. "What do you mean you had a feeling?"

"That's just it. I can't explain it. My magic isn't future-telling or anything. But in the pit of my stomach, I felt I should spend a night at home. Of course, I was home all day and eventually came to find you...but this is very unlike me."

Silence fell over them as Sierra pondered what he said for a moment. "You know, this is going to sound crazy, but just hear me out." Sierra sat on the couch, Aodhan sinking into the seat next to her.

"So, you believe humans are differently evolved Fae, right?"

Aodhan confirms with a nod.

"As humans, we have this thing called intuition. It's where something bothers you, or maybe you feel you should do something, but you don't have any rational reason to do that thing you feel you should do. We don't have magic, so this is one of the few unexplainable things about our nature that somehow works to protect us.

"Most humans brush off their intuition because it isn't always right. But sometimes it is, and especially as women, we often have to rely on that intuition to protect us—when we are meeting men for dates, for example. Because we have nothing else. As a result, women tend to be more in tune with their intuition than men. But men often think we are crazy when we mention it."

Aodhan remained silent, his gaze resting on his hands in his lap.

Feeling self-conscious, Sierra asked, "Am I making sense?"

Aodhan swallowed. "Yes. Too much, actually."

"What do you mean?"

"Well, you're saying all humans have this feeling, right, though it is stronger in women because they use it more often?"

"Yes, well, most anyway. I'm sure there is someone somewhere who will say they don't." Sierra rolled her eyes, thinking of all the idiots who live on the internet these days just to harass or bother other people.

Aodhan glanced at Sierra, his green eyes boring into hers before continuing. "So, if I have suddenly developed this intuition, it would mean I am gaining a common human trait.

Remember how I said I believed the Fae were losing their magic because they were intermixing with humans more?"

Sierra nodded, setting her hands on Aodhan's, sensing whatever was rolling over in his mind was upsetting him.

"Well, what you just said would mean that maybe it isn't the intermarrying that is thinning the magic. It would mean that we are simply evolving as humans did. Just more slowly, for some reason. Or maybe we are even evolving differently. Or I suppose something else could be at play, but either way, what I think to be occurring isn't really occurring."

Sierra didn't know what to say. For all her years studying medicine, this wasn't something she had an answer to, but she did have one thing to suggest. "Maybe you aren't evolving to humans, but rather developing an intuition because you can no longer rely on your magic to protect you. It could be a sort of... backward evolutionary advantage?"

Aodhan didn't answer, removing one of his hands from underneath Sierra's to rub his face.

After a few moments of quiet, he finally turned to face her. "I really wanted to spend tonight with you, but Braan said my father would try to contact me again later. So, I should go. But I will see you for our date tomorrow, right?"

Sierra smiled slightly, but it didn't meet her eyes. "I understand, you should go. I'll see you tomorrow."

Aodhan nodded, grabbing her chin, and pressing his lips to hers so firmly it took Sierra's breath away. "I'll text you, okay? I'll let you know how the contact goes."

"Okay. And either way, I'll see you tomorrow after work."

A smile overtook Aodhan's face, his eyes becoming even brighter than before. "Yes, and I've got special plans for us. Until tomorrow."

Sierra opened her mouth to ask what they were, but before she could, Aodhan disappeared from sight, apparently shifting back to Braan's.

With a sigh, Sierra made herself comfy on the couch and

grabbed the remote. But before she could dig through the visual sludge on Netflix to find something good, her phone vibrated from where it was tucked in her messenger bag.

Thinking it was Aodhan, she jumped up to grab it, only to see her mother's name on the screen. Her shoulders dropping in disappointment, Sierra pressed the green answer button and held the phone to her ear.

"*Hola, mamá. Como estas?*"

"Oh, now you want to talk to me? It would be nice if my *hija* would call me from time to time, but nooo, she's too busy in the big city—"

"*Mamá*, we live in Dallas." Sierra cut off her mom's dramatic speech, hoping it was the end of it, but of course, her mom was not to be dissuaded from her petition for attention.

"—and it's so far, we can't even visit. Why, I'll be an old maid when you return." A sniffle came through the other end of the line, but Sierra knew it was likely fake.

"Mama, I'll be back in a year and a half. You will be exactly 55." Like most women of Hispanic descent born in the early 70s, Sierra's mother had children very young and close together, meaning she was not an old mother, at all. Though anyone listening in on the conversation would think she was on her deathbed with the way she was acting.

"Even Maria makes time from being a *doctora* to come see me. But noooo, it's too much for *mi* Sierra."

Taking a deep breath to keep her cool, Sierra replied, "Mama, I am going through a similar program to Maria. Remember when she was in medical school how busy she was?"

"*Si*, but she became a *doctora*, and what are you becoming, *hija*? Do you even know?"

Sierra sighed. This was the same argument they had when she had entered the program a few months before. "I am not sure, *mamá*, but I may become a medical researcher. Something which is just as important as a doctor, I just won't see patients."

Sierra's mother let out a *hmph* from the other end of the

phone, and Sierra knew it was no use, so she tried to change the subject.

"How is Diego, *mamá*? Are things better?"

"*Sí, sí*, he has come to visit his *mamá* and make amends. And he will attend mass with the family on Saturday."

Sierra pulled the phone away from her ear to look at the date. Saturday was *Día de Los Muertos*, which is why her family would be attending mass. "Ah *sí, mamá*, that's great. Light a candle for me, *por favor*."

"You could come light the candle yourself."

Just when Sierra thought they were making progress. "*Mamá*, it is a 13-hour flight to Dallas. I cannot just get on a plane for every holiday."

"*Y la Navidad*?"

La Navidad was Christmas. But Sierra knew at this point, she didn't have the money to buy a flight to return to Dallas for Christmas.

"I don't think so, *mamá*. I will come in the summer for a week or two, though."

That was clearly not the right answer, as another sniffle came through the line, and this time, Sierra could tell her mom was crying on the other end. "I cannot believe you won't be here for *Navidad*. What have I done to deserve this, *mi hija*?"

Sierra closed her eyes slowly. Her mother had always played the guilt card, but it seemed to be escalating lately. She just didn't seem to understand that Sierra had her own life, which she had to be allowed to explore. Deciding to take the path of least resistance, Sierra muttered an apology in Spanish.

"Your apology means nothing. I do not understand why you can't put your family first. Or at least before your studies," she huffed.

Sierra knew it was no use, but she tried anyway. "*Mamá*, I am my own person. I love our family, I do, but I have to be allowed to be on my own for some time, too. This year, I am very far away, but once I finish this study, and have a job, I will be able to visit for more holidays."

"Hmph. Fine," Sierra's mother replied. "I will see you later then." And with that, the line went dead.

Sierra scrolled through her contacts, debating on contacting Maria or Diego to see if they could talk any sense into her mom, but she was exhausted and didn't have the mental space to speak to one of her siblings tonight.

Though it was early, Sierra didn't much feel like dinner, and doom scrolling on her phone in bed sounded heavenly. With a click, she shut off the TV and slipped on her pajamas. She would worry about how to deal with her mother's dramatics tomorrow.

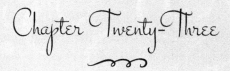

Chapter Twenty-Three

The next day at work, the hours dragged on forever, the hand on the analog clock in the employee room barely seeming to move. Sierra couldn't tell if it was because she was excited about her date with Aodhan later or simply because it was a slow day in the library. She was so distracted by her dreamy thoughts that it wasn't until a blond girl came into the library dressed as Little Bo Peep that Sierra realized it was Halloween.

As she had told Tyler, Sierra hadn't really cared about Halloween, well, ever, but as she looked around and noticed that even some of her coworkers were wearing fun jumpers and hats that represented various book and movie characters, she wished she had paid just a little bit more attention so that she could've done something fun too.

Ah, well, there was always next year.

Other than realizing too late that it was Halloween and feeling like someone had purposely slowed down time, the day went smoothly; Sierra reshelved books, took her lunch break, then reshelved some more.

Sierra was shelving what would probably be her second to last cart of books when a man approached her.

"Excuse me, miss?"

Sierra turned, catching her breath as she realized the man was wearing a black beanie. As quickly as her mind flashed to Aodhan, the thought dissipated as she realized the man was nothing like Aodhan. First of all, he was wearing some type of old-fashioned sweater, which definitely didn't match his hat. He was also quite tall and looked a bit older than the average student. Sierra surmised he was possibly a Ph.D. student. "Are you looking for something?"

He cleared his throat. "Yes, I was wondering if you had any books in old Gaelic?"

Sierra drew her eyebrows together. Of course, on the day Aodhan wasn't working at the library, what she assumed was a Ph.D. student would need a book in the language only he spoke.

"We do. I have to apologize, though; I don't speak old Gaelic, so I'll take you to the area, but then you are on your own."

"I'll manage."

Sierra set the book in her hand on the cart and started walking toward the part of the library where they kept the Gaelic books, the man following silently behind her. So silently, in fact, she had to glance over her shoulder once or twice to ensure he was still there. Each time she looked over her shoulder his eyes bore into hers. He was looking at her so intently it was unnerving and Sierra walked a little faster hoping to get him out of her hair sooner rather than later.

As they rounded the corner, Sierra was trying to brush off the weird vibes she was getting from the stranger when he suddenly pushed her up against the bookcase, putting his hand over her mouth.

Panic set in immediately, and Sierra started struggling against him, trying to remove his hand from her mouth so she could scream, but his hold was firm, his hands like iron.

Sierra's mind flashed back to her talk with Aodhan about strength yesterday, and she rolled her eyes up to the stranger's face, focusing on the beanie. *Could he be Fae?*

While she had been afraid before, Sierra's heart sank to her stomach as she realized this probably wasn't a human holding her. She continued to struggle, hoping her adrenaline would magically make her stronger as it did in the movies, but the stranger didn't budge.

It seemed like time had slowed to a crawl, but realistically, Sierra knew that she had likely only been in his grip for a few seconds. In a last-ditch effort, Sierra raised her knee, intending to go for his balls, but before she could connect, the stranger pinched her neck, and the world in front of her eyes swam before everything went dark.

Sierra awoke a while later in the pitch-black feeling as if she was spinning. She brought her hands to her head to see if she could stop the sensation, only to realize her hands were stuck together. She struggled against whatever kept her wrists pressed together, but she couldn't tell if it was rope, duct tape, or something else.

Letting that thought go for a moment, she brought her tied hands to head level, running them along the side of her face. The smoothness of tape glided over her cheek, and she felt the cloth covering her eyes. Well, that answered both her questions; it was dark because she was blindfolded, and her hands were taped together with duct tape.

Now that was out of the way, Sierra took a deep breath to center herself before she panicked, and tried to take in her surroundings with the senses she did have access to.

When Sierra was a kid, her mother had been convinced one of her children would one day be kidnapped. As a result, Sierra had taken a few self-defense classes over the years. While she had already made one mistake, which was allowing the kidnapper to change her location, she knew it wouldn't be long before Aodhan noticed she was missing. She also knew she needed to figure out her new location, and fast, so she could start working on an escape plan, or leave clues for someone who could be looking for her.

Sierra inhaled deeply, trying to work out the scent filling her nostrils. It smelled like burned rubber. That, and the fact that she could tell she was in motion, led her to believe she was in a vehicle of some kind.

She wiggled around, but wherever she was, was flat, and she had been able to move her bound hands to her face, which meant she wasn't on a seat or on the floor of the back of the vehicle, unless it was a type of van. Sierra moved her bound hands around her head, but she didn't encounter any walls. Then she lifted them up a few inches, and her hands came into contact with hard metal.

She was in a trunk.

Sierra took another deep breath, glad that her mouth wasn't taped shut, but she also knew that if it wasn't, her captor likely had an idea in mind to control her noise, or that there wasn't anyone around to hear her scream.

If this had been just any kidnapper, Sierra might have tried screaming anyway, in the hopes he had misjudged her, but Sierra was reasonably certain at this point that her captor was not human.

So that left only one option, and that was to figure out what he could possibly want from her and figure out a way to use it to bargain for her freedom, or a way to outsmart him when the time came. Sierra ran over all her conversations with Aodhan, Braan, and Kaye in her mind. Had any of them mentioned dangerous Fae?

She didn't think so.

The only time they had even spoken about Fae and humans together was when discussing the loss of Fae magic and the fact that only humans were servants in the Fae world.

Was this man taking Sierra to become a servant? Was that what this was?

She certainly hoped so, as that would give her an option to

escape. If he was taking her for more nefarious purposes, she was out of ideas.

Sierra felt tears behind her eyes at the thought of the things he could be planning to do with her, but she forced herself to push those thoughts away and remember that Aodhan was coming for her. There was no way he would accept that she had ditched their date. Plus, he was picking her up at the library, so he would notice she wasn't there right away.

Yes, Aodhan was likely already on his way to rescue her. With that comforting thought in mind, Sierra let herself be carried off to sleep with the rocking motion of the car. She would get out of this. She had to.

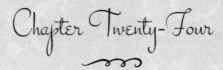

Chapter Twenty-Four

Sierra woke to the light of sunrise pouring into the trunk as whoever had kidnapped her pulled it open. While she still couldn't see anything but light from behind the blindfold, she could feel the cold wind whipping around her and smell the salty scent of the sea. They weren't in Dublin anymore, and if they had been driving all night as Sierra suspected, they could be in Northern Ireland by now.

The kidnapper grabbed her arm roughly, pulling her from the trunk. Sierra opened her mouth to start screaming.

"Don't bother. No one will hear you." His harsh voice cut through her thoughts, but Sierra decided she didn't want to take the chance and screamed anyway.

It didn't last long before some kind of cloth was shoved in her mouth, effectively choking her.

"You brought this on yourself," the kidnapper grumbled as he began to pull Sierra through the grass.

Although she couldn't see much from behind her blindfold, Sierra began cataloging anything she could sense to use later when she escaped. There was no way this was the end for her, she wouldn't allow it to be.

The kidnapper was pulling Sierra so roughly her legs began to tangle in the long grass they were walking through, and Sierra stumbled a bit. This didn't deter her captor, as he only began to pull her more roughly, resulting in him practically dragging Sierra.

Using this to her advantage, Sierra put her bound hands along the ground to try and feel her surroundings. Unfortunately, the grass was sharper than anticipated, and Sierra soon felt the sharp sting of her hands being sliced open by the tiny blades.

Trying to hiss in pain but unable to do so with the gag in her mouth, Sierra ended up coughing instead, causing her kidnapper to come to a stop. At least, she assumed that was what was going on until the air around her changed.

At first, Sierra thought she was being pulled through a clear waterfall, but she realized the sensation she was feeling wasn't wet, rather more of a vacuum. But then, as suddenly as the sensation started, it stopped, and the air around Sierra felt heavy, warm, and moist; three things she knew were not characteristic of the air in Dublin.

That's when the thought finally hit her. She had been brought to Sidhe, or The Hills as Aodhan described it. Unless there was another secret world that she hadn't been told about, in which case she was truly screwed.

Sierra didn't have much time to evaluate what was around her before she was roughly shoved onto something made of wood, the impact jarring as her entire body came into contact with it. Sierra grimaced but couldn't say anything, thanks to the gag.

At least, she thought, *Aodhan can come in here and find me.* She just hoped he figured it out quickly, as she had no idea of the strange man's intentions.

The wood beneath her began to move, and Sierra figured she had been thrown in some sort of wooden cart or wagon. Although the situation wasn't ideal, and Sierra was scared out of her wits, she couldn't help but wish she wasn't wearing a blindfold so she could at least see the world into which she had been taken so forcefully.

The ride continued for what felt like days but was probably

only an hour or two, if that. Sierra's shoulder was pressed uncomfortably into the wood, and her neck ached from sleeping in a trunk the night before. Trying to find something to pass the time, and keep her mind off the pain, Sierra began running through the homework assignment she had been planning to complete that weekend. It wasn't all that interesting, and she knew it likely wouldn't matter anymore since she doubted she was leaving here alive, but at least it temporarily lessened the pain and gave her something to focus on.

The cart finally rolled to a stop, and just as roughly as she was tossed in, Sierra was pulled to a standing position, though her kidnapper remained silent. She almost wished she hadn't screamed now so she could at least ask him what was going on.

Sierra's feet stumbled over the uneven ground, the man keeping up his brisk pace whether her feet were on the ground or not. When the dirt beneath her feet became cold, smooth stone, Sierra knew they had entered some kind of structure.

"Ah, what have we here?" A new voice that wasn't that of her kidnapper reached Sierra's ears.

"Sir, I believe I have found the girl to break the curse." Her kidnapper spoke up from just behind Sierra. She really wished he would remove her blindfold so she could see who she was talking to.

"You have now, have you?" the second voice questioned. "Well, remove her blindfold so I can see her face."

Before she could register what was happening, her blindfold was removed, causing a bright light to stream into her eyes. As much as she wanted to look around, Sierra was forced to close her eyes because of the brightness. After a few moments, she blinked, trying to allow her eyes to adjust. A man stood in front of her, but he was still blurry as she attempted to focus.

"Ah yes, this is the woman my son spoke about."

At the word 'son' Sierra's ears perked up, and she blinked furiously until she could finally see the form standing in front of her.

The man was well dressed in the kind of suit Sierra expected to see in a fairytale. But that wasn't what caught her eye. Rather, it was his pointed ears, wide jaw, and green eyes, reminiscent of someone else she was familiar with. *Aodhan*.

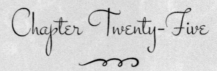

Chapter Twenty-Five

Sierra's heart stopped. Standing before her was Aodhan's father. The man in front of her looked so much like Aodhan that she couldn't breathe.

Still frozen in shock, her mind rewound the last few minutes as she looked at her surroundings. She was in a structure built of large gray stones. The floor was partially covered by a long red rug, and a similar red tapestry hung on the walls. The ceilings were high, and lanterns rested every few feet, casting light in even the darkest corners. Everything around her was reminiscent of the medieval castle structures Sierra had seen in her books in grade school.

She wanted to believe that this was an odd and crazy dream, but she knew the alternative was that she was still knocked out in some man's truck, and at this point, she would take the weird dream castle rather than consider the only other plausible option.

Suddenly, her mind snapped to something she had heard just moments before. What did Aodhan's father mean by 'the woman his son had spoken about'?

And what did her kidnapper mean by her being able to break the curse?

Something about this situation was very wrong, and Sierra knew it was probably going to get worse before it got better.

She was so busy tearing through her thoughts, trying to unravel what could possibly be going on here, that it wasn't until Aodhan's father was right in front of her that she even noticed he had moved. Sierra's instinct was to step back, but her kidnapper was right behind her, forcing her to remain where she was as Aodhan's father visibly evaluated her face, eyes, and hair.

"Hm." He rolled a strand of her dark hair between his fingers.

Sierra's heart was attempting to break out of her chest, but she wasn't sure what she should be feeling right now. On one hand, Aodhan had told his father about her, which was something most women were happy about. But on the other hand, she was 99% sure she wasn't able to break some Fae curse, so this could be about to get ugly.

Aodhan's father finished his evaluation and stepped back, snapping his fingers simultaneously. A woman appeared next to him, and Sierra quickly noticed how her ears weren't pointed, indicating she was likely human.

And likely a servant, her heart reminded her.

Aodhan's father motioned to Sierra. "Get her cleaned up and prepared for the ritual."

Ritual? Sierra didn't like the sound of that. But it didn't matter because her hands and mouth were still restrained. She could do nothing but follow as the woman motioned for her using a sweeping hand motion Sierra was somewhat familiar with.

The woman was about Sierra's height, with mousy brown hair that was braided down the center of her back. She wore a simple green dress that was loose around her curves and stopped just before the top of her feet, clad in simple black slippers which didn't look like they would keep the cold of the stone floor out.

Sierra was so busy evaluating the dress she didn't notice that the woman had stopped, until she collided with her back in an embarrassing way that almost had her toppling over if she hadn't, equally embarrassingly, grabbed the woman's shoulder at the last second with her bound hands. She tried to mumble a sorry as she removed her hands, but it came out a bit like a moan with the cloth still in her mouth.

The woman didn't say anything, and her eyes didn't even rise to meet Sierra's, as she opened a wooden door and ushered her inside. More questions bubbled at Sierra's mouth, but they, too, were blocked by the cloth. She watched as the woman began to heat water over a fire in large black pots before pouring it into a gray wash basin that looked to be made of stone.

Sierra felt a bit of shame as she just watched the woman cart buckets of water from the fire to the tub to the pump in the corner of the room and back. She wanted to offer to help but figured it wasn't allowed even if she had full use of her hands.

After what had to be 20 trips, finally, the tub was full of water, steam curling from the surface, and the woman motioned for her to get in.

Sierra raised her eyebrows, looking from her tied hands to the woman. Clearly, she couldn't get undressed like this.

The woman noticed her predicament and quickly left the room, closing the door behind her. In a few moments, she was back with a small knife, and she quickly sliced through the bindings on her wrists.

The moment her hands were free, Sierra yanked the cloth from her mouth, trying to swallow, but her mouth tasted like sandpaper, and her salivary glands had apparently thought they didn't need to work because it felt impossible to get enough saliva to do so.

Oblivious to her struggle, the woman motioned to her clothes and the tub. Sierra rolled her eyes and began undressing, still trying to get some form of moisture in her mouth so she could communicate, but to no avail. Not seeing any other solution, Sierra pointed to her throat and said, "Water," but it came out hoarse.

The woman appeared to understand her predicament, however, and she pointed to the pump near the fireplace, which she had used to fill the buckets of water before heating them over the flame.

Without a second thought, Sierra rushed to the pump, lifting the handle up and down as she had seen the woman do several times, bending down to stick her head beneath the trickle of water that appeared a few moments later. She didn't even care that the stream of water increased, splashing all over her face and clothes. She was about to bathe anyway; at least that's what she assumed at this point.

After she had let copious amounts of the cooling liquid slide down her throat, Sierra righted herself, looking back at the woman who had filled the tub. She now looked annoyed, probably not expecting Sierra to drink that much.

Now that her mouth felt back to normal, Sierra did the first thing that came to her mind, and she stuck out her hand to the woman for a handshake. "I'm Sierra," she said. "And you are?"

The woman just looked at the tub, ignoring her hand.

"Maybe if you tell me what we are doing, I can better understand?" she tried, but the woman just stood and looked at the tub.

After another moment of watching the woman staring at the tub, Sierra figured she'd better get moving, and she bent down to pull off her shoes, socks, and jeans, shuddering at the look of her legs pocked with red lesions. She knew the woman would likely be afraid, as most people were when they saw her skin, but it served her right for not even introducing herself.

Sierra pulled her sweater and undershirt over her head, waiting for the questions that were certain to come now that she, and her lesions, were almost fully exposed. But to her surprise, the woman said nothing, she just continued staring. It was really starting to scare Sierra, if she was honest.

With a final sigh, she unhooked her bra and slid her underwear down her legs before stepping toward the tub and over the rim. The water was warm but not hot, and Sierra immediately ducked beneath the surface, trying to rub away the invisible grime she felt from spending the night locked in some weirdo's trunk.

She tried to relax in the warm water, but the fact that she was in some unknown world, about to be part of some ritual she didn't understand, wouldn't allow her to relax.

After only a few minutes, the woman ushered for her to leave the warmth of the tub, holding up a sheet of white gauze. Sierra was certain they were curtains, until the woman began to drape them around her, and Sierra realized it was actually a dress.

It was like something out of a Greek movie. The dress was flimsy and thin, but there were a few layers to hide her more intimate parts. The dress came over each shoulder, before converging at her breasts to make a long skirt which fell to the tops of her feet. A matching piece of fabric was tied beneath her breasts to gather the fabric and give her shape.

Although she was sure the dress was beautiful, the only thing Sierra could focus on was her spotted skin, which was visible on her exposed chest, and the entirety of her arms. She hadn't worn something this revealing in years, and the white color only seemed to draw attention to the angry red marks on her skin.

Sierra wanted to express her concerns about how she looked, but within moments the woman was dragging her out the door and along the corridor, barefoot and wearing nothing but the gown. Sierra felt weird without any underwear, but honestly, that was the least of her worries at the moment.

After a few turns, they came to a room that was entirely barren besides a large stone brick which occupied the center and reminded Sierra of what they laid bodies on for viewings in medieval times. For the first time since she arrived, Sierra worried she might really be in trouble, and that this could be the part where she was going to die. Even though this was Aodhan's family, and Aodhan had clearly spoken to his father about this, the room in front of her wasn't screaming anything akin to safety.

Before she could theorize too much about the pending ritual, the woman led her forward, having her sit on the giant brick. As she did so, a few men, along with Aodhan's father, entered the room. Sierra played with the material of her dress nervously.

As soon as the men and Aodhan's father came to a standstill, he began to speak, but in old Gaelic, so Sierra couldn't understand what was going on. Instead, she counted the men who had appeared with Aodhan's father, counting six total. They were all dressed in long robes that touched the ground, far different from the fancy medieval suit Aodhan's father wore.

As Aodhan's father finished his speech, the woman directed her to lay back on the stone. Sierra nervously glanced around the room, but she didn't see any sort of weapon that might lead her to think her death was imminent. Either way, she realized that lying down probably wasn't the best idea, so she quickly sat back up again.

This angered the woman, who quickly began yelling at her in old Gaelic and motioning for her to lay back down. Sierra shook her head. "I don't know what's going on."

Aodhan's father chuckled from where he stood off to the side. "My apologies. I forgot you don't speak old Gaelic. Now lay down so we can perform the ritual."

"I would feel better knowing what this ritual is," Sierra insisted, remaining in her seated position.

"It's nothing serious. We just have to take some of your blood to put on the altar for Gaia."

Sierra cocked her head to the side. On the one hand, this appeared to be extremely ominous and dangerous, but at the same time, he didn't say she would die. Or was he just omitting that fact?

Deciding to be on the safe side, she asked, "How much blood will you take?"

The king held up a small stone bowl. "Only enough to fill this bowl."

Sierra looked at the bowl. It was bigger than the tubes at the doctor's office, but she would probably be fine. Deciding it was best not to start a fight with the father of the man she was falling for, despite her doubts about his odd ritual, she lay back on the table.

As soon as she was prone, the weird men in robes rushed forward, each one grabbing one of her limbs, and one man holding her head in place. Sierra regretted her decision to be complacent immediately and tried to sit up again, but it was too late, and the men were too strong.

The sixth man, who wasn't holding one of her limbs, came to stand over her with a small knife, and the bowl Aodhan's father had held, and Sierra realized her fatal mistake.

She hadn't asked *where* they would take the blood from.

With a grimace, she decided it was best to face this with her eyes closed. So, she pressed them tightly shut, turning her head to the side, which the man holding it allowed.

Before she could think of anything else, a searing pain shot through her arm, so sharp that her back arched and her eyes flew open of their own accord.

Sierra immediately wished she hadn't, as she saw the knife cutting the major vein on her arm, which she had learned during her studies could definitely kill a person.

The man doing the cutting must've had that same knowledge, however, as he only made about a one-inch incision before turning her arm so her blood could drip into the bowl.

Sierra felt sick. But as she looked away from the blood spurting from her arm, she noticed the other men observing the skin of the limb they held in place, their eyes clearly seeing her lesions.

Feeling incredibly self-conscious, Sierra decided squeezing her eyes shut once again was the only solution to the current situation. Although she hadn't been religious for years, she began to pray, deciding to direct her prayers to this Gaia she didn't know, as it was probably better that she prayed to a god in this world rather than one who had never answered her pleas in the world she had come from.

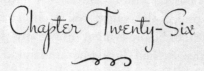

Chapter Twenty-Six

Once the bleeding procedure, or ritual, or whatever they called it, was finished, Sierra assumed she would be led somewhere to rest or relax until Aodhan figured out she was here and came home to give some answers.

She couldn't have been more wrong.

After they finished, two men came into the room, grabbing her roughly by her arms without seeming to notice her cut was still bleeding. They didn't even offer her a bandage or anything, as she assumed they would. They simply grabbed her arms and began leading her through more of the stone structure.

They tossed her roughly into what she could only assume was a prison cell, judging by the iron that crisscrossed the window in the wooden door and the fact that it was locked tightly behind them.

"Great, just fucking great," Sierra mumbled to herself as she stood in the middle of the room with her hands on her hips. Apparently, not only was she the answer to some backward prophecy, but she was also going to be held as a prisoner for the foreseeable future.

It was a small room, and the floor was made of dirt, so she was either underground, or on the bottom floor of the stone structure. There wasn't any sort of bed, just a pile of blankets in the corner, which looked less than comfortable. The opposite corner held a bucket, which Sierra could only begin to imagine what it was used for.

Noticing the blood running down her arm from the still-open wound, Sierra pulled the gauze belt from around her waist, folding it a few times before tying it on her arm. For once, all the bandaging practice she had during her undergrad came in handy. Careful not to tie it too tightly, Sierra held her arm to her body while she used her other arm and teeth to tie the bow. At least now it would hopefully clot quickly.

With a sigh, Sierra began to rearrange the blankets to try to make something decent to sit on. But the more she thought about the events of the past 24 hours, the more panicked and anxious she became. So, at some point, she simply wrapped one of the blankets around her and the gauzy dress she was still wearing, and sat on the second blanket, leaning against the cold stone wall.

Now that she actually had a moment to herself, everything of the past 48 hours sunk in. How had she gone from the high of having sex with Aodhan for the first time, to here?

At some point, Sierra must've drifted off, as she awoke to the clinking of a key in the lock of the cell door. Thinking that Aodhan must've finally shown up, Sierra stood up from the blanket nest she had made, trying to brush the dirt from the white dress, but she quickly realized it was useless. This wasn't the type of dress one re-wore after sitting on a dirt floor.

The door swung open to reveal the two men who had dumped her here, who knows how many hours before. At least Sierra assumed they were the same men; they were all dressed the same, so it was hard to know. Sierra's heart fell, but she still held out a small sliver of hope that had taken root in her heart that perhaps they would lead her to Aodhan, or maybe they were just keeping her here until her room was ready.

She knew that last thought was far-fetched, but she had to hold on to something or she was liable to fall over the edge into the pit of emotional self-pity, and she knew from past experience, once she sunk to those depths, she wouldn't be motivated to do anything to help herself out of her current predicament.

For the second time in what Sierra hoped was the same day, the two men roughly dragged her through the maze of stone hallways. Sierra tried to soak in what information she could as they moved, hoping to begin to memorize the layout, but it was no use. She was in an unfamiliar land and an unfamiliar building, and nothing seemed recognizable from where they had been before.

The two men stopped in front of another wooden door, and Sierra held her breath as they pushed it open, immediately releasing it as she realized it was a storage room.

Dried plants and leaves hung from every available surface, and in the center, there was a table with a mortar and pestle, as well as supplies that she assumed were used to cut and prune plants.

Sierra was so busy observing what the room held as far as supplies went, she didn't notice an older woman stand from a stool by the fire until she was walking toward them. She was shorter than Sierra by an inch or two, with dark hair that was pulled behind her head in some type of knot, revealing her pointed ears. Sierra couldn't explain it, but she felt that the woman was older, even though she looked fairly young. Whether it was her wisdom Sierra was sensing or the way she carried herself, it was clear this woman knew a lot. She wore a simple black dress with some form of protective covering on top made out of what looked like leather.

The men holding her exchanged a few words with the woman in old Gaelic before they directed Sierra to sit on the stool by the fire. Once she sat, they released her arms, leaving the room and closing the door behind them.

"Hello, I am Slaine," the woman said, her words heavily accented.

"Sierra," she responded quietly, wondering where to start with all the questions she wanted answered. She decided to forego pleasantries and just go for it. "What is going on here? Why am I here?"

Slaine sighed. "They don't keep me informed of all their doings in this castle, but you are in this room normally used for healing."

"Healing?" Sierra tilted her head to the side, glancing for a second time at all the plants in various states of being dried, some of which hung only a few inches above her head.

Slaine motioned to her arm, to the spots Sierra had almost forgotten were there due to the craziness of the last few hours. "Your...rash."

Sierra shook her head. "It's not a rash...it's a disease."

"I know," Slaine replied.

Okay, now Sierra was confused.

"My magic knew immediately when I saw you that this wasn't something I could heal. But those two guards are waiting outside to take you back to the dungeon when we are through, so the least I can do is give you a few moments of peace."

Well, that answered that question at least, Sierra was indeed being held prisoner.

"Why are they keeping me here?"

Slaine shrugged, turning to one of the tables to work with a few of the plants lying there. "I can't say for sure, but if I had to guess, it's probably because the king has been crazed in recent decades trying to break the curse that is taking their magic."

"So, there is a curse then?"

Slaine finished what she was doing, turning to hold out a plate, which Sierra now saw contained slices of apple and orange. "No dear, there is no curse. At least I don't feel one—and normally I can tell when a creature or being has been cursed." She motioned for Sierra to take one of the slices, before taking one herself and sliding a second stool up to the fire.

"You should tell...tell..." Sierra suddenly realized she didn't know the name of Aodhan's father.

"Conlan," Slaine cut in, clearly sensing Sierra's predicament. "And I have. Many times. If you haven't noticed, he isn't a man who listens to anyone, really."

"Is he the king?"

Slaine picked up another piece of fruit, watching as Sierra did the same. "There isn't really a king here. There used to be, but a few hundred years ago, we replaced the monarchy with a panel of highly ranked advisors who make decisions for each part of Sidhe. Unfortunately, the members of the panel are still chosen based on noble birth, but at least the power is more equally balanced, and there aren't any more of the internal wars which once plagued these lands as regularly as it rained." Her eyes stared off into the distance as she was reminisced about past times. "But yes, Conlan is on that panel."

Sierra took a bite of the apple slice in her hand, nearly humming at the delicious taste. Fruit in the human world never tasted this good. "Well, I guess I just have to wait until Aodhan comes then."

Slaine's eyes widened, and she set the plate down on the table to take Sierra's hand. "He didn't come with you?"

Sierra shook her head. "No, some Fae I don't know kidnapped me."

Slaine appeared even more surprised by that. But before Sierra could ask her more questions or ask how she spoke English so well, the door swung open, and the two guards stepped inside.

They exchanged a few words in old Gaelic, with Slaine speaking the most. Whatever she said apparently meant it was time for Sierra to leave, as she was suddenly roughly escorted from the room the same way she had entered.

Sierra wanted to protest, but she didn't know what good that would do, considering they didn't even seem to speak English. Either way, she decided to try.

"You don't have to be so rough with me."

Nothing changed, and the men didn't release their tight grips on her biceps.

"I'll walk with you if you just let me go," she tried a second time.

Again, nothing. Sierra wondered what they thought she was going to do. Even if she did run, she had no idea how to get back to her world, or what she would even do when she got back since Aodhan had said the entrance to Sidhe was quite remote and far from any human villages.

Aodhan would come for her, she was sure of it. And this whole strange situation would be cleared up. It had to be some terrible mistake. It had to be.

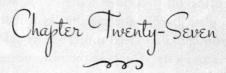

Chapter Twenty-Seven

Sierra wasn't sure how much time had passed in her cell, but it was enough that she was forced to use the bucket in the corner. The two guards had brought her some sort of pastry with vegetables in it at some point. It was good, but not enough to calm the growling in her stomach.

There were no windows in her cell, and she truly had no idea what day it was, or whether it was day or night even, when the guards came a second time to collect her.

Clearly, they didn't speak English, as she was roughly dragged through the castle a third time, though this time she recognized the route, and was relieved when they stopped outside Slaine's door.

As soon as she was seated on the stool and the door was closed behind the two guards, Sierra turned to Slaine, questions burning in her irises, but she had no idea what to say, or how to ask.

Slaine noticed her dilemma. "I told them I would need to treat your 'rash' every day for the next few days."

"So, it was yesterday when I was last in here?"

Slaine nodded a second time. "I'm afraid so."

Sierra looked around the room, taking in the many plants she didn't recognize. "I'm sorry I didn't ask yesterday, but are you a healer?" She vaguely remembered Aodhan speaking about the healers in Sidhe and Slaine talking about magic being able to heal the day before.

"I am, the only healer on staff in this household, in fact." She replied, her hands busy cutting more fruit, which she was arranging on a plate just like she had the day before. "I'm sorry I don't have anything more to feed you. They would be suspicious if I asked for extra meals." She held the plate out to Sierra, who immediately grabbed several of the slices and began putting them in her mouth.

"It's okay," she said around the food crammed in her cheeks. She knew she needed to slow down, or she would choke, but she had never felt this sort of desperate hunger before. She hadn't eaten dinner on Friday, and it was now Sunday, and all she had eaten the day before was that pastry they brought. She was ravenous. "This fruit is delicious."

Silence settled over the two women as Sierra ate as quickly as possible without choking. When the plate was clean, she looked up to find Slaine observing her curiously.

Breaking the silence, which had suddenly grown awkward, Sierra asked, "So, where did you learn English?"

Slaine smiled. "Most Sidhe learn it these days, as long as they have an education." She stood to stir a large pot that was hanging over the fire. "It used to not matter if they did or did not speak English when your world spoke the same as us here, but now, without English, they can't leave. Otherwise, humans would become suspicious. It was made a decree that all Fae schools and tutors teach their students English about 100 years ago."

Sierra tried to imagine what it would be like to meet someone who spoke only Old Gaelic in Ireland, but then she realized that people who moved abroad probably felt the same way when they went to a country that spoke a language other than theirs.

"That makes sense," Sierra agreed, before changing the subject. "Have you heard of Aodhan arriving?"

Slaine shook her head sadly, sinking into the stool opposite the one Sierra was sitting in. "I'm afraid it won't be that simple."

"What do you mean?"

"Well, Aodhan's job, per se, is to help his father break the curse. The fact that he didn't accompany you back tells me Aodhan and Conlan had a disagreement about something...and that something was probably you."

"Wait...what?" Sierra felt the last glimmer of hope for her rescue drain from her chest.

Slaine set her hand on Sierra's shoulder. "Aodhan was supposed to bring back anything that could help his father. Whether that was a person, book, or other material. The fact that you came back without him tells me he is likely in trouble with his father."

"So...he won't come?"

"I didn't say that." Slaine grasped one of Sierra's hands, not seeming to notice, or mind, that they were a bit sticky from eating the fruit. "He may have already come back, but Conlan may have punished Aodhan for not bringing you himself, especially if he believes you are the key to whatever fake curse he's dreamed up this time."

Sierra hung her head, feeling the tears build in her eyes. "I... I..."

"I know. But don't panic. I'm working on a plan to get—" Before Slaine could finish her sentence, the door was pushed open, and the guards came in, collecting Sierra as before.

Sierra kept her eyes on Slaine as she was dragged out the door, wishing they had more time, but she knew better than to say anything because, based on what Slaine had said, it was very likely her guards were just pretending not to speak English.

Once she was thrown back in her cell, the tears she had been fighting while she was with Slaine began to pour down her face. She had been so sure that Aodhan would be able to rescue her, but now it was likely that he was in trouble of his own. Sierra would need to figure out how to get out of here without him, and fast. She began looking through her cell, looking for anything that could help her escape. Besides the bucket (which had been emptied while she had been out) and the two blankets, she had nothing, which severely limited her options for an escape.

As she was thinking, Sierra glanced down at the white gauze gown she still wore, grimacing at how dirty it was. She hadn't been offered anything to change into, nor had she been given her old clothes back. While it was fine for now, it certainly made escaping difficult, considering she didn't have any shoes and had no idea what season it was outside.

Sierra thought back to the first day she had been brought here, trying to remember if it had been cold when she was transported from the entrance to this castle. Now that she thought of it, while she couldn't remember how she felt temperature-wise, she had been kidnapped without her jacket, wearing just her sweater and jeans. While that didn't mean it was summer, it also meant she would probably be okay running without a jacket, though the dress offered much less coverage than her sweater and jeans.

Sierra winced as she remembered her running skills, which were next to nothing. She had never been much for jogging, and she doubted she would be able to outrun her well-trained guards. This meant she only had one option left, and that was to sneak out without them noticing and hope she could make it far enough away that she could hide before they noticed.

Surveying the tools she had on hand again, a plan began to formulate in her mind.

Chapter Twenty-Eight

When she heard the clicking of the key entering the lock on the door, Sierra quickly paused her work, tossing one of the blankets over the hole in the corner, which she had been working on all day. Hoping the darkness, which was barely broken thanks to the single lamp on her cell wall, would help to hide the dirt under her cracked nails, Sierra leaned up against the wall just as the door swung open to reveal the two guards.

Repeating the same pattern as the two days before, the men each grabbed one of her arms and began to move quickly from the room. At least Sierra knew this was a normal occurrence now, and she was at least able to somewhat prepare for her daily dragging. Just like the two days before, she was roughly deposited in Slaine's dim work room, and the guards quickly removed themselves to the hall before closing the door behind them.

"You're looking a bit worse for the wear," Slaine commented as soon as it was safe, taking one of Sierra's hands in hers, and observing the dirt under her nails, which were also cracked and bleeding. For a moment, Sierra debated sharing her plan with Slaine, but although the woman was kind, she did not yet trust her enough not to turn her in to Aodhan's father.

"It's very dirty in the cell," Sierra replied, figuring that was a safe enough comment, especially considering the state of her dress, which was now becoming more brown than white. Plus, there was still the fact that she wasn't wearing any undergarments, and she was sure her period was likely to appear any day now. While Sierra had never been regular, her body was always good at making sure the irregularity lined up with the most inconvenient times.

Slaine prepared a plate of fruit again, which Sierra had to restrain herself from consuming in a single bite. Slaine also handed her a cup of water, which she swallowed in one gulp before holding it out for more. There had been no pastry this morning or last night, and the pit in her stomach only continued to deepen.

The room filled with the sound of the crackling fire, which was much welcomed after a night of digging in the cold dirt. Once the plate of fruit was gone, Sierra set it aside and turned to Slaine.

"Have you always lived here...in Sidhe?" she asked, hoping she didn't butcher the name too much. Aodhan had always let her refer to it as The Hills, which was better with her obvious American accent, but she was unsure if that translation was widely known here.

Slaine nodded. "I was born here. To a human father and a Fae mother. Even with magic, in Sidhe you often remain in the same social class as your parents, unless you marry someone above your social class or have above-normal levels of magic. My mother was a healer, and since my magic is also of the healing nature, here I am."

Sierra didn't want to ask, but she knew the answer would plague her if she didn't. "Are you here...by choice?"

"Yes. As a healer, working for a wealthy family is much preferred to working for a village. At least here I am paid in coin and decent lodgings instead of being paid in cattle and home-cooked dinners."

Sierra understood. Without modern constructs like insurance, it was likely a town healer would be paid in whatever the town had, even if the pay was non-monetary.

"And Conlan wasn't always like this," Slaine added.

The corner of Sierra's lips ticked down in confusion.

Slaine sighed before continuing, "He was once a nice man, but as he aged, he became more concerned about the failing magic and, in particular, the fact that he held very little. The Fae lifespan has also been shortening as a whole, and I believe he fears death."

Sierra mulled over Slaine's words for a moment, thinking of some of the lectures she had attended at Trinity College for her masters. "But even if it was a curse affecting the Fae, and he managed to break it, does he believe the results will be instantaneous enough to extend his own lifespan?"

"I'm not sure. I think he may believe that, but I also believe he may just be doing this out of love for his children."

Sierra wasn't so sure. Based on what Slaine had told her, it was likely Aodhan was in trouble with his father for not turning her in. That didn't sound like love to her. But maybe it was because of Aislin. "Does...Conlan...have a good relationship with Aodhan's sister?"

"Brother," Slaine corrected, confusing Sierra as she was sure that Aodhan had mentioned a sister. "And no, he does not."

"Aislin?" she asked, to clarify.

"Aislan, now," Slaine replied. "He began his transition a few months ago. Aodhan likely didn't know, but he had always been supportive of Aislan doing what felt right to him.

"Conlan is not supportive of the transition, sadly. He also blames Aislan's desire to transition on the fact that magic is waning. He acts as if the whole reason Aislan chose to transition was because he didn't have much magic, but I can assure you that wasn't the case at all. I'm afraid Conlan has started to use the fading of magic as a scapegoat for several unrelated issues in his life."

Sierra gritted her teeth. She hated when people put the blame on something that was clearly unrelated. Her mother did the same thing, blaming Diego's social issues on him not attending church, when it was, in fact, more likely that Diego was having problems due to disagreements with their mother herself. The thought of her family made Sierra realize they were probably worried, but for some reason, while she felt guilty that they would worry, she also felt a small amount of satisfaction that they couldn't call and blame her for her own disappearance.

"But that's what I wanted to tell you yesterday before it was time for you to leave." Sierra's eyes moved from the fire to Slaine as she continued. "Aislan left the castle, but he still has connections. I have sent word to him through the information grapevine. If anyone knows how to get you out and find Aodhan, it's him."

"He'll rescue me?"

"I don't know what he will do." Slaine motioned to Sierra's dirty nails. "Continue your plan. It may be a while before Aislan is able to come for you. I don't know what his plans will entail either; I just know that he is cunning, and adept at getting around the rulings of his father, as he has been doing so for a long time."

Sierra was about to ask for more information, when, like the days prior, the door was rudely pushed open, and she was collected by the two guards.

Once she was redeposited in her cell, Sierra resumed her digging. The dirt floor was hard-packed, but she was pretty good at using her short nails to get her hand in and remove the dirt clump by clump. To avoid having an obvious pile of dirt by the corner, each clump she removed she repacked in the ground around her room, trying to make it as even as possible so no one would notice the random appearance of more dirt.

She had yet to make it to the bottom of the wall, and she wasn't even sure this was an exterior wall, which could prove problematic later. Either way, she didn't see another solution, so she continued her excavation.

On and on she dug, only pausing once when the door to her

cell opened enough for a bit of bread on a plate to be passed through. Sierra devoured it quickly, before resuming her task. Unsure whether it was night or day, she continued digging despite the mounting pain in her nail beds, squealing in excitement when she finally reached the base of the stone wall. Now, she would just have to dig deep enough for her to fit underneath, then dig up the other side.

Sierra was exhausted, however, and decided it was time for a little sleep. She would continue her plan tomorrow. If all went well, she hoped she would only be imprisoned here for another two or three days at most.

She could do this. She had to. She refused to die in this cell.

Sierra awoke to the sound of a key in the lock, rising quickly to ensure her hole was covered before the guards entered the room. She felt she had only slept a few hours, but the thought of seeing Slaine and having some food for her stomach was enough to perk up her tired body.

When the guard grabbed her arms, Sierra winced as their hands encircled her biceps. It made sense that she was a bit sore after the hours of digging the day before. She just hoped she was able to push through the pain to dig again today.

Her hope quickly died, however, when she noticed the guards were taking her on a different path than normal. As they continued to take more turns around corners Sierra wasn't sure she recognized, her mind began to go wild, thinking of all the things she could do or say if she was being brought to Conlan directly.

All of these thoughts tumbled through her heart as she was instead pushed into the room containing the tub which she had bathed in upon her arrival. Like before, a woman stood and motioned for her to get in the bath as soon as the guards released their grips.

Although she hoped this was just because her dress was now officially brown, she feared it was likely because they planned to take her blood again. Stripping herself of the gauzy gown, Sierra stepped into the tub, quickly concealing her dirt-packed nails beneath the surface. She cleaned what dirt she could, hoping it wouldn't be too obvious that she had been passing her time trying to dig out of her cell.

It wasn't until she was handed a bar of soap that Sierra noticed that her arms didn't look like they normally did, covered in red spots, and lesions every few millimeters. Instead, the spots had begun to fade, almost from the inside out, with her normal skin peeking through the center of each lesion, which were now no more than pink rings.

Sierra couldn't believe her eyes. For years, the spots had inhabited her skin, and now they were disappearing of their own accord, without Sierra needing to take a pill or use one of the creams the doctor had given her. Sierra resumed her washing, trying to think of anything else that could have caused this miraculous almost clearing of her skin. By the time the small bit of soap was gone, Sierra had come to the conclusion that the Sidhe realm itself must be healing her, or perhaps the fact that she hadn't eaten much besides fruit and bread for the last few days was the answer.

Sierra would've liked to spend more time in the bath, looking at her clearing skin and enjoying the enveloping warmth of the water, but within a few minutes of her using the last of the soap, the woman beckoned for her to rise, pulling a new white gauze gown over her head.

With a sigh, she glanced down at the dress as the woman tightened the waistband. They must've had multiples of these on hand, as Sierra's brown one was still in a pile on the floor by the tub. She glanced around, hoping to see something that resembled underwear, only to be disappointed. Before she could ask the woman who had handed her the dress, the guards were back and leading her down the hallway.

The little hope she held out that this was just a chance for her to wash and change disappeared the moment she was pushed into the room with the stone slab, and she braced herself for what was coming.

Sierra rolled her eyes as she was led to the slab and held down just as she had been before. This time, Conlan wasn't even there, and it was a different man who collected her blood. She couldn't be sure, as her eyes had been pressed closed the entire time, but Sierra was pretty sure they took more than before. From a medical standpoint, Sierra knew she would be fine, but she also knew that taking someone's blood made them hungry and fatigued, so she may not be able to dig the rest of the day. She promised herself she would try anyway.

The moment Sierra stood, she knew she had been correct in her assumptions. She felt lightheaded, and was forced to lean on the shoulder of the guard as they led her back to her room. Unlike before, their dragging tactic didn't work because of how light-headed Sierra felt. She could tell this annoyed one of the guards, as he huffed when they practically had to carry her the last bit to her cell. She wanted to make a smart remark, but she found she was too tired to even do that.

By the time they arrived at her dungeon cell, or wherever it was they were keeping Sierra, the two guards were carrying her between the two of them. As they leaned down to place her on the ground, Sierra tipped her head back, her eyes making contact with one of the guards.

For a moment, Sierra thought she really was losing it, as Aodhan's emerald-green eyes looked back at her. But then she blinked, and his face transformed to the point where it didn't truly resemble him. Sierra shook her head. She had clearly lost too much blood.

But then, to her shock, the guard held a finger to his lips in the universal 'quiet' symbol, before releasing her shoulders and stepping away.

Sierra mustered all the energy she could to push herself into a sitting position, but by the time she did, the door was swept closed, and the room echoed with the telltale click of the lock. Sierra's vision swam a second time, and she decided that as much as she wanted to dig today, she would sleep first. Just for a few hours...

Chapter Twenty-Nine

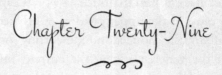

Once again, Sierra awoke to the sound of the door shifting open. Except instead of the usual two guards, this time there was only one standing within the arc of light the opened door allowed into her room.

Sierra moved into a sitting position, her muscles tightening in response, letting her know she had been sleeping longer than she had anticipated.

Before she could fully deduce what was going on, the guard was by her side, helping her to her feet. Sierra assumed it was time to visit Slaine, but to her surprise, the guard led her out of the cell in the opposite direction of where they usually went.

Sierra looked over her shoulder just to be sure, but before she could decide whether she should be worried, the guard grabbed her arm tightly and began speaking in a low, urgent whisper.

"Don't look back. We must be quick."

Sierra wanted to ask why, or where they were going, but her intuition told her this was the time to remain quiet.

The guard led her through several hallways of doors resembling the one where Sierra had been held the past few days. On and on they went, until at last the guard pushed open a door that led to the exterior. Directly in front of the door was a small patch of grass, that ended at what looked like a fast-moving river, sparkling in the dim light of the setting sun.

"Can you swim?" the guard asked.

Sierra looked back at him to notice he wore a cap pulled down low, obscuring most of the upper portion of his face, probably to hide himself if anyone noticed him escorting her out. Sierra looked back at the water, noticing the current pulling it along rapidly, creating small swirls in the surface of the water.

"I can, but I'm not a strong swimmer."

"It will have to do." The guard pushed her toward the water. "Stay in the river until it narrows. You will see a large boulder on either side. One of the boulders has a crevice in it where you can stay until I can come for you. There will be food and water waiting for you there."

"But wait, who are you?" Sierra asked, as he pushed her toward the water.

"No time for that now. I'll see you later."

Sierra wanted to argue, but she must've still been weaker than she realized because the next thing she knew, she was falling, and the cold river water was closing over her head.

In a panic, Sierra's stiff limbs began to move, pushing her towards the surface. By the time she broke through, gulping down a few breaths, she looked back to see that the bank where she had entered the river was already empty, and the door to what looked like a castle, now that she could see it fully, was closed. Sierra stretched her toes, only to find the river was too deep for her to reach the bottom.

Trying to stay in control of her panic, Sierra moved her arms in an arc motion to situate herself so she could see the direction the river was flowing. She hadn't swum in years, mostly due to her insecurities about her skin while wearing a swimsuit, but she found the instinct came back to her quickly.

The river was moving quickly, and Sierra knew she had to come up with a method of flotation before she tired herself out from treading water. So far, she had kept her head above water with a forward crawl, but she wasn't sure how far she had to go to find these boulders the guard spoke of.

Sierra looked at both sides of the river. The banks were steep, and she wouldn't be able to climb out here. Not that she planned to, as she had a feeling she could trust the guard who helped her, but it would be nice to find a branch or something to keep herself afloat.

Although she thought of going closer to the bank to see if something was, by chance, hanging over the river's edge up ahead, she also knew how dangerous the current could be if she was pulled into a tree on the bank and unable to get to the surface to breathe. Based on that knowledge alone, Sierra was certain that she needed to stay in the center of the river and just hope the boulders the guard spoke of weren't too far away.

As she made this decision, she also came to the realization that her adrenaline was wearing off, and the river water was very cold, especially on her wound, where she had been bled the day before. With a grimace, Sierra realized she might be facing an infection later, depending on the status of the water around her. In the rapidly dimming light, she couldn't see anything in the water, which was probably for the better. She didn't know what kind of animals lived in Sidhe waters, but if she saw anything moving around her feet right now, she was liable to scream, possibly compromising the escape she had been gifted.

Time seemed to go on forever as Sierra battled to keep herself in the center of the river, and to keep her head above water. Just when she thought that she couldn't make it any further, two boulders the size of small huts on either side of the river came into sight. The light was mostly gone from the sky at this point, and Sierra knew it was a miracle she had seen them at all. A few minutes later and it would have been too dark for her to make sense of anything around her.

She made her way to the bank on her right before realizing that the guard hadn't specified which boulder would have the supplies. She would have to check one first, and if it wasn't there, she'd have to make her way across the river to the other. Luckily, the river was becoming shallower as she moved toward the edges, and Sierra was able to stand within a few feet of the bank, so it shouldn't be too hard to cross the river again if needed.

As soon as she rose out of the water, the gauzy dress clinging to her body, Sierra's teeth began to chatter in the chilly evening air. While it was warmer here in Sidhe than in Dublin, the river water had been cold, and the air on her skin was giving her goose bumps.

Sierra only hoped that the mystery guard had planned for this and would have a blanket or something for her to change into stashed in the crevice.

Approaching the boulder, Sierra started at the side closest to the river, walking around it slowly, looking for any opening. She ran her hand along the rock, ensuring she wouldn't miss anything as the sun officially set, leaving her in darkness. The rock face was smooth beneath her callused hands, indicating it had once been in the water itself.

Unfortunately for Sierra, she reached the river on the other side of the boulder rather quickly, meaning she had made the wrong choice. Trembling, Sierra grit her teeth as she walked back to the area where she had exited the water. It was completely dark now, with no moon to speak of yet, and crossing to the other side would be dangerous. But Sierra knew that staying here without shelter would be equally as dangerous.

Seeing no other option, Sierra waded in as far as she could before pushing off the ground and swimming for her life to the other side. While the current did catch her, as she expected, she had entered far enough upstream that she was able to make it to the other bank just before the boulder. Sapped of energy and now officially without adrenaline, it took everything Sierra had to crawl her way up the bank. At one point, she had to stop and lay in the mud for a moment before she could continue.

Finally, once her entire body was out of the water, Sierra rose to her knees and began wringing out the parts of the dress she could reach so the water wouldn't weigh her down. It was only getting colder, and one glance at the rising full moon told Sierra she needed to get to the crevice fast, before any nighttime creatures in Sidhe began their hunting.

Just as before, Sierra started feeling the rock by the river and made her way around the boulder. This time, there was a distinct crack in the boulder about halfway through illuminated in the moonlight. The entry wasn't large, but Sierra could just squeeze herself through, cursing her hips as the fabric of the dress caught on the edges of the rock.

Inside the rock was pitch black, except for the small sliver of light the moon allowed in through the crack. Sierra reached her hand out in front of her, only to encounter nothing. She began feeling her way around on her hands and knees, concluding that the rock was completely hollow. During her exploration, Sierra found a small leather sack, which she opened to discover a large piece of material which she assumed was a blanket, something that felt like bread, and a water skin. She drank the water greedily, forcing herself to save some for later, and ate the bread as quickly as she could manage without choking, before trying to figure out what to do with the blanket. She knew the best thing to do would be to peel off her dress and put on the dry material. Even though she realized that was the best option to prevent hypothermia, she also couldn't bear the thought of the guard coming back to find her naked.

In the end, Sierra's sense of preservation overcame her insecurity, and she peeled off the dress, wrapping the cloth around her bare shoulders. In any other situation, she would hang the dress to dry, but she knew that wasn't an option here as it could alert an enemy to her location. So, she spread it out across the ground in front of her as much as she could with the restricted dimensions of the boulder, before leaning up against the rock wall and curling herself in a ball for warmth.

The boulder kept her body heat trapped inside for the most

part, making Sierra glad she hadn't given up on the riverbank. Although she knew she had just slept for at least a day, and that it was probably better to stay alert, Sierra's eyes felt heavy. Soon, they were drifting closed of their own accord, and Sierra fell into a dreamless sleep.

Chapter Thirty

When Sierra awoke, daylight was streaming in through the crevice, landing on her dress, which was still laid out in the middle of the boulder. Although the light inside the rock was still dim, Sierra could now see around her haven, taking in the fact that it was mostly barren, except for the leather satchel and water skin she had tossed aside last night.

The mysterious guard hadn't come for her yet, and Sierra's stomach grumbled, making her wish he had stashed more food for her. She decided to double-check the leather bag, only to find it was indeed empty. Water would have to do for now.

After she nearly emptied the water skin, Sierra reached out to touch her dress. It was almost dry, which she supposed was the benefit of the fact that it was made out of gauze. Sierra shifted the dress so a different part of it was in the sun before curling up in the cloth again which she could now see was actually a cloak, with a small clasp for securing it around her shoulders. She didn't know how long she should wait here before venturing out, but she knew she should at least wait for nightfall, as someone was more likely to see her if she ventured out in the daylight, and she didn't think she was that far from the castle.

For the first time since her kidnapping, Sierra wondered about her family, where they were, and what they thought of her being gone. She also thought about Aodhan, kicking herself for over-looking all the red flags during the beginning of their relationship. While she knew he wasn't to blame for all of this, she grimaced as she remembered how he had treated her. Even though he had made some adjustments to said red flags as they got to know each other, she should have recognized the signs that he came from a different upbringing and known that he was probably bad news.

With a sigh, Sierra realized that even if she had thought better of associating with Aodhan, she didn't regret anything that had happened. She just hoped that they were both able to get out of this alive. If they did, then Sierra would worry about what choice words she would need to say to Aodhan.

The day dragged on, and although Sierra welcomed the time alone with her thoughts, the noises outside the boulder would filter in from time to time, causing her to panic and press herself as tightly into the corner as possible, just in case someone happened to glance right into the crevice of the boulder. Sometime during the day, when the sun was high in the sky, Sierra slipped her dress back on. While it was completely dry, she still wished she had something else to wear besides the flimsy dress, which was clearly a better fit for a ball or ceremony than wandering through the woods.

Sierra had no idea what time it was, but by the time the sun began to sink from the sky, the water skin was completely empty, and she began to debate whether it would be safe to collect water from the river in the setting sun, before it became pitch black once again. Then there was the question of finding food, which she wasn't even sure she could do. Even if she did have an idea of what plants were safe for humans in the regular world, she had no idea what type of plants she would encounter here in the Fae realm.

Lucky for her, Sierra was saved from making that decision when a dark form ducked into the crevice a few minutes later. They wore a cloak so Sierra couldn't see their identity, but the way they sank to sit next to her made her think they were friend rather than foe.

Once they were seated, they slipped the hood from their head and a pack from their back, revealing a face that was similar to Aodhan's, from what Sierra could see in the fading light. While their facial shape was thinner than Aodhan's, without the wide chin, Sierra could see the matching emerald eyes, high cheekbones, and curly brown hair, which clearly ran in the family. The individual was dressed as a guard, but his frame was slim, and Sierra was pretty sure he was the one who had helped her.

"Aislan." He dipped his chin. "I believe you know my brother."

Sierra nodded, relief flooding her veins at the fact that she had escaped Conlan's home and whatever weird ritual he had been holding her for. "Sierra." She lifted her chin. "But you already knew that."

He smiled. "Yes, I think everyone knows it now," he responded, keeping his voice low. Sierra figured that while they were relatively safe in this boulder, it was better to be safe than sorry. "I'm sorry about my father, by the way."

"It's not your fault," Sierra responded, keeping her voice at the same volume as Aislan's.

Aislan looked away. "I know, but I still can't believe he has taken things this far."

Sierra couldn't keep the question that was burning in her chest inside any longer. "Where's Aodhan?" Sierra asked.

Aislan's face conveyed a sad look, and Sierra grit her teeth as his eyes searched the interior of the boulder for the answer he clearly didn't want to give her. "I'm not sure. After Slaine alerted me that you were here in Sidhe, I contacted Braan via the waters to verify that he wasn't in the human world anymore."

"And?"

Aislan shook his head. "He disappeared the morning after you were taken likely realizing what your absence meant."

Sierra grimaced. While she had been hoping that Aodhan would rescue her, and she was currently mad at him for his deception, the thought of him being locked up somewhere made her chest ache.

"He wasn't in the dungeon where I found you. I checked every cell, but they must be holding him elsewhere," Aislan continued. "There aren't many places in Sidhe that can hold our kind...with the shifting and all...so they likely have him locked up in the general prison, but—"

"But what?" Sierra asked, even though she was afraid of the answer.

"He might also be in the isolation prison, where the seriously dangerous prisoners are placed."

Something about what he said sunk its claws into Sierra's mind. "Is he...dangerous?"

Aislan's eyes grew wide. "He didn't tell you?"

"Tell me what?" Sierra felt a cold chill settling in her veins.

Aislan shook his head. "It's not my place to tell you, but... yes...you could say Aodhan is dangerous."

Sierra's eyes grew wide. "Why?"

Several emotions flitted across Aislan's face as he clearly debated on what to tell her and what to hold back. Finally, he came to a decision. "Aodhan told you that our people are losing our power, right?"

"Yes."

"Well, he's one of the few exceptions. He is more powerful than both of our parents."

Sierra felt her mouth drop open. "Wait, what? But he said that your grandparents..." Sierra trailed off as she tried to recall Aodhan's exact words when they had spoken about his magic.

"He wasn't lying. Our grandparents were more powerful than our parents, and in most families, the magic has declined steadily with each coming generation...except for Aodhan. While he isn't more powerful than our grandparents, he was born with more magic than our parents. Which is odd because magic is hereditary."

"What about you?"

"I was born with barely any. Less than our mother, the way it should be, as she is the one our power came from."

Sierra leaned back, resting her head against the cool stone. It was hard to wrap her head around all this magic stuff, and she could sense there was something Aislan wasn't telling her. "Why is Aodhan so powerful?"

Aislan shrugged. "No one is sure. But my father has sent him to many places over the years to find out the reason."

"And has he?"

"We don't know, he has stopped being forthcoming with his findings."

Sierra thought of the Aodhan she knew. For the past month she had known him, he had been quiet and reserved, and she had needed to force information out of him several times. It was hard to imagine him as ever being forthcoming. "Why?"

Aislan pursed his lips, obviously coming to the part he was keeping from Sierra. "You'll have to ask him when we find him. After all, he became this way a few months ago. After he met you."

Now Sierra was really confused. Her Tinder date with Aodhan had been at the end of September...and it was now just the beginning of November. They hadn't known each other for months, as Aislan was insinuating. While she debated letting that stay quiet, she knew that in their situation, withholding information would do neither of them any good.

"You must be mistaken." Sierra's voice came out a bit hoarse. "I only met Aodhan a little over a month ago."

Aislan nodded in agreement. "I know. But Aodhan has

known of you since last year, when he visited a seer." Sierra cocked her head to the side in confusion. "A seer is someone who is paid to look into a Fae's future using their magic, sometimes called a fortune teller in your world. Aodhan went to the seer to see if he would eventually find the cause of the loss of magic in Sidhe."

"And what did the seer see?"

"You. She showed him you."

Chapter Thirty-One

Sierra and Aislan sat in silence, although Sierra's mind was screaming at her for various reasons she could barely keep straight. On the one hand, her stomach was about to eat through itself, as she hadn't had any food since the day before. On the other hand, a seer, a kind of fortune teller, had seen her in Aodhan's future, which was a massive development in this twisted situation.

A few years previously, Sierra had left her family's religion because she had seen it for what it was: deceptive. And now, here she was, sitting in another realm most humans didn't know existed, speaking about people who saw the future for money. Mentally, she couldn't wrap her head around how any of this was possible. She even pinched her wrist discreetly to make sure this wasn't some messed-up dream. But she was, in fact, awake, and more confused than she had ever been before.

"What do you mean, she saw me?" Sierra asked, her voice cleaving through the heavy silence, now that darkness had completely fallen.

"He didn't give me details," Aislan's voice replied from the darkness. "All I know is he asked if he would solve what has been lowering the magic in this realm, and the answer was you."

"Hmm. Are you sure?"

"I don't know all the details of the vision, I'm simply repeating what Aodhan told me. Shortly after his visit to the seer, he went to Dublin, which is apparently where he knew you would be."

But Sierra hadn't been in Dublin at that time. She had only arrived for the fall semester in August. "But I wasn't there yet."

"I know. I talked with Aodhan frequently. He was waiting for you. He would've waited for you no matter how long it took, I'm sure."

The cogs in Sierra's mind started to turn, piecing together the last few days with this new information. She drew in a shaky breath. "What...what was he supposed to do when he found me?"

The tension stretched between them, and it felt like an eon passed before Aislan replied, "He was supposed to bring you back here."

"So your father knew about the vision then?"

"Yes."

"And Aodhan planned to bring me back here when he left for Dublin?"

"Yes."

It was starting to come together now, why she was here. "But he didn't?"

Aislan let out a long breath. "He stopped answering our calls in September, near the end."

Around the time they had actually met. "Why?"

"Your guess is as good as mine," Aislan murmured. "But I sense it had something to do with meeting you."

Sierra was silent. Something in her chest clenched at the thought of Aodhan changing what he planned to do all because of a failed Tinder date, from which she had stormed out after just a few minutes.

The path her heart began to venture down at that thought was too painful, so she decided it was time to change the topic. "What's the plan for rescuing Aodhan?"

"I thought you'd never ask." Sierra could hear the smile in his voice even though she couldn't see it. "We will leave in a few hours to begin heading toward the general prison."

"You're sure he's there?" Sierra remembered the earlier part of their conversation where he had mentioned there was also a high-security prison.

"No. But it's closer and easier to access. So, we will start there."

Right on cue, Sierra's stomach growled loudly.

"Ah, I see I was right to grab some provisions." Aislan began rustling around in the darkness, only to press something round into Sierra's hands. She took a bite, the sweetness of the apple tasting like heaven on her tongue.

"I didn't know how much you could carry," Aislan continued. "And I was a bit limited on what they wouldn't miss. But I got us a second water skin and at least dinner for tonight."

Sierra was almost too busy taking bites of apple to respond, but she made herself swallow so she could ask, "How far is it? To the general prison?"

"Two or three days at most if we walk quickly."

Two to three days didn't seem too bad. At least this wasn't some three-month-long journey through the woods. Reaching the core of her apple on all sides, Sierra rested her arm on her dress, which reminded her of something else she wanted to ask.

"I know this is going to sound dumb and shallow, but did you bring anything else for me to wear?"

"Um." Aislan cleared his throat. "Yes and no." Sierra felt excitement bubbling up in her chest, but before she could get too excited, Aislan added, "There isn't much clothing that will not be missed, so I brought you another dress, the same as the one you are wearing."

Sierra groaned.

"I know. But they have 50 or more of these on hand, and they come in every size...so they are easy to steal."

"Have you ever worn one?" The words came out a bit harsher

than Sierra intended but she just wanted him to know how uncomfortable they were.

"Yes, actually."

Sierra immediately wished she could retract her previous accusation.

"All women in Sidhe wear a similar gown for nature ceremonies or rituals. Of course, they come in other colors, but white is thought to be the color of innocence and purity when one is seeking the approval of Mother Nature. So more and more white ones have been made in the past few years."

Well, that explained a lot. Sierra had almost forgotten for a moment that Aislan had recently transitioned. Besides the voice that was slightly higher than Aodhan's and the thinner frame, Aislan truly was the man he wanted to be. But before his transition, he had likely been subjected to the exact same torture Sierra was now.

"I'm never wearing white again after this."

"I understand. And honestly, I'm not even sure Gaia likes white anyway."

"You speak as if you know her." Sierra heard rummaging again, and the apple core in her hand was replaced with some sort of baked pastry, which she greedily bit into.

"I do. When a Fae wishes to change gender, as I have done, we must have a meeting, called a ritual, with Mother Nature. It's different for everyone, but at my ritual, I spoke with Gaia, and she agreed I had been improperly assigned my gender at birth, and she allowed me to change."

Sierra polished off the last of the pastry crumbs on her hand, almost regretting that she had eaten it so fast. "Aodhan made it sound like asking Gaia for something isn't easy to do."

"It's not. It takes a lot of courage, and often, if she doesn't approve of your request, you could find yourself with a curse—or worse."

Sierra wanted to ask what could possibly be worse than a

curse, but she had a feeling the answer was death, so she kept her mouth shut.

"It took me months to get up the courage, which is why Aodhan didn't know, and I didn't want to tell him until it was complete in case I ended up with a curse or something. After I changed...I wasn't welcome at home anymore, so I haven't been able to call. I didn't even know things had gone wrong until Slaine sent a message."

Sierra's heart bled for him, and she reached out in the darkness to put her hand on his shoulder. "Where have you been living since then?"

Sierra swore she could hear Aislan's smirk even in the pitch black of the boulder interior. "Oh, right in the castle under my father's nose. That's actually the best part of all of this. He kicked me out, giving me a few hours to gather my things. Instead, I gathered a few guard uniforms, and now I live in the barracks with the rest of the guards."

She remembered the night after the second ritual, when she had sworn she had seen Aodhan's eyes but thought it was just because of the blood loss. "I knew I had seen you before."

Aislan laughed. "I do my best to avoid Conlan, because he would know in an instant if he saw. But it turns out it's reasonably easy to get assigned to the dungeon and stable duty, as most guards prefer to be inside rather than dealing with the elements."

Well, that explained how he knew about the dungeon door.

"Won't they notice you are missing the next couple of days?"

"No. We get a certain amount of leave each year, so I am currently visiting my family as far as they know."

Aislan stood from where he was sitting next to her, leaning toward the crevice in the boulder. "It's almost time. Are you ready?"

Sierra nodded. "Yes, do I need to carry a pack?"

"No. If I left with two, that would be suspicious. So, I'll carry the one pack we have for the both of us."

Sierra rose to a standing position, only to grimace as the rocks dug into her feet. "You didn't bring shoes by any chance, did you?"

Aislan groaned. "I forgot you were barefoot."

Sierra wracked her brain for what they could possibly do about the no-shoe situation. While she wasn't against going barefoot, she knew it would slow them down as she picked her way over rocks and other things on the ground. Plus, she had seen the forest on either side of the river. It hadn't exactly seemed like a safe place for going barefoot.

"Let me feel your feet."

Sierra agreed, and Aislan leaned down, feeling every side of her feet. Sierra realized he was taking a form of crude measurements.

"Alright, I have an idea. You stay here. I'll be back soon."

"Okay, be careful."

"I will," Aislan replied before slipping through the crevice and into the dark night.

Chapter Thirty-Two

It felt like hours later, even though it was more likely that only a few minutes had passed, when Aislan slipped back into the crevice in the boulder later that evening. He pressed two firm but delicate forms into Sierra's hands, paired with a quick apology.

"There weren't many options that would fit you. These are slippers, but they will protect your feet from the ground a little, at least."

Sierra assured him it was alright as she slipped them on her feet. After the events of the last few days, the last thing she was going to complain about was the availability of suitable footwear for their midnight forest trek as fugitives.

Sierra began to rise to her feet, testing the shoes. While they weren't the thickest, they would at least protect her from thorns and rocks as they traversed the forest, and they fit her well enough. She moved toward the crevice in the boulder, but Aislan stopped her with a hand on her shoulder.

"I have to warn you. Because we don't eat animals here in Sidhe, they aren't as scared of people as they are in your world, and it is likely we will see quite a few. Some of the breeds that exist here are large. Most of them are harmless. Unless I tell you, never run, as many of the harmful ones are motivated to give chase."

Sierra gulped.

"In most cases, just stay still. Most of the species we encounter won't hurt you."

"But some will?" Sierra's voice was shaking.

"Yes, but I will direct you in those situations. Most animals are just curious. While there are some predators, they must all be dealt with differently, and we don't have time to go through all the ways to deal with them before we leave."

Sierra felt cold fear seeping through her veins, but she knew that if she wanted to survive this world and rescue Aodhan, she didn't have much choice. She quickly shook out her limbs and flexed her fingers, a tactic she had learned during her undergrad studies to quell test anxiety. Sure, this was much different than an anatomy test, but she hoped it would at least help settle her nerves a little.

"Are you ready?"

"Yes," Sierra replied, and slipped out into the night. It was a dark night, the moon shrouded by clouds, and Sierra couldn't see at all. "Is it always this dark?"

"No. I had hoped we would have some moonlight to help you. But since we couldn't count on it, and you don't have Fae night vision, I have prepared a backup plan."

Aislan slipped a cloth around her wrist, tying it loosely. "I am tying the other end to my wrist. There's some space so we can walk comfortably. If there is an emergency and we need to hide immediately, I will tear the fabric. If this happens, hide anywhere you can manage and stay there. I will find you when it is safe."

Sierra nodded, and once Aislan was sure the wrist cloth was secure, they were off.

It quickly became apparent that traversing the woods this way would be more difficult than they anticipated. Not only was Sierra nearly blind, but she was constantly tripping due to not being able to see the ground in front of her. While Aislan tried to catch Sierra as much as he could, there were several times when Sierra's hands met the ground in front of her, and within a few short hours, her hands and knees were covered in cuts and bruises.

Regardless, Sierra didn't complain, doing her best to remain quiet lest they attract some animal she would rather not see. Still, the sound of them breaking through the underbrush covering the forest floor filled the night to the point that Sierra hoped that no one was looking for them, as it was painfully obvious where they were. The night was cool, but not cold, and sweat coated Sierra's arms and neck as she struggled to keep up with Aislan's quick pace and stop from tripping over her dress.

At some point, they broke through the tree line into what looked like a meadow in the moonlight, which was finally breaking through the clouds. Aislan pulled her to the side, keeping them in the shadows of the woods as he pulled out one of the water skins. "Drink."

Sierra gulped down the water, sighing as the cool liquid calmed the pounding of her chest.

"I have an idea," Aislan whispered, but before Sierra could ask what the plan was, he leaned down, ripping off some part of Sierra's dress. The cool evening night brushed up against her ankles, indicating he had made her dress shorter, stuffing what he tore off into his rucksack.

Sierra wished she had thought of this sooner, as when they started moving again, it was much easier to lift her feet, and she only tripped about half as much as she had previously.

As they crossed the meadow, Sierra made the mistake of glancing around to notice numerous eyes glowing in various colors from the forest around them. While she had never been afraid of snakes or spiders like many women were, she was pretty sure she could see teeth gleaming in the moonlight, and she shuddered.

She was so busy trying to think of what kind of animal with pink eyes could be watching their journey that she didn't notice Aislan had stopped, and she collided with his back. As she was flung backward, she looked up, eyes widening as she realized why they had stopped.

In front of Aislan, a herd of large animals was crossing the meadow. They were as tall as an elephant and equally as wide, but unlike the large animal she had seen in the zoo as a child, these elephant-like creatures had curled tusks and eyes that gleamed cerulean blue.

"Holy shi—" Aislan's hand slapped over her mouth as the creatures paused their crossing, and all turned to look at the pair of them.

"Don't move," Aislan whispered harshly, trying to stop her limbs from shaking. Whether they were quaking from fear or exhaustion, she couldn't be sure.

The blue eyes evaluated her and Aislan for what felt like an hour before they turned and resumed their journey.

Once the creatures had left the meadow, Aislan dropped his hand from Sierra's mouth.

"What were those?" Sierra gasped for breath.

"Elipags." Aislan helped Sierra to her feet. "They're not carnivores, but they can be dangerous if we get too close, as they are very territorial."

"I'm guessing they are similar to elephants in the human world?" Sierra whispered back as they began walking again.

"I'm not sure. I'm not familiar with elephants."

Sierra realized it was unlikely that the Fae had ever encountered one in Ireland, even if they had left Sidhe. "Do the Fae ever leave Ireland if they leave Sidhe?"

"I'm not sure. No one I know ever has. But I don't know everyone in Sidhe."

That reminded Sierra of another question she had been meaning to ask. "How many people live in Sidhe?"

"It's not like your world. We don't count. But we also don't procreate as prolifically as humans, so I suspect our population hasn't changed much over the years."

It wasn't the answer Sierra wanted, but she could sense she

was annoying Aislan with her constant questions, so she decided not to ask for a more specific answer, though she was itching to know.

"I will say there are 13 seats on the council, one of which my father occupies. There is one seat for every region of Sidhe." Aislan offered, clearly sensing Sierra's dissatisfaction with his previous answer.

"And what region is this?"

"*Fuinseog*, a region known for its enchanting forest and ecosystem of beautiful creatures."

They approached the edge of the meadow ahead, indicating the small amount of vision Sierra had was about to be obscured by the trees once again.

Just as they were about to step into the tree line, two shadows emerged from the trees to block their path. Panic sank in her gut, like a stone in the water, as Sierra realized that they may be about to be captured. Just as she was preparing for Aislan to cut the cloth so she could make a run for it, one of the shadows spoke.

"It's good to see you again, Sierra."

Chapter Thirty-Three

As the shadow spoke, three things happened in Sierra's mind simultaneously. First and foremost, her feet began to prepare to run for her life. She also began to wonder if she shouldn't have trusted Aislan so easily, and perhaps this was a betrayal. But at the glint of vibrant red as it caught in the moonlight, Sierra's heart both leaped for joy and calmed in recognition.

In front of Sierra stood Braan and Kaye, both dressed differently than when she had last seen them in the human world, now wearing long pants and what looked to be an old-fashioned long-sleeve dress coat, similar to what Aislan was wearing.

Before she could remember that she was indeed currently attached to Aislan, Sierra ran toward Kaye to give her a hug. Luckily, Aislan seemed to anticipate what she would do at the sight of her friend and stepped forward a few steps so the line between them wouldn't pull taut.

As Sierra folded her arms around Kaye, she felt some of the tension leave her muscles for the first time since the night she had been kidnapped the week before. "I am so glad to see you," she whispered into Kaye's hair.

"I'm glad to see you as well. We were so worried."

Sierra pulled back, looking at Braan over Kaye's shoulder but not wanting to let go of her friend.

"I see you two got my message." Aislan's voice came from behind Sierra.

"I just can't believe Conlan would do something like this," Braan chimed in, stepping forward to place a hand on Sierra's shoulder. "We are glad we were able to find you two."

Kaye looked around them. "Aodhan?"

Aislan shook his head. "No, that's where we were going next. I'm not 100% sure where they are keeping him, but we will try the general prison first."

"We will come with you," Braan said, as Aislan stepped past Sierra to take the lead.

"We will have to catch up later," Kaye explained to Sierra as they once again prepared to enter the forest. "It's better that we are quiet."

Sierra nodded in understanding, and the four began to make their way through the forest, pausing for a moment for Braan and Kaye to tie their arms together so Kaye could be guided by Braan. What little Sierra had been able to see in the meadow was once again obscured by the inky black of the forest.

As the air around her grew heavy, Sierra remembered what Aislan had said about the forest being enchanted, and she now knew what he meant. The air surrounding them was warm and moist, and she could sense the life around them as they passed through the forest— not just the trees and plants, but almost as if the forest itself was breathing.

Although their group now had twice the number of people, Sierra noticed with a grimace that the sound of them moving through the forest hadn't changed, meaning she was likely solely responsible for the noise she did hear, despite her best efforts to be quiet.

With four of them, their pace was slowed slightly because even though Braan could see in the forest without issue, Kaye was in much the same predicament as Sierra, though her better shoes kept her from tripping quite as frequently as Sierra tended to.

The forest grew more dense the further they went on, and soon Sierra could feel the branches slicing into her arms as they passed. While the first few didn't bother her, soon, the branches began catching on to the already existing scratches, causing her to wince in pain and slow her pace.

After one such nasty cut, Sierra came to a stop, her right hand automatically coming to cover the slice on her left arm, her teeth gritting in pain.

Aislan came to a stop as well, but it was too dark for Sierra to judge whether he could see the problem.

"My arms," Sierra whispered, hoping the scent of blood wouldn't attract anything that was lurking in the underbrush.

Aislan didn't answer, but Sierra heard shuffling before he thrust something made of cloth at her. "Stay still. I'm going to untie the band so you can put this on."

She felt his fingers brush lightly over her wrist, tapping it when he was done so she knew she was free. Holding the garment he had handed her, Sierra began to explore the garment with her fingertips, trying to figure out how best to put it on. It wasn't something she had worn before, and Aislan must've grown impatient because, within a few seconds, he was directing her arms into different armholes and buttoning up the front for her.

As soon as the front was secure, Aislan was tying the cloth around her wrist again, and they continued to make their way through the forest. Since Aislan had said he didn't have any other clothes, Sierra could only assume that she was wearing one of his garments now, and she hoped that he was faring better with the sharp branches than she was.

They traveled through the trees for what Sierra was sure was hours. In fact, at one point, she began to wonder if the sun had indeed already risen, but the forest overhang was just too dense for them to notice. Just as she was about to ask for a break, convinced her legs would give out at any moment, they came to a stop at the base of a large tree. Or at least what Sierra assumed was a tree.

"You two go first," Aislan hissed at Braan, and Sierra heard a frantic rustling in the darkness.

As soon as the rustling stopped, Aislan turned to her. "Climb on my back."

Sierra knew Aislan was taller than her, but he hadn't looked near as built as Aodhan, making her a bit self-conscious as to whether he could carry her weight or not.

"Are you sure?"

Aislan scoffed. "Of course, I'm Fae. We are built strong."

Sierra mentally slapped herself for even asking. Of course, it wouldn't be a problem.

Aislan wrapped her legs around his waist, untying her arms so she could put them around his neck. Sierra couldn't be certain, but she was pretty sure he was no longer wearing a shirt, which meant he had given her his clothes earlier as she had assumed.

"Hold on tight."

Sierra did, apprehensive of what they were about to do. She suddenly felt herself moving upwards, at least she thought they were, but she wasn't exactly sure how they were doing so.

As they made their way higher, the pale pink light of dawn began to filter through the trees, confirming for Sierra that it had still been the night before and she was indeed more out of shape than she thought. As she looked around, she could see that the forest wasn't truly that dense. It was then that she became aware of the magical buzz around them increasing. Or maybe it had been there before, and she had just been too scared to notice it. Either way, she could feel the reverence and enchantment of the forest in a way she hadn't been aware of, as the frosty light of dawn filtered through the trees, illuminating the ground like water through a strainer. The chirping of birds reached her ears, and she saw a few bursts of color out of the corner of her eyes as they flitted their way through the trees.

When she looked back around, she noticed that Aislan was

holding on to a rope and pulling them up a tree with his upper body while his lower body walked up the large trunk. She would've marveled longer at his impressive strength, but at that moment, they broke through the tops of the trees to reveal a small wooden house perched atop of the tree they were climbing.

Sierra looked around in wonder, noting the way most of the trees stopped at a certain height, creating the blanket that shielded the light of the moon from the forest floor below. Several trees had grown above the height of the forest, and besides the tree-house they were headed for, there were a few others a bit further on, which she could see poking out from the canopy. Beyond, purple mountains rose ominously in the direction she thought they had been headed. As she craned her neck to look at where they had been, she noticed a castle rising on the far horizon, past the edge of the trees. Since she had only seen it from the outside once, Sierra assumed that was where they had been keeping her, but she couldn't be sure.

Aislan reached the top of the rope, where there was a hole in the deck of the tree house for them to pass through. "Get as close to me as possible," Aislan said, not sounding out of breath at all, almost making Sierra doubt he had just climbed up this massive tree with a person on his back, even though she had been there the whole time.

She felt the wood of the desk brush her back as they passed through. Aislan stepped to the side and helped her off, lowering her onto the deck as he pulled the rope up from below so no one else could follow.

In the light of the rising sun, Sierra couldn't help but gape as she looked around them. It was almost as if the ceiling of the forest created a sea, and the few houses that were visible were boats floating in the gentle morning breeze. The deck they stood on belonged to a small, one-story treehouse made of smooth wood paneling with an eaved roof. It looked to her as if someone had taken a small hunting cabin and placed it on top of a tree. The windows were purple glass, which glimmered in the light of the rising sun. A brightly colored bird, which looked akin to pictures Sierra had seen of a Toucan in the human world, let out a chirp from its large beak as it settled on one of the porch railings. It ruffled its feathers, allowing one to fall, which Sierra bent down to pick up. As she lifted it, she noticed the way it glinted in the sun, displaying rainbow colors that shimmered and changed as she shifted the feather from side to side.

"What is this place?" Sierra squeaked out, unable to take her eyes from the unique feather.

Aislan smiled as he replied, "Welcome to *Teach Crann*."

SAILEACH

CUILEANN

CAORANN

DARACH

To Sine, Coll, Gioleach, Biethe, and Eidnean

NOG

Sceach Gheal

Funiuin

Teach Crann

ISEOG

To Human World/Ireland

Chapter Thirty-Four

As it turns out, the outside appearance of *Teach Crann* was deceiving, for when Aislan led her into the house, she found that it was a spacious home complete with a small kitchen, living room, dining area, and bathroom, if you could call it that. It was rudimentary at best, nothing like the bathrooms Sierra was used to in the human world. While there was some type of apparatus that flushed using a pull handle, there was a simple bowl and pitcher to operate as a sink and an old-fashioned bathing tub, which would need to be filled manually with pitchers of water. The house also had three bedrooms, which Aislan showed her so she could rest after she used the facilities.

As he opened one of the bedroom doors, Sierra's jaw dropped.

The room had a large bed in the center, akin to a king-size in the human world. It was decked out in a black silk comforter, with red sheets peeking through from underneath. The room was lit by what looked like fireflies in jars, though Sierra couldn't be sure from afar. While the room wasn't heavily decorated, there were some green and gold vines painted on the wall here and there to add some color to the brown wood. Sierra immediately noticed a door on the far side of the room, which led to a private bathing chamber.

"Are all the bedrooms this big?" Sierra asked as she headed for a second door in the bathroom.

"No, this is the one for the owner of the home. The other two are a bit smaller and don't have a private bathing chamber."

Sierra's hand paused where it rested on the door handle. "But I don't own this treehouse."

Aislan's response came at the same time that Sierra opened the door to reveal a closet filled with men's clothes. "I know, but Aodhan does."

Sierra was aghast. "I thought he lived in the castle with your father?" She stepped into the closet, running her hands over the soft fabrics.

"He has a room there too. But this is a place where he can come to get away from our father when he needs to. He bought it in secret a few years ago. I've been hiding out here since our father doesn't know about it when I have to leave my ruse at the house from time to time."

Sierra turned from the colorful clothes until her eyes met Aislan's green ones. Her heart ached as she wished that they were the green eyes of Aodhan instead. "Are you sure he's okay with me staying in his room?"

Aislan smiled. "Of course. If I know Aodhan, which I do, there is nowhere else he would rather you stay. Plus, besides my room, there's only one guest room, which Braan and Kaye are staying in, so unless you want to bunk with them..." Aislan trailed off suggestively, but Sierra could tell by his tone he was kidding.

Sierra chuckled. Something about Aislan's demeanor reminded her of her younger brother, Diego. But before she could delve too deep into the meaning of those thoughts, which were sure to be painful, she yawned.

"Rest a bit. We will meet in the living room in a few hours to discuss how we proceed from here."

Sierra made her way to the large bed as Aislan slipped out the door, closing it behind himself. As she peeled back the covers and got comfy, she sighed in contentment. The bed was so soft and comfortable it felt like she was being tucked into a cloud. Before she could follow that thought further, she drifted off into a dreamless sleep.

~

Sierra awoke hours later from a dead sleep, groggy and unsure of where she was. As she lay in the plush red bed, looking at the room around her in confusion, it took quite a few minutes for the events of the night before to come back to her.

Once they did, she sat up slowly in bed, grimacing as she realized she was still in the white dress, and she had laid in Aodhan's pristine bed without even removing it. She would have to offer to wash the sheets before they departed.

Rising from the soft and silken sheets, Sierra noticed some clothing laid out on the end of the bed. The clothing wasn't large enough to be Aodhan's, but it looked too large to belong to another woman of her size.

Willing to do anything to get out of the white dress, Sierra stripped down, sliding the leggings up her legs and pulling the jacket top over the top of her body. It didn't exactly fit, but at least she would be able to move more easily than she had the night before.

Walking over to the window, which was covered with a dark curtain, Sierra slid it open slowly, her eyes meeting the dim light of sunset. She had slept the whole day away.

She stood there for a few moments longer, willing the stress of the past few days to leave her muscles, but of course, it was useless. She wouldn't truly be able to relax until she saw Aodhan again and was able to sort out exactly what had happened. It would also help if she was out of the danger of being captured by Conlan. Sadly, she had no idea when that would be. Admiring the golden glow of the sunset over the trees, she remembered the time and her task and readied herself to join the others in the main room to see how the planning had turned out, since she was pretty sure she had missed it at this point.

Opening the door, she found Braan, Kaye, and Aislan huddled around a small wooden table, arguing in hushed voices. The moment the door creaked open, Braan and Aislan paused, their Fae hearing clearly coming in handy.

"Good morning, or should I say evening?" Aislan offered, motioning for Sierra to join them around the table.

"Sorry, I guess I was more tired than I thought," she apologized sheepishly.

Kaye waved her hand in the air. "Don't worry about it, we only got moving about an hour ago. Trapezing through the forest all night will do that to you."

Sierra approached the table to find a colorful map spread out over the surface. Her eyes widened at all the names of the unfamiliar towns and territories. Sidhe was much larger than she anticipated. Her eyes searched the surface of the map, but nothing familiar came into focus. "Where are we?"

"Here." Aislan pointed to the far-right side of the map, colored green with foliage. "Even in Sidhe, *Teach Crann* is one of the best-kept secrets, so you won't find it on many maps."

Sierra nodded. "Is it still in *Fuinseog*?"

"Partially, but some of the buildings are in *Funiun* territory, and others in *Sceach Gheal.*" He pointed to an area in the forest. "The borderline between the three territories is in the forest below *Teach Crann.*" Braan clarified. "Which is good for us because the specialty prison is in *Sceach Gheal.*"

Sierra looked at Aislan. "But I thought you said Aodhan would be in the regular prison?"

"That's what we are currently disagreeing about. I think Aodhan is in *Cuileann*, at the main prison there." Aislan pointed to a larger town on the coast. "But Braan is pretty sure he's in *Sceach Gheal.*"

"Is there any way to know for sure?" she asked hopefully.

Aislan shook his head. "No, that's the problem. Basically, we have a 50/50 chance, and we don't want to waste time by going to the wrong one."

"My vote is that we go to *Sceach Gheal* since it's only half a day away from here," Braan said.

"But if he's in *Cuileann*, and we get caught at *Sceach Gheal*, we won't be able to rescue him at all until we figure out how to get ourselves out of the strongest prison in Sidhe."

"So, just to make sure I'm following, Aodhan could be in either prison, but *Sceach Gheal* is closer to our location but also more dangerous, meaning if we fail, we are all screwed. But, if we check *Cuileann* first, and he isn't there, we've wasted time and energy on the two days it takes to travel there from here." Kaye pointed at each location as she mentioned it before raising her eyes to meet Sierra's. "And splitting up isn't an option?"

Aislan shook his head. "We need all four of us to even have a chance at *Sceach Gheal*, but it is possible that two people could likely be successful at *Cuileann*."

"I don't get it," Sierra interjected. "What makes *Sceach Gheal* such a big deal both for prisoners and for us to break someone out?"

All three sets of eyes in the room came to rest on her. "*Cuileann* is a basic Fae prison, similar to the one I broke you out of. It is run by the Fae and human servants who are easy to outmaneuver and manipulate," Aislan explained. "*Sceach Gheal* is run by Typhon."

"Who's Typhon?" Sierra asked.

Aislan shook his head a second time. "Don't they teach you anything in the human world? Typhon is the child of Gaia, also known as the father of all monsters. He's a snake and human shifter. He also has many dragons in his employ, guarding the prison. They are faster than Fae, often smarter, and they breathe fire. Typhon is often rumored to be more snake than human, slithering himself into places where he doesn't belong."

"And in the past few years, there have been several instances where he took prisoners just because he wanted to, and most of them were never seen again."

Sierra's eyes grew wide, and she hastily looked back at the map. "And you think we truly have a chance to break Aodhan out, if he is there?"

"Well, everyone has to have their weakness, right?" Braan said pointedly at Sierra.

"Okay, and what's Typhon's weakness?"

"Humans," Aislan said pointedly. "Imagine being one of the only human creature shifters in Sidhe. Supposedly, Typhon is a true immortal, unlike the Fae, and he's been living in the mountains since the beginning of time. He has gotten lonely, and human visitors are the only ones allowed in his court without an invitation."

"Oh." The room was quiet as Sierra absorbed the knowledge. "So, I have to go to *Sceach Gheal* then."

"Yes," Aislan confirmed. "But Aodhan would kill me if he knew I sent you in there alone, so Kaye has to go as well. Sidhe is dangerous for humans without Fae protection."

"And where Kaye goes, I go," Braan cut in. "And now you see how we came to the conclusion that we can't split up."

Sierra turned from the table to observe the last of the sun's golden rays sinking behind the edge of the sea of trees. She turned their predicament over in her mind a few times, coming to her own conclusion before turning back to the group. "I know where we should go."

Chapter Thirty-Five

"**W**here?" Aislan asked eagerly.

"Aislan," Sierra turned to Aodhan's brother. "Do you think your father would really punish Aodhan for betraying him, or do you think he probably just wanted to scare him a little?"

Aislan rubbed his chin with his hands. "I think he would probably just want to scare him a little; after all, he is the favorite child."

Sierra nodded in agreement. "I don't know your father well, but I know my parents, and although they frequently get angry, they usually just want to scare a little sense into me. Therefore, I think it is unlikely that Conlan actually sent Aodhan to *Sceach Gheal*, if it is as scary and difficult to escape as it sounds."

"I agree," Aislan said. "I think he is in *Cuileann*." Braan raised one eyebrow, still clearly thinking that *Sceach Gheal* was the better choice, but he let Aislan continue. "It's safer to traverse the forest during daylight hours, so I vote we stay here for the night and leave in the early hours of the morning."

Sierra bit her lip. While she would much rather be able to see where she was walking, she was also still a bit worried she was being hunted. "But what about Conlan?"

Aislan shrugged. "Honestly, at this point, there's enough forest that the chances of running into him are very slim, and I doubt he would search for you for more than a day. Either way, we will be careful."

Kaye stood up from the table, putting her hands on the wood surface. "Now that we've settled that, how about we have some dinner and take some baths?"

All of them nodded enthusiastically, and Sierra followed Kaye into the kitchen while the men folded up the map. "Need any help?" she asked.

Kaye smiled. "Actually, I've already got something in the oven, so most of the work is done, but I'm glad you followed me." She looked over Sierra's shoulder to ensure the men were occupied before lowering her voice. "I wanted to make sure you were okay and that nothing happened that you couldn't tell Aislan about."

Sierra was glad that Kaye was checking in on her, even though it was unnecessary, "No, I'm okay; mostly just scratched and bruised but nothing serious happened. I actually got in some good thinking time while I was locked up, believe it or not," she joked.

Kaye's eyes searched her face for a moment; looking for what, Sierra was unsure of. But she nodded and then turned to the black iron oven, where Sierra could see a flame behind the rack holding whatever their dinner was. "If you're sure. You know you can always talk to me, right? I'm a girl's girl, so I'll always side with you."

"I'm sure," Sierra assured her. "Now let's eat!"

Dinner turned out delicious, though Sierra wasn't sure what it even was. It was some form of casserole filled with potatoes, mushrooms, and some other vegetables she had never seen. Either way, they all took seconds and thirds, scraping the bottom of the pan when it was eventually empty.

After dinner, they sat in the living room, discussing the route they would take the next day. Well, everyone except Sierra discussed, since she had no idea where anything was in Sidhe.

As they sat there, Sierra felt herself getting tired. She had slept all day, but yawn after yawn kept passing her lips. After fighting it for a while, she finally gave up, standing to announce she was going to bed.

While Braan tried to argue that she had slept all day, Aislan understood, bidding her goodnight as Kaye rose with her to work on filling a much-needed bath.

Sierra watched as Kaye added a few pots of boiling water to the tub, adding room temperature water to help dissipate the heat. Although Sierra's skin was now almost completely clear from her psoriasis, she stayed dressed out of habit, leaning against the wall as Kaye worked to fill the tub.

"Can I help in any way?" Sierra asked, feeling bad that she wasn't lugging her own water for her bath.

Kaye shook her head. "No, I'm almost done." She patted Sierra's shoulder as she returned to the kitchen for the final bucket of boiling water. "When you're done, allow the water to cool completely before you release the plug. The water goes right to the tree, and we wouldn't want to burn it."

Sierra nodded, thinking how cool it was that they recycled their bath water directly to the forest. "How does the water get up here anyway?" Sierra hoped that Kaye wasn't lugging it up from the ground below by the bucketful.

"A type of hose that runs up the side of the tree. It's made from old tree roots, so it blends right in. But of course, we can't cover the full tree with them, so most treehouses have only one tap, though some have two."

Kaye turned to leave, but Sierra had one last burning question she couldn't brush off.

"You talk about this place as if you've been here before."

Kaye smiled. "I have. Aodhan spends a lot of time here, and

he and Braan have been friends since I've known Braan, so whenever we come to visit, we stay here."

Sierra didn't say anything else as Kaye closed the door behind her.

Glad to finally be in water which was for bathing, and not preparing her for bloodletting, Sierra didn't waste any time slipping off the loaned clothes and sinking into the water. She wasn't sure how Kaye did it, but the water was the perfect temperature.

Using the soap that had been left for her, she quickly scrubbed herself and washed her hair, marveling at how smooth her skin was. It had been lesion-pocked for so long, it was an absolute luxury to be able to run her hand up her arm without stopping.

The water seemed to stay warmer much longer than was natural, and Sierra briefly wondered if the tub carried an enchantment or if it, too, was made from a special material to help it fulfill its purpose.

Either way, after some time, she climbed from the tub, wrapped a towel around herself, and headed into the bedroom to find that Kaye had managed to put fresh sheets on the bed while she had been bathing. A large tunic was laid out on the bed, likely belonging to Aodhan, along with some undergarments that resembled boy short underwear in the human world. Sierra was so tired that she didn't really care who the tunic or undergarment belonged to as she pulled them on and slid into bed.

She must've fallen asleep quickly because the next thing Sierra knew, it was pitch black in the room, and she could hear a rustling sound in the dark. Kaye must've removed the lighting jars or shut them off somehow. She was so sure it was Kaye cleaning up after her bath that Sierra rolled over to her other side, intending to go right back to sleep.

It wasn't until she felt the covers being pulled back and a

warm body slipping into bed with her that she realized something was off, and within a millisecond, her mind snapped awake. Sierra yanked herself back from whoever was in bed with her, yelling as she ended up on the floor. It was still pitch black as Sierra fought her way to her feet, her legs tangled in the luxurious sheets she had been praising just hours before.

Once she was standing on her feet, her back against the wall, she realized whoever it had been wasn't trying to grab her or put a hand over her mouth as she expected from a kidnapping. Debating whether to yell again, or to use her words, Sierra finally decided on the latter. "Wh-who's there?" She stuttered, her voice coming out way weaker than she intended.

"It's me."

For a moment, Sierra's mind was confused. The voice sounded so familiar but much lower than Aislan's—

"A-Aodhan?" she asked in shock.

He must've been fixing the lights, or turning them on or whatever, because a moment later, the jars illuminated the room in a low yellow glow that glinted off Aodhan's chiseled jaw, his eyes looking ocean green rather than their usual emerald.

Sierra wasn't sure what he was expecting him to say as they stared at each other in the dim light after what had been a terrible week—or was it two? But it certainly wasn't the "yes" that came out of his mouth as he crossed the bed, coming to stand in front of her.

Sierra's breath came out in ragged gasps as her sleep-addled brain tried to catch up to what was going on. "Is this a dream?" she asked in a breathy whisper, as Aodhan's hands came to rest on either side of her face.

"If so, we are having the same dream, I suppose," he replied, pressing his lips to hers.

Chapter Thirty-Six

J ust like their first kiss, outside the pizza restaurant almost a month before, it took her a minute to come to her senses. The situation was different now, as they were technically dating, but it had been a long two weeks, and much had happened as a result of the man kissing her, so Sierra didn't want to wait for answers.

Although she was enjoying the feel of Aodhan's hard body pressing up against hers while her back was to the wall, she slid her hands between them, pressing hard on his chest until his lips detached from hers and he took a step back.

Sierra opened her mouth to demand some answers, but before she could say anything, a voice called from the doorway, "What the hell are you doing here, motherfucker?" Braan looked peeved, some sort of battle axe gripped in his fist that was lifted above his head. "We were just about to launch a massive rescue mission, and your ass is chilling here in your treehouse?"

Aodhan held up his hand, eyes wide at the sight of three people standing in the doorway. "Listen. I'm a bit confused as well, as I didn't expect you all to be here, though I guess I should've known something was up when the main rope was nowhere to be found." Braan crossed his arms, his left eyebrow lifted in disdain. "But I promise I was imprisoned up until this morning, and I did, in fact, at some point need a rescue mission."

Braan cocked his head to the side. "We're listening."

Aodhan might've been about to respond, but then his eyes landed on the face over Braan's shoulder. "Aislin?" he squeaked out.

Aislan lifted his chin defiantly. "It's Aislan now."

"Wow, I...uh..." It was clear Aodhan didn't know what to say about the current development of events. "Congrats. I'm proud of you, *deir-dearthair*."

Sierra didn't speak Gaelic, but she was pretty sure Aodhan had just made a gender correction in their language.

"We can catch up on the family matters later. Aodhan, you need to tell us how you are standing in this room right now." Braan had lowered his axe-bearing fist, but it was clear he was not excited about being woken up for this development of events.

Aodhan's eyes turned back to Sierra, taking in the fact that she was wearing nothing but his shirt and was still somewhat pressed up against the wall. Her legs were quivering, thanks to the adrenaline of thinking she had been about to be abducted for the second time in two weeks.

"Yes, I'll explain, but please let me talk to Sierra first."

Braan's chin protruded a fraction as he gritted his teeth. "Fine. We will wait out here, but make it fast." The door closed behind him with a click.

Aodhan turned back to Sierra, and she could see the flame igniting in his eyes as he took in the state of her undress. Before he could say anything suggestive that would cause them to dive right back into bed, she stepped to the side, sinking down to sit on the edge of the bed. "Don't even think about touching me," she spat with as much venom as she could in her current state, but it came out shaky as the adrenaline was still flowing. "You owe me an explanation."

Aodhan nodded. He sat beside her, leaving a few inches of space, and turned to face her. "I'm so sorry, Sierra. You are right; I owe you an explanation, but please, first tell me what happened since I last saw you."

"No," Sierra snapped. "You can find out what happened to me after you explain the process of trying to woo me based on the predictions of a seer!"

Aodhan winced. "You've been talking to Aisli-an, I see."

"Yes, so you'd better start explaining."

Aodhan sighed, running one of his hands through his curly brown hair, which was much more unkempt than the last time she had seen him. Now that she wasn't in panic mode, Sierra was able to take in the fact that he was wearing similar clothes to Aislan, but they were all one color, a dull gray that didn't seem to fit his complexion, and there was stubble across his chin, suggesting he indeed had been locked up. Sierra also noticed his eyes looked bloodshot; at least she hadn't been the only one losing sleep.

"I don't know where to start," he edged.

"The beginning," Sierra replied firmly, bending one of her legs to mirror the way Aodhan was sitting so she could face him. She crossed her arms over her chest, but then became aware of how mean she probably looked, so she released them, clasping her hands together in her lap instead. She didn't know why her heart was in her throat at the thought of what Aodhan would say, but she could barely swallow over the bundle of nerves. She knew, though, that this feeling wouldn't go away until they discussed everything, as uncomfortable as the conversation might be. Sierra had learned a long time ago that avoiding difficult conversations only made things worse. They were like a band-aid, best ripped off sooner rather than later.

"Well then," Aodhan reached out his hands as if to touch Sierra's face, but he quickly thought better of it, resting them on the bed in front of him. "I should start by telling you that my father wasn't always this way. Once upon a time, he was friendly and kind, or so my mother says. I wasn't conceived yet. But he's over 500 years old now, and that kind of time, well, it changes a person. During his time, he watched as his world was irreparably changed for a reason he didn't—couldn't—understand."

Aodhan paused, motioning to the room around them. "Once, Sidhe was a land filled with nothing but magic. Just crossing the barrier would allow you to feel it in the air. Most Fae used magic to go about their daily tasks, often not just having one gift, but three or four, depending on the magic their parents possessed when they were conceived.

"But over the course of my father's lifetime, magic began to fade, and the older he grew, the more rapidly it faded. As a member of the council, many of the citizens began to look to the council for answers, thinking they could find a solution to the draining magic. Over time, the pressure grew even more immense."

"But I thought you said your father was born with weak magic?"

Aodhan nodded. "That is what I believe, but Fae don't usually have magic when they are young, and it develops during puberty. My father is convinced his magic failed to develop, although it is much more likely that he was born with very little magic to begin with.

"When I came along, my father was even more disgruntled to find that while I developed strong powers, it was still nothing compared to the generation prior to my father, and when Aislan developed even less magic..." he trailed off. "Well, about 50 years ago, his previous passion project became an all-out witch hunt. He was convinced that the Fae were cursed by some ancient being. First, he thought it was because we had disobeyed Mother Nature at some point, but slowly, the blame turned to the practice of intermarrying with humans. He believed that the loss of magic was a punishment from Gaia for marrying outside of our race.

"But the thing is, Fae and humans once lived side by side, and

I truly don't believe the intermarrying was that big of an impact, except for in those lines where the Fae repeatedly married humans. Which, while it does occasionally happen for the Fae that stay in Sidhe their entire lives—it is truly rare—usually, the magic in the bloodline would bounce back in the next generation." Aodhan lifted his eyes from his hands to meet hers. "And there was another major problem with this theory. As my family has weak magic, and we haven't had a human marry into our line for generations, it meant this couldn't be the true reason the Fae are losing magic.

"And so, my father began going through old texts, often taking me along with him. I grew up thinking that magic was something the Fae were owed for being Fae, and that it was an absolute crime that it had been taken from us, no matter the reason behind it.

"But then, about two years ago, I started to look at how my father was treating Aislin. Not just on the surface, where he was cordial but cold, but I could truly see how he consistently brushed aside Aislin's thoughts or feelings without hearing them out first. And for the first time in my life, I began to doubt the path my father was on. I didn't think that Fae should be treated differently solely because of their level of magic, something that is completely out of their own control.

"Then, about a year ago, my father asked me to journey north to a seer who is well known in Sidhe. When I got there, she wasn't anything like I expected. She seemed young, maybe one or two centuries, and when I walked in, I could tell she already knew all about me. Before I even sat down to explain to her why I was there, she said, "She's waiting for you." And I was more confused than I had ever been.

"But then she put my hands on her temple and showed me images of you. She showed you shelving books in the library, walking down the street, and sitting by the wall, eating your lunch. As your images passed through my mind, I must confess my first thought was how beautiful you were, and then the second thought was how alone you were. I never saw anyone else with you. I can't deny I was attracted to you, but at the time, I was more attracted to my father's approval, so I didn't even ask the seer what she meant when she said you were waiting. I just went back to my father and told him that the answer was a girl in Dublin, and I described you to him.

"I knew you were human. I saw your rounded ears in the visions I was shown, and at the time I really didn't think much of humans, to be honest. I didn't share the same hatred my father does, but to me it made no difference. You were going to bring my father's approval; I was sure of it. I never...not for a minute did I even think that maybe the seer had meant for those images to be just for me. That you were meant for me, irrespective of my father's plans. My mind had never worked that way before.

"Then I arrived in Dublin, and you weren't in any of the places where the fortune teller showed me, and for the first time in my life, I realized I might have made a hasty decision. I should've asked about when you were, and, more importantly, who you were.

"I was about to give up after about six months of waiting, when, at the end of the summer, I just happened to be walking across campus, and I happened to look at where I had been routinely checking for you. And there you were, leaning against that brick wall, looking at your phone, and I realized you were even more beautiful than you had been in the seer's visions. I also realized I neglected to remember that I could feel your emotions. For the first time in my life, I felt immense loneliness looking at you. I wasn't sure at first if it was truly coming from you, or a byproduct of my own emotions at always seeing you alone. But I began to visit the places of the visions, and you were often in many of them, and the loneliness remained.

"I was at a crossroads. Something told me to go back to my father and report that I had gone to find you in the wrong century. But something held me there. I felt as if the threads of fate had meant for me to find you. So, after the third or fourth time of seeing you, I went home and asked Braan what I should do.

"To my absolute shock, he recommended I download some app called Tinder. Which I did, and he taught me how to use it. It took me almost a month of shuffling through all the pictures on there, until I saw yours, and when I matched with you, I didn't know what to say. Suddenly, I realized that while I knew you, and some of the things you did, you knew nothing about me. I beat myself up over what I should say to you for a few days, and it was this mentality and debating with myself that made me late to our first date, and I'm sorry for that.

"But then I met you, and you became more than just some attractive stranger in a vision; you were this fiery, intelligent, human being, and I wanted to be around you more than anything I'd ever wanted before. Reading your emotions made me feel things I have never felt here in Sidhe. Even so, something told me that I needed to stay away from you and that my father would eventually take you away from me no matter what I wanted. It was this constant war waging inside myself that caused my behavior—and your confusion—the first month we knew each other, and for that, I'm also sorry."

Sierra looked up at Aodhan, his eyes meeting hers. She was about to say something, but he pressed a finger softly to her lips and continued, "Maybe I should've stayed away. But the longer I spent with you, the more I couldn't bear to leave, even though you hated me. Then, that day in the library with the drunk guy...I felt your absolute shame and horror when you knew I had seen your skin, and the idea that people, your own race of people, had made you feel that way about something that was out of your control was so abhorrent to me.

"I know you never told me, but I could tell that men, specifically, had made you feel bad about it before...and it was then I knew that I would spend the rest of your life trying to convince you to see yourself the way that I see you, a demure light that deserves to shine brightly in the never-ending darkness of life."

Sierra's heart melted as surely as the tears flowed down her cheeks. Before she could think of the consequences of what she was about to do, she leaned up, pressing her lips to Aodhan's, and the world around them faded. And so they were, two souls who had found their fates strangely intertwined in the tapestry of life.

Chapter Thirty-Seven

Aodhan kissed her back like a man starving, his hands coming to rest on her hip and shoulder as Sierra ran her hands up his chest.

Aodhan leaned into the kiss, using the hand on Sierra's hip to guide her back to lay on the bed. With a mind of their own, her legs came to wrap around his waist, wanting him closer, feeling his hard length pressing into her center from beneath his pants.

Without breaking the kiss, Aodhan slid his hands under the shirt she was wearing, one going to her already moist center, the other coming to rest on one of her nipples. "I need you," he whispered against her lips.

Sierra was far beyond coherent sentences at this point, but she knew better than to sleep with a guy without some form of protection. Breaking the kiss, she tried to collect her thoughts to convey why she had stopped. "I...uhh..."

"I've got us covered," he murmured, sliding open the drawer to the right of the bed to pull out a small glass jar of what looked like small rolled-up leaves. "You can take one as well if it will make you feel comfortable. They're for all genders."

Sierra nodded as Aodhan placed one in her hand. She wasn't sure if she should swallow it or chew it, but her question was answered when she placed it on her tongue, and it melted immediately, a sweet taste sliding down her throat. It was a weird sensation, that was for sure, but it was still better than many of the human birth control methods that required the woman to go through pain and stress on behalf of the man.

As soon as the liquid was gone from her tongue, Aodhan's mouth was on hers again. "It takes a few minutes to take effect," he told her, kissing a path down her neck. "Can I take your shirt off?"

Sierra nodded vigorously as Aodhan undid the buttons and slid the shirt from her shoulders. She expected him to say something at the sight of her clear skin, but he didn't even seem to notice as he continued his kiss path down her body until his lips came to rest on her clit through the odd underwear she had been wearing.

Sierra gasped as he bit gently, something no guy had ever done before, before sliding the underwear off. Although she expected his bite to hurt, the result was the opposite, tingles spreading through her hips and center as he bit a second time. It usually took much longer than this for her to reach orgasm, but his words about how he felt about her had been enough to get her worked up, and within a few strokes of his tongue, Sierra was falling over the edge, gasping in pleasure as she orgasmed.

Aodhan worked his way back up her body with kisses, stopping to knead her breasts and place each nipple in his mouth briefly. His stubble brushed against her sensitive skin, her back arching toward him.

"Has it been a few minutes yet?" she asked, breathless.

Aodhan continued kissing her neck. "Just a few minutes more, to be sure."

Taking that as her cue, Sierra sat up, pushing Aodhan into a sitting position. Before he could ask what she was doing, she slid her hands under his shirt to pull it over his head. While he finished taking the shirt off, her fingers undid the laces on his pants before sliding a hand in to clasp around his shaft.

Aodhan let out a groan. "You're going to be the death of me, *mo grá*."

Sierra pressed against the material of his pants with her other hand, indicating he should slide them down over his hips. As he did so, she leaned down, taking him into her mouth. He let out another groan as her lips came into contact with him.

She kept her hand at the base of his cock, only taking part of him into her mouth. Aodhan's hand came to rest on her hair gently, not being forceful, controlling the pace as her head bobbed over his shaft gliding in and out of her mouth.

Within a few minutes, Aodhan could wait no longer, and he pushed her off him, onto her back on the bed. "Are you ready?" he breathed.

Sierra nodded, out of breath. Aodhan spread her legs and pushed himself into her center in one smooth move, pausing to allow her to adjust. As soon as Sierra moaned in pleasure, he began to move in slow, deep strokes, leaving both of them breathless.

"Oh, Aodhan," Sierra gasped. "I'm close." She didn't know how it was possible that she was already this close to a second orgasm, but within seconds, she was falling over the edge for a second time. Aodhan continued his pace, thrusting into her slowly, making sure the top of his pelvis rested on her clit, giving her the friction she needed to come.

"Come on, you can come a third time for me," he whispered into her ear, even as she was still recovering from the most recent orgasm. He reached between them, pressing a finger to her clit, and Sierra felt the pressure building again.

"That's it. Come for me," Aodhan demanded in a husky voice.

With a small cry, Sierra came for the third time, and Aodhan wasn't far behind, collapsing onto his forearms and kissing her neck as he spilled into her.

It was a few minutes before Sierra regained her breath enough to speak again. "I see how it is, distract me before we can finish sharing stories."

"Hm?" Aodhan asked, lifting his head so his emerald, green eyes could look into hers. "I distracted you? More like you distracted me. We didn't even get to the part where you explained how you got to Sidhe."

He had a point. "Fine, we agree that we both distracted each other then?"

Aodhan nodded, sitting up and slipping himself out of her. He reached to the side of the bed, grabbing a towel to clean them up. Sierra noticed he was already hard again.

"Didn't we just have sex?" She inclined her chin to his cock.

"Yes, I must've forgotten to mention that us Fae males recover quickly," he explained.

"How quickly?" Sierra demanded.

Aodhan motioned to his dick. "Maybe a minute, two at most. As you can see, I am already ready for round two."

Sierra's eyes widened at the prospect, and she felt her vagina clench in anticipation, the traitor, but before she could follow that thought too far, she came to her senses, moving away from Aodhan and snatching the discarded shirt to cover herself with.

"Nice try, trying to distract me again, but no more sex until we finish story time. I'm serious." Sierra tried to put on her most serious face, but Aodhan just chuckled.

"You're cute when you're trying to be serious." He reached up and flicked her nose gently.

Sierra held up her finger. "I am serious. Now, tell me how we got here."

Chapter Thirty-Eight

Aodhan stepped off the bed to pull on his pants before slipping beneath the covers and motioning for Sierra to sit with him. Sierra slid under the covers, leaning her head back on his shoulder.

"So, on Friday, we were supposed to have our date. I spent a little extra time getting ready, because I wanted to take you to this really fancy restaurant Braan had told me about. He knew about our date because I had asked him to arrange some things while we were out so I could take you back to my place after." He took a deep breath.

"Everything was going well until I got to the library just before closing, and you weren't there. I asked Mona, and she said you had been there, but maybe you had left a few minutes early because it was slow. But when I went into the break room and saw your messenger bag, I knew something was wrong right away." It was Sierra's turn to take a deep breath as the events of that night flickered behind her eyes, but she kept quiet; her time to talk would come later.

"Before panicking completely, I checked the bathrooms and the microfilm room, just in case you had ventured away from your usual duties. But by the time Mona was ready to lock up, I knew something had happened during your shift. I took your messenger bag with me and went to your place to see if you had gone home sick enough to forget your bag or something.

"But then you weren't there either, and I really started to panic. You are a creature of habit, and I couldn't think of anywhere else you could possibly be other than the places I had already checked, especially because you always stuck to the plans we made previously, even when I was late. So, then I went to Braan.

"Braan helped me call the Dublin police, just in case it was someone human who had taken you, so they would be looking for you there. But deep down, I already knew. My father had gotten tired of waiting and must've sent someone to collect you."

"Did he know what I looked like?" Sierra asked.

Aodhan nodded. "Before I left for Dublin, I had made a sketch. You hadn't meant anything to me then, and I didn't realize then how dangerous that could be.

"I asked Braan and Kaye to stay there in case you came back and that I would 'call' them using the waters as soon as I reached my father's place in Sidhe."

"But you never made it," Sierra surmised.

"No, my father had anticipated my every move. They were waiting for me when I crossed the border into Sidhe."

"Who was?"

"Guards from *Cuileann*. My father had labeled me as a dangerous criminal and said to detain me by force until further notice."

Sierra's eyes widened. "How did you get free then?"

"Well, that's the thing: while my father had labeled me as a criminal and asked the *Cuileann* advisor, Fearghal, to hold me until further notice, *Cuileann* is its own province, and they have their own laws. They believe in a fair trial system, similar to the ones in the human world, and when requests for elaboration on my crime went unanswered, they eventually let me go. I didn't know how many days had passed, but I assumed I was there for four or five days.

"At first, I went back to my father's place in *Fuinseog,* but I knew that if he saw me, I would be in trouble, so I used a servant's entrance to see Slaine, who I knew could help me figure out where you had gone, and she told me that she had been in contact with Aislan. She wasn't sure where he was planning to take you, and she isn't one of the few people who knows about this place. So the next part was just by chance, but I decided to come here to hide out, get some sleep, and plan my next move. Then I saw the rope was up, and I thought maybe I had guessed right and Aislan had brought you here.

"And here we are." He smiled, gripping me a bit tighter. "Now it's your turn."

"Before I begin, let me just specify that next time we are separated and I'm not expecting you, please don't just get into bed with me, that was terrifying."

"Noted," Aodhan replied. "But know that I don't intend to be separated from you ever again."

"As much as I wish that were true, you know as well as I do that it's bound to happen at some point."

"Fine," groaned Aodhan, clearly not liking the idea of being separated. "Now continue with your story."

"Well, some of it is...muddled, because I was drugged or knocked out." Sierra felt Aodhan stiffen below her as a low snarl emerged from his lips, displaying his displeasure at the thought of Sierra being hurt. "But best as I can tell, I was taken from work Friday night, a little before closing, but whoever took me drugged me almost immediately, so I was out until Saturday morning...I think."

"When I awoke again, I was in the trunk of a car, and then I slept more until I was taken out sometime during the day, likely at the entrance to Sidhe. I was blindfolded and bound, so the man who took me practically had to drag me across the border.

"Once we crossed into Sidhe, he put me into a cart, and I was taken to your father's home, or at least I assume it was your father's home."

"If it is where you saw Slaine, then yes, it is."

"I was prepped for some ritual that Conlan was convinced would break the Fae curse, but either it didn't work, or Conlan saw my skin and thought that my condition was the reason it wouldn't work."

At the mention of her skin, Aodhan reached down, running his hand over her arm. "Your skin, it's clear." His eyes were wide.

"Yeah, you didn't notice before when I was naked?" Sierra asked incredulously.

Aodhan reached his hand down to touch her thigh, clearly surprised by the smooth skin he felt there. "No. When I'm with you...I can't explain it, but it's your soul that I am attracted to, not your body. I'm too distracted by who you are as a person to notice something trivial like your skin."

Sierra turned to look at Aodhan, her eyebrows raised.

"I mean, I find your body beautiful as well, but beauty is a subjective thing. You are the most beautiful woman in the world to me in the way you speak, think, and breathe. I am happy that you are more comfortable with the way you look now, but I am attracted to you no matter your appearance."

Sierra felt herself blushing, "I-I'm flattered."

Aodhan placed a kiss on the top of her head. "Now tell me what happened next."

Sierra continued the story, telling Aodhan all about the dungeon, as well as her time with Slaine. Eventually, she got to the part where Aislan rescued her and their trek through the jungle.

"And now, I'm here," she finished, with a fake flourish.

Aodhan was silent for a few minutes, clearly taking in everything she had said, his arm running a languid path up and down her arm. "I know this might be hard for you, but can you tell me exactly what ritual my father was performing? I'm trying to figure out what prophecy he thinks he's fulfilling."

"He, uh, took some of my blood, twice, while I was tied down to this stone podium." Aodhan's grip on Sierra's arm grew tight —so tight that Sierra had to wrap her own hand around his to get him to loosen his grip. "It's okay, I'm okay, I survived, and I'm here," she whispered, to calm Aodhan.

"I know," he said at last. "I just can't believe he thought he could hurt you and get away with it."

"You have to remember, Aodhan, that not everyone knows how you feel about me."

Aodhan opened his mouth to argue, then quickly shut it again, and Sierra knew she was right.

As if someone had been listening from the other side of the door for a good time to intervene, Aodhan and Sierra were interrupted by knocking.

"*Isteach*," Aodhan called, and Braan poked his head in the door.

"While I'm glad to see you two catching up, we really do need to plan what we are going to do next."

"You're right," Aodhan agreed. "Give us a moment to get dressed and we will be right out."

Braan closed the door. "I'm timing you, so just one minute is all you get," he called through the closed door, clearly reading both Sierra and Aodhan's minds, both of which were currently contemplating if they could have a second round before it was time to join the others.

"We will have more time for that later, I promise," Aodhan said as he stood from the bed and pulled on a shirt, before heading to the closet and tossing some leggings to Sierra. "Those will probably be a bit big, but I'd rather my friends not see you in just that shirt."

Sierra slid on the pants, which, indeed, would barely stay on. Crossing the room, she peeked into the closet until she found a pair of pants with laces similar to what Aodhan was wearing. She eased the chord from the pants, tying it around the top of the pants as a makeshift belt to keep her pants in place.

"This will hold for now, but it probably won't work for when we travel from here."

Aodhan nodded, clasping her hand in his and heading for the door. "We will cross that bridge when we get to it, okay?" Opening the door, the two of them stepped into the common room to join the others.

Chapter Thirty-Nine

"**I** vote we imprison Conlan and let him see how he likes it," Braan suggests to the groans of Aodhan and Aislan.

"I already told you it won't be that easy. Someone would let him out; all of *Fuinseog* loves him," Aodhan argued.

"I vote we visit the other provinces and get him kicked out of the council, that will lower his influence," Aislan suggested.

"We don't have the time to journey to 12 different provinces and convince them to vote out Conlan. We would need 7 of the 13 to side with us to get a majority vote." Braan rubbed his chin, while staring at the map on the table.

After a quick catch-up, the five of them immediately began debating strategies for what they should do next and how they could get Sierra back to the human world. Unfortunately, the entrance to the human world was in the forest on land that belonged to *Fuinseog*, though it was likely they could go through *Darach*, a neighboring province, to get there without being detected by Conlan. The problem was that Conlan likely had the entrance guarded 24/7, knowing Sierra would need to use it at some point. Additionally, leaving wouldn't really solve the problem, because as long as Conlan lived, he had unlimited resources to come after Sierra again and again, and there was no way she and

Aodhan could always be on their guard. Plus, Sierra didn't like the idea of putting the innocent lives of her family and coworkers at risk by returning to her former life without resolving the problem completely.

The problem was that they either had to get rid of Conlan, or at least get him voted off the panel that made decisions for Sidhe, because then someone else could try and convince the panel that keeping a human prisoner wouldn't solve their problem. They could also try to solve the diminishing magic problem, but Aodhan was convinced that there was no problem—it was simply time and interbreeding taking its course—which is why he preferred not to try that route since it wasn't an immediate solution.

Also, Sierra wasn't really sure what was waiting for her in the human world at this point. She'd been gone for over a week, and the police had been contacted, meaning her sudden reappearance would raise questions she couldn't answer. Not to mention that she was behind in her classes now and would likely spend a month trying to get her master's back on track.

Basically, there was no easy solution beyond hiding out in the treehouse and ignoring the rest of the world, which they couldn't do forever.

"Why don't we at least try to find the prophecy your dad is convinced Sierra is a part of, to see if we can prove him wrong?" Kaye suggested, for what was at least the third time.

Sierra had stayed mostly quiet, not knowing enough about Sidhe and its inhabitants to know how they could help.

"And then what? Risk that we somehow convince him to take a different human? The vision of the seer has him convinced that Sierra is the answer," Aislan shot back.

"Maybe you could try to just talk to him about it, Aodhan?" Sierra suggested, the entire table falling quiet in shock before breaking out in laughter.

"Everyone knows you can't talk to Conlan about anything." Braan rolled his eyes.

"Fine," Sierra conceded. "But I think we should at least split up so we can pursue two solutions at the same time or visit multiple provinces if we are truly trying to turn the vote against him."

"I agree," Kaye piped up, winking at Sierra from across the table.

"Wait." Aislan pinched the bridge of his nose. "I just thought of something. What if we visit the seer again?"

"In hopes of what solution?" Aodhan grumbled.

"That maybe she could tell us more about why Sierra was seen as a solution in the first place? Maybe she could even clear things up for Conlan."

Sierra leaned her elbows on the table, placing her head in her hands. Something was niggling at the back of her mind, like she should have an idea of a solution, but she couldn't get it to become clear in her mind.

"Maybe. Or maybe if Sierra is the solution, she knows how," Kaye added.

"Yeah, and what if she says killing Sierra is the only solution?" Braan said, before slapping a hand over his mouth.

So quick that her human eyes couldn't follow, Aodhan had Braan in a headlock, and his face was turning purple. "Don't you dare say those words in the same sentence ever again, do you understand me?" he demanded.

Braan was unable to speak, but he managed a feeble nod and a tap on Aodhan's arm, which must have been a sufficient enough agreement for Aodhan, because he released him. Kaye immediately stood to check on her husband.

Sitting back in his chair, Aodhan placed his palms flat on the table. "Here's what we're going to do. Sierra and I will go to visit the seer. Maybe she does know something that can help us." He paused, making eye contact with the other three before continuing, "In the meantime, the three of you will do some reconnaissance to find out what prophecy it is that Conlan thinks he is fulfilling with Sierra's blood. Okay?"

They nodded in unison.

"Then we will meet back here and decide our next move. At least then, we will have more information and be able to choose our next move more wisely."

"That's a good plan," Aislan conceded.

"I know," Aodhan smirked. "You three can decide when you are leaving. Sierra and I will head out at first light."

Sierra glanced at the window, grimacing as she realized that daylight was likely only an hour or two away at this point.

"After we visit the seer, we will meet you wherever you go. Then hopefully we can either implement a solution, or make a plan for convincing Conlan that Sierra isn't the answer."

Aodhan rose from the table. "In the meantime, Sierra and I both need to get what sleep we can." He points at the table. "Leave a note with the name of where you intend to go when you leave, just in case you don't make it back." Aislan nods solemnly in agreement.

Without another word, Aodhan pulled Sierra back into the room, closing the door behind them and pressing her up against it, placing a searing kiss on her lips. "As much as I am aching to take you again, we really do need some sleep before we begin our journey."

Right on cue, Sierra yawned. "You're right."

Making her way over to the bed, Sierra undid the cord belt, allowing the leggings to fall to the floor before sliding into bed. Aodhan slipped off his shirt before doing the same, pulling Sierra into his side so she could rest her head on his chest.

"Sleep well. See you in a few hours," he murmured into her hair.

"You too," Sierra replied, before drifting off to sleep.

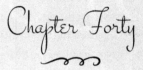

Chapter Forty

When they arose the next morning, the other three had already left, leaving a piece of paper with a single word on the table.

Fuinseog.

Apparently, they figured the best library to check was the one that Conlan would have the most access to. Sierra just hoped they had a plan for sneaking in and out without getting caught; the last thing she wanted to do was lose her new friends this soon.

Aodhan and Sierra dug through his wardrobe, but there was nothing that would work or be remotely comfortable as they traversed the forest. In the end, Aodhan raided Aislan's closet, coming back with a few items that fit slightly better: a pair of simple pants and a long-sleeved tunic, which was probably fitted on Aislan, but hung off Sierra like an oversized dress. Either way, she wouldn't complain; at least she didn't need to hold up the pants with a cord.

They didn't say much as they each consumed a piece of bread with sweet red preserves that Kaye had left for them, and Aodhan prepared a pack with a few supplies.

"So where is this seer?" Sierra asked, as Aodhan packed a second, smaller bag for her to carry.

"*Funiun*, about a day's walk from here, though we will likely need to split it into two days for you."

Sierra felt bad that she wasn't as fast as the Fae, but at least they wouldn't be too set back by her slow pace, considering the others likely had two days en route to get back to *Fuinseog* since they, too, had a human slowing their pace.

"Where will we spend the night?" Prior to this adventure, where she found herself camping in a boulder out of necessity, she had never been much of a camper or an outdoors girl at all. It just wasn't a thing in Texas.

"I'm hoping we can find a cave or an overhang, but I haven't been this way in over a year, and I've never had to camp on the way, so I'm not exactly sure what there is along our route."

That didn't make Sierra feel any better, but she knew they had very little choice at this point. Sliding the bag Aodhan had packed for her on her shoulders, he gave her a quick peck on the lips before leading her out the door and pulling her onto his back, just as Aislan had done when they had come up.

As Aodhan situated the second backpack on his chest, Sierra took one glance back at the tree house. She could see why Aodhan chose to spend most of his time here. Even though it was small, it was peaceful, and being above the trees made it seem like the rest of the world was non-existent, even though there were tree-house neighbors less than 100 feet away.

Sierra held tight to Aodhan's neck as he began to lower them through the hole. With two backpacks, it was a bit tighter than before, and it took them a moment or two to get everything clear. Once they were through, Aodhan deftly repelled down the tree, reminding her that he had been here many times over the years.

Sierra jumped off Aodhan's back, brushing herself off as she looked around the forest, which was shrouded in shadow. Apparently, daylight didn't make a whole lot of difference with such a dense tree ceiling overhead. The small amount of light filtering through the trees did give the forest a magical look, making it feel less menacing. Sierra was able to appreciate it all a bit more this time around, as she was no longer worried about Aodhan.

Aodhan let her look around as he used his Fae senses to orient them. It was easy to get lost in the dense wood, which is why he was reasonably sure that Conlan wouldn't waste resources searching for Sierra here; it was too risky, and too easy to get turned around.

"Before we go," Aodhan said, breaking the peaceful silence of the forest, "I'm sure Aislan explained a bit about the animals in this forest, but don't run from anything, and stay quiet if we encounter any animals."

"I remember," Sierra assured him.

"Good," Aodhan replied, placing the palm of his hand against Sierra's cheek and leaning in to kiss her forehead. "I forgot to tell you how thankful I am that you are here with me."

Sierra arched one of her eyebrows.

"Most women would run screaming in the other direction, or straight up refuse to come with me at this point. I appreciate that you are meeting this problem with me head-on, even though it technically isn't your problem to solve."

Sierra grabbed Aodhan's wrist, which was resting on her face. "That's what people in a relationship do, you know. They accompany each other, even on the journeys they would rather not take."

"Oh, so we're in a relationship now?" Aodhan teased. "I thought we were...what's the human term? 'Just dating'?"

Sierra smacked his hand away from her face playfully. "After being imprisoned by your father and dragged across a foreign realm to help you solve your family problems, we'd better be in a relationship. Otherwise, I'll be headed home to Dublin right now," Sierra joked right back.

Aodhan threw back his head and laughed. "Alright, I guess we are in a relationship. Now, let's resume our journey to the seer."

Sierra nodded in agreement as Aodhan slipped his hand into

hers. "I don't have the band as Aislan did, but I'll keep a firm grip on your hand, alright?"

"Alright," Sierra responded, and before she could blink, they were off, moving at what she would consider a jogging pace through the forest.

Unlike her last adventure trapezing through these woods, she was able to see, taking care to step, instead of trip, over the various roots and rocks in their path. She had also acquired some boots, though they were much too big for her. But with socks stuffed in the toe portion and the laces tightened, she was able to keep up much more efficiently than she had been in the slippers Aislan had acquired.

It was much easier to traverse the forest in daylight, as she wasn't as nervous about what she couldn't see, and she wasn't solely reliant on the feel of the pull of her arm. Instead, she was easily able to visibly follow Aodhan, ducking when low-hanging branches emerged on their path.

Although the journey was far from enjoyable, when Aodhan announced it was time to stop for lunch, Sierra didn't feel nearly as fatigued as she had thought she would. Sinking down onto the large rock where Aodhan had laid out their measly lunch, they both began to dig into the bread and fruits he had packed. Sierra wasn't sure what type of fruit they were eating, but she assumed it was something native to Sidhe as she had never seen anything quite like it before. It was round and a bit fuzzy, like a peach, except it was bright green in color. When she bit into it, the sweet juices started rolling down her chin, and she almost moaned in ecstasy.

"Oh my God, what is this?" she asked Aodhan.

"*Serwil*. It's a fruit that grows here in the forest."

"Wow, it is delicious."

"I know." He smirked before biting into his own *serwil*. "But don't fall too much in love with them because I only brought two. It's just bread after this."

Sierra flashed her eyes at Aodhan. "Scared I'm going to want the *serwil* more than you?"

"I would be, if they weren't so limited." He smirked. "They're a treat, even here in Sidhe."

Sierra was too busy stuffing her face to answer. By the time she was done, her fingers were covered with a light green liquid, and she saw no choice but to lick them clean.

Aodhan groaned at the sight. "Are you trying to kill me? Doing that when I have to keep my hands to myself for the foreseeable future?"

Sierra laughed. "It's not my fault you packed a messy fruit. Maybe keep that in mind when you're packing lunches in the future." Sierra looked down out of habit to check if there were any crumbs on her shirt, and when she did, she noticed a small furry face looking at her from the bush.

The animal was brown, or mostly brown, and covered in fur. It looked like an American badger, but at the same time, Sierra had never seen one in real life, so she couldn't be sure. Trying to alert Aodhan without scaring the animal, she discreetly dug her elbow into his side.

"What—" he started, before turning his head to see the small animal observing them from the brush. "Ah, you've attracted a badger, I see. They're carnivorous, but lucky for you only to small animals."

"Should I be afraid?" Sierra asked, keeping her eyes trained on the badger.

"Yes and no. Yes, because I haven't seen one look at a human like that, ever, but no, because I promise he won't be eating you. He's intrigued."

True to what Aodhan said, the badger ventured further out of the bush, sniffing around the base of the boulder they were seated on. In between sniffs, he would glance up at Sierra, obviously hoping for some sort of handout.

"He likes you," Aodhan surmised before digging in the pack. "But I don't have anything on hand that he would like to eat."

Sierra nodded, tramping down the urge to hold her hand out to the badger. This wasn't a house cat or dog; it was just as likely to bite her finger as it was to let her pet him. "I'm sorry," Sierra apologized in a low voice to the badger. "I want to pet you, but I don't think you would like that."

As if it understood her, the badger nudged the bottom of her shoe. Sierra looked to Aodhan for advice to find him staring at the badger with his mouth agape. "I have never seen a badger do that."

Sierra looked back at the badger, giving it a smile. "Maybe next time we meet, I'll have something for you, buddy."

The badger, as if he understood her, turned, and scurried off into the bush.

"Well, that was...interesting," Aodhan said, once the badger was out of sight. "Once you are finished, we should probably start moving again."

Sierra looked down at her empty hands. "I'm finished, I suppose. You're sure you aren't hiding another *serwil*?"

Aodhan stood, pulling the backpack up on his shoulders and holding out a hand to help her down off the rock.

Then they were off again, passing through the trees, and over rocks and tree roots. Sierra had no idea how Aodhan knew where they were going, it all just looked like forest to her. Every bend they came around looked like the last, and it wasn't as if they were following any path.

They were moving at a pace that was a bit too fast to be comfortable, so they couldn't talk. Plus, Sierra figured they still had to be careful to stay off the radar of any creatures, or people, who might be inhabiting the wood.

Soon, the sunlight began to fade, and Sierra found herself tripping from time to time. She gripped Aodhan's arm tighter, but if he noticed the fading light or her steadily increasing clumsiness, he didn't mention it.

At some point, it became pitch black, and she was tripping

every other step. "Aodhan," she hissed, trying to be quiet but knowing she couldn't go much further.

"I know," he whispered back. "I'm just trying to find us somewhere slightly safe to spend the night."

Sierra didn't like the sound of that, but she knew that they didn't really have a choice. Safe places to sleep in this forest were probably few and far between.

Just when she thought she couldn't go another step, Aodhan stopped, pulling her close to him so he could whisper in her ear. "This tree trunk is hollow, but an animal could be living in it, so I need to look inside alone. Stand right here, keep your hand on the tree trunk, and don't move a muscle."

Sierra nodded, feeling strangely empty and cold when his warmth left her back. Suddenly, everything in the forest became scarier. The darkness felt like it had teeth of its own, and the rustling of the leaves intensified. The pace of her breathing increased, and she placed the hand that wasn't on the tree trunk on her stomach in an attempt to slow it.

Aodhan couldn't have been gone long when he once again touched her elbow and began to direct her around the tree, but Sierra felt all her breath whoosh out of her in relief.

Aodhan didn't say anything as he silently guided her into the tree trunk, which had apparently been uninhabited. It was pitch black as he maneuvered them to where they could sit on the dirt with their backs against the interior of the tree trunk.

"I can't risk lighting a fire in here, so let me know if you need help finding anything." Aodhan kept his voice low. "We are also cornered, and need to keep quiet, so we don't attract anything with our echoing voices."

"Um, what about...bathroom needs?" Sierra asked in a whisper.

"Just go on the other side of the tree, keep your hand on it, and don't let go. I'll stand nearby in case you need help."

Now that she was sitting down, even though it was in a hollowed-out tree in a strange forest, Sierra felt incredibly tired, like she could sleep right away. Seeming to read her mind as he always did, Aodhan pressed what felt like a bit of bread into her hand. "Eat, then you can sleep."

Not one to argue when it came to food, Sierra ate her slice of bread in a few bites. As soon as she was done, she felt around in the dark for Aodhan's face, giving him a quick peck before drifting off to sleep on his shoulder.

Chapter Forty-One

S he awoke the next day, with her limbs entangled with Aodhan's, as he ran a calming hand over her hair. "Did you sleep well?" he asked in a low voice in her ear.

"Mm-hmm," Sierra murmured, it being too early to formulate a response that included words. She kept her eyes closed, focusing on the way his hands felt as they ran through her loose black curls. Although Sierra had always hated her skin, she had always loved her hair. It was the kind other women wished they had. A mix between wavy and curly, it fell naturally into loose curls no matter what the weather was outside or how she had slept.

Aodhan's hand drifted lower, falling from her hair to her backside, giving it a slight squeeze.

"Are we in a rush this morning?" she whispered, her voice laced with hope as other parts of her body awoke at his touch.

"We only have about half a day's travel to the seer, so I think there's time," he whispered back, his hand creeping between her legs to press against her clit. At the feel of him brushing her through the fabric, arousal immediately pooled in her core.

"Here, open your mouth," he whispered.

Sierra trusted Aodhan, and did as he asked, unsurprised when she felt the same melting tablet on her tongue. "You brought them with you?"

"Why would I leave them behind?" Aodhan asked, swallowing his own tablet.

Before Sierra could ask more questions, he was pressing her up against the inside of the tree, trailing kisses down her neck. With the hand that wasn't rubbing her between her legs, he guided one of her hands to his cock, already straining at the laces of his pants. "I dreamed of you last night, and it was torture to wait for you to wake up."

Sierra let out a gasp. "That feels good," she moaned, as she rubbed him through his pants.

"Hm, think you can come for me this way?" Aodhan said in a low murmur, his breath fanning against her earlobe.

Feeling her orgasm already building in her core, Sierra could do nothing but nod. Aodhan continued his ministrations, pressing against her clit lightly as he moved his hand back and forth between her legs at the same rhythm with which she stroked him with her hand.

"Come on, come for me, *mo grá.*"

At the sound of his nickname for her, Sierra toppled over the edge, digging the fingernails of the hand that wasn't on his cock into Aodhan's shoulders as she came. It took her a moment to regain control of her breathing as she panted in Aodhan's chest, trying to stay at least somewhat quiet in case they still had to be cautious.

Aodhan was paying attention because the minute she was done, gasping for breath, he repositioned them, so his hard cock was pressed between their bodies as she sat on his lap.

"Are you ready for me?"

Sierra nodded, reaching down to undo the button on her pants. Aodhan helped her slip them off before pulling off his own pants.

Lifting her as if she weighed nothing, he placed her on top of him, easily guiding himself between her slickened folds. As he slowly sank her down, Sierra moaned in ecstasy, placing her hands on his shoulders once again so she could have the leverage to move.

Aodhan began to move beneath her, thrusting up into her as she pressed herself down. They found their rhythm quickly; the only sound in the tree was their breaths echoing back at them.

"You feel too good," He huffed. "I won't last much longer. You need to come again, *mo grá*."

Sierra gripped his shoulders harder, pushing her clit forward against his body to get some friction to fuel her pending orgasm. Within a few seconds of the adjusted position, Sierra was coming hard, fighting the urge to call out his name.

Not a moment later, Aodhan exploded as well, spilling himself inside of her with a gasp. He was also finding it difficult to be quiet, having to bite Sierra's shoulder to keep from moaning loudly with his orgasm. It would probably leave a bruise later, but she didn't care.

Sierra collapsed on his chest, and Aodhan wrapped his arms around her. They sat in silence for a few minutes, enjoying the feeling of each other.

"You know," Aodhan broke the silence, "I hate the situation we are in now, but I wouldn't want to change a thing and run the risk of not meeting you."

"I feel the same way." Sierra's voice came out a bit husky, and foreign to her ears. "After all, who wouldn't want to have sex in a hollowed-out tree trunk?"

Aodhan tossed his head back and laughed. "You never cease to entertain me."

Sierra shrugged. "That's what I'm here for: entertainment."

He lifted his eyebrows suggestively. "Do I get to pick the type of entertainment?"

"We just had sex." Sierra rolled her eyes, knowing he could still see it in the low light.

"I told you, we Fae have insane recovery times. I'm ready for round two."

"If we do another round, I'm going to need a nap. Then we will never get to the seer."

"You're right," Aodhan agreed, shifting Sierra off him and handing her her pants. "Just hold on to those for a moment. I'll check outside; you can relieve yourself, then put them on."

Sierra nodded. This was the one thing they didn't tell you about the adventure of outdoor sex: not having a way to clean up afterward.

Aodhan swiftly stood, tugging on his pants, before peeking out through the opening of the trunk. "It's clear," he called over his shoulder. "I'll stand a few feet forward to give you some privacy."

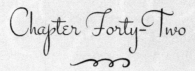

Chapter Forty-Two

Relieved and satisfied, she pulled on her clothes so they could get on their way. They each gobbled down some of the bread and nuts from their food stores, which were running low, and then Aodhan went to fill their water skins in the stream, leaving Sierra in the tree so he could use his Fae pace to get to the river and back as quickly as possible.

When he returned, he helped Sierra get her pack on her shoulders before asking if she was ready. She nodded in response, and Aodhan took her hand, and they were off at the same pace as the day before, Sierra struggling to keep up. If she ever got to go back to her old life, she was seriously going to hit the gym.

It was brighter than the day before, and Sierra tried to take in what she could as they passed through the forest. There were all types of birds and flowers that she wished she had more time to watch and study. Hopefully, someday, she would be able to, maybe at some distant point in the future when she was no longer in danger.

She quickly brushed off the thought. They were going to solve this issue soon; she was sure of it.

~

Unlike the day before, the journey went quickly, and all too soon, Sierra found herself staring at a small wooden home in the middle of a clearing in the enchanted forest. Aodhan had them stop in the tree line, turning to her before they proceeded.

"I have to warn you. The seer, Fia, is strange, but there is no reason to hide anything from her. She knows all, anyway."

Sierra's eyes widened.

"She can see the future, the past, and sometimes I think she can see other beings that we don't." He took a deep breath. "She might say some things that terrify you, but I promise she is just trying to convey what she knows in the best way possible."

"I understand." Sierra swallowed as Aodhan took her hand for the second time that day and led them at a leisurely pace to the door of the building. Before they could knock, the door opened, revealing a beautiful woman in a floor-length purple gown. Her golden hair fell in two long braids down her back, and while she was clearly Fae, Sierra could sense something else about her, but she couldn't put a name to what it was. This was likely the strangeness that Aodhan had mentioned.

"Aodhan, Sierra," she said, greeting each of them with a bow of her chin, before moving aside to let them into her home. "I've been waiting for you," she said in perfect English, which was almost spooky after weeks of hearing the Sidhe-accented English spoken by everyone around her.

Aodhan pulled Sierra into the house, which looked on the inside just as she suspected it would from the outside. The living room and kitchen were small and sparsely furnished. There was a stone fireplace, however, with flames crackling even though it wasn't the least bit cold. The kitchen held a wooden table with just two chairs, and similar appliances to what Sierra saw in Teach Crann. The wall above the counter was filled with shelves, lined with colorful bottles of all shapes and sizes, and containing all manner of things. Some looked like food, and others Sierra hoped weren't food, because they certainly didn't look edible.

"Make yourselves comfortable." Fia motioned to the purple

couch in the living room, which didn't look strong enough to hold both her and Aodhan, but when they sat down, it didn't so much as creak. Fia picked up a wooden chair from the kitchen, and placing it before them, she sat.

"You have questions."

Sierra was glad that Aodhan had warned her, as she was much less creeped out than she would have been had she just gone in blind. The one thing they hadn't talked about, however, was whether Sierra would be talking, or Aodhan would be.

As it turns out, there was no need to discuss, as Fia took Aodhan's hands and placed them on the sides of her head. Sierra had never been a jealous woman, but something about the motion made her a bit uncomfortable.

Maybe Fia could hear her thoughts, because without even a glance in Sierra's direction, she said, "I'm just showing him what I saw before. Before he went to find out."

Sierra nodded as Aodhan's eyes drifted closed. She assumed he was committing to memory what he saw, or perhaps looking for details he had missed previously.

"Would I be able to see too?" she asked.

"I'm afraid not. I can only show people the future which pertains to them. Meaning I could show you what I saw for your future, but I can't show you what I am showing Aodhan now."

Sierra understood, and for a moment she wondered if she did, in fact, want to see her future. There was something inherently scary about being presented with the concept of being able to see what would come next in life. What if it was something she didn't like? Would she be able to change it?

Aodhan's eyes snapped open, glancing to the side to focus on Sierra, before looking back at Fia.

"Sierra," he gasped. "I can't believe I never asked this before, but what is your master's thesis on?"

Sierra cocked her head at the odd question, but answered anyway. "I'm evaluating some of the variables in life which, when changed, can extend the human lifespan."

"And have you made any discoveries yet?" he asked, his eyes drifting closed again.

"Yes, and no, I just started the lab work, so the details on my experiments won't come back for a while, plus they are on mice, so some of it will be conjecture anyway. But based on some of the similar studies which I am reviewing, I believe there are several variables that can extend the human lifespan when observed early enough in life."

Aodhan's mouth was agape. He couldn't believe he had never discussed this with her before. "What are they?"

"Well, diet, for one. Vegetarians or pescatarians live much longer, and are much less prone to diseases than those who consume meat. And if you look at the blue areas on earth, the regions where humans live the longest, they are all the areas where the diet is majority pescatarian. And the only meat they occasionally eat other than fish is chicken or eggs, meaning no red meat at all."

Sierra couldn't hide the emotion in her voice; this really was her passion project and she rarely got to speak about it in length. "Another factor I am looking into is exercise, as well as living in a familial unit, or with another being for the entirety of life. So far, similar studies have concluded that those who stay active, and don't live alone, live longer than those who do. This is most clearly seen in Italy, on Sardinia, and in Ikaria, Greece, two of the blue spots I spoke of. In these areas, it is common for young adults to live with their family until marriage, and from there, live with their partner together, often with the parents in the home, or with siblings, so they almost never live alone and almost always live in homes of at least four adults.

"Of course, there are other aspects and variables too, and I am evaluating them in the same way, but I believe these are the three aspects I'll be focusing on. There is also a genetic aspect, which I can't always account for, but I'm trying to focus my thesis on the variables that someone could control if they wanted to live a longer life."

Aodhan's eyes moved between Fia and Sierra. "Hm."

"What did you see?" Sierra asked. "Maybe I'll recognize something you didn't."

"Well, I saw you just as I did before, but this time instead of focusing on the background to try and figure out your location, I looked at what you were doing. Fia's visions are a bit like a slideshow," he explained. "I saw you in a lab, and writing, and in a classroom. But now that I know you, I figured that these actions must have some significance, because you aren't in your home, or the library, which are both big parts of your life."

Sierra's mind began to whir, like different pieces of a puzzle falling into place all at once. She thought over the topic of her thesis, and the struggles of the Fae over the last few centuries and how they could possibly connect.

"Aodhan," she breathed. "You told me that Fae were traditionally vegetarian, is that still the case?"

It was Fia who answered, "The Fae used to be solely vegetarian, but with the technological advancements of the human world, and the traders who cross the border with some regularity, many have started eating meat and animal products, not as regularly as humans, but from time to time."

Sierra turned that thought over in her mind. "In the human world, there had been a trend of getting married later in life, which has led to many humans who, in previous generations, wouldn't live alone long before marriage, now spending many years by themselves. Has something like that changed here in Sidhe?"

Aodhan nodded. "Yes, marriages used to be arranged by parents to preserve bloodlines, but the practice was, for the most part, discontinued over 100 years ago, mostly because it was thought to be cruel to arrange marriages and often led to a lot of infidelity, which further thinned the bloodlines. Though some Fae in positions of power still arrange suitable marriages for their children."

Sierra tilted her chin down. "And have the Fae become less physically active?"

Fia shrugged. "That I can't say for sure, but I will say that just as the humans have had their technological advancements that lower hard labor, so too have the Fae."

"Then there's a possibility that similar factors to those affecting the human lifespan could also be affecting the Fae magic. I can't say for sure; I would need to perform some studies, and they would likely take, uh," Sierra swallowed uncomfortably, "Hundreds of years to complete because your lifespan is already so much longer than a human's.

"I would also need to do some research, talking to Fae scientists here, as well as looking at any previous studies which may have been performed."

Aodhan ran a hand across his forehead. "There are some Fae scientists, most of whom live in *Saileach*. I could take you there and see what the records have on hand." His voice was somber, probably at the realization that Sierra's mortality could be a major preventing factor in their research, and the fact that this wasn't quite the quick fix they had been hoping to find.

Sierra took a deep breath and looked at Fia. "Can I see my future, please?"

Fia nodded. "Be prepared to see things you may not like."

Sierra's eyebrows shot up nearly to her hairline. "Have you already seen?"

Fia shook her head. "Once I touch you for the first time, I'll be able to look into your future on a regular basis, but since I haven't ever met you until today, I've only been able to see your future as it connects to Aodhan."

Sierra gulped.

"I can look first without showing you, if you would like?" Fia offered.

Sierra shook her head. "No, I'll be fine. But I want to ask: is what you see set in stone?"

It was Fia's turn to shake her head. "Far from it. The future I show you now is your current future. If you change paths, it will change. But know that intentions aren't taken into account, just actions. For example, if you see your death and then think about eating a healthy diet, the future I see won't change until you actually begin to do so and there is a change within your body. This makes my gift excellent for long-term predictions, but terrible for telling the immediate future or helping someone make critical decisions."

Sierra drew her eyes to Aodhan. "Have you already seen your death?"

Aodhan nodded. "I have."

Sierra waited for him to elaborate, but he didn't. He either wasn't scared of his impending death, or believed he could change it. This thought made Sierra's thoughts spiral to the fact that he may have already seen her death, and panic snaked through her insides. Realizing she needed to rip off the band-aid and get it over with before she freaked out anymore, Sierra turned to Fia. "Alright, I am ready."

Fia dipped her chin, before placing Sierra's hands on either side of her head. "Here we go," she whispered.

The room around Sierra faded into white, and appearing before her she saw a series of 3D images. The first was of her and Aodhan, and she was dressed in a gown like she had worn while imprisoned, but this time it was red, and Aodhan was dressed in very fancy attire, almost like a prince in a cartoon fairytale. They were clearly having a ceremony of sorts, and she wondered if it was their wedding.

Before she could question too much, the vision changed, showing her with Slaine. Sierra looked dejected and she assumed they must've been discussing something sad, but with a quick glance at her future self's skin, Sierra could see it was still clear— no lesions in sight—so that couldn't be the reason.

The next image was of her and Aodhan having sex in the tree-house. Sierra felt herself blush but knew that Fia wasn't judging her. Sierra tried to look more closely to see if she had aged some in this vision in comparison to the previous ones, but it was hard to tell in the dim light.

The fourth image was of her in a large library, Aodhan sitting at a table behind her. They were both reading large books and scrolls, and making notes on parchment. Sierra figured this was her trying to complete her research.

The fifth image came, and things in the future began to grow darker. Sierra and Aodhan were engaged in a battle, both of them wounded, before the picture flashed again, and she was in another cell, eerily similar to the one she had spent time in just the week before.

Sierra's heart rate began to pick up, and her breathing grew labored, even as she reminded herself that Aodhan was right there with her. She felt his warmth as he scooted closer, but he didn't touch her, and Sierra figured it was probably for good reason.

The sixth image came, and Sierra was running through the enchanted forest alone, but it was impossible to see who was chasing her. It was dark, but she could see well enough to recognize the signs of fear on her own face as she ran.

The seventh image came, and Sierra felt all the air leave her body, beginning to feel lightheaded. She was lying on the forest floor, and she didn't need anyone else to tell her that this was the last image, because she could see it. She could see she was nearing the end. Her lips were moving, maybe as a silent prayer to the God she had reconnected with in her last moments or maybe to Mother Nature; she couldn't be sure.

She tried to see if there were signs of aging in her face, but to her horror, she didn't look much older than she did now. Sierra let out a whimper, and Fia dropped her hands from the side of her face, the room slowly coming back into focus. Sierra was aware of the tears falling down her cheeks, but she was powerless to stop them.

"I can only show you what I see. I don't know when this will happen," Fia apologized.

Sierra grimaced. She couldn't decide what hurt more: the fact that her future was only seven images long and likely close to the end, or the fact that it didn't include finishing her studies or seeing her family in the human world again before her death.

"How many images does Aodhan have?" Sierra asked in a whisper, the tears continuing to flow.

"Hundreds," Fia answered solemnly.

Chapter Forty-Three

Sierra wondered if this was what people felt like when they were diagnosed with cancer, and told they only had a few months left to live. While she obviously didn't have the same hard limit they were given, facing the fact that her death would be coming soon was more challenging than she had anticipated. She had thought she was prepared for this, but she was wrong.

Sensing her emotions, Aodhan dropped his arm over Sierra's shoulder and pulled her into his chest. "Don't panic. Remember, this is just the future of your current path. If we make a change, there could be more images."

Sierra nodded into his tunic, but the tears wouldn't stop. She knew she would fix this—she had to—she just wasn't sure how, since their current path had felt like the only one that would get her out of the clutches of Conlan, but it appeared that it as it was, it wouldn't work.

Fia rose from the chair and headed into the small kitchen, quickly stirring some powders into mugs. She made three, carrying them back to Aodhan and Sierra, placing one in each of their hands before sipping her own.

"It's a calming brew I make. It's all natural; don't worry."

Sierra sipped the beverage from where she was tucked into Aodhan's chest. He held her with one arm, quickly downing the drink in the other before setting the cup on the side table and running his hand up and down her back in a soothing motion.

"We had planned to head to my father after this, either with a solution to the loss of magic, or to meet up with our friends to help us devise a plan that didn't end with my father imprisoning Sierra again."

Fia nodded, her face going blank for a few minutes. Sierra furiously wiped her cheeks. The tears had stopped coming, at least, but she needed to calm her emotions and take some deep breaths so they could come up with a new plan.

Fia's eyes came back into focus. "I haven't checked your father's future in a long time, but I did check for him back when he was a younger man, before you were born."

Sierra's felt her eyes widening as she realized that Fia was older than Aodhan, and possibly even older than Conlan. Aodhan's eyes were wide too, which made sense as he had told Sierra earlier that he thought Fia was only 200 at most—so apparently they were both mistaken.

"But, I just checked, and it doesn't seem like much has changed for him in the past three hundred years," she continued. "Even with the birth of you and your brother,"—Sierra was surprised that Fia already knew, but then again, she had probably been the one to show Aislan that everything with his transition would go okay—"You would think it would change, but your father has apparently been on the same path in life for a long time."

Aodhan didn't say anything, continuing to rub Sierra's back.

"So, what are we going to do?" Sierra finally pulled away from Aodhan's chest, placing her arms on his chest while he moved to grip her shoulders.

"I'm not sure. I need to think on this a bit and come up with a new plan." His eyes moved to the window, where the light had begun to dim at some point during their conversation. "Let's stay here for the night. Tomorrow, we can discuss this more, after we've had some sleep."

Sierra let out a yawn at his words, realizing that running through the forest and crying had zapped all her energy. But as soon as she was done yawning, she realized that Aodhan had just invited himself to stay at Fia's place. "Wait, are you sure that's okay?" She looked at Fia for confirmation.

Fia's eyes sparkled. "Of course it is. I already saw you would be spending the night and made up my extra room." She rose from the chair and motioned for them to follow. "I'm afraid it's not much, but I don't often have overnight guests."

She led them into a room that was very similar to the one Aodhan had at Teach Crann. Though sparsely decorated, it had a wooden bed with small side tables on either side and a wooden dresser across from the bed with a large mirror perched on top.

"I only have one wash facility, and it is the door across the hall." Fia looked at Sierra's clothes, which were not in the best shape, considering they both didn't fit, and she had slept in a hollowed-out tree the night before. "I did foresee that you would need clothes, and I set aside a few items that should hopefully fit you. I'm closer to your size than Aislan, I think."

A smile emerged from Sierra's lips at the thought of finally wearing clothes that fit after all this time. "Thanks so much; that would be amazing."

"I'll go get them. In the meantime, you two clean up."

Aodhan led Sierra across the hall, where the washroom was located. Similar to Teach Crann, there was a water basin, and a large tub, as well as something resembling a toilet. Unlike the tree house, it gave the impression that this place had multiple sources of running water. Making it easy for Aodhan to begin running a bath.

"No hot water, unfortunately. That's something the humans definitely have on us," he joked. "But while this is running, I'll get some kettles going in the kitchen, okay? I'll be back in a minute;

you just relax." He placed a kiss on the tip of Sierra's nose before slipping out into the hall.

Sierra began stripping off her ill-fitting clothes, admiring her clear skin in the bathroom mirror.

Fia returned before Aodhan, reaching an arm into the bathroom, a robe grasped in her hand. "This is for tonight. I put an outfit for tomorrow in the bedroom."

"Thanks, Fia," Sierra replied, grabbing the robe, and holding it up to see that ,while it was still a bit long, it was more her size than anything else she had worn since coming to Sidhe.

Aodhan returned next, two steaming kettles in his hands, which he added to the bath. "Two more should do it. I'll be back."

Sierra nodded, turning off the faucet as the water drew close to the brim of the tub. She stuck her hand in, surprised to find that the water was warm. Two more of the large kettles of water Aodhan was bringing would indeed make the bath hot.

The door creaked as Aodhan slipped in a second time, dumping the water from the kettles into the tub. Instead of walking them back to the kitchen as she expected, he simply set them outside the washroom, closing the door.

"Get in." He motioned to the tub, as he began to disrobe.

Sierra didn't need any more encouragement as she stepped over the edge, sinking into the water. It was heaven on her muscles, which were sore from so much overuse, and it was a balm for her soul, which was still reeling at the thought of her grim future.

Sierra closed her eyes and leaned her neck on the rim of the tub. She didn't even open them when she felt Aodhan step into the tub, seating himself between her legs directly opposite of her. He was a bit too tall for the tub, and he had to keep his legs bent, but he also appeared to relax as he leaned back against the side of the tub.

Aodhan didn't say anything, and Sierra was glad. She needed a little time to just be in her mind and not worry about the world around her. Aodhan seemed to sense that, even though she didn't voice it, and he simply rested one of his hands on the side of her foot underwater, rubbing calming circles, his eyes closed as well.

Sierra ran over everything in her mind, trying to think of a way to solve their current predicament while also changing her path in life enough to change her future. She thought over everything that had happened since she came to Sidhe, replaying each conversation in her head.

She must've gotten distracted, because the next thing she knew, Aodhan was nudging her. She opened her eyes to see a bar of soap held out in her direction.

"You should wash so you can get to bed."

Sierra nodded mutely, taking the soap, and running it slowly over her arms, her energy zapped from the events of the day.

Seeming to notice her lackluster approach to washing herself, Aodhan deftly extracted the soap from her hands and began helping her wash. It wasn't anything sexual, just him helping her get clean. He even helped her wash her hair, massaging the soap into her scalp just the right way, and tipping her chin back with his finger as he poured water over her hair to rinse it out.

"You're good at this," she whispered at some point.

"At being a decent human being and knowing how to bathe? I'm glad you think so." His tone was light, and Sierra appreciated that he was trying to cheer her up. But she was afraid that nothing would lighten her current mood.

When he was done, he picked up a towel from nearby, holding it out to her.

Sierra looked him straight in the eyes. "I'll get out on my own. I'll meet you in the room in a few minutes."

Aodhan smiled. "Alright, I'll see you there." He leaned down to give her a peck on the lips before exiting the room, closing the door behind him.

Sierra sat in the tub a bit longer, before rising to dry herself with the towel Aodhan had left behind. During the last few moments of the bath, an idea had come to her. She wasn't sure if it would work, and it would involve getting Fia on board.

She sucked her bottom lip in between her teeth as she considered the rest of the plan. It involved a small amount of deception, specifically deceiving Aodhan, and she hoped he wouldn't be too mad when he found out. But if she was going to have a fighting chance, no—scratch that—if they were going to have a fighting chance at having a future to enjoy together, it would have to work.

Slipping on the robe, Sierra snuck out the bathroom door, heading to the kitchen on a hunch, hoping that Aodhan wasn't listening too intently.

She was in luck. Fia was sitting at the table poring over a scroll while sipping out of a mug. Her eyes connected with Sierra's as soon as she entered the room.

"It just might work," she whispered, her eyes sparkling.

Chapter Forty-Four

Sierra awoke from a deep sleep to a knock on the door. Aodhan was out of the bed in a flash, pulling on his pants as he crossed the room. Sierra tried to rub the sleep out of her eyes as quickly as possible.

Aodhan yanked open the door to reveal Fia, clad in a robe similar to the one Sierra had worn prior to crawling into bed. Remembering that she was wearing nothing other than the undergarments Fia had given her, Sierra quickly pulled the blanket up over her exposed chest.

"What is it?" Aodhan asked, clearly knowing this wasn't some sort of social call.

"Conlan. His future has changed."

Aodhan looked over his shoulder at Sierra.

"He's planning to come here. We have to think of what to do, and fast." Fia's voice grew louder and more urgent.

Sierra gulped, trying to figure out how she could slide out of bed and put her clothes on without dropping the blanket covering her.

Fia somehow knew what she was thinking. "No, Sierra, I think you should stay here."

Sierra scrunched her eyebrows in confusion. This wasn't what they had discussed the night before.

Fia turned to Aodhan. "Leave Sierra here. I can hide her if he makes it here before you and Aislan are able to intercept him."

"But we don't have a plan." Aodhan grimaced, remembering the time he had just spent escaping prison.

"I know. But there isn't time to create one. You need to leave now if you're to intercept the others." She took Aodhan's hands and placed them on her head, showing him something in his future.

Aodhan's mouth drew down into a frown. "Let me say good-bye; I'll be out in a few minutes."

Sierra wasn't sure if she was supposed to hear that, but she did, and it made her heart clench.

Aodhan closed the door and turned back toward the bed, crossing the room quickly to embrace Sierra, placing a passionate kiss on her lips.

"It wasn't my intention to separate us, but after what Fia showed me, it's for the best. She will tell you more after I leave."

Tears prickled at the corners of Sierra's eyes.

"Hey, look at me." He tilted her chin up so his emerald-green eyes could connect with her brown eyes. "We will figure this out. The others will have a plan, I'm sure of it. Just stay with Fia, okay?"

Sierra couldn't help it; a tear slid down her cheek.

"Don't cry," Aodhan begged as he kissed her a second time. "We will see each other again, I promise."

"Don't make promises you can't keep," Sierra whispered, thinking of the future she had seen the night before.

"I only ever make promises I intend to keep," Aodhan replied firmly. "We will see each other again, okay?"

Sierra hugged Aodhan one final time, before he broke away from her to slide on his clothes. Sierra grabbed her new clothes and began slipping them on as well.

"Remember," Aodhan said, turning back to her one more

time as he prepared to leave. "No matter what, stay with Fia. I will come to you when it is safe."

Sierra didn't reply as Aodhan closed the door and made his way down the hall. She finished dressing, stopping by the mirror to try and make her hair somewhat presentable, but by the time she made it to the kitchen, Aodhan had already left. Fia was sitting at the table, stirring another beverage, a second cup placed at the empty seat across from hers.

"You did the right thing," Fia assured her, as she slid into the empty seat, grabbing the mug.

"I know," Sierra sighed. "It was just a lot harder than I thought to let him go."

Fia placed a hand on Sierra's. "It's never easy to let go of those we love."

Sierra opened her mouth to argue that she didn't love Aodhan, that they had just started dating, so how could she? But she found the words wouldn't come.

In fact, the more she thought about it, the more she realized she did love Aodhan. Burying her face in her hand, Sierra groaned.

"It's okay. He knows. You didn't have to tell him."

"But I should have, now, before he left, just in case."

Fia shook her head. "No, it might have changed his mind. You did the right thing. Like I said, he already knows. No ordinary woman puts her entire life on hold to follow a man around to try and save his world. If you didn't love him, you would've gone back home the minute it was even suggested."

Fia was right; Sierra had been acting in Aodhan's best interest for the last few days. Of course, what they were about to do now was in her best interest, but it was also in hopes of making a change to the future she had seen last night.

"So, is Conlan really coming? Or was that the only way you could think to get Aodhan away?" Sierra asked Fia. Their planning the previous night had been brief; as Fia had seen the plan and there wasn't much to discuss, but she had mentioned that she would come up with a way to get Aodhan to leave so Sierra could put her plan into action.

Fia shook her head. "I wasn't lying; you know as well as I do that the Fae can't. Conlan's future hasn't necessarily changed, but I did see a shift last night. That shift, however, had nothing to do with the two of you, so I showed Aodhan some of the images from his future which happened to overlap with his, and he made his own inferences."

"But isn't that technically a lie?" Sierra thought back to what Aodhan had said, about how the Fae could kind of lie, but typically didn't.

"If he had asked me to swear on it, we would have been in trouble, yes, but that's also why I came in the middle of the night. I couldn't warn you in advance because I needed your reaction to be real as well."

Sierra had to hand it to Fia; her plan had worked flawlessly.

"So, what's next?" Fia looked at Sierra, anticipation creeping over her features.

"Wait, you don't know what my plan is?"

A slow smile grew on Fia's lips. "No, I don't, but I do see lots more images for you now, some of which are activities of us together, but it's hard to know what is happening when."

Sierra felt a smile steal over her features as well. "It was that easy?" She felt her heart rate speed up. "To change my future?"

Fia held up her hand, "Not so fast. Remember, this is the future I see for your current path, but you and Aodhan taking different paths has already made some changes, yes."

Sierra tried to calm her excitement, not wanting to get ahead of herself, considering this was the easy part of her plan. "Well, I... uh...need to know information about the ritual of asking Mother Earth for something."

Fia's eyes grew wide. "You're going to ask her...now?"

Sierra had assumed that Fia had seen the ritual in one of the images in her future. "Yes. I honestly just want to talk to her, but I figure if I'm going to go through all the trouble and face the possibility of a curse, I might as well ask for what I really want."

"And what's that?"

"To be able to spend at least a few hundred years solving the magic problem in Sidhe."

Chapter Forty-Five

As it turns out, the ritual of asking Mother Earth, or Gaia, for something was far more intensive than Sierra had mentally prepared for. The entire first day, Fia simply coached her on what to say, if Mother Earth deigned to come.

"So she doesn't always come when summoned?"

"Do you?" Fia shot back.

Sierra couldn't help but laugh. "Okay, you have a point. I guess I just thought this was more of a sure thing."

"It isn't sure at all." Fia let out a breath. "Not only do we have to hope that she shows, we also have to hope she speaks English."

"What—?" Sierra hadn't even considered the fact that these rituals probably usually happened in Gaelic. "But if she is some type of...God, wouldn't she speak all languages?"

Fia shook her head. "You've been spending too much time believing in the human god. They like to make him all-knowing and adaptable to all cultures, but Gaia, well, she is more a presence rather than a being. I'm not sure how she interacts; I've never done the ritual myself."

Sierra groaned. "I should've asked Aislan more when I had the chance." That reminded Sierra of something else. "What about the ritual clothes? Do you have those?"

Fia nodded. "I've got one for myself, which I think you will fit. But to be honest, I'm not sure it's even required. It's just something we've always done, so we continue to do it. But I'm pretty sure if you showed up naked, it could still go on as planned."

"Did you have something you wanted to ask her?" Sierra asked, not meaning to change the subject, but feeling that she should get to know Fia better, especially if this wasn't something that could be accomplished in a day.

Fia nodded. "I...uh...had a partner a few hundred years ago, and I wanted to ask Gaia for something for him."

Sierra raised her eyebrows. "But you didn't?"

She shook her head. "He left before I had the chance."

"Left where?"

Fia's eyes grew glassy. "To the life which comes after this one."

Sierra didn't know what to say. She wanted to ask for more details, but she wasn't sure if that was appropriate in this situation.

"It's okay," Fia assured her. "It was a long time ago."

"And you never met anyone else? In the time since?"

Fia gave her a watery smile. "I wasn't meant to. He was the only one for me, I know it."

Sierra turned that thought over in her mind for a moment, before another pressing question bubbled up. "But, didn't you see it coming?"

"I don't see my own future, Sierra. That is something the mother seemed wise enough to bless me with."

"But didn't you see his?" Sierra couldn't believe that barely a month ago her biggest worry was avoiding Aodhan, and now here she was, in another world, discussing how futuristic visions worked with a woman who had lost the love of her life decades before.

"No. He didn't want me to look, he wanted life to be a surprise: that is why we were such a good match." She gazed, unblinking, at the wall, as she reminisced about the past. "Could you imagine me trying to meet another Fae and then explaining that I see the future and them not wanting to know every minute of every day if it's changed?"

She had a point.

"Saor was different, even from the beginning. He just wanted to be in the present. He knew what I could do, but he didn't ever want me to look at his future, because he didn't want me to give it away by accident. He wanted to live life on the edge and take the difficulties as they came."

"Can you turn it off then?"

"Somewhat. Most Fae, when they are adolescents, are instructed by a trainer or family member to control their abilities and only use them when they want to. This was more important back when our abilities were stronger, and one tantrum could cause a tornado, but I was born with strong powers, and so my parents ensured that I could block them when needed. Otherwise, it would be impossible to function in society. I would have visions of the future whenever I touched someone, and that would've eliminated the possibility for me to have a life partner at all."

Sierra understood. Now that she thought about it, it would be incredibly annoying to see someone's future anytime you touched them. Sierra wanted to ask about Fia's parents, but she figured she already knew the answer.

"Alright, back on topic." Fia directed Sierra's attention back to the scroll. "You need to be careful how you word things. Especially if she grants your wish. The last thing you want to do is leave yourself in an unexpected situation due to asking for the wrong thing."

Sierra bit her lip; she hadn't always been the best at saying the right things at the right time.

"You also want to say as little as possible. Keep your answers short."

"Okay." Sierra rubbed her neck. "What kind of stuff might she ask?"

"I can't say for sure—it's different for everyone—but historically, she must ensure that your intentions are pure. If they are not, that's when she doles out the curses." Fia must have noticed the horror on Sierra's face because she added, "It's what keeps the balance. Otherwise, everyone would just ask for everything all the time."

Sierra nodded, squinting at the scroll in front of her. She really wished that she had learned Gaelic at some point in her life, but then again, in the human world, it was useless outside of Ireland. Actually, it was fairly useless within Ireland as well, unless you happened to work in the library, where there were several old texts in Gaelic to organize.

"Alright, I'm going to make us something to eat," Fia announced, tilting her head to the window where the sky was just beginning to show hints of sunset. The entire day had passed, yet Sierra was no closer to being ready for the ritual than when the day had started. "In the meantime, you start working on what you are going to say to Gaia."

Chapter Forty-Six

The second and third days with Fia passed much like the first. The women spent most of the day sitting at the table, poring over whatever scrolls Fia could find on the topic of rituals involving change that had to be asked of Gaia. Since they were all in the ancient Fae form of Gaelic, Sierra mostly listened as Fia translated, jotting down notes whenever she thought of something that could be good to say if she was successfully able to catch the interest of Gaia.

While they were busy most of the day, there was still plenty of downtime for Sierra to stare out one of the small glass-paned windows into the forest, wondering where Aodhan was. There was no word from him, nor anyone else in the group, and Sierra couldn't decide whether this was good or not-so-good news.

As she watched the sun fade from the sky at the end of the third day, Sierra cradled a mug in her hands and delved into the thought of what would happen if she was successful at the ritual within the next few days.

She would be Fae, and she would belong in this world. She would be the closest thing she had ever known to immortal, and she would be stronger and faster than she had ever dreamed of being. There was also a chance that she would be cured of the auto-immune condition she had battled since childhood and would never have to worry about the appearance of her skin again.

But her mind kept turning back to thoughts of her family.

If this was successful, she would never be able to see them again.

Well, that wasn't exactly true, but she knew she would only be able to see them for a few years before they began to question why she wasn't aging. And while it was possible she could pretend she had found some groundbreaking information during her master's studies, she also knew there was no way she would be able to hide her pointed ears from her parents long term.

Sierra had never been a hat wearer, and she knew the minute she tried to go home to Dallas in a beanie like Aodhan wore, her mother would know something was amiss.

Sierra's heart was heavy at the thought of not seeing her family again, but in the same way, she felt slightly liberated. She wished she had left things on better terms with her mother and siblings, but at the same time, she had not truly fit into their lives for far too long.

"They'll never let you go." Fia was standing beside Sierra, her light blue eyes reflecting the pink and purple hues of what little sky they could see between the stretched branches of the imposing trees surrounding Fia's small abode on all sides.

"Of course not," Sierra replied. "Families aren't supposed to let you go." She had yet to ask Fia to see her new future, and honestly, she didn't want to, not until the ritual was complete. This was the path she had chosen now, and she didn't want anything to draw her away from it, even if it ended in ruin. "I just hope they'll eventually learn to move forward without me."

"If you want my opinion, you shouldn't let someone else's ideas dictate who you want to become."

"But I didn't—"

"You didn't have to." Fia cut her off. "Your future has been fluctuating. I know this is a hard choice, but you need to choose what will make you truly happy, regardless of what anyone else thinks."

Silence settled between them for a few moments until Fia turned to face Sierra, flashing a small, sad smile, before looking away once again. "You want to know what happened to my family." It wasn't a question.

"I can assume."

"It's not the same," Fia replied, her eyes tracking something in the trees that Sierra's human eyes couldn't see. "As you know, it's rare for Fae to have more than one child."

Sierra gave a slight dip of her chin that was almost a nod.

"But I am something even more rare. I was a twin." The way Fia said the word 'twin' made it feel as if all the air was suddenly sucked out of the room. A ghostly chill wove its way down Sierra's spine.

"Fae twins only come every few hundred years, and even then, they are usually two halves of a whole: one the sun, and one the moon, both very powerful in their own right, but also complements to each other. A single soul born into two equal parts.

"When my sister and I were born, we were exact copies of each other, an identical pair, which you call identical twins in the human world." Fia inhaled. "We were both powerful from a young age, but we both manifested the same power."

"And that was a problem?"

Fia shook her head. "It's an abomination, a misdistribution of power. We couldn't both live—Gaia wasn't going to allow it—and my parents knew that from the minute our powers manifested as mirror images of each other."

Sierra didn't even know Fia's twin, nor had she known Fia for long, but her heart bled for the woman standing next to her.

"We didn't have long together. She died shortly after our powers manifested. Her lifespan wasn't even what humans wouldn't consider a full one."

"How did it happen?"

Fia shrugged. "It was sudden. I went to wake her up one morning, as we both still lived with our parents at the time, and she had faded into the next world sometime during the night."

The air in the room was heavy; Fia's despair a sour taste on Sierra's tongue.

"Nothing was ever the same after that. My parents faded not long after, and after meeting Soar and he passed on, I found the only joy I had left in life was to be alone. Because at least when I'm alone, I can pretend that maybe there was some mistake and that she will walk through that door any moment, smiling at me over some secret.

"But when other Fae are around, and I see their sad looks pointed in my direction, the illusion is broken, and I know she isn't with me anymore."

Without thinking, Sierra put her hand on Fia's shoulder, in an attempt to comfort her. "Loss is never easy, whether you have 80 years or 800 years." Sierra hadn't dealt with the loss of a twin, or anything close to that magnitude, but with the way her heart twisted in her chest, she was beginning to think she had somehow absorbed some of Aodhan's empathetic power over the last couple of weeks. "And I don't know how the Fae afterlife works, but many in the human world believe that when someone dies, they are able to watch from the other side as you continue to live, enjoying your life in spirit, as they experience peace in the next life."

"Do you believe that?" Fia asked.

"I'm not sure," she answered honestly. "I thought everything in this world had an answer, until a few years ago I learned that wasn't the case. And ever since, I've been trying to come to terms with the fact that there may not be an answer for everything, and sometimes you may have to go about your life wondering."

"I didn't tell you all this to make you sad," Fia replied. "I'm telling you so you can be prepared. Becoming nearly immortal may seem like a blessing; if Gaia grants it. But it's also a curse all on its own, because if someone you love leaves this life before you, you must live with the grief even longer. And because all your friends and family are human, someone you love will undoubtedly leave this life before you."

Sierra didn't say anything more as Fia backed away from the window, leaving Sierra alone to watch the final fingers of light fade from the sky. Fia's words had hit home, except Fia had forgotten one crucial detail.

Sierra had never really had any friends.

Later that evening, they sat by the fire, the silence between them having grown comfortable over the past few hours as both remained sequestered in their thoughts.

"Fia, can I ask you something?" Sierra didn't take her eyes away from the flames.

"Yes."

"Am I making a mistake?" Sierra tried to swallow past the lump in her throat, but even though she had been drinking Fia's concoction all night, she found her throat suddenly parched.

"I can't answer that." Fia's voice was even, a stark contrast to the wobbling Sierra felt on the inside. "Only you can decide which path is right for you. But if you are proceeding with the ritual, we should try the day after tomorrow. We shouldn't waste time."

Fia rose from the couch, walking away without a word, leaving Sierra alone with her thoughts.

The decision she was about to make was a fork in her life; she could feel it. If she went through with the ritual, her life was going to change drastically. Either she would walk away with a curse and then rush to figure out a way to stop whatever was going on in Conlan's mind before he captured her again, or she would walk away a Fae and say goodbye to her human life forever to enjoy a possible future with Aodhan, whom she loved, but wasn't exactly sure was her life partner just yet.

Sierra truly had no idea which to pick, and she wished Aodhan was here, but she also knew that he would likely try to talk her out of putting her life on the line. But it was her life, and Fia was right; she had to make this decision on her own.

But why did it have to be so hard?

Chapter Forty-Seven

As it turns out, Sierra's decision was made for her later that night when Fia burst into her room holding a lantern, shining a dim orange glow that didn't quite reach the corners of the room. Sierra felt a sense of déjà vu as she rubbed the sleep out of her eyes and pulled the blanket up to her chest.

"Fia? What's wrong?" Her voice was muddled with sleep.

"Something has changed. Conlan is coming now; I'm not adjusting the truth this time."

These were the same words she had uttered a few nights before to convince Aodhan to leave. "Are you sure?" she asked.

"Yes. I don't see Aodhan, but you need to prepare to start the ritual now."

Sierra's eyes were drawn to the window, where it was still pitch-black outside. She couldn't even make out the trees from the inky blackness of the sky. "But...what if I'm not ready?"

"If you don't go now. There won't be another opportunity." Fia pulled a red bundle from beneath her arm. "Wear this."

Sierra knew better than to continue questioning Fia, and quickly rose from bed to pull the dress over her head. In her mind, she was silently running through the notes she had made the last few days. While she would have preferred one more day to truly flesh out what she was going to say, she knew there wasn't time.

Last night, Sierra had gone to bed in a state of indecision as to whether she would go through the ritual or not. She had been torn between the permanence of it, versus the benefits. But it looked as though fate had made her decision for her. Something for which she was both grateful and slightly annoyed.

As the dress slid over her body, Sierra grimaced at the familiar feel. It was just like the dress she had worn in the dungeon, but the dim glow of the lantern revealed it was a darker color. Sensing her question, Fia answered, "It's red."

"Red?" They had discussed how different colors meant different things for this ritual.

"Yes, for passion, sacrifice, and intent."

The words didn't make much sense to Sierra, but she figured that Fia knew what she was doing. As soon as Sierra had run a brush through her hair, Fia grabbed her arm and led her towards the backdoor.

"Go straight into the woods, until it feels right. Stop there and begin your conversation with her. If it is meant to be, she will come."

Sierra nodded mutely, not wanting to mention the fact that she couldn't see anything, so it was just as likely that she ran into something that could eat her as she was to summon Gaia. She just hoped that it felt right quickly, so she wouldn't have to wander too far.

With a few last well wishes, Fia pushed Sierra out of a door at the rear of the house. Sierra looked back over her shoulder just in time to see Fia nod before she closed the door, sealing Sierra out with the night.

Figuring there wasn't much else to do but go forward, Sierra put her hands out in front of her like a zombie and began walking away from the house. The night wasn't cold, per se, but it wasn't warm either, and goosebumps prickled their way up her bare arms as she made her way toward the trees, step by step.

After a few minutes, Sierra had worked out a rhythm. It was slow going for sure, and it wouldn't protect her from anything that wanted to eat her, but it kept her from tripping and falling flat on her face.

First, she would put a foot out in front of her and feel for any uneven ground or tree trunks that might be in her way. Then she would reach out with her arms and feel. Once she got to the tree line, she was able to go from tree trunk to tree trunk this way, doing an ample job of getting herself through the forest with no vision whatsoever.

From time to time, her foot would encounter vines or bushes, and she almost ran straight into a tree trunk that was abnormally close to another, but for the most part, she was currently unscathed.

Sierra didn't know how long she continued like this, but at some point, it became a habit, and she was able to devote her mind to other thoughts, like the reality that she had no idea where the right spot for the ritual would be.

When she had discussed this with Fia, she had assumed it would be daylight and that she would wander until she found a place of beauty or reverence, but now that it was night, she would have to rely on her other senses, and her intuition, to know when the place was the correct one.

Just as her feet were starting to feel like lead weights, it happened. She left the trunk of one tree to touch another and what felt like a feather-light caress made its way down her spine. The night sounds of the forest had also quieted, the air around her heavy with reverence. This was the place.

Figuring that Mother Nature wouldn't mind if she sat down before beginning their talk, Sierra felt around the area to see what was available. To her dismay, there was no rock or tree root that even resembled suitable seating, so after a few minutes of searching, Sierra sank to the ground at the base of the large tree her hand had been on.

"Well, here it goes," Sierra said out loud, breaking the grave silence of the night. Hopefully, she would be able to get through her entire speech before something came to eat her. "Hi, um, Gaia, or Mother Nature, whichever you prefer to be called. It's me, Sierra."

Sierra paused, waiting to see if someone would speak back, but after several moments of nothing but silence, she continued, "You, uh, may not know me, but I'm human. I came here from the human world probably about a week ago now, but anyway, I'm studying why and how humans age, as well as some possible solutions, as part of a master's program in Dublin."

Sierra didn't think it was possible, but in that moment, the forest around her grew even more silent. In fact, the only sound was Sierra's heart, which was pounding in her chest, and she was pretty sure that every creature in the forest could hear it.

"But, back to the point, I'm here because Conlan is convinced I'm the solution to the Fae aging problem. I'm not sure if that's true or not, but a friend of mine can see the future, and she showed me that my death is coming soon, soo...I'm here to see if it would be possible for me to become Fae, so that I could take the time to try and solve this issue more before...my death."

The last two words came out as a whisper. Sierra had never really pondered her own death before, and hearing the words come out of her mouth was weird. She swore that she could still hear them, as if the wind had picked them up, and decided to continually swirl them around her ears.

Sierra wasn't sure if she had said the right thing, and she had no idea if Mother Earth had heard her. Maybe she had picked the wrong spot after all? Or maybe she had already been cursed. Could one feel a curse when they were given, or was it something you noticed after a bit of time? These questions and more swirled around in Sierra's head, but no answering voice came.

Sierra wondered what to do now. She had entered the forest

without a plan to go back, and it looked like Mother Earth didn't want to talk to her. She hadn't marked her path at all, and even if she had, she assumed Conlan was on his way to Fia's right now, and she had no option to return.

As she was plotting her next move, Sierra heard a sound coming from the underbrush. Knowing that nothing good could come from that low, Sierra drew her knees into her chest, tucking her feet beneath the red gown. In her head, she repeated the mantra, "Please don't eat me," at least six times while the rustling continued.

Finally, it stopped, only for Sierra's eyes to latch on to a pair of glowing pink eyes, much too close for comfort. Sierra considered screaming, but before she could do so, a small animal emerged.

I know who you are.

The voice was feminine and seemed to come from inside Sierra's mind. Taken aback, Sierra bit her lip and looked around at her surroundings nervously.

That's when she realized something—she could actually *see* her surroundings.

Sure, it wasn't quite the same as daylight, but her eyes were able to pick up on sources of light she hadn't been able to perceive before. The shapes of the forest at night emerged from the inky darkness in front of her eyes.

Wait a minute.

With a shaky hand, Sierra reached up to feel her ears, as the glowing pink eyes of what she could now discern was a badger watched her from a few feet away. She started at the bottom, brushing her earlobe before running her finger up the side of her ear, only for her jaw to drop open as she felt her ear continue to slightly above where it used to, now coming to a slightly pointy tip.

Sierra couldn't process the thoughts; her mind was in a state of shock. How had her ears changed without her feeling them?

You're not done yet.

"I'll do whatever is needed." She offered the strange internal whisper, her voice sounding foreign even to herself.

Be prepared to pay the price.

The voice whispered inside her head. But before she could ask what the price was, or second guess her decision, everything went black; her last thought of the glowing pink eyes slowly coming closer, and the bolt of pain shooting down her spine.

Chapter Forty-Eight

Sierra opened her eyes to see streaks of sunlight weaving their way between the branches of the trees. The light pink sky was barely visible as a light wind caressed the various levels of the tree branches that stretched above her head.

Sierra didn't know how long she lay there, appreciating the nature around her, until the events of the night before came rushing back. She shot up, running her hands over her body and face.

Well, other than the pointed ears, everything felt the same as it was before. Holding her arm up to inspect it closely, she rolled her wrist back and forth. There were no signs of the lesions, but then again, there hadn't been any before the ritual either.

Secretly, Sierra hoped that this meant she would never have to worry about them again, but she also knew that there was a chance that they were just gone temporarily, as her skin had been clear prior to the transformation. There was also the fact that Gaia had mentioned a price. Though she didn't remember much of the initial pain, she was a bit worried there was some long-term cost she should be preparing to pay. Of course, there was the fact that she probably couldn't see her family again, something which she was currently trying to repress. She would deal with those implications and their corresponding emotions when she wasn't sitting in the middle of an unfamiliar forest.

Sierra rolled her neck, realizing the more she moved, the more aware she became of the aches in the various parts of her body. It felt somewhat akin to sore muscles. She groaned as she pressed her hand against one particularly sore muscle on her flank. It had been a while since she had felt this kind of pain.

Once she finished inspecting her body, she began to look at her surroundings, groaning with each step. Seeing it for the first time in daylight, it made total sense why this place had been the right spot.

Although the ground was dirt riddled with rocks every few feet (something her aching muscles reminded her of as she looked around), just beyond where she lay was a small pool that reflected the trees and the color of the dawn sky, and the air here was quiet and more peaceful than other areas of the forest she had been in previously.

Remembering her final moments with the pink eyes, Sierra crouched down to look underneath the bushes, but there was no sign of the badger.

As soon as her short investigation was done, Sierra realized two things simultaneously: one, becoming Fae had not improved her sense of direction any as she still had no idea where she was, and two, it was highly possible that she had been asleep, or knocked out, for more than just one night. Her muscles felt so stiff that she may have slept through two nights, and possibly an entire day. If her stomach or bladder were any indication, then this was certain to be the case.

Sierra stood, walking over to the water. Refreshed after a splash to her face and a long cooling drink, she caught her reflection in the water and evaluated the planes of her face. Although her ears confirmed she had transformed to some extent, the rest of her still looked the same. Sierra was still wearing the red dress, and although it was dirty for having laid on the ground for who knows how long, she had to admit that it suited her.

After she had finished drinking and washing what she could while remaining fully dressed, Sierra stood and looked around, wondering what she was supposed to do now. It didn't seem very safe to just start wandering the forest, but she knew she couldn't just sit here either. Her stomach growled its agreement.

Sierra closed her eyes and stretched out her arm, her pointer finger making her body one large spinner. Then she spun around a few steps. When she opened her eyes, she was slightly dizzy, but this was the way she was going to go.

Figuring this was probably a dumb idea, but not seeing any other option, Sierra began picking her way through the forest in the direction she had pointed. A feeling in the pit of her stomach told her that she should hurry, but she had no idea why, and it was difficult not to get distracted by every flower and plant she saw as she passed through the forest. Even though she didn't look any different, her eyesight had changed, allowing her to see the intricate forest details more clearly than she ever had before.

Sierra came across several bushes with fruits, and while she was too afraid to eat something she didn't recognize at first, eventually overcome with hunger, she ended up shoving some sort of berries from a bush into her mouth as fast as she could, hoping she wouldn't regret it later.

The day passed quickly as Sierra simply enjoyed the world around her. She noticed that she no longer felt fatigued as quickly as she had as a human, and when the sun began to set, she continued on her way, enjoying the sights of the forest courtesy of her new night vision.

Toward the end of the day, she came across a clearing in the trees, and there were small floating lights hovering at about the height of her chest. She tried to get closer to investigate if the lights were made by large bugs, or something else, but every time she came close, the lights floated a respectful distance away. After trying this several times, she decided just to sit and enjoy the beauty of the lights, letting go of the fact that she didn't know what they were. She was so busy focusing on the lights that it wasn't until a large shadow fell over her shoulder that Sierra realized she wasn't alone.

With a gasp, she tilted her chip up to see one of the elipags looking down at her curiously. Sierra held her breath; she had no idea what she was supposed to do around these things. She was sure Aislan had mentioned before, but as she racked her brain, all she could remember was that they were herbivores but still dangerous.

Sierra remained still as the creature lumbered in front of her, moving its large limbs slowly as if it didn't have a care in the world. She hadn't been this close when she was with Aislan, and it had been dark, so she hadn't noticed before how the animals were covered with a short layer of fur, which made a spotted pattern across the elipag. Without realizing what she was doing, Sierra raised her hand, running it across the side of the creature. The fur was soft and delicate, and she couldn't help but think this Sidhe creature was some type of weird elephant leopard hybrid.

The animal turned to look at her, not seeming to mind that Sierra's hand was on its side. Its blue eyes glimmered, but Sierra swore she could see a smile on its face.

Need a ride?

Sierra's hand flew to her mouth as she let out a surprised squeak.

"You can speak?" she gasped.

The creature merely tilted its head. *Not your language, no.*

What kind of non-answer was that? Sierra waited for the creature to whisper something else in her mind, but she had a feeling this wasn't really speaking so much as understanding. Remembering the way the badger had spoken to her during her ritual, she wondered if this was a connection with nature she now possessed.

Something like that. So, ride?

Sierra bit her lip to stop from squeaking a second time in shock as she nodded. "Yes please."

The creature lowered one of its massive legs, dipping its right side toward Sierra. Even though it was much closer than before,

Sierra still wondered just how she was supposed to get up. She didn't have to wonder long, as soon the creature had pushed her onto its back with its trunk.

When she was situated comfortably, or at least as comfortably as she could be without a saddle or something to hold onto, the creature resumed its lumbering pace across the meadow.

Where to?

"I'm honestly not sure. Do you know of a small house where a woman lives?"

Sierra couldn't say for sure, but it seemed like the elipag dipped its head.

"If so, I need to go there."

We know.

Sierra felt her eyes grow wide at the words in her mind, suddenly remembering that these things traveled in herds. Chancing a glance over her shoulder, she noticed the trail of elipags behind them, all of their glowing blue eyes resting on her.

You'll grow used to it.

Sierra desperately wanted to ask more questions, but she had a feeling whatever this connection thing she had didn't work that way. Suppressing her urge to question what was going on around her, Sierra took a deep breath, trying to just be in the moment as she had been when she awoke and when she had first seen the floating lights in the field. But it was easier said than done, as the moment she was able to get it out of her head was usually the moment when she noticed she was on a creature much larger than herself, several feet off the ground.

Just when she was about to give up on getting out of her head, Fia's house came into view, and Sierra felt a smile spread across her face at the fact that the elipags had known where they were going. She made a mental note to ask Fia about the mental capabilities she was experiencing once inside.

The elipag she was riding brought her close to the door before dipping a leg again so Sierra could slide off. She had to admit getting off was much easier than getting on.

See you soon.

The words tickled her mind as the elipag waved its trunk and disappeared back into the trees, the rest of the herd following suit. Watching the elipags from this angle, she wondered if they had some sort of magic powers with the way they moved through the trees. They were so wide, and Sierra knew from experience that the trees were much closer together than they looked, as they had scratched her arms when she had been on foot with Aislan. But the elipags were unbothered, and they moved silently, with no sounds of breaking branches in their wake.

Yes, definitely magic, Sierra concluded before turning toward the door.

Now that Sierra thought about it, it was a bit weird that Fia hadn't opened it already. Hadn't she seen that she would return?

"Fia?" Sierra called out, not sure if knocking was a thing in Sidhe.

When no sounds reached her more sensitive ears, Sierra turned the knob in her hands, entering the small home. The sitting room was just as she left it, a fire burning low in the hearth, indicating that Fia had been here at some point in the last few hours. Sierra tried again. "Fia?"

She heard something that sounded like a step, and she spun toward the sound, but it was too late. Someone grabbed her around the waist, locking their arms so she couldn't move; at the same time, someone put a gag in her mouth and something over her head that obscured her vision.

Sierra tried to struggle, and she knew immediately that these weren't humans based on how strong their grips were. She tried kicking her legs, but they were grabbed by a third person, who quickly picked up her feet to move her out of the house.

She was being kidnapped. Again.

Chapter Forty-Nine

Sierra had to admit, although she hadn't had much time to explore the Fae strength and heightened senses, she felt far less scared during this kidnapping than her previous one.

The thought caused her to chuckle to herself. Only someone with her luck would be kidnapped twice in a matter of weeks—and be making a joke about it.

Sierra tried to pay attention as she was moved, but this time, she was carried for the duration of her transportation over the shoulder of a male she assumed was Fae. As a result of being carried like a sack of potatoes, her head was lower than the rest of her body, and it was all Sierra could do to keep from vomiting from all the jostling and jiggling. She couldn't decide if it was the position upsetting her stomach, or the unknown berries she had eaten earlier that day. Either way, the last thing she wanted was to make it even harder to breathe than it already was with the sack over her head.

At least this kidnapping, they kept her conscious for the entire event, which was good, because Sierra was able to gauge more accurately how far they were going, but it was also bad because it meant they likely knew who Sierra was and that she wouldn't be able to find her way back to Fia's on her own.

She hoped that if Conlan was the one behind this kidnapping, she would be able to speak to Slaine again. Braan, Kaye, and Aislan were supposed to be somewhere in Fuinseog anyway, and she was sure that if Slaine could get word to them, they would help her escape.

At least Sierra didn't have to wonder for long who had kidnapped her because a few minutes later—which felt more like hours—she was dumped unceremoniously on a stone floor, and the bag removed from her head.

"I was wondering what happened to you."

Sierra's eyes raised to meet Conlan's as he glared down at her with obvious disapproval.

She didn't really know what to say, but she didn't even have time to respond before Conlan used a long wooden stick to lift her chin so he could take a look at her face from his seated position a few feet away.

"Well, this is unfortunate. I imagine you are useless to me as a Fae." He snapped his fingers at the man next to him. "Lock her up with the others."

Sierra's heart stopped.

What others?

She didn't have to wait long to find that out either as she was dragged through the castle. She hadn't been to this section of the castle before, but she had a feeling it was some kind of more advanced dungeon.

The four guards dragging her attached her wrists to iron cuffs, which were on the wall, before placing similar cuffs that were attached together around her ankles. It was dark in this room, but with her new night vision, Sierra could make out the other forms hanging in much the same way she was on the other walls. She also took notice of the hard stone surface of the floor beneath her, as opposed to the dirt of the other dungeon.

As the men finished locking her up, one of them spat at her feet. "We found your little escape attempt," the guard spat, and Sierra closed her eyes just in time for him to kick her in the ribs.

Sierra moaned in pain, trying to move her hands to hold her side before remembering they were locked tightly above her head.

"Don't try anything funny. These are Fae chains, so you won't be able to break out or shift even if you try," another guard snapped in perfect English. Apparently, they had just been ignoring her before. They must've considered her worth their time now that she was Fae, something which made Sierra's insides twist.

Sierra didn't say anything, instead focusing on breathing through the pain in her ribs and the gag in her mouth. It was likely that she had a broken rib from the kick, since she hadn't been able to brace herself before his boot had made contact. She just hoped that the rib hadn't punctured anything to cause internal bleeding.

Sierra's mind churned. She had never asked Aodhan if Fae healed faster, but since they were so long-lived, she assumed it must be so.

The four guards just laughed at her obvious pain before pulling the gag from her mouth and moving toward the large iron door, closing it securely behind them after they vacated the room.

As soon as the door was closed, Sierra remembered the other forms hanging on the other walls. She lifted her head, trying to blow her hair out of her eyes to make out who was in the dungeon with her. Her eyes focused on the form closest to her, blinking a few times as her vision blurred.

"Aislan?" she whispered, seeing the curly brown hair and thinner frame that Sierra had come to associate with Aodhan's brother.

"Sierra?" He lifted his head, revealing what looked like a split lip, his face covered with bruises.

"Are you okay?" she gasped out before remembering his traveling companions. "Are Kaye and Braan...?"

Aislan tipped his head to the left.

"We're here too." Braan's voice sounded pained from his position across the room, and he didn't lift his eyes to meet hers. Sierra's eyes caught on the third form, the furthest away from her. Kaye was in the darkest corner, and she lifted her eyes to look at Sierra but didn't say anything, likely due to having human vision and being unable to see in the inky blackness.

"What happened?" Sierra gasped out.

Aislan shook his head lightly, grimacing in pain. "We were captured on our second day here. We had snuck into the library the first day without issue, and we thought no one had noticed, but the next day, when we tried again, guards were waiting for us."

Sierra grimaced. "And Aodhan?"

"What?" Kaye's voice was shaky. "He's with you."

"No." Hope bloomed within Sierra. "He was with me until a few days ago, but then he came to find you."

"Well, we haven't seen or heard from him," Aislan answered. "And if he left a few days ago, he should be here. Slaine is feeding us information, and she hasn't mentioned Aodhan at all. She would have told us if he came looking for us, and he would have gone to her first. Everyone knows she has all the connections and runs one of the largest underground information networks in Fuinseog."

Sierra felt something tighten in her chest. "So, if he's not with you—and he wasn't at Fia's cabin—where is he?"

Chapter Fifty

Aislan shook his head. "We have no idea. Hopefully, this means he is still in a position to rescue us, or I'm afraid—"

Sierra cut him off. "Don't say it. We will find a way to escape with or without Aodhan."

Braan groaned from across the room. "Did you, or did you not hear them say these are Fae cuffs? That means they are immune to all types of magic, and our increased strength is useless against them."

Sierra was quiet for a moment, but no matter what Braan said, she refused to believe she had come this far—to have basically sacrificed her entire human life—just to rot in a Fae prison. "If you have that attitude, you will never find a way out. Where there is a will, there is a way."

The words were out before Sierra even realized it, and the fact that the last part was something her mother had always said when she had been struggling in school made her heart clench. She pushed the feeling aside. She could mourn the past and the decisions she had made later.

"Let's start by taking a catalog of what we have," Sierra suggested.

"You mean absolutely nothing?" Aislan snapped back.

Sierra's eyes searched his beaten face before drifting to Kaye, who hadn't said anything else. "That's not true at all," Sierra insisted. "First of all, we have each other, so that is something. I can almost guarantee they won't consider how powerful a team can be when everyone works together.

"Second," she continued, pausing as a wave of pain rolled through her midsection. The pain overall was lessening, and she hoped that meant she was healing. "Aodhan said most Fae have gifts. Aislan, you can sense emotions, right?"

"Yes, but I don't see how that is going to help."

"Just listen," Sierra said, she was getting a little annoyed by Braan and Aislan's negative attitudes. "Braan, what is your magic?"

Braan didn't even lift his head. "I'm a dream catcher."

Sierra's breath caught. "A what?"

"Dream catcher," he said again. "I can see other people's dreams. I can also send dreams or stop certain dreams from happening. Back when the magic was stronger, those with my gift could also make changes to dreams as they were happening. My father could, but I have never mastered that aspect of the magic."

Sierra breathed out. "Do you think you could send Aodhan a message through a dream?"

"I don't think so. I need to be fairly close in distance to use my talent. Though the distance does increase when I am trying to affect the dreams of someone I know well."

The wheels in Sierra's mind were turning at full speed. They obviously hadn't noticed yet that she was also Fae, or if they had, they hadn't said anything. But either way, they had more variables at hand than they thought.

"Okay, could you affect the dreams of Conlan, maybe?"

"Possibly," he answered. "I've been sending dreams to Slaine —that's how we've been communicating with her."

"Hmm..." Sierra thought out loud.

She didn't know if it was the confidence in her previous statements, but Braan finally looked up, his eyes immediately settling on her ears.

"You...changed..."

At his words, Aislan and Kaye lifted their heads, and Sierra grimaced at the sight of Kaye. Being human, it was clear she was not able to sufficiently heal between beatings, and she looked worse off than both Braan and Aislan. She didn't say anything before lowering her head, probably because she couldn't see Sierra anyway.

"So, what is your magic?" Braan asked.

Sierra wasn't really sure how to explain what had been happening, but she figured if anyone could put a name to what she had been doing, it was Braan. "I'm not sure," she started, "But when I was making my way here, I was able to...communicate with the elipags in the forest."

"So, you can communicate with animals," Braan surmised.

"Something like that."

Now Braan was the one *hmm*ing as he, too, realized their situation may not be as bleak as they originally thought.

"Also," Sierra added, "When I was captured, I was at Fia's house, and she wasn't there. I assume that means she saw what was going to happen and escaped. So, we aren't the only ones that know we are here."

Silence settled over as the four of them began to consider the possibilities. Aislan spoke up first. "I have an idea." Braan turned to look at him. "There's bound to be an animal, such as a rat, around. Perhaps Sierra could communicate with it and get it to bring the keys."

"That could work," Braan commented before Sierra could even get a word in. "But I don't really like the idea of leaving our future in the hands of a rodent."

"I agree," Aislan continued, "Which is why, in the meantime, you'll be sending dreams to whoever you can reach. If you can reach the guards, you could send them good dreams to distract them and increase our chances of any key they have on hand being stolen. You could also send dreams to Slaine; maybe she could help on the other end somehow."

Sierra had to admit, Aislan was definitely on to something. "Could you at least try to send dreams to Aodhan and Fia? Maybe if they are nearby, you could send a dream of us here, so they know where we are."

"I can try," Braan replied. "I was never close to Fia, but I have met her a time or two, which could help if she isn't close, but I also feel she likely already knows, so it might be better to concentrate my efforts on Aodhan."

"At this point, I think anything we try is better than waiting for someone to realize we are here and make their own rescue plan," Sierra said.

"Well, I've already been sending dreams to Slaine, so she knows at least, but I can send new dreams now showing you are here, as well as your magic. Maybe she will have some ideas we haven't thought of."

"I wish there was something I could do to help," Kaye said at last, and Sierra immediately realized why she hadn't been talking much before. Her voice was gravelly, and it sounded like each word pained her, which was probably true.

"There's one more thing you should know, Sierra." Aislan's voice was pained.

Sierra's heart dropped to her stomach. "What is it?"

"Conlan has been taking other humans since you escaped."

Sierra's throat constricted in shame. This was all her fault.

Aislan, sensing her emotions, shook his head. "You aren't to blame. It's his own delusions that are causing him to do this."

Sierra knew that, deep down, but it didn't quell her despair. "Is he taking them from the human world?"

Aislan pressed his lips together.

"We think so," Braan said sadly from across the room. "If he was taking the humans who are servants here in Sidhe, another council member would say something and make him stop."

"Are...are they okay?" Sierra had to force the words out.

It was Braan's turn to swallow a lump in his throat, his eyes drifting to his injured wife. "I don't...Slaine has shown me that she will see them once, but then not again. It's a new human everyday..." He trailed off, answering Sierra's question.

Silence and tension filled the cell as they all realized how gruesome this situation was becoming.

Sierra pushed the thought aside, knowing that dwelling on it wouldn't change what was happening. "Are you all...tortured here?" Sierra asked. Looking around the room, a second idea formulated in her mind.

"Unfortunately," Aislan replied. "We had already thought about options for escaping when we were removed from the room, though it seems like Conlan had considered that too by ensuring that we are never allowed to leave."

Sierra mentally reviewed her last experience being imprisoned by Conlan, figuring her new idea was likely not to work, but she knew Kaye would feel better about the situation if she had a job like the rest of them. "In my experience, during my last imprisonment, it didn't seem like Conlan, or the guards, had much idea of what humans really needed to survive."

Aislan raised his eyebrows.

"I, uh..." Sierra hesitated. Although she was learning to be okay with her disease, she was so used to not speaking about it that it was a little hard to get the words out. "When I came here, I had a disfiguring skin condition. Conlan thought that was the reason the prophecy wasn't being fulfilled, and he sent me to Slaine for her to heal it." She took a deep breath. "But Slaine, like myself, knew it wasn't an illness, but a deeply rooted internal disease that was incurable. Regardless, they brought me to Slaine daily for healing. So here's my idea..."

She looked over at Kaye, who once again had her head down. "Kaye, you should play dead—well, as close to dead as possible. Of course, we can't stop your heart, but if you stop responding and breathe as little as possible, I think there is a chance they will take you to Slaine for healing."

Braan was now staring at Sierra intently. "And if they don't care and leave her here to die?"

Sierra tried to shrug instinctively but found she couldn't with her arms restrained as they were. "That's a risk we have to take. There may also be a chance they dump her in the forest." Sierra grimaced at the thought of Kaye being dumped in her current state. "That wouldn't be ideal, obviously, but maybe Fia would see it, or Aodhan would find her. I would also try to pass information through my animal communicating abilities. But either way, it is a risk Kaye would have to be willing to take."

Before Braan could argue more, Kaye opened her mouth. "I'll do it." Her eyes shifted to her husband's shocked face. "I know that it's risky, but anything is better than sitting here and wondering how much more torture I can take before it really is the end. At least in the forest, I'll have a chance, however slim."

Braan's lips pursed together, he clearly didn't want to put his wife in danger, but he also seemed to realize that they didn't have many options, and being here was just as dangerous as being dumped in the forest injured.

"Alright, it's a plan," he said at last.

Chapter Fifty-One

None of them knew how much time had passed before the guards entered the room again, but as soon as they heard the sliding of the metal lock on the door, they put their plan into action.

Kaye hung her head, closing her eyes, and slowing her breathing as much as possible.

Six guards entered, splitting off into smaller groups, with a single guard headed toward Kaye and Sierra, and two guards each for Braan and Aislan.

The guards began saying things in Gaelic as they aimed a kick for the same side as before. Sierra still didn't understand Gaelic, but she could assume from their tone that it was some kind of insult. Sierra gritted her teeth, breathing through the new wave of pain that washed over her as she tried to keep an eye on what was going on elsewhere in the room. It looked like Aislan and Braan were interrogated in addition to the beating, though Sierra couldn't be sure because of the language barrier.

Her eyes reamined focused on Kaye. She winced as a punch landed on her left cheek at the same time that Kaye was kicked. Sierra's vision swam, though the punch didn't hurt as much as it might have had she been human. When the moisture cleared from her eyes, she watched as the guard lifted one of Kaye's legs, only for it to fall lifelessly to the floor. Sierra had to hand it to her; Kaye looked close to dead, her head hanging at an angle that did not look comfortable in the slightest.

The guard said something, and immediately, the rest of the guards stopped their attacks and headed over to see what he was speaking about. Sierra watched quietly, unable to see what was going on with the six Fae guards crowded around Kaye, blocking her view.

Sierra couldn't follow their conversation, but she figured that Braan and Aislan would alert her if something went wrong.

It took a few minutes, but finally, the men shifted, revealing a Kaye slumped over, her arms detached from the wall manacles.

Four men each took a limb, another opening the door so they could carry Kaye through. The one remaining guard said something to Braan, to which he began begging in Gaelic. Sierra held her tongue, trying to stop the twist of fear wrenching through her gut. Was their plan going horribly wrong?

Braan continued his pleading in Gaelic, the guard saying things in response, until he, too, exited the room, the metal door closing behind him and the lock slipping into place. As soon as Sierra was reasonably sure he was not coming back, her question burst forth. "What are they going to do?"

"I'm not sure," Braan replied. "They did think she was close to death, and I begged them to take her to a healer, saying I would do anything."

Sierra gulped, but she knew Braan had done the right thing; the guards would have been suspicious if he hadn't reacted in response to his wife being nearly dead.

"We need to think of some fake information for you to reveal if they come back," Aislan said. "Since I doubt they will reveal what they're going to do to her."

Sierra swallowed. This was part of the plan she hadn't considered, the fact that they wouldn't really know what was going on beyond the confines of the cell until much later.

"I could tell them Aodhan went to Fia's, but clearly they already know," Braan suggested.

"I think it's better if you just tell them the truth," Sierra interjected. "Honestly, our original plan is shot anyway. Just say you came here and that the plan was for Aodhan to meet you here in a few days."

"But that would alert them to up the guards on watch."

"I agree with Sierra. At this point, they are likely on the lookout for him anyway, if he isn't here," Aislan replied. "If we say he is coming here, they might even pull some guards off the search, which could make things easier for Kaye to escape."

Sierra could tell that Braan didn't like the idea of betraying his friend, but she knew they didn't have any better ideas, and there was too much at stake.

"Plus," Aislan added, "if I know my brother, and I do, he will already know to be careful, so we won't be changing anything by revealing that he is headed this way. I also assume they are keeping Sierra as bait, so it won't really matter in the end."

"You're right," Braan agreed.

"We should focus on the next part of our plan," Sierra suggested. "I can't tell if it's night or day, but Braan, what do you have to do to influence dreams?" She looked around the darkened room, but there was no window, nor even a crack in the stone revealing light.

Braan sighed. "It would help if we knew if it was night or day, as I have to cast a mental net to see who is dreaming in the vicinity. I can start casting at random and see if I can get a general idea. More people will be dreaming when it is actually night. I assume Slaine keeps a more regular schedule, though healers that work in private residences like this can be called for at any time."

That left Sierra's part of the plan. She looked at Aislan. "Do you think there is a way I could cast my communication abilities?"

Aislan thought for a moment. "I don't know anyone else with this type of magic, but I'm sure you could. I just wish you had more experience with magic; this may be hard since you've only used it once before."

"Twice," Sierra corrected.

"Like it makes a difference," Aislan snapped back. "But let's stay focused. Maybe take yourself back to how you were feeling and what you were doing when the elipags helped you in the forest."

Sierra closed her eyes, mentally turning back time to the moment she was sitting in the field. She hadn't been actively thinking of how she needed a ride; the elipags had just known. They had also just known where she needed to go. But that entire day, she had been thinking about how she needed guidance or a plan. Maybe she had been projecting those emotions?

Sierra decided it was worth a shot, and tilted her head back, trying to clear it of all the noise. *I need help. We need to get out of here; we don't know how to escape.* She thought these few thoughts over and over, willing the feeling to flow through her body. She wished she was on the dirt floor rather than the stone, as she had a nagging sensation that her connection to nature via her transformation had played an essential role in her communication with the elipags.

Then again, maybe her need would transit through the stone to any animals touching the stone in the same way? Realizing that her thoughts of 'how' were distracting her from her need, she quickly pushed them away, putting her trust in the creatures of this strange world to answer her call.

Thoughts whirling, Sierra drifted off to sleep.

Chapter Fifty-Two

Sierra was having a strange dream in which she was watching herself from across a dark stone room where she was being held prisoner as a small mouse was investigating one of her legs, its whiskers tickling her skin, but when she tried to move her arm to scratch, she couldn't, because her arms were bound.

Sierra's eyes flew open as the sensation increased, her eyes searching the stone floor for the mouse, which was indeed by the side of her leg. Sierra had always been averse to rodents, and it took everything in her to tromp down the scream that crawled up her throat. This mouse was clearly friend, not foe, and she needed to remain calm.

Her eyes caught Braan's across the room. He was awake and staring at her, *and he probably sent me that dream*, Sierra realized.

Before she could ask him to confirm, the words of the mouse drifted through her mind.

Help is needed.

Just like before, Sierra couldn't find a way to respond, so she just nodded her head, hoping whatever magic was at work would communicate the answer to the mouse.

We cannot break the bonds.

"Do you know someone who can?" she asked in a whisper, which made it a little less weird even though she knew she was communicating with the mouse mind-to-mind.

Yes, wait for the sign.

"What sign?" Sierra asked, but it was too late, and the mouse was scurrying off under the door. How it fit through a crack that was barely a sliver, Sierra had no idea, but she was thankful that it could.

"And?" Braan's voice cut through her thoughts.

"It said it didn't know how to break our bonds, but it knew someone that could. It said to wait for the sign."

"What sign? And what are we supposed to do when said sign appears?" Aislan asked, now awake as well.

"I'm not sure," Sierra grimaced. "This talking to animals magic thing isn't as clear-cut as you would think."

"It looked pretty cool to me," Braan said in Aislan's direction.

"It is, but it's not like I can communicate full sentences, it's more of an impression on my mind, and it's usually very short and not very clear."

"It makes sense if you think about it," Braan explained. "We assume that communicating with animals would be easy, but animals don't have the same diction or verbal structure that we do, and often they communicate complex emotions with a single sound. Like a single bark of a dog can indicate he is angry and about to attack. So, when your magic translates, it probably does its best, but it may be taking a single sound of the animal and trying to put it into an understandable sentence. It's quite remarkable, really."

Braan was right. Sierra hadn't had a whole lot of time to explore how her magic worked just yet, but the fact that it would be very difficult to translate the sounds of animals into words made sense. It also was unsurprising that they wouldn't gender their speech, as humans did.

The good news was they didn't have to wait long for the sign. Soon, there was a sound a bit like an avalanche in the distance.

"Do you think that's the sign?" Aislan asked.

"I assume so," Sierra replied.

The noise grew louder, as if the avalanche was moving closer.

"Uh...do you think we should be concerned?" Aislan's eyes were wide with panic.

Sierra wasn't sure if they should worry or not, but she figured being nervous wouldn't help anything. "I'm sure the animals know what they are doing."

Aislan scrunched his face in what was either concern, or disagreement at the sentence Sierra had just uttered.

She opened her mouth to argue, but just then the stone beneath them began to shift and move, almost like an earthquake.

"I'm regretting this decision immensely." Aislan looked around nervously, but Sierra saw that Braan had a smile on his face; he was enjoying this.

As the rumbling came to a peak, the wall behind Sierra began to rattle, her body moving with the movement of the wall, causing her teeth to chatter together despite her efforts to hold them together.

Before she could process another thought, the stone wall behind her collapsed inward, the chains around her wrists snapping just in time for her to lean forward and cover her head with her hands. She tried to cry out to Aislan and Braan in warning, but she couldn't be sure any sound passed her lips as the wind was knocked out of her. It was a good thing Kaye was no longer here, as Sierra was sure this would have killed her.

As quickly as it began, the rumbling stopped, and Sierra heard the sound of stones scraping against one another as they were shifted and lifted off her. As soon as she was able to lift her head, she did, only for the blinding outdoor light from the pale sunrise to filter into the room, revealing the form of several large elipags as they used their trunks to move stones off her and Aislan. From his spot across the room, Braan was mostly spared, but his wrists were still cuffed to the wall behind him. Sierra looked down at her own arms, which were now free thanks to the fact that the metal cuffs had been attached to stones, which were now in pieces around her.

Sierra brushed herself off and stood, fighting to pull her chained legs free as they were still attached at the ankle beneath the stones.

As soon as part of the restraining chain was revealed, the elipag closest to her used a tusk to snap it in half. She could move freely now, although the heavy metal cuffs remained firmly around her ankles. Another elipag was busy helping Aislan with his ankle chains as Sierra rushed across the room to Braan, her fingers brushing over his cuffs, trying to figure out how to get his wrists released. Sierra could see a keyhole, but they really were Fae-proof because, as much as she tried, she couldn't pull the metal apart even a small amount so Braan could slip his hands out. Sweat soaked Sierra's face as she tried, both from her effort, and because of the heat in the room thanks to the three large elipags behind her.

We will try.

The words floated through her mind, and Sierra backed up a few steps as the elipag came up and slipped the curled edge of its tusk beneath the metal, cutting Braan's hand, but if it hurt him, he didn't say anything. The cell had appeared to be small before, but with the elipag in front of Sierra and the two behind her, there wasn't any room to breathe. The elipag pulled back, snapping the metal easily before moving on to the next one, doing the same thing before breaking the chain that connected his feet.

Sierra nearly whooped with joy, but she knew that they needed to get out of there quickly before anyone came to investigate.

Mouse prepared distraction.

Sierra nodded once in response as the trio made their way to the edge of what used to be their prison.

Looking back over her shoulder, Sierra realized that Conlan wouldn't be able to use that cell again anytime soon, watching as

Braan and Aislan stepped through the massive round hole in the wall.

Braan gasped, his breaths coming in short pants. "We need to find Kaye."

Aislan shook his head, "There's no time. Hopefully Slaine has her and we can come back for her later."

Braan bit his lip and Sierra knew how hard it was to leave someone you loved, but she also knew that Aislan was right. She placed a hand on Braan's shoulder, "We will find her I promise."

Braan frowned, but nodded and turned back to the group of elipags. The elipag, which had undone Braan's cuffs, leaned a leg down so she could climb on its back. The other two were doing the same, and Braan was already moving to climb on one, while Aislan looked at the creature in front of him with apprehension clouding his features.

"Just get on, we don't have time."

That was all it took, and Aislan climbed on as the elipags made their way back to the small herd waiting a few feet away. As the three elipags joined the formation, they began to move back toward the forest.

"Where are we going?" Braan called out as they entered the trees.

Sierra's arms ached and tingled from being above her head for so long, making it a bit difficult to hold on, but the elipag noticed, slowing its pace slightly.

"I'm not sure," she called back.

"See if they know Teach Crann," Aislan suggested.

Sierra figured that was as good of an idea as any, and she pictured the treehouse in her mind, trying to project it as she had before.

We know.

Sierra smiled at the elipag's response, chancing a single glance over her shoulder at where they had come from, but the view of the castle was already obscured by trees.

Chapter Fifty-Three

The elipags dropped them off at the base of the treehouse, lingering for a moment to use their tusks to snap Sierra's ankle chains before they disappeared silently into the forest. Aislan climbed up first, followed by Sierra, who could now climb on her own, and Braan came up last, struggling a bit as his injured hands had not yet healed. Once they were all through the hole in the deck, they collapsed against the side of the house. The same bird Sierra had seen before tilted its head at them curiously from its spot on the balcony railing.

"Is that bird always here?" Sierra asked once her breathing had calmed.

Yes.

The word floated through as Aislan looked over to see the bird she was talking about. "No, but I think Aodhan might give it snacks sometimes, so it does visit frequently."

Sierra didn't mention the conflicting answers and wondered what snack the bird could possibly want, but she knew once she figured it out, she would definitely give it one.

All the snacks.

The bird blinked as the words came through. Sierra made a

mental promise that she would get it something as soon as she could.

Aislan was the first to stand, holding out a hand to help Braan. His hands had stopped bleeding, but they were still red and puffy where the tusk of the elipag had hurt his wrist trying to free him. "If we ever do that again, I'm requesting to be imprisoned on the exterior wall," he joked.

Sierra rolled her eyes as Aislan twisted the knob of the door and let them into the cabin. "It's not locked?" she asked curiously.

"It is," Aislan corrected her. "The doorknobs are spelled to only allow Aodhan and I. You couldn't come here without one of us, unless we hired a Fae locksmith to respell them."

Sierra raised her eyebrows. She wanted to ask more about the powers these Fae locksmiths had, but realized they were all exhausted and now wasn't the time.

Sierra made her way over to the sitting area, collapsing on the couch. All of this running and transforming and being imprisoned was taxing. She wished it would just slow down a bit, but she knew that until they found Aodhan, it wouldn't.

As she thought his name, she jumped up from the couch and ran over to the main bedroom, twisting the door open. Only the empty bed greeted her. She mentally chastised herself. If Aodhan had been here, he would have already come out to greet them.

"He's not here," Aislan explained, as if Sierra couldn't have already deduced that herself. "Otherwise, the rope wouldn't have been down. Especially if he was hiding out."

Sierra knew he was right, and now she was feeling pretty dumb that she had hoped he would be here.

"Don't worry, we will find him. But first, we need to find out what happened to Kaye."

Sierra's hand flew to her mouth as she realized she had forgotten all about her during their escape. What had become of the human woman?

"I'm going to do some dream reading and see if I can get any information." Braan said as he sank into a chair at the table.

Sierra glanced outside to notice the setting sun. *Time flies during escape attempts*, she supposed.

"I'll take a look around the forest," Aislan volunteered. "Sierra, why don't you see if the bird on the porch knows anything."

Sierra nodded, heading to the kitchen. "Let me get it a snack. I promised I would."

The small kitchen didn't hold much, and Sierra figured that without a fridge, they probably consumed a lot of dry foods. She pulled open the curtain to reveal some baking supplies sparsely occupying the shelf behind it. Unfortunately, she didn't have that kind of time.

"There should be some dry fruit over there." Aislan pointed as he headed toward the door.

Sierra found a small sack of unidentified dried fruit leaning on the countertop. She shook some out in her hand, tossing it in her own mouth, before shaking out a second handful for the bird. As she headed to the door, she watched as Braan grabbed some for himself as well.

Back on the porch, Sierra couldn't help but glance around at the rest of Teach Crann as the setting sun cast beautiful shades of pink and yellow all around them. The bird was impatient, however, and it quickly flapped its wings, taking off a few feet only to settle on Sierra's shoulder, dipping its head down to nudge at her closed fist.

Mine.

Sierra opened her hand, allowing the bird access to the dried fruits, which it ate one at a time in quick succession. As soon as it was finished, Sierra focused her mind on her question about Aodhan, referring to him both by name and as the man of the house, in case names weren't a thing in bird speak.

We hear rumors.

"What rumors?" Sierra asked quietly, afraid to hear the answer.

The bird seemed to hesitate, maybe looking for a way to say it, or maybe not having a word for it at all. When the answer finally came, it was just two words.

Snake human.

Chapter Fifty-Four

AODHAN
7 DAYS EARLIER

With every step that Aodhan took away from the house, he felt like the whispers in the trees grew louder. While he couldn't exactly make out what they were saying, it sounded like a combination of the words 'danger' and 'turn-back' in his language.

Aodhan had heard rumors over the years that the trees in this forest were enchanted, and the forest itself was named after that fact, but if that truly were the case, he wondered why they had just now decided to start whispering to him. Concluding that the whispers he was hearing were simply his own subconscious wishing for him to turn back, he blocked them out and continued on his way.

Aodhan kept the whispers out by thinking of Sierra. He meant what he had said to her back in Teach Crann; she was unlike any woman he had ever met. Sure, his father had tried to introduce him to various Fae females over the years, but none had ever caught his fancy like Sierra. Mostly, they just threw themselves at his feet, as if they had no self-respect and were just waiting for a male to walk all over them in exchange for a stable future.

For a while, Aodhan had thought this was just what females,

Fae or human, were like, especially when he had first journeyed to the human world at the beginning of the year. He had liked Kaye from the moment he met her, and for a second he had thought that maybe Fae women had been his problem, but after spending some time on campus, he had quickly learned that many human women were just like the Fae ones, willing to do anything to get a man to date them— even sacrificing their own values. Kaye had been a diamond in the rough that Braan had been lucky to find.

It was these experiences that had led him to treat Sierra so terribly the first few times he had met her. He had assumed she was just another dumb woman that he would easily be able to coax into coming back to Sidhe with him, and he hadn't thought he would need to put in too much effort.

The reality, of course, had been so far from what he had imagined. Not only had Sierra stood up for herself, and the value she saw in her time, she had even gone on a rampage to try and knock him down a peg. While her attempt was admirable, it had just made her all the more attractive to him, and he had found himself falling fast.

So fast, in fact, that at some point, even before she had met Braan and Kaye, Aodhan knew he would never be bringing her back to Sidhe, to be subjected to his father's strange ideals and beliefs that women, especially human women, were meant to be used as the Fae saw fit.

Now that Aodhan thought about it, it was his father's ideals, which Conlan shared with most of Sidhe, that had gotten them into this situation in the first place. As far as Aodhan could see, it was time for some changes around here, and he was ready to do what had to be done to make them.

With a new breath of determination, Aodhan picked up his pace on the route toward Fuinseog. He wasn't exactly sure where Aislan, Braan, and Kaye would be, but he assumed if he made covert contact with Slaine, she would be able to guide him in the right direction. Hopefully, the trio was laying low and not getting into any trouble.

Aodhan was so distracted by his thoughts and trying to ignore the sounds of the forest whispering in earnest that he didn't realize that he was surrounded until the scent of the first unfamiliar Fae reached his nose, causing him to stop in his tracks.

Standing in place, Aodhan turned in each direction, his nose lifted slightly in the air, only to realize he scented not just one, but five unfamiliar scents.

"Who's there?" he asked, knowing he was far too outnumbered to try and fight his way out of this. He was going to have to try the diplomatic approach.

"I'm sad to hear you don't remember me, Aodhan." A man slipped out from behind a nearby tree; the way he moved immediately caused the wheels to turn within Aodhan's brain. "After all, I thought we were future colleagues."

"Typhon," Aodhan whispered, sensing someone behind him, before everything went black.

To Be Continued...

To Be Continued...

IN BOLD BY HOPE E. DAVIS

Coming December 16th, 2024

Sierra

Sierra's life had been upended and changed in ways she could have never imagined. But would her newfound confidence and belief in herself be enough to help her escape the clutches of evil and bring much-needed change to Sidhe?

Aodhan

Captured by the last person he expected to become his enemy, Aodhan is faced with a choice: stay in prison and wonder what became of Sierra and his friends—or make a deal with the devil himself, which could change his path in life forever.

From Author Hope E. Davis comes the sequel and conclusion of Sierra and Aodhan's story which began in the NA Fantasy, Demure.

Please Review

Did you enjoy reading Demure? As an Indie Author, your reviews mean the world to me and the future of my author career.

If you could please leave a review on whatever platform you purchased Demure on, as well as on Goodreads, I would be forever grateful.

Pronunciation Guide

If you would rather just pronounce them in any way you want, that's fine too! This is only for those who want to be over-achievers!

Names:

Aodhan—a-ode-hawn

Aislan—ash-lan

Braan—brawn

Fearghal—fair-el

Teach Crann—ch-auch kr-anne

Fuinseog—foo-in-shog

Sceach Gheal—sk-ee-uh gee-al

Saileach—say-luck

Fearnog—fee-are-knock

Funiun—foo-ee-noon

Cuileann—quill-un

Caorann—ka-o-ran

Darach—da-are-uck

Sine—shu-nuh

Coll—cull

Gioleach—ge-o-luck

Biethe—Be-the

Eidnean—e-duh-nan

Phrases:

Isteach—ish-te-ach

Mo Grá—moe-gra

Deirfiur--draw-fur

Dearthair—drae-har

Also by Hope E. Davis

Mystery/Thriller Novels

Deceptive Perfection

The Fate of Ava Miller

Before Now

You Can't Run

Fantasy Novels

Demure

Bold (Coming December 2024!)

Buy books and extras at hopeedavis.com.

Acknowledgments

Edited by: Sarah Lemcke

Cover by: Caroline Leger

Beta Readers: Kaye Hardy, Catie O'Neil, Haley Laundry, and Kathryn Kincaid

About the Author

HOPE E. DAVIS

Demure is Hope's fifth novel. When she isn't writing, she is busy traveling the world, trying new foods, or hanging out with friends. She is also an avid reader and always looking for her next life-changing fantasy read.

A graduate of Metropolitan State University, Hope grew up in Colorado but currently calls the Netherlands her home. To find information about her other novels and be notified of her newest releases, follow Hope on Twitter @thehopeopera, Instagram @hopeedavisauthor, TikTok @hopeedavisauthor, and Amazon: Hope E. Davis.

Printed in Great Britain
by Amazon